EVIL IN THE SHADOWS

The Adventures of Pat Patton Series

EVIL IN THE SHADOWS

The Adventures of Pat Patton Series

ROGER FENTON

Octopus Publishing Company

A Division of Octopus Enterprises LLC

P. O. Box 132

Covington, GA 30015-0132

Octopuspublishingcompany.com

Library of Congress Control Number: 2015903124

Rev. 4 – Aug. 6, 2018

ISBN: 098244334x
978-0-9824433-4-7

DEDICATION

This book would not have been possible without the help of my good friend, Rick Hawkins, a true man of God.

ACKNOWLEDGMENTS

Thanks, Geleta, for encouraging me to write this book. She published <u>Joel's Adventure at Sea</u> in 2013.

TABLE OF CONTENTS

PROLOGUE

Evil in the Shadows is the 2nd book in the Adventures of Pat Patton Series. Book 1, "Death to the Novice Attorney," ended in a graveyard.

The funeral was held on a dreary day with light misty rain and ground fog. The preacher said a few words before the man was lowered into a pauper's grave, but only the two gravediggers were there to hear his words. One man could be seen in the area, standing in the shadows of some large oak trees, clenching and unclenching his fists.

"I loved you, Skinny. We lost Jeb as kids when that damn Burr-Head Edwards killed him 26 years ago. Now that you and Jeb are gone, I don't have no brothers. Skinny, I'm going to get them for you! Hear me? I'm going to get them for you!"

He stood there until after the casket was covered and the men had left. It was drizzling harder when he walked over to the grave. A temporary marker, pushed into the ground, said: "Arnold 'Skinny' Anderson, Born: March 1, 1938, Died: Dec. 20, 1980."

"That damn attorney and his girlfriend killed you, but I'm going to get them. I'll get them. I'll really get them!" shouted the man.

The dark clouds turned ominously thicker. The thunder growled, and lightning speared the sky.

The first 5 chapters of "Evil in the Shadows" covers the early years of the antagonist and is meant to show the lack of conscience and depravity of the Anderson brothers.

PREFACE

Many hours of research were spent to make sure events, music, and other things are accurate as to the time period, namely around 1980.

Much of what you will read was derived from the author's actual law practice experience with similar characters and events. However, literary license allowed him to exaggerate, change, or totally fabricate some characters and events to make Pat's story more interesting, and humorous. A tender love story weaves through it.

<u>Death To The Novice Attorney</u> is the first of <u>The Adventures Of Pat Patton Series</u>. Pat recently passed the Bar. Bad luck comes when he represents the ex-wife of a cold-blooded killer in an adoption case. Two people have a profound influence on his life: Shirley, the woman who loves him, and Skinny, a vicious sadistic killer, who hates him. Shirley wants to marry Pat while Skinny wants to murder him.

<u>Evil In The Shadows</u> is the second in <u>The Adventures Of Pat Patton Series</u> and continues the story as Pat's nerves suffer when Skinny's brother, a more depraved and cruel killer, hunts Pat for revenge.

<u>Mr. Clean: Serial Killer</u> is the third in <u>The Adventures Of Pat Patton</u> <u>Series.</u> A predator, who loves to play cat and mouse games before the actual kill, has Pat in his sights. Will Pat and his true love survive this latest threat?

CHAPTER 1

The Early Years

On Monday, July 4th, 1955, the three Anderson brothers were on their way to celebrate their youngest brother's birthday. Jefferson 'Jeffie' Davis Anderson had turned 14, 5'8" and 150 pounds.

They were riding in their older brother Jeb's 1946 Ford Pickup truck. He had bought it for $50. The tires were bald, the radiator leaked, the motor burned oil, the battery was on its last legs, and the brakes were worn. The body was a combination of surface rust and dents.

Edward 'Skinny' Anderson was the middle brother. At age 17 he was 5'9" tall but weighed only 125 pounds. He had dead-looking gray eyes and a pockmarked face.

Jeb was a good-looking boy, 5'11" tall with an average build and weighing about 165 pounds.

The youngest sibling was Charlotte, a sweet 13 year old girl, who was nothing like her worthless brothers.

All three brothers were known to be vicious and to be avoided at all costs. Their favorite sport was hurting people, or animals, whichever were handy at the time. The boys had taken after their 240-pound stepfather, a quarrelsome drunk who liked to pick fights. He was killed in a barroom fight two years earlier. Their mother was never home because she was always working two jobs trying to support her children.

"Hey, Skinny, what's we gonna to do for excitement on brother Jeffie's 14th birthday?" asked Jeb.

"Don't know," answered Skinny. "Get him drunk maybe?"

"Now that I'm 14, I want some of that Red Man chewing tobacco you guys use."

"Here you go, kid," said Jeb, handing him the pack. "We're getting low on money, so soon we'll have to roll another drunk or bust some more vending machines."

"Red Man's some good stuff," announced Jeffie, coughing between words. "Now I'm ready for a few beers."

"Let's stop at old man Henry's, 'cause he always sells you beer, Jeb," said Skinny. "And get some more chewing tobacco."

"You got it," agreed Jeb, as he managed to squeal the bald tires, then turned into Henry's Grocery store.

A few minutes later, Jeb came out with not only a grin on his face but also 12 cold cans of beer and a pack of Red Man.

"Now that we got beer and more tobacco, we need to teach the kid how to spit. Right, Skinny?"

"Right, and I've been thinking of us havin' a spittin' contest," said Skinny, popping open a beer.

"Good idea," agreed Jeb, aimlessly driving down a dirt road, "but what we gonna use fer a target?"

"What about that nigger kid over there?"

A young black boy, about 10 years old, was walking home from the store on the side of the road. They pulled over and stopped beside him.

"Need a ride, boy?" yelled Skinny with a twisted grin.

"No, ah, no sir," stuttered the boy.

"Get in the back of the truck, boy!" commanded Jeb.

The youngster was afraid not to do what he said. He thought about running, but the ground was rough and wooded, hard on his bare feet. The boy knew they would really like that, because it would give them an excuse to attack and beat him. He got into the back of the truck and sat down in the bed, full of junk, tools, old beer and used oil cans.

"Let's head for the point now that we got us a target," directed Jeffie.

"It's your birthday, Brother," answered Jeb as he turned off onto another side road, which led to a lake about a quarter of a mile into the woods. The point was a piece of wooded land that jutted out into the lake for about 100 yards.

Jeb came to a noisy stop, jumped out and ordered, "Okay, boy, out of there, and move fast when I talk to you!"

"Y-y-yes, Sir," replied a very frightened voice.

"Get the rope and Coke case out of the back of the truck," yelled Jeb.

"M-m-mister, please, don't hang me, Sir. I didn't never do nothin' to you. Please, Mister, please!" cried the young boy as Jeb held him by the collar and pushed him forward.

"Look, boy, you do exactly what we tell you to do and maybe we let you live!" said Skinny, who had the rope and the wooden Coke case in his hands. "What you got in mind, Jeb?"

"There's a low tree limb. Throw the rope over it."

"We gonna hang us a nigger?" questioned an excited Jeffie.

Skinny did what Jeb told him to do. Then Jeb had the young boy stand on the Coke case, which was on its side.

"Please, please, please, Mister, don't hang me!" cried the boy, as he stood on the unsteady Coke case. It was four or five inches wide and little over a foot-high.

Tears ran down the black face as Skinny put the rope around the boy's neck and tied a knot. Jeffie threw the rope over a limb and tied the other end to a smaller tree. Jeb drew a line in the dirt about six feet from the boy.

"Now listen up, boy! As you can see, the Coke case isn't very steady. You fall off, well, that's your problem!" announced Jeb with a sick grin. "So, you had better be still as I explain the rules to my brothers here. The target is his nose, boys, and the first to hit it with a good gob shall be declared the winner!" laughed Jeb.

"What a great idea!" exclaimed Skinny.

"Jeb," said Jeffie. "What a great way to have us a spittin' contest. Give me another beer. Whoopee!"

"Okay, since it's Jeffie's birthday, he gets to go first. Aim high kid, as beginners usually fall short," urged Jeb.

Jeffie chewed more Red Man and got a big mouthful of juice. He puffed up and let it rip. It hit the boy in the chest. making him flinch and almost fall off the Coke case. Tobacco juice was running down his shirt.

"I told you to be still, boy! Now you keep doing that and you're gonna to hang yourself! Hear me, boy? Hang y-o-u-r-s-e-l-f!" yelled Jeb with almost uncontrollable laughter. The beer was having its effect on all of them.

The boy was so scared he wet his pants. They all thought that was funny and had another good laugh over it.

"My turn," said Skinny," as he worked the chew in his mouth. He let one go and it hit the boy right in the forehead. The juice ran down his face. "Missed, damn it!"

"Okay, let the master try," said Jeb.

He let go a big wad of tobacco that hit the boy on the side of his nose, with some of it going into his eyes.

"I win, I win!" yelled Jeb.

"So you do," bellowed Skinny. "Hey, Jeffie, come here." Skinny led a wobbly Jeffie to about two feet away from the boy.

"Now see if you can hit him in the nose from there," urged Jeb.

Jeffie worked up a big chew, but said, "I'm not feeling too good."

"See if you can hit him from two feet and we'll leave," said Jeb. Jeffie got him right in the face and then got sick.

"Okay, boy, we're going to let you go now, but if you ever mention this to anyone, we'll bring you back down here to finish the job. Understand? We know you, boy, and we know where you and your damn family live. Tell anyone and we'll kill all you niggers and burn your damn house down!"

Skinny untied the rope from the tree and Jeb removed the rope from around the boy's neck, and then pushed him off of the Coke case.

"Now get the hell out of here and keep your mouth shut! As your prize, we're going to let you live!" laughed Skinny and the rest joined in.

When pushed, the boy fell off the case and onto the ground. He quickly picked himself up and ran down the road, sobbing, shaking and trying to wipe the tobacco juice from his face.

"Look at that coon run!" laughed Jeffie.

"We ought to do this every night! You won't forget your 14th birthday, will you, Jeffie?" asked Jeb, still laughing.

"Sure won't!" said Jeffie, thinking of what they could possibly do on his 15th birthday.

CHAPTER 2

The Brotherhood

"What I really want to do is join the 'Brotherhood,'" said Jeffie, and then he threw up again.

"Man, I would love to get into that organization, too," chimed in Skinny, "but they won't let guys our age go to a meeting, or at least I never heard of anyone our age going to one. Boy, just think, all them important people, masks, hoods, and cross burnings. The secret hand shake, and nobody, but nobody messes with members of The Caucasian Brotherhood!"

"I'm afraid it's wishful thinking. They would never let us attend a meeting, let alone join," sighed Jeb.

"Maybe I got a way we can get in," said Jeffie, squinting as he thought.

"Well, listen to him, Skinny, our little brother thinks he knows how to get us in The Brotherhood." Jeb rolled his eyes and laughed. But when Jeffie, little Jeffie, told his big brothers what he had in mind, they didn't laugh anymore. They looked at him with disbelief.

"What do you think, Jeb, are we going to the meeting tomorrow night?" asked Skinny.

"Man this is big time but I'm in if you guys are," said Jeb.

"I'm in," agreed Jeffie.

6

"Me, too," chimed in Skinny.

"Then that settles it," said Jeb. "I know just the place to look. Listen guys, we got to do it tonight, 'cause the meeting is tomorrow night at the old Griffin Airport. You know, the old abandoned one off Sistrunk Road."

"Right, Jeb, and with fireworks tonight, everybody will be watchin' them, not us," said Skinny.

"Little Brother, you are something else," said Jeb, playfully messing up Jeffie's hair.

"Soon as it gets dark then, we'll do it. Right, Jeb?" asked Jeffie.

"We sure will, and it just might get us into the meeting."

* * *

Later that night the boys drove to Griffin, parked the beat-up pickup truck and walked through some woods to some old deserted buildings. They located an alley where black winos would sleep off a bottle of Ripple, or Morgan-David.

Griffin was a cotton-mill town with a multitude of shotgun houses, stores, and alleys and its share of destitute inhabitants. The boys found several men in various states of intoxication.

"No good, Jeb, we need to find one alone," said Skinny, shifting a baseball bat to his left hand.

"You're right," said Jeb, "let's come back later. In the meantime, we can play bus stop baseball."

"I get to ride shotgun," yelled Jeffie. "After all it's my birthday."

"Okay. Jeffie, I'll sit in the middle," said Skinny.

They walked through the woods and back to the truck. Skinny gave his baseball bat to Jeffie and took the hatchet Jeffie was carrying.

"Remember, keep it straight out and low. We want to knock 'em down, not kill 'em. Be prepared for the jolt. Keep your arm flexible and don't drop the bat. Got all that?" laughed Jeb, as he gave all of them another beer. "This stuff is really getting warm."

Jeb started the truck and they went downtown. The boys drove slowly and spotted a black woman holding a bag of groceries, waiting for a bus.

"There's your target, Jeffie," yelled Jeb with excitement in his voice. "I'm keeping it at a steady 25 mph, so you can't miss."

As the truck approached the bus stop, Jeffie held the bat straight out, about three feet off the ground. The black woman was standing sideways, looking up the street, so she didn't see them coming. She was hit in the left arm so hard she whirled around and down, landing on her groceries. She tried to get up, and held her left arm as though it were broken. The boys saw her fall down and the groceries go everywhere. They continued on down the road as though nothing had happened, laughing all the way.

"Way to go, Jeffie!" exclaimed Jeb. "Now let's get the hell out of here before the cops come."

They went to another convenience store, which would not sell them beer, so it was back to Henry's Grocery. After pooling the last of their money, it was barely enough to buy a six-pack of beer, another quart of oil for the truck, and two dollars' worth of gas. Now they all were broke.

"Shall we try the alley again?" asked Skinny.

"Might as well," answered Jeb as he put the truck in gear and headed for the spot they previously had parked.

They all got out, Jeffie still holding the baseball bat in his hand. A walk through the woods brought them to the deserted buildings and the alley they had checked out earlier. Skinny now carried the hatchet. Fireworks could be seen lighting up the distant sky in the east side of town, probably at the fairgrounds. However, they had more serious business to take care of now. Jeb noted it took longer to walk there this time because it was dark and hard to see. They would have to take that into consideration when it was time to leave.

As they approached the alley, Jeb looked around to make sure no one was watching them. Not seeing anyone, he turned on the flashlight from his truck and shined it in the alley. An old black wino was sitting looking at them like a deer staring into the headlights of a car. He was alone.

"Unless you gots a bottle, get the hell out of here! I's was here first!" snarled the old black man with slurred speech.

"Say, old man, that's not very neighborly of you," answered Jeb, as he motioned Jeffie to get behind the man. The old man sensed grave danger, even in a wine stupor.

"H-h-here, take w-what's l-left of dis b-bottle and leave dis old m-man a-alone," said the old man as he stood up.

"But, Uncle Tom, you weren't very neighborly to us, so we just can't let it go, now can we?" asked Jeb, as Jeffie worked his way behind the wino. The old man's dark eyes registered terror as Jeb pulled out a knife, but that's all he ever saw because little brother Jeffie was swinging his baseball bat.

* * *

The next morning the boys looked in the paper and read about a gruesome murder of an old black man who was found in an alley with his head caved in and body mutilated. The police confirmed that this was no ordinary murder. They were withholding information, pending a full investigation and notification of next of kin. The police also admitted they had no leads and no motive. Robbery could not be ruled out as no valuables were found on the body, but he probably did not have much to take in the first place.

"Stupid cops!" laughed Jeffie, as he read the newspaper. "Of course he had somethin' to take."

"Next of kin, my ass. That old wino didn't have no one or he wouldn't have been living in that alley. Nobody will miss him. Man, we did our country a service," said Jeb.

"Hey, Jeffie, don't forget to burn that baseball bat," cautioned Skinny. "It has dried blood all over it."

"Already did, man. Early this morning. My head hurt so bad I couldn't sleep, so I got up and went out back and started me a fire in the 55-gallon drum, and put it in with a bunch of dry tree limbs."

"Good thinkin'," said Skinny.

That night the boys went to a meeting of The Brotherhood.

"Hey, Jeb, you got the jar?" asked Skinny, as they parked the pickup.

"Jeffie has it."

"Here's yours, Jeb, and one for you, Skinny."

They were allowed in the meeting and instantly became legends, as they each used a black human finger for admission. No member ever went to the police, as they knew it would be their death warrant.

CHAPTER 3

Ed Edwards

The brothers were accepted into The Brotherhood and an exception was made concerning their age. They were allowed to go with the men to some cross burnings, and other Brotherhood business.

One day Jeb was talking to Bubba Hawkins, a big illiterate red-neck. He was as strong as an ox and just as dumb. Bubba worked at a local gas station and was telling Jeb, and Bo Cane, the son of the local mortician, about a problem in Griffin.

"A black man, by the name of Ed Edwards, is now a manager of a gas station and convenience store. Jimmy's Come'n Get It, you know, the one located on the south side of town in the black area. Also the blacks are goin' out of their way to do business with him, and it's costin' my boss lots of money. But that ain't the worst part. You ain't gonna believe this but the damn coon is married to a white woman!" exclaimed Bubba.

"How could a white woman stoop that low?" asked Bo.

"The question is, what is The Brotherhood going to do about it?" asked Jeb.

"We gonna have a specially called meeting next Sat. night. Make sure you're there. Daddy is spreading the word, and he's calling it a war council."

"Damn bitch, ah, ought to have her ass kicked."

"A whole lot more than kicked," replied Jeb.

"You're right but it is up to the board of The Brotherhood to decide what to do with them. Although your little brother Jeffie might have some ideas because his idea got y'all into The Brotherhood in the first place," said Bo.

"I can tell you this though, if somethin' ain't done soon, ah, they're gonna to get brave and start wantin' white men's jobs and white girls!" exclaimed Bubba.

"Why don't you call your daddy? He's on the Supreme Council, and a State Senator. Ask him if he thought they would mind us giving them a few little subtle hints in the meantime?" asked Jeb.

"Good idea. I'll use the pay phone 'cross the street."

Bo, a nice-looking man, was a leader only because of his father's position. He was afraid of his father and did his best to please him.

"Daddy? It's me. Bo. Bubba, Jeb, and I have been talkin' about the gas station situation. I don't want to say too much on the phone, but you know what I'm talkin' about, don't you?"

"Yes, go ahead; tell me what it is you want."

"I know the situation will be discussed at length by some very important people, as far as what to do about it, but do you think they would mind if we gave them some subtle hints in the meantime?"

"No, Son, I don't think so, as long as it's not something drastic. Just be careful, that's all. You can fill me in tonight."

"Okay, Daddy. See you later."

Bo sauntered back across the street giving the other guys a thumb's up.

"He said okay but nothing drastic."

"I know where that bitch parks when she goes to the grocery store," said Bubba. "I watched her go to the Big Deal, right beside the Simplex gas station I work at. I ain't got no problem, unless we was busy, takin' off a few minutes to key her car."

"Man, you got to point them out to me, 'cause I don't know what she looks like, or him neither," said Jeb, "except she's white trash."

"Ah, she ain't too bad lookin' for bein' the low life she is. Ah, blond hair, nice boobs and butt, a little overweight, and about 20 years old. She came in the station a few times to get gas. Ah, guess she was runnin' too low to go buy it from her black husband's place across town. Ah, anyways, she always keeps that skirt hiked up where I can see the gold mine. I always make sure I take a long time washin' her windshield," smiled Bubba. "Ah, her old man manages the station and store over at, ah, Saunders and Eden. He even has two whites workin' for him. If you see a black face takin' your money, that's him."

"That black SOB ain't takin' no money from me!" Bo had a mean look in his eye.

"Same goes for me, but we need to go see what this burr head looks like. What do you say we go to the south side and get us a coke?" said Jeb, looking at Bo with a twinkle in his eye.

"I guess the price of a Coke would be worth it to check him out. Maybe I can get one out of a machine," answered Bo.

"Come on, we can take my truck. Bubba, you want to come?" asked Jeb.

"Can't. Gotta work, but if I see her go to the store, I'm goin' to key that sorry excuse of a car!"

The boys picked up Jeffie and Skinny, and headed for Jimmy's Come'n Get It. They were amazed at the business, which was at least twice as much as at the Simplex where Bubba worked. It was the only place in town where a black managed a store and gas station. It was only a two-pump station but had cars backed up, with a young white high-school kid pumping gas and taking the money inside. He would check your oil and also wash the windshield. Now a second white could be seen helping him, an older man who looked to be a little slow.

"Ready for that drink?" asked Bo.

"Let's do it," answered Jeb.

"They went in and there were about ten customers in that little store.

"There he is!" Bo pointed to a black man behind the counter taking money. "That must be him."

Ed was very black, had a nice smile, and was taller than either Bo or Jeb and weighed about 20 pounds more. He looked to be in his very early 20's.

Most of the customers were black and Ed smiled and thanked them as he rang up their purchases.

"Let's get a drink out of the machine outside. I don't want to give him even a penny," said Bo.

"Me either. Look at that white woman smiling at him and saying you're welcome after he thanked her for her business. Doesn't that just make you sick?" asked Jeffie.

"Sure does," answered Bo.

They went outside, got a drink out of the machine and looked around at this busy little store. Amazing, but not right. It would have to stop.

"I'm finished and saw enough! You ready to go, Jeb?" asked Bo.

"Let's go back in. I got an idea," said Jeffie.

They followed him in and Jeffie went up to Ed.

"What kind of place you running around here anyway? I put change in the machine out there and it took my money. Same goes for my friends here. We want our money back," spoke Jeffie in a very loud, angry voice.

"But I saw you and your friends through the window and all of you had drinks in your hands."

"Boy, are you calling me a liar?" glared little Jeffie, leaning toward Ed.

"Lookie here, Sir. I don't want no trouble. Here's a refund for the drinks." Ed opened the cash register and put the money on the counter for Jeffie.

"Bo, can I borrow that handkerchief you got in your pocket?"

"Sure," said Bo as he handed a crumpled rag to him.

Jeffie made a big show out of carefully picking up the change, one coin at a time, with the handkerchief, and wiping each coin very thoroughly before placing them in his pocket. Ed and his customers just looked at him. Everyone felt the tension.

Jeb and Bo turned around, and as they were walking out, deliberately ran into a stack of displayed bakery goods and knocked them over. Bread, cakes, and pies went all over the floor. They made sure to step on some of the pies.

"Oh! How clumsy of me!" laughed Jeb, as he walked out of the store. Bo was right beside him.

Jeffie smiled, and then pissed in the cracker barrel.

As the boys went out, customers, both black and white, helped Ed pick up the baked goods.

Going to their truck, the boys saw a black man get out of his car and go toward the store.

"Hey, you, you, boy!" demanded Jeb. "What time does this place close?"

"It be's around 11:00, Mr. White Folks."

Without thanking him, they got in Jeb's truck and left.

"I guess we showed him, didn't we," exclaimed Jeb.

"Hell, yes! Jeffie sure put on a show. I can't wait to tell the boys about it. Man, did you see all that stuff go flyin' all over the place?" laughed Bo. "Then to top it off, Jeffie pissed in the cracker barrel!"

"And the burr head had to go pick it all up. Maybe now he'll leave white folks jobs to white folks. On second thought, maybe he needs another lesson," said Jeb. "Little Brother, sometimes you surprise the hell out of me!"

When Bo told his father about their visit, Mr. Cain nodded his approval.

"I'm having supper with two out of the five members on the Supreme Council. Since the three of us are a majority, I intend to bring up your visit and suggest another, shall we say, stronger hint in the near future. I'll let you know what they say when I come home tonight.

"You should have seen how busy that place was, Daddy. We can't let that go on, or soon all of them coons will want manager jobs, and be tellin' white people what to do."

CHAPTER 4

The Beating

When Mr. Cane came home he told Bo he needed to talk with him.

"Son, it was unanimous. When I told my two friends what was going on, we called the other two members and had an emergency meeting. We all agreed that the sooner something is done the better. They want you and your friends to pay the coon another visit tonight, if possible. You boys have been given this honor because you have taken the initiative to check out this disgraceful situation and attempted to do something about it.

"Bo, I'm really proud of you. Now, I've got something else. Here's a map showing a small farm owned by the same man who owns Jimmy's Come'n Get It. They want you to pay him a visit, too, and give Jimmy one of your subtle hints. And here is something else. A leather pouch filled with lead shot; otherwise known as a black jack."

"What am I supposed to do with it?"

"Use it to put the coon in the hospital!"

"But Daddy, niggers are hard-headed. I need a piece of lead pipe."

"You got a point, son, but we don't want to kill him. Not yet, anyway. Now go call your friends. Maybe you can get him at closing time, unless the store closes at 9:00."

"No, it doesn't close until 11:00. We'll do you proud, Daddy."

Bo called Bubba, and Jeb, who was to inform Skinny and Jeffie that he'd pick them up in his car at 9:45. They were excited at the attention given them.

16

"Boys, we get Burr-Head Ed tonight. Hey, man that rhymes, Burr-Head Ed," laughed Bo. "Then tomorrow we pay a visit to a certain farm."

"It's only 10:00 and the Come'n Get It doesn't close for another hour. Why don't you drive by that jerks farm and check it out before we pay a visit to Burr-Head Ed?" asked Jeb.

"Yeah!" echoed the boys

Bo drove over to Jimmy's small 40-acre farm. It was on a dirt road, with the house sitting far back off the road. The moon was full and they could see several cows grazing in the pasture. A sign said they were Polchin Registered Cows.

"Guys, I'm wondering how much a nice big Polchin Registered Cow like that is worth?" asked Jeb.

"At least several hundred dollars," answered Bo. "Why, are you thinkin' what I'm thinkin'?"

"How many .22 bullets would it take to kill something that big?" asked Jeb.

"That would sure get his attention. The sinking of the U. S. S. Cow!" laughed Jeffie.

"I can't wait!" grinned Bubba.

"Me neither," agreed Jeffie.

"Time to go," said Skinny.

When they got to Jimmy's, shortly after 11:00, the station was closed and Ed was out back hosing down some garbage cans. Jeb parked down the street. Bo, Skinny, Jeffie, and Jeb went around back, while Bubba, who Ed never saw before, went to the front. Jeffie was a lookout.

The water from the hose washing out the cans made enough noise that Ed never heard the boys come up in back of him. His attention was on Bubba who was asking for change.

Jeffie left his lookout post and snuck up about ten feet behind Jeb, and then Bo brought the lead-shot bag down over Ed's head with all of his strength. As Ed started to fall, Jeb caught him under the arms, and held him up.

"Okay, guys, let him have it!" yelled Jeb.

Bubba and Bo took turns giving the unconscious Ed a severe beating. Then Jeb let him drop to the ground.

As Ed was laying unconscious, bleeding from the mouth and nose, Jeb said, "My little brother has something for you."

Jeffie kicked Ed several times and dumped a half-full can of garbage over him. Then taking Jeffie's lead, they all pissed on him.

They all laughed as they returned to the truck.

"Man, he has a head like a rock." Bubba was looking at his bruised knuckles. "But I sure got him good!"

* * *

The next thing Ed remembered was waking up in the hospital. His beating made Page 3 of Section C of The Clayton County Daily News. Ed stayed in the hospital for three days, suffering from a mild concussion, three cracked ribs, and numerous cuts and bruises. He also had two loose teeth and 14 stitches. He was back to work three days after being released from the hospital. Jimmy would only allow him to work half days for the first two weeks. They really hurt him.

The Brotherhood was overjoyed at the job the boys did on Ed. He went back to work as a symbol only, because he was heavily taped up with the cracked ribs and stitches in his face. He sat at the cash register and rang up the sales. What they didn't like was that Jimmy let him go back to work, and the fact Ed was now a celebrity in the black community. Jimmy's Come'n Get It was busier than ever.

"Bo, it's time to teach Jimmy a lesson. I like your cow idea. Go do it, Son," said Mr. Cain.

That was all the boys wanted to hear. Jeb went to Sears and bought two straight lawnmower mufflers and a roll of duct tape. They had two .22 semi-automatic rifles, and he took off the front sights with a small screw driver. Duct tape was wrapped around the end of the barrel, so the inside of the pipe of the muffler fit over the taped barrel of the rifle. More duct tape was used to secure it to the barrel. They now had very crude silencers, which worked rather well because .22's weren't very loud anyway.

Jeb had the two rifles loaded and 200 rounds of spare ammunition. Because they only had two rifles, Skinny had to watch.

The cows were standing beside the fence as they drove up. When they got out of the car, the cows shied away, moving about 20 feet from the fence. Jeb and Bubba had the rifles while Jeffie stayed in the car with the engine running for a quick get-a-way. They picked the biggest cow and emptied both rifles into it. They held 18 rounds each. The rifles made little noise and the cow didn't know what was happening. It was walking in circles, mad with pain, but did not go down. They reloaded and again emptied both rifles into her. Finally she went down, bellowing in pain, with fluids seeping out of a multitude of wounds. Altogether they were there only five minutes and quickly left the scene while the cow was still alive, laying there in agonizing pain.

The Clayton Daily News carried a story of Jimmy finding one of his prized Polchin cows shot dead from at least 75 gunshot wounds. The Humane Society was up in arms and vowed to find the person responsible for this vicious act. It was attributed to sick young vandals, but Jimmy knew better, as he got a note telling him to "get rid of the nigger." He was not to go to the police if he knew what was good for him and his family. The cow shooting drew more outrage than Ed's beating.

Jimmy felt he had little choice. He let Ed go, which really made Ed mad, not at Jimmy, but at the guys who did this to him and Jimmy. He called the police, the FBI, the newspapers, and any black organization that would listen to him. He was really stirring things up. That's when the Brotherhood decided to get rid of him for good.

Several days later, when he went to work on Monday, Bubba got his chance to key Ed's car, from the tail light to the head light on the driver's side. Then, with the side of his hunting knife, he jammed a wooden match into the driver's side door key-hole. Now Ed's wife would not be able to lock her car. Next week he'd do the other side if she was stupid enough to park in the lot beside his station again. They would learn not to mess with The Brotherhood.

CHAPTER 5

Dynamite

Andrew Cain called his son into the office of his funeral parlor.

"Son, I got something for you. You remember the lessons you got a few weeks ago on how to handle dynamite?"

"Sure, Daddy."

"You'll find five sticks, 100 yards of wire, caps, and a plunger in the trunk of my car. The Supreme Council has voted to blow Mr. Loudmouth's trailer, along with him in it, to Hell and back. You and your friends have done such outstanding work that you have been selected for this honor. I don't have to tell you that all of you are headed for leadership positions in this organization. One Council member wanted to bring in an outside shooter, but the rest of us felt you boys could handle this job just fine.

"Place the charge between the living room and bedroom areas under the trailer. Then run the wire from there into the woods. Cover it the best you can. When he and his lowlife wife come home, push the plunger."

The boys started watching the trailer and wrote down the times Ed and his wife came and went. She worked as a waitress and her hours were set. Ed got a job at a small garage changing oil and tires, even though only two weeks had passed since the beating and he was still in a lot of pain. He needed to work and did what he had to do. They did not know that after getting out of the hospital, he bought a used .30-.30 lever-action rifle along with plenty of ammunition. Then still in pain, he went out in the woods several times and learned how to shoot.

The boys worked in shifts to learn Ed's habits. They noticed one that could be his undoing. Ed and his wife had the habit of turning on a porch light when they left and turning it off when they got home. The two Fridays the boys watched were apparently payday as Ed took his wife out to eat at a black- owned restaurant.

Jeb decided to set the explosives and run the wire the following Friday night. From a side road, about 75 yards away from the trailer, where the boys planned to put the plunger, they could see the porch light go on or off. When it went off, they would push the plunger.

The trailer was watched until the porch light came on and Ed's car left. No one at the other trailers appeared to be home either.

Jeffie stayed with the van as the get-a-way driver, and Jeb went through the woods to plant the dynamite. He placed five sticks of dynamite, enough to blow the trailer to the moon, under an area believed to be between the bedroom and living room. Blacks lived on both sides of Ed, so who cared if they were blown up along with the Edwards.

While Jeb did his job, Bo ran the wire to the plunger while Skinny followed, covering up the wire as best he could with leaves, grass, and sticks.

Slowly they made it back to the van without being seen by the neighbors. When they got back, Jeffie seemed worried.

"Man, I just got a scare while you were gone. A cop car went by me real slow, looking at our van, but he couldn't get a tag number 'cause I put mud over the plate."

"That was smart," said Jeb with praise.

"How long ago," asked Bo, as he started to hook up the wires to the plunger.

"Only a few minutes ago. Damn, here he comes again!"

The road snaked around and almost doubled back on itself, so they could see the headlights long before the cop car got near.

"Let's get the hell out of here! I'll grab the plunger," yelled Jeb. "Maybe they won't see the wires."

Jeffie was only 14 but an accomplished driver. The boys jumped into the van and sped off. The police were suspicious and stopped where the van had been parked. They found the wires and followed them to Ed's trailer. There they found the dynamite.

"Almost wish we didn't find it," said one police officer. "You know whose trailer this is, don't you?"

"I know whose it is and what you mean, but the Feds have been snooping around ever since that nigger shot off his mouth. We better call it in."

The dynamite and wire were taken as evidence but they never called the FBI.

When Ed and his wife came home, a cop car was sitting out front. The police told them what happened and both thanked the officers.

After the police left, Ed made the decision that they would have to find another place to live. His wife was really scared and he was plenty worried, too. These guys were out to kill him and his wife! It took a few minutes to sink in, but when it did, he got the shakes.

The boys were really pissed that the police messed them up. They needed to regroup and try later, but first they decided to harass Ed again. They would get together the next night at Moe's Grocery where Ed usually stopped after work or when they were out of something. It was a little store about a half mile from his trailer. When he came in the store, they intended to be there.

* * *

The next evening the rain poured down when they got to the store. They had the two .22 rifles that were used on the cow and a 20-gauge shotgun in Bo's trunk.

Ed got his umbrella, with the metal end sharpened to a point, and ran from the trailer to his car. His wife was out of bread again. When he got to Mo's, Ed picked up a loaf of bread and walked to the counter, aware of the white guys scowling at him. Ed recognized Jeffie, standing near a side window, from the confrontation at Jimmy's.

"They don't serve niggers in here!" yelled Jeffie.

Here we go again, thought Ed.

He looked straight ahead and threw a dollar on the counter, enough for two or three loaves of bread. He started to back out of the store when Bubba lunged at him. Trying to defend himself, Ed shoved the tip of the umbrella into Bubba's side about an inch deep. Bubba backed up in disbelief.

"The nigger stabbed me!" yelled Bubba, with pain in his voice.

Bo and Jeb stopped short.

Ed backed out the door and ran for his car. He went home the back way, looking to see if he was being followed. The sky was clearing now, and he saw no one behind him.

When he got home, he told his wife what happened, loaded the .30-.30 rifle and just waited. He knew they would come.

The boys pulled up to Ed's place in Jeb's truck. Jeffie and Skinny were told to watch from a distance. Maybe they could learn something. Jeb had one of the .22 rifles and Bo had the other. Bubba had the 20 gauge shotgun and was in the bed of the pickup.

When the two semi-automatics and the shotgun started rapid firing, the noise sounded like war. Bullets were flying everywhere, glass was breaking, and the smell of gun smoke was in the air. During the first volley, Ed's wife was hit in the head with a .22 bullet, but fortunately for her, it was a glancing blow which cut a two-inch furrow in her forehead. Ed was enraged when he saw his wife hit, and his windows shattering. He grabbed the loaded .30-.30 and returned fire.

When the smoke cleared, his wife had been hit again in the arm, and the trailer looked like a piece of Swiss cheese. Miraculously Ed was not hit, but two white men lay dead and a third seriously wounded. The nigger had shot back! Later the third man had also died - - Bo, Bubba and Jeb.

* * *

Ed was arrested for murder. The trial was held four months later. An all-white jury took less than two hours to find him guilty of three counts of murder. He was given a life sentence.

Mr. Cain laughed when he learned of the verdict. He had avenged his son. He had Judge Harris Nesbitt in his pocket and members of the Brotherhood had friendly chats with all 12 jurors and the witnesses before the end of the trial. Although he wanted the death penalty, he knew it would bring too much attention from the Feds. It also was easier to convince the jury to vote guilty.

"Merry Christmas, Burr-Head," said Mr. Cain with a big smile on his face.

CHAPTER 6

Louie Lake

In 1980, Pat Patton became an attorney at the age of 30. He was a hard worker and put himself through law school. In 1980, Pat had been in law practice only seven months, but had acquired considerable fame. In his first jury trial he defended Sammy Joe Washington, one of the three infamous *Five-O'Clock Traffic Bandits* who held up a bank and, in their attempt to escape the police, threw several paper bags of roofing nails out their car's open sunroof onto I75. This created a monstrous five-o'clock traffic jam on a Friday afternoon. Sammy suffered the delusion that he was Moses. He carried a stick which he thought turned into a snake, which told him what to do.

During the robbery trial, a man named Arnold "Skinny" Anderson was out to kill Patton. Skinny had grown into a 40 year old career criminal.

One of Pat's first cases was an adoption. Skinny's ex-wife had remarried and her new husband adopted Skinny's two children using Pat for their attorney. A cold-blooded killer, and a poor excuse of a father, Skinny, believed the attorney, and all other involved in the adoption, stole his kids. In his attempt to kill Pat and his girlfriend, Shirley, Skinny was killed.

During the *Five-O'Clock Traffic Bandit's* trial, Skinny called in several threats to the judge's office while the trial was in progress. This story made not only state-wide news but also national news. The press and the public ate it up. When Skinny burned Pat's Mustang convertible,

Pat called Skinny a coward on TV, which had made the reporters run for the phone.

Now divorced and dating a divorced Assistant DA who he plans on marrying, he is slowly maturing but still loves a good joke or prank.

* * *

January 1981

"So when is the big day, Boss?" asked Julie, Pat's secretary.

"Shirley says she and her mother can have things worked out for the wedding to take place on Sat. March 7th. That's only about eight weeks away but Shirley's mother has lots of help from the ladies at the Solid Rock Christian Church. The only problem I can see is the weather. March in Georgia can be anywhere from sunshine to a blizzard.

"Jeez, Boss, I wouldn't worry about that. I'm sure everything will be fine."

"What do I have on the calendar today?"

"You're a lucky guy. Shirley has it all; looks, education, personality, and comes from a wealthy family."

"I am lucky. Now, what do I have on the calendar for today?"

"I heard you the first time, Boss, but you know how us girls get all sentimental about weddings."

"Julie!" said Pat emphatically but with a smile.

"Okay. In about 15 minutes you have one Louie Lake. He's out on bond for shooting up telephones."

"What?"

"That's right, Boss. He used some kind of gun to blow a hole in pay telephones and take the money. At least that's what I gathered when I asked him what kind of a case he had. He's charged with Criminal Damage to Property, and Theft."

"Yeah, and he'll probably want to pay me in coins, too." said Pat while laughing.

Julie was 28, very pretty, trim, well built, and came up to Pat's shoulders. Although a natural blond, she was very intelligent. Julie was married to a cop named Ralph and had served time in jail for a traffic death that was her fault. In the rain she ran a stop sign she did not see.

"Say, Boss, how's the shoulder coming along?"

"That buck shot Skinny put into my left shoulder is still bothersome, but the doctors say I will be good as new in time. I'm glad it wasn't my right shoulder. I had to temporarily stop bowling."

"I'll buzz you when he gets here," promised Julie as she left Pat's office.

Later, Julie brought the new client into his office. He looked to be about 40, and was a nice looking man, who spoke very distinctly and deliberately, and brought a copy of his arrest warrant and a copy of the police report.

"Have a seat, Mr. Lake. I give prospective clients 15 free minutes," announced Pat, starting a timer, "and then we go on the clock at $125 per hour. I need to tell you that up front."

"That's fine, Mr. Patton, but I want you to know I didn't come here haphazardly. I did my research and found out some very interesting things about you. You are very intelligent and care about your clients. I called Mrs. Washington, and she was kind enough to talk to me about your representation of her son in the *Five-O'Clock Traffic Bandits* case. She was very high on you, sir. Your girlfriend, and I understand also your soon-to-be wife, is an Assistant DA with Clayton County. Her father, Dr. Greg O'Kelly, is a well-known wealthy doctor, who is a good man and active in his church. And the way the two of you stood up to Skinny, and shot it out with him, brought a lump in my throat. This was especially true when you called him a coward on national TV for burning up your car and Mr. Butterworth's house. And speaking of Herb Butterworth, he is a former Clayton County Chief Asst. DA and also gives you advice on how he would handle a case."

Pat was dumbfounded! He thought, *What was a man of this apparent intellect doing shooting up pay phones? That was for dumb kids.*

"Yes. You surely did your homework, Mr. Lake. But why did you do something like shoot up pay phones? The police report says ten counts of Criminal Damage to Property and Theft."

"First, Mr. Patton, here is $125. I want to make certain you are retained, at least for an hour. Is that fair?"

"Alright, Mr. Lake, I am officially retained for one hour and your attorney client privilege just kicked in."

"Mr. Patton, I frankly don't believe the DA has enough to make these charges stick. Did I do it? Yes, but not a pay phone, or ten pay phones. I did it to hundreds of them in several states. I'm really a burglar and armed robber by trade, but I hit pay phones about three nights per month for household money. Three nights work will bring in about $1000 per month. Each phone takes me about 90 seconds and will net an average of $35 per phone tax free. So you can see I average about $1000 for 40 minutes work. Now, of course, there is a little more to it than that, as I have to drive to each phone booth and when I've gotten the money, I have to put it in my kitchen sink with Clorox to get rid of any powder burns on the coins."

"You also have to pay for a car and gas, but I don't understand powder burns."

"No car expenses; I use a stolen car. To get at the coin box, I use an 8-mm rifle. I go into the booth, point the gun about 6 inches from the lock and pull the trigger. The 8-mm really does a job on the coin box, so when I pry on the sides with two large screwdrivers, it pops right out. I take the whole coin box. Believe it or not, it does not hurt the telephone. I've made long-distance phone calls by putting in coins that come right back out where the coin box used to be, and then use the same coins over and over again for the call."

"But doesn't the bullet ricochet and come back to hit you?" asked Pat.

"No, but I've gotten lead splatter in my arms several times. I always wear safety glasses and ear plugs."

"How about the noise from the gun?"

"You would be surprised. No one ever seems to pay attention to it. Anyway, I'm in and out in 90 seconds. Oh, and you asked about the powder burns. When I shoot, remember the barrel is only a few inches from the coin box."

"Doesn't the bullet ruin the coins?"

"Some of them are ruined, but the majority are fine."

Pat took a deep breath, rubbed his eyes and sat up straight. Then he offered Louie a Hershey Bar and had one himself.

"I read over the police report and it says they found an 8-mm rifle in your car. Also you were in the same area where several telephones were hit."

"That's all true," acknowledged Louie with a proud grin, "but that's all they have."

"Tell me what happened," said Pat quietly with interest.

"The cops have suspected me for a long time and had a judge ready to sign a search warrant if I were stopped for anything. I had hit my ten phones for the night, had dropped the coin boxes off at a friend's place, got rid of the stolen car, and was going back home when I was pulled over supposedly for making an illegal turn. I hadn't made a turn for at least a mile. I was in the area of the phones that were previously hit, and it was yours truly driving; so they stopped me and asked to search the car. Of course I refused, but they had a search warrant in no time. When they opened the trunk, they found the rifle but were shocked when there were no coin boxes," laughed Louie.

"It does sound like a weak case on the surface. How about shell casings, bullets, witnesses, or someone getting your tag number," asked Pat, "and fingerprints?"

"I never leave shell casings, the remains of the bullets are untraceable fragments, there were no witnesses, and a tag number is out because the car was stolen and driven by a friend. They got me in my own car and I wear gloves."

"Well, this case should not get past the preliminary hearing, or even if it does, at least the grand jury should no-bill it. You understand the judge at the preliminary hearing can do only one of two things: bind it over to the superior court, or dismiss it. If it's bound over, the grand jury has to hear evidence and they in turn can do only one of two things - - indict you or no-bill the case. No-bill literally means it is dismissed. Indictment simply means you now have to deal with the district attorney who can accept a plea of guilty for a deal, try the case, dismiss it, or decide not to prosecute it."

"Yes, Mr. Patton, I understand all of that."

"If you want me to take this case, I will need a $1,000 retainer, which would entitle you to eight billable hours of my time, plus any expenses I might incur representing you. I will keep track of my time and any time over eight hours will be billed at the rate of $125 per hour. If I get it done in less time than that, I get to keep the entire amount because it is a non-refundable retainer. If you want to retain me, I have a contract which spells all of this out."

"Give it to me and I'll sign it," said Louie, as he pulled out his wallet and gave Pat another $875.

"Before I forget, we also need to check out the search warrant. I know you said they didn't find anything, but we may be able to suppress the 8-mm rifle and the ammo they found," said Pat as he gave Louie a receipt for the money.

"Right. Check it out, because I think they were harassing me. They took my rifle and I want it back."

"Louie, if I can call you that, you are taking an awful chance for $35 when you hit one of those pay phones. You never know who is watching."

"Pat, if I may call you that," said Louie smiling, "again you would be surprised. No one ever seems to see anything. And like I said, I'm in and out in 90 seconds."

Pat took down the information he needed to open a file on Louie. Before he went into law practice he had no idea that some people thought like Louie.

After a firm handshake, Louie left and Julie came bouncing in.

"So you got another one, huh?"

"I surely did, but what a bizarre case! Shooting up pay phones in telephone booths. Can you believe that?"

"Jeez, Boss, after several months in this office, nothing surprises me. Oh, and the stories I hear from Ralph. As Mindy, says, 'My dad puts them in jail and momma's boss gets them out.'"

"I'm not surprised anymore either, but it's still bizarre."

"So, how are you and Shirley doing after the Skinny ordeal? I notice you still favor your left arm."

"Julie, both of us are having trouble sleeping, and I get the creeps thinking about him. That man was evil personified. A cold-blooded killer."

"I know, Boss. He sure had nerve - - busting out of prison and killing two men doing it. Then burning down Herb's house and destroying your Mustang. And then the way he called the courthouse made me sick, lying about your mother having a heart attack and your dad being in a car wreck!" Julie was working herself into being really angry.

"Slow down, Julie," cautioned Pat with a smile. "No use getting upset over something that happened in the past and which you have no control over."

"I know, but just thinking of Skinny infuriates me! And him killing those poor police officers, trying to kill the Johnsons, and then coming after you and Shirley!"

"There you go again. But I know what you mean, because he was as rotten as they come. What else do we have today?" asked Pat, trying to change the subject.

CHAPTER 7

Ed, 26 Years Later

"Boss, you know I always try to keep your Friday afternoons free. Nothing more is scheduled today, but a man named Ed Edwards insists on coming in. Do you know him?"

"Sure don't. Did he say what it was about?"

"No, Boss, except he says he was sent to prison illegally for over 20 years. He sounded black over the phone. Still doesn't ring a bell?"

"No. Never heard of him."

Rhonda poked her head in the door. "Pat, the guy who's been calling all morning is here. He says he is not leaving until you agree to see him."

Rhonda Rogers, Herb's secretary was 45 years old, plain- looking, a little overweight, very loyal to Herb, and an overall good employee. Pat leased space from Herb.

"Ed Edwards, a black guy?" interjected Julie.

"That's him. You want to see what he wants or do I tell him you're not available?" asked Rhonda.

"He's got me curious. Tell him I'll be with him in a few minutes. Julie, we're done. Please explain the first 15 minutes are free, but it's $125 per hour after that."

"Jeez, Boss. This guy is like a hemorrhoid; he won't go away."

"Julie, you should be ashamed of yourself!" Pat smiled.

"With that last comment by Julie, I'm gone," stated Rhonda with false modesty in her voice.

Pat was very busy, but this Ed character intrigued him. He buzzed Julie and told her to send him in.

Ed was a very black, black man, middle aged, and looked to be in good physical shape with a build similar to Pat's. He had the odor of beer on him and his eyes were bloodshot.

Julie introduced them and they shook hands. "What can I do for you, Mr. Edwards?"

"I wanna thank you fer seeing me, Mr. Patton. Mrs. Washington's friend said dat you was de man dat I needed to see. You helped Sammy and maybe you can help me."

"What was her friend's name?"

"I don't know what her friend's name be but she goes to Mrs. Washington's church."

"Well, Mr. Edwards, why don't you briefly tell me what you want me to do for you."

"Everybody calls me Ed, Mr. Patton."

"And everybody calls me Pat," broke in Pat.

"Uh, Pat, ah, I gots to tell you I don't have no money. I don't want to, you know, be cheatin' nobody."

"Ed, you still have ten free minutes, so please tell me what brings you here."

"Mr. . . . ah, Pat, ah, I just gots out of prison on parole. I been der for the past 26 years for killing three white Brotherhood members. You probably heard of dem, ah, Pat, 'cause dey was some real bad dudes dat, you know, hated us black folk. Anyway, I killed dem fellows, but only 'cause dey was shooting up my mobile home and had done shot my wife in de head. I killed dem in self-defense."

"Why were they after you, Ed?"

"'Cause I was de first black manager of a gas station and store and I's was only 21 years old. And, ah, 'cause my wife was white. Dis was 26 years ago."

"That would sure do it. Let's see, 26 years ago would have been back in 19 . ."

"It be 1955," interrupted Ed.

"You brought me some paperwork on your case?"

"Yes, sir. It's de papers from what de court person with dat little typin' machine wrote during my trial."

"Yes, the transcription. Have you read it?"

"No, Sir. I can't read or write."

"If you say it was self-defense, Ed, why would a jury convict you of murder, as it says here?" asked Pat with a creased brow.

"Sir, it was an all-white jury, and I was married to a, you know, white woman. You gots to remember dat dis was back in 1955. I'm sure dat de Brotherhood got to dem, or some of dem was members, too. Could be de judge was, too. I don't know. One of dem boys dat I killed was de son of one of de richest men in town. He were also a senator."

Could this be true? Did this man serve 26 years in prison for defending his wife and home? Come to think about it, I heard the name Brotherhood connected to Skinny during the trial last month. Is this déjà vu?

Pat started looking through the indictment and the transcript of the trial. The 15 minutes were long gone. He was convicted of murdering Roy "Bubba" Hawkins, Bo Cain, and Jeb Anderson. *Jeb Anderson! Could it be?*

"Ed, this Jeb Anderson. Did you know him?" asked Pat uneasily.

"I knows him, or rather knew him. He was one of de three dudes dat tried to pick a fight with me in my store. Dem boys knocked over a store display when dey left. Stuff went flying all over de place. De young one even pissed in de cracker barrel! People in de store helped me pick it up. Dem white folks helped me, too. De other two, dat Bubba and Bo, be with him. I been told dey always hung out together. Everybody knows Bo 'cause his daddy be a rich man what owns a big funeral place. I knows it be dem three what shot Jimmy's cow and got me fired!"

"You lost me, Ed. But first, did Jeb have a brother or brothers?"

"I don't know, Mr. Pat. All I knows is dat dey hung out together."

"Okay, now what about the cow?"

"Jimmy's registered Polchin cow. I think I's pronounced dat cow name right. One what cost a lot of money. My boss, Jimmy Cross, had a little farm wif some cows. He was told to let me go and wouldn't do it, so his cow was shot. I don't mean just shot, but it was shot about 80 times from what I was told be in de newspapers. Dey used .22 guns. But dat was after I got out of de hospital."

"I'm confused again, Ed. What about the hospital?"

"After I closed up de store at night dat I was managing and was washing . . ."

"Wait a minute. I don't mean to interrupt, but you told me you can't read or write. How could you manage a store?"

"I can't read or write, but I'm real good wif dem numbers. I can count real good, and I had a label from everything we sold taped in a note book with de name and de price. I look at names like you do pictures. I could read some names like Coke or beer. Most of de things in de store I just looked at dem and knew dat it was chicken soup, or spaghetti, just by de way it looked. Lots of folks thought I could read."

"Okay. I understand. Now, what about the hospital?"

"At closing time I goes out back and hose out de garbage cans after I'd emptied dem. One night dis Bubba guy comes up and ax for change. Dats de last thing I remember until I woke up in de hospital. Later, I found out it was de Bubba guy. Anyway, when I was getting him some change, wham! My lights went out. Dey must have beat me when I was out 'cause I had bruises all over, a concussion, some cracked ribs, 14 stitches, and even foot-prints on my shirt. I never did see who hit me! It must have been one of de other guys Bubba hung out wif. Dat Bo, or dat Jeb. I had loose teeth, too."

"Wow! Ed, you're telling me that members of the Brotherhood harassed you, beat you up so badly that you were hospitalized, got you fired, attacked you and your wife in your own home, shot your wife in the head, and then you got convicted of murder for defending yourself and your wife?"

"Yes, Sir, dat's right. Dey also tried to blow us up."

"What!"

"Dey done hooked dynamite up to my trailer and, you know, ran wires from it down to de road. Lucky fer me some cops come along before dem boys, and I'm sure it was dem same boys what done it, set it off. If dem cops wouldn't have come along when dey did, I would be one dead nigger!"

"Ed, that will be all for now as it's almost lunch time."

"Is you gonna help me?"

"Can I keep this paperwork for a few days? I want to look over it, read the trial transcript, and do some research. Then I can give you an answer."

"You can keep it, you knows, a week or a month if you wants to. I just need help. I sure 'preciates your time. You gots my telephone number. I stays wif my mama."

Ed got up and Pat shook his hand. When he left, Pat went out of his office to see Julie.

"Hi, Boss. You get retained?"

"He doesn't have any money, but I'm tempted to take the case anyway. If what he is telling me is true, and it should not be hard to check it out, he spent 26 years in prison for defending his home! This guy is either a gigantic victim or a gigantic liar. And since you're sitting down, I'll tell you one of the men he killed was named Anderson!"

"Jeez, Boss. You think he was related somehow to Skinny?" asked a surprised Julie.

"I don't know, but I'm going to be at the library after lunch to see what the newspapers say. It happened in Griffin, which is in Spalding County, but it's not more than 25 miles from Jonesboro. A trial that big should have made the Clayton County newspapers. I'll look at newspaper stories around Aug. 1955 when those men were killed. I should be able to get a good idea of what happened."

"What are you going to do tonight? I understand Shirley has this girl thing she is going to do with her best friend, Kathy."

"Right. It's called getting-together-with-momma-and-the-ladies-to-plan-our-wedding. You will be getting an invitation. And speaking of Kathy, Shirley is thinking of fixing her up with Eb. What a pair they would make!"

"Like I said, Boss, it's a girl thing," laughed Julie.

"Eb, who is now my part-time roommate, is coming over and it's the boy's night out."

"Geez, Boss. That sounds scary! You guys have a knack of getting into trouble," smiled Julie.

"Me and Eb? Why, Julie, we wouldn't dream of – of – of - . . ."

"See you later, Boss," said Julie, shaking her head.

Pat smiled because he was looking forward to getting together with his roommate, and best friend, the Great Eb.

CHAPTER 8

Research

After lunch, Pat was at the library when the doors opened. He would have gulped down his lunch and gone sooner, but it was closed from noon to 2:00. The librarian directed him to the area where they kept microfilm of old newspapers. She showed him how to find a dated newspaper on the film and how to use the reader. Then she guided him to where he could find copies of the Clayton News Daily and The Evening News, which long ago had merged. They were all filmed under Clayton News Daily, which made looking up dates much easier.

He started in July 1955; but, after skimming all of the July news pages he found nothing. However, under Sunday Aug. 7, he found a small article on the beating of a black man named Ed Edwards. He was found out back of Jimmy's Come'n Get It by a customer who had run out of gas and coasted into the station. He saw lights on inside and hoped someone was still there after closing time. The article said Ed was unconscious when taken to Clayton General Hospital.

The Aug. 10th edition had a small article saying Ed was released from the hospital with a mild concussion, some cracked ribs, and numerous cuts and abrasions. The article also said the police had no leads on who did it, but the motive of robbery had been ruled out because Ed had $27 and change in his pockets, and nothing appeared to be missing from the store.

So far it jives with what Ed told me.

The next article Pat found was dated Aug. 13th and merely said Ed went back to work at Jimmy's. On Aug. 15th there was a story about Jimmy's cow being shot around 80

38

times with a small-caliber firearm. The veterinarian said it apparently suffered a great deal of pain and died slowly. Again, no motive, or suspects.

His story is still holding up.

On Aug. 26th, under police news, Mrs. Edwards had reported someone had keyed her car from the headlight to the tail light. Then on Aug. 27th, the newspaper reported that someone placed several sticks of dynamite under Ed's trailer. During a routine patrol, the police spotted a suspicious vehicle parked along the side of the road. When they approached it, the vehicle, believed to be a van, took off. They were too far behind for pursuit. When they stopped where the vehicle was parked, a wire was found going about 75 yards to the Edward's mobile home and was connected to dynamite.

A bomb squad from neighboring Atlanta was called in to defuse it. The explosives expert said it looked like a professional job because of the way the dynamite, with an igniter placed in one of the sticks, were located between the living area and the bedroom areas, underneath the mobile home. The sticks of dynamite were wrapped together and taped to the top of a steel beam, which would direct the blast upward to the mobile home.

The explosive experts estimate the results of an explosion of five sticks of dynamite would have been a completely destroyed mobile home and could have wiped out the two units on both sides of it. Anyone inside the trailer or anywhere near would surely have been a fatality.

This case was getting really scary! Then the big story leaped out at him from the issue dated Aug. 28th, 1955. Pat's heart was racing as he found the story concerning the shooting.

The headline read: "Negro Kills Two White Men and Seriously Wounds Another." Pat read: There was an earlier confrontation between the colored man and the three white men. One of the white men was Bo Cain, the 18-year-old son of a prominent mortician and state senator. Another was Roy "Bubba" Hawkins, age 18, who said the colored man stabbed him without cause. Apparently these two men, along with Jeb Anderson, went over to Edward's trailer to talk with him about the stabbing. According to friends of the deceased, when the men arrived at his home, Edwards opened fire on these defenseless men. Cain and Anderson were killed and Hawkins was shot and later also died.

"How numerous bullet holes got in Edward's mobile home, or how his wife was injured was unclear.

"The viewing of all three men will be held from 7:00 PM to 9:00 PM on Aug. 29, 1955 at the Andrew Cain funeral home. The memorial service and funeral will be held at 2:00 PM on Aug. 2, 1955 at the Cain Memorial Gardens."

The article went on to tell about surviving relatives, but one name jumped out from the microfilm when Pat saw it. "Mr. Jeb Anderson is survived by his mother Marie Anderson, a sister Charlotte, and brothers Arnold Anderson and Jefferson Davis Anderson."

Could it be?

Pat gathered up his notes and had the librarian print out the major articles for him and left. Back at the office, Pat called his friend Lt. Keller.

"Lt. Keller here, how can I help you?"

"This is Pat Patton. As usual, I need your help."

"Hi, Pat. As you know, we members of the CCPD are here to serve the public," laughed Lt. Keller. "What do you need?"

"I just took in, or should I say will probably take in, a case that involves a black man, who claims to have been convicted and given a life sentence for the murder of three white men, when he was protecting his wife and property. I did research at the library and the back issues of the Clayton Daily News seem to confirm what he told me. He was a store manager and married to a white woman, but this was back in 1955. Lt., they beat this man and put dynamite under his mobile home, but luck was with him as the police found it before it was set off. However, what jumped out at me was the name of one of the men killed. One was 'Jeb Anderson' and the newspaper said he had brothers by the names of Jefferson, and Arnold!" said Pat, stopping to let this sink in.

"Are you trying to tell me this case is coming right back to Skinny?"

"That's what I'm hoping you can find out. I need you to see if our Skinny, who we both know was named Arnold, had brothers named Jeb and Jefferson. If he also had a sister named Charlotte, that would clinch it."

"Are you at your office?"

"Sure am."

"Let's see, it's now 4:00. I should have an answer for you within an hour. Stay by your phone."

About 45 minutes later Lt. Keller called back.

"Pat, it's hard to believe, but you hit the nail on the head. Your client, or prospective client, killed one of Skinny's brothers back in 1955. His name was indeed Jeb, who was 18 at the time. He was a suspected member of the Caucasian Brotherhood, or just Brotherhood, as were the other two. I called a friend who is a retired sergeant with our department, and he told me they were a force to be reckoned with back then. Many influential people were either members or supporters. He remembered the shootout as he was one of the officers called to the crime scene. He said that when he got there he found two dead white men and a third severely wounded.

"The black man's mobile home was full of bullet holes, his wife had been shot in the head, and all of the windows had been shot out. Two of the men had semi-automatic .22 rifles and the third had a shotgun. He said there were shell casings all over the place. Apparently they reloaded at least once and each rifle held about 20 rounds. That meant a minimum of 50 or 60 shots were fired by them, plus the other guy with the shotgun. Numerous empty 20-gauge shotgun shell casings were found.

"He went on to say the murder charge sure smelled to him because if the black man indeed shot down unarmed men, how do you explain the two rifles, a shotgun, and at least 50 or 60 bullet holes in the mobile home? He thinks the jury was afraid to vote not guilty."

"This case gets stranger by the minute! Say, what was your friend's name, and do you think he would be willing to talk to me?"

"His name is Retired Sgt. Lorne Orris, and he already agreed to talk to you."

Lt. Keller gave Pat his address and telephone number.

"How's Herb's house coming?" asked Lt. Keller.

"I went by there the other day and all the debris from the fire Skinny set was gone, a new floor over the basement was finished, and walls were going up. They are working fast. I'm absolutely amazed, as they have only been working on it a few weeks. Skinny has been dead now for over three weeks and he is still haunting Herb; he's haunting all of us!"

"About quitting time, isn't it?"

"Right, Lt.," said Pat looking at his watch. "Shirley should be here anytime now. We're going out to eat and then she's going with her mother and Eb is coming over to the house."

"How is your old roommate?"

"You know Eb. He's impossible. Shirley plans on fixing him up with her best friend, Kathy. I've met her and she is about as scattered as Eb. Good looking, too. Maybe they will be a good match. Shirley went to school with her from 1st through 12th grade."

"See you, Pat. I'm meeting my girlfriend for supper, too. You know her, Dottie Albert, Judge Musselman's secretary."

"Why you sly fox; she is a real nice lady! How long has this been going on?"

"For about three months. I'm surprised you haven't heard. Have fun and I'll let you know what I find out from Sgt. Orris. Oh, before you go, did you hear about the man who embezzled several million dollars? His lawyer told him not to worry, because he would never go to jail with all of that money."

"So, what happened?"

"His lawyer was right. When the man went to jail he didn't have a penny to his name. Bye, Pat."

Pat hung up when in walked this very attractive 29-year old woman, long blond hair, green eyes, about 110 pounds, perfect skin, and dressed fit to kill, filling a white sweater and skirt like most women only dream about. She came in and plopped down on Pat's lap, put her arms around him, and gave him a big kiss.

"Gosh, Shir, you need to be more careful or you won't make it to your mother's.

"I know, I can feel that worm turning into a snake!"

"You shameless hussy. What am I going to do with you?"

"That's easy, my lord. Keep me serviced!"

"I'm not believing you!" laughed Pat.

Shirley laughed, too, as she got up from his lap. She loved to tease him, but she certainly wasn't just a tease. Shirley loved Pat deeply, and the bonding they went through, when both of their lives were at stake, made their love for each other even deeper. Pat felt the same about her.

Shirley complemented Pat perfectly. She was intelligent, had a fun-loving personality, came from a Christian family, and was an accomplished pianist and tennis player. Both were attorneys, but Shirley was an assistant district attorney for Clayton County. She was also a hunter and had a much larger mounted deer head than her father or Pat. Even though she came from a family with money, and her father was a very well-known plastic surgeon, she was very down-to-earth. Her mother, Grace, was a registered nurse. Shirley's parents were good people and were active in their church and also did volunteer work with a children's hospital and a veteran's hospital.

"Okay, Shir. I'm ready to let you buy me supper."

"Not on your life, Buster. I'm an old-fashioned girl, not a women's libber. You do the buying!"

"Well, you can't blame a guy for trying to pull it off. Can you?"

"Seriously, Hon, if you're running short, I'll buy."

"No, Shir, I was just teasing you back for that earlier premeditated, rather successful attempt at the worm-to-snake transformation."

"Let's go to supper. I'm getting hungry," said Shirley with a devious smile.

"Mexican, Chinese, steak house, or Burger Doodle?"

"How about the Brave Bull Cantina?"

"You got it. Come hop in my trusty Mustang."

Pat had given Shirley's father the check he received from the insurance company when Skinny destroyed his previous Mustang and asked him to find another car for him. Greg had the connections to get a good deal. He got Pat a '67 Mustang Convertible with a bored out and highly modified 351 Cleveland engine. This was a body off of the frame restoration, which was very expensive. Pat knew there was no way his old car was worth half as much as the '67 but Greg refused to let Pat put up additional money.

On the way to eat, Pat turned on the CB radio hoping Pick'em-Up-Man was on the air. Pat had been giving him a hard time on the radio for the last few months as he pretended to be *The Gay Blade.*

". . . . and since this is payday, good buddy, I'm going to stop for a cold 12-pack. Come on," said MoPar Man.

"Hey, gang, I'm coming, too, and you got the Sheet-Metal King here."

"Hey, Pick'em-Up-Man, which store you headed for?"

"How about Charley's? We all go there."

"Okay with me," said Sheet-Metal Man.

"Come on, Pat. Do your thing!" urged Shirley, who loved to hear Pat and Eb harass Pick'em-Up-Man.

Pat picked up the mike and proceeded to do a perfect imitation of a very gay man called The Gay Blade.

"Sa-a-a-y, Pick'em-Up-Man, you big sexy hunk. This is your s-w-e-e-t-h-e-a-r-t," said Pat with a heavy lisp.

"Oh, no! Not you again, Blade? You are ruining my reputation with my friends!"

"And you are h-u-r-t-i-n-g my feelings, handsome. I just got done buying a sexy-tight-fitting pair of bikini panties to wear just for y-o-u, Honey."

"What do you want from me Blade?" asked Pick'em-Up-Man in an exasperated tone. "If I catch you, I'm going to kick your ass good!"

"I think he already got it," laughed Sheet-Metal King.

"Up to the hilt!" joined a laughing MoPar Man.

"Sounds like a serious love affair to me, boys," said Eighteen-Wheel Willie, his laughter apparent.

"Just remember one thing, Boys, he's m-i-n-e!" said Pat in his sexiest lisp.

"This is too much!" laughed Sheet-Metal King, "Why don't you two go someplace private?"

"I've got to go, Sugar! Ta, ta! Ten four, sixty-nines, and all t-h-a-t!"

"Did you hear that, fellows? Ten four and sixty-nine's," asked Sheet-Metal King in uncontrollable laughter.

Pat and Shirley laughed themselves silly. Pick'em-Up-Man was putting on a macho man show for his friends. They had caught him with a little limp-wristed guy in pink pants when they went out of town to a movie. He had begged The Blade not to tell on him.

"Let's follow them," egged on Shirley.

"You're going to make us both late."

"If we're short on time, we can always eat at the local Burger Doodle instead of The Brave Bull. Charley's is only a few minutes away."

"You win, but I can't let Pick'em-Up-Man see me, because of the time I met him face to face, right after The Blade put the can of beer with a love note on his car hood."

". . . and I'm sorry fellows, but I got to head for home right after I get the beer. Got something important to do. Hot date with a 36-26-36 tonight," said Pick'em-Up-Man.

"Let's follow him home," said Shirley.

"You're going to get us both in hot water."

"Think of how you can describe his house on the CB next time you catch him on the air."

"Sounds good to me. Okay, Sweetie, let's do it. You might have to call your mother and I might have to call Eb to tell them we're running late, but what the heck."

They pulled in the last parking space at the end of Charley's lot, and about two minutes later along came the boys. Pick'em-Up-Man was in his pickup truck, a brand new 1981 Chevy. They got out, went inside, bought their beer, looked at the girlie magazines a few minutes, and then came out.

As Pat explained who was who, Shirley said, "So that's what they all look like."

Pick'em-Up-Man left and they followed him home. He lived in a typical subdivision in a brick house, with a carport, three bedrooms, and 1 ½ baths. They slowed way down about a half block away and parked when they saw him pull in his driveway at 14th Street and Greenwood Way. A car was parked in front and out stepped the little limp-wristed guy. Sure enough, he had on tight pink pants again. Now they knew Pick'em-Up-Man lived in the Greenwood Valley sub-division.

The little guy hopped in the passenger's side of the truck. Apparently they were going somewhere.

"He's getting bold now," laughed Pat, as they pulled away, circled the block, and went to The Brave Bull.

In the restaurant they ordered the usual, a Special 2 - -burrito, rice, and beans.

"I probably shouldn't eat beans since I'm going over to Mother's and meeting with her friends."

They both laughed.

* * *

Neither one of them would laugh if they knew what Jefferson Davis Anderson, Skinny's younger 40-year-old brother had in store for them.

CHAPTER 9

Brown Sugar

Pat and Shirley finished eating and he dropped her off at the courthouse to get her car. She was going to her parents place for a meeting with her mother, Kathy, and other friends to make wedding plans, while Pat went to his house to meet with his part-time roommate, Ebenezer, or Eb for short. He was about the same size and build as Pat but had dark hair. He worked as a paint and body man for a Ford dealership in Atlanta. Eb was a good-looking and fun-loving man, but a recent divorce had him drinking too much.

He was spending much of his time at his girlfriend's house, but they were having problems and a breakup was on the horizon.

Shirley stayed at Pat's modest 1250 sq. ft. house most of the time now, but when she was at her apartment, Pat stayed with her.

Pat pulled into his basement garage and went upstairs to the living area. This was the house where Pat and Shirley shot and killed Skinny. Shirley shot first, then Pat finished him off.

"Eb, I'm home," yelled Pat as he put a cold 12-pack in the refrigerator along with a pack of Hershey Bars.

"Over here in the den."

Pat went into the den where Eb lay on the couch watching TV.

"Running a little late tonight, aren't you?" asked Eb, as he put on a Herb Alpert 8-track tape. As he sat back down Eb had a beer in one hand and a cigar in the other.

"A little. Shirley wanted to follow our old friend, Pick'em-Up-Man, to his house."

Pat told Eb the story.

"Do you think he still might be in the area and on the air?" said Eb as he did a little dance to the music.

"He's always on the air running his mouth, but – let's see, five minutes back to Shirley's apartment, another five to say good bye, another five to stop to get the beer, ten to get home, and I've been here another five. Let's see, that would have been about 30 minutes ago when I was by his house. He's probably long gone, unless he got a phone call or something. Why do you ask?"

Eb jumped up and said: "Come on, let's get in my truck and take a chance. It's time he met *Brown Sugar.*"

They laughed and ran for the door. Pat's house was at the bottom of a hill, so Eb waited until they got to the top before he tuned around the band. Sure enough, Pick'em-Up-Man was on the radio.

"That's him, Eb; I'd know that voice anywhere!"

Apparently the same gang had planned this CB rendezvous earlier when they were buying beer. Eb picked up the mike and started talking as soon as he found an opening. Eb had the ability to imitate any type of voice or dialect.

"S-a-y-y-y, Pick'em-Up-Man," said Eb in a very good black feminine sounding lisp. "This be your sweetheart, Brown Sugar. Come on, Handsome."

"What! Who the hell is Brown Sugar?"

"That's not what you said to me behind the bowling alley the other night. You remember when we became very good f-r-i-e-n-d-s!" said Eb with a black-sounding lisp.

"Hey, Sheet-Metal King. Are you believing this? First, The Gay Blade and now Brown Sugar." Mopar Man laughed so hard he could hardly talk.

"Gay Blade!" yelled Eb with an outraged black lisp.

"Is you cheating on me after I gave you all of my brown sugar?"

"This here (laughter) be Eighteen-Wheel Willie, (laughter). In all my days on the CB radio, I have never heard anything like this!"

"Look, you black queer! I don't know what the hell you're up to, but you're about to get your ass kicked if I find you."

"But, Sugar, I'm sure you can find something better to do than kicking it," said Eb in his sexiest black lisp.

That brought out more laughter from the guys and made Pick'em-Up-Man furious.

"A-g-g-g-g-g-g-g!" screamed a hurting Pick'em-Up-Man. Unknown to the gang, just as he had keyed the mike to speak, the little man in the tight pink pants had hit him where it hurts. Pick'em-Up-Man had to pull off of the road.

With pain in his voice they heard, "I got to go. Pick'em-Up-Man out!"

Pat grabbed the mike and angrily said: "Hey, Brown Sugar, this be The Gay Blade, and if I find you with my Pick'em-Up-Man, I'm gonna scratch your black hussy eyes out!"

He quickly handed the mike back to Eb, whispering for him to keep it going.

"Oh! Listen you white dog turd. I'll fight for my m-a-n! He's my steady. We're engaged!"

"I'm not believing this," laughed Sheet-Metal King. "He has salt and pepper faggots fighting over him!"

"This day is one for the record books. I can't wait to tell my trucker buddies," laughed Eighteen-Wheel Willie.

"Hey, fellows, this here be the MoPar Man, and I think old Pick'em-Up-Man will be hiding under a rock for a few days, or maybe in a hospital if both the Blade and Sugar get a hold of him!"

"That's right, you two-timer," screamed The Blade.

"And that goes for me, too!" yelled Brown Sugar.

"What did I do to deserve this?" pleaded Pick'em-Up-Man as he fought off the little limp-wristed man in the tight pink pants, who was demanding to know who the Blade and Brown Sugar were and why he was involved with those hussies.

"What fun!" said Eb, "as he turned off the CB radio. "Say, Pat. I have some of those delayed-action firecrackers you gave me. Pull them out of the glove box and we'll find somewhere to dispose of them on the way home."

"How about Mean Mable's flower box? I went by there the other day and she has some kind of winter flowers blooming in the big flower box on the porch railing."

"Good idea, but we would have to get out of the truck to plant them."

"No problem. Let's see. You've got three in here. That should tear it up fairly good," laughed Pat.

Mean Mable was a neighborhood woman who didn't like kids and, in fact, didn't much like anyone. She was the kind of neighbor who children loved to make up stories about. Typical was a dead body buried in the basement, or a prisoner locked in her attic.

Pat had some twine that, after it was lit, would smolder around three minutes per inch, so Pat knew how long it would take to smolder down to the fire-cracker fuse wrapped around it.

"Hey, Eb, what's two 30-year old guys doing planning something like this, anyway?"

"Trying to relive their childhood, I guess. You weren't around then, but when I was growing up, we kids all thought Mean Mable was a witch."

"There's her house and I see a parking spot across the street about two houses down from hers. We should be able to see good from there." They parked and got out of the truck with about nine minutes left on wicks lit with the cigarette lighter in the truck. Eb had two and Pat had one.

They walked to her house, quickly pushed the three firecrackers down into the dirt in the flower box, which was shoulder high, and quickly walked away. They walked about a half block and doubled back on the other side of the street to watch the fireworks. They got into Eb's truck and waited. About a minute before they were set to go off, a group of Girl Scouts went up on the porch with one of their mothers, apparently to sell something.

Just as Mean Mable came to the door, three explosions and flash-bulb type light occurred almost at the same time. Flowers and dirt were flying everywhere. Girls were screaming, Mean Mable came out on the porch cussing, and pointing a finger at the girls and the woman. The leader gathered the girls in a corner which made Mable cuss even more. Then one of the girls wet her pants.

It was sheer pandemonium, and neighbors on both sides came out to see what was going on. Girl Scouts were walking down the street with Mean Mable pointing her finger at them and cussing a blue streak. No one suspected the two laughing men in the truck as they drove away.

"How were we supposed to know those Girl Scouts would come along at that time? I mean, they weren't even in sight when we placed those charges," exclaimed Eb.

"All I know is I'm getting too old to do this much longer. But - - did you see the expressions on their faces? They will be talking about it for weeks!"

"It was kind of hard to see their faces, but with the porch light on, I caught some of it," laughed Eb. All the neighbors were laughing at Mable, too."

"This has been too much for one evening, what with *The Gay Blade, Brown Sugar*, and now blowing up Mean Mable's flower box. Let's go home."

"Right! I got to take a leak like a race horse. The beer has been working on me."

CHAPTER 10

Jeffie and Reb

Earlier, when Pat dropped Shirley off at the courthouse to get her car, unknown to him, a man in a 1967 Camaro T-Top had been watching them. He noted Pat's looks and compared them with newspaper pictures of him. He did the same with Shirley and commented to himself that she looked even better in real life. He followed Pat home, while a man in a 1971 Chevy pickup truck followed Shirley. She got to her parents subdivision and was waived through the gate by the guard who knew her. For some reason, the guard thought the man in the pickup was with her and also waived him in. Shirley drove down Entrance Road, then turned on North Lake Drive, and finally arrived at the cul-de-sac where her parents lived.

Reb, the man in the pickup truck, could hardly believe what he was seeing - - a beautiful large brick house, and on a lake to boot. Some of their estate he couldn't see because of the shrubbery. What a place!

I can't wait until I, ah, tell Jeffie! This broad is really living the good life. Enchanted Lake Estates no less!

The two men met later at the Silver Slipper, a biker's bar, outside of Jonesboro. The man in the Camaro was Jefferson Davis Anderson or Jeffie, as he was known. He was now around 40 years old and a former mechanic for Dixie Airlines. A little over average height and weight, he kept in shape lifting weights. Jeffie kept a crooked smile on his face most of the time, which was almost a smirk. He now wore a full beard, moustache, and long hair tied in a ponytail.

Jeffie was never in trouble with the law, not because he didn't break it, but he was both smart and lucky. He was a smart-ass, a bully, and liked to slap women around. At 14, Jeffie helped his brothers kill an old black man. He loved to get into fights he knew he could win, but tended to shy away from a fight with a *real* man. Jeffie had little or no conscience, which, coupled with his high I.Q., made him a very dangerous adversary.

The man in the pickup truck was Johnny "Reb" Carter. He was 36 years old, 6' 3", and weighed 260 pounds. Reb had a large frame with a barrel chest, was not handsome, and was a high school dropout with below-average intelligence. He was a follower and was almost like Jeffie's shadow. Reb would cut your throat if Jeffie told him to do it.

Both men were members of the Confederate Motorcycle Club, an offshoot of The Brotherhood. Reb owned a Harley chopper, which he had stolen and changed the identification numbers. He called it his wife, his kids, his everything. Reb never served in the military, as he had a wife and four children, all of whom he deserted some years earlier. Every once in a while, he would show up to see them. Reb worked as a framer, building houses, although his supervisor had to constantly tell him what to do. He wasn't smart enough to do much on his own but could lift lumber and swing a hammer all day long. He was a good worker when not hung over.

"I found out where Patton lives," said Jeffie. "How 'bout you?"

"Man, ah, you wouldn't believe the place she lives at," answered an excited Reb. "It's a great big place on a lake. Lots of them there fancy big houses all around."

"That must have been her parent's house, man. He's a big shot doctor of some kind and has lots of money. I read that in the newspaper. The article also said she don't live with them anymore. It's good to know where they live though, 'cause it might come in handy. Did you mark it on the map like I told you?" asked Jeffie as he spit tobacco juice into an empty beer can.

"Ah, I couldn't find it on that map you gave to me, Jeffie. But I wrote down the two streets where this house is, like you told me. Ah, just like you told me."

"Man, give me the map and the street names."

"Ah, Jeffie, they's in my truck.

"Well, then go out and get them, Dumbass!" commanded Jeffie, while chewing on his ever-present toothpick."

"Ah, sure, Jeffie."

Reb went back out to the truck and got the map and notes he had jotted down. He couldn't read the names of the streets very well, but knew the letters of the alphabet and copied down the street names from the signs. He had an uneasy feeling when he went back into the bar. Although Reb was not very bright, he had extraordinary instincts and senses.

When Reb came back, Jeffie was watching a year-old Clint Eastwood movie on TV. *Every Which Way But Loose* featured Clyde, the orangutang, which Jeffie loved.

"Ah, I got the map for you, Jeffie, and I copied down them names of them streets real careful like. Ah, Jeffie, I got a funny feeling when I came in here, like someone was watching me. You know, I felt it with the hair what's on the back of my neck."

"Sit down, Dumbass. You're just imagining things."

When Spike, the bartender, brought their beer, he carefully laid a small envelope that was under a napkin on the table and shoved it toward Jeffie, who nodded to him. Jeffie handed Spike the folded menu, but it now contained payment for the speed, crank, or meth. It was known by all three street names.

"Reb, my good buddy. We gonna get high tonight!"

"What ya talkin' about?" asked Reb, who had no idea what was going on. However, Reb usually had no idea what was going on. That's why he had Jeffie to tell him what to do.

Jeffie showed Reb the envelope and made a fast gesture with his hand while saying: "Zoooooom!"

"Yeah, man, alright!" yelled Reb with a big smile.

"Next we gotta find out where Little Miss Tight-Ass lives.

They finished watching the movie, drank another beer, lit up a cigar, and left to get high.

* * *

While Jeffie and Reb were at the bar, Pat and Eb were at Pat's house, unaware he had been followed home earlier in the day.

"Hey, Eb, when I was reading the Bible this morning, I found out the meaning of the name Ebenezer. Do you know what it really means?"

"Not really."

"Next time you get out your Bible, read 1st Samuel 7:12."

"I will, I will already! Now tell me what it means!"

"Get this. Your name means *The Stone Of Help*!"

"So, now you're calling me a rock head, huh?"

"No, but that might explain why you're so weird! Anyway, it had to do with the Lord helping the Israelites defeat the Philistines."

"I'll read about it tonight. Say, how about some piano and drums?"

"Okay, but let me finish this Hershey bar, then we'll pop two tops and get with the program."

They played for about an hour, Pat on the piano and Eb on the drums. Neither one of them were accomplished musicians, but they had a good time.

"Say, Pat, how about a Red Neck or a Diamond number?"

"Okay, but I don't want anyone getting hurt, either physically, mentally, or emotionally."

Eb found a Zeke located at a well-known redneck trailer park and dialed the number.

"Speak to me, Hoss. You got Zeke," said a deep male voice.

"You being a kool cowboy and all, I want to give you a tip."

"Who the hell is this and what the hell you talkin' 'bout?"

"Your best friend, that's who."

"You don't sound like nobody I knowed."

"No man," said Eb, spitting into a beer can, "your hound dog is your best friend."

"What 'bout Budweiser?"

"I hain't talkin' 'bout no beer, man. I talkin' 'bout a hound dog."

"Budweiser is my dog's name."

"I knowed that, I jus was a-teasin' ya," said Eb with a laugh.

"Get on wif it man, dis ole coon gotta hot mama a-waitin' fer him."

"You 'bout to lose ole Budweiser."

"What! How that be?"

"The county commissioners, cowboy. They passed a vicious animal law. They now considers all hound dogs to be vicious animals and them guys is wantin' $1000 fer the license fee. 'Course most cowboys can't afford that, so they will jus have to get rid of them."

"But - - - but, Budweiser is old! He don't even have no teeth no more."

"Son, iffin I was you, I'd get on the phone and give them snakes a piece of my mind!"

"Thanks fer the tip, ole buddy," and a sad sounding Zeke hung up.

Pat was laughing as Eb tried to keep a straight face.

"Here's one in the Diamond exchange. The Black Knight's Poolroom in Atlanta," said Eb as he dialed the number. Eb was so good that even a black person couldn't tell he was a white guy.

When the number started ringing, Eb signaled Pat to pick up on the extension before a man with a deep voice answered.

"Hello, you gots de Black Knights Poolroom. Talk!"

"Say, Baby, dis here be Leroy for de Black Power Ball Committee. We's decided dat you gonna sell 50 tickets to de ball, what wif you being a successful businessman and all," said Eb in a convincing black voice.

"What de hell you be tryin' to pull, nigga?" said the voice. "You ain't gonna be demandin' nothin' from me, understand?"

"Look, Man. We be gonna send a man down der to your place and you will buy 50 tickets or else! Does I make myself clear, you black dumbass!"

"You show your black ass here and I gonna stick a shotgun up it an pull de trigger!" said the deep black voice as he slammed down the phone.

"Well, I guess he told you. Didn't he?" stated Pat.

"I guess he did," said a laughing Eb.

About that time Shirley came home.

"Hi, Guys, what have you been up to?"

"Oh, nothing, just spending a quiet night at home." However, Pat's big grin was a giveaway.

"Right, and the Devil drinks Holy Water, too," said Shirley with mock concern. "You two, a quiet night? Come on!"

"Alright, Shir, we did go out for a little while, just to help an old lady across the street," said Pat.

"Or to blow up her flower box," chimed in Eb.

"What! Just what have you two goofballs been up to, anyway?"

They told her about Mean Mable's flowerbox and about the encounter between The Gay Blade, Brown Sugar, and Pick'em-Up-Man. She enjoyed the story but was concerned.

"Honey, you need to cool it some. Can you even imagine the dim view the Bar would take on a fairly new attorney, or even an old one for that matter, blowing up an old lady's flower box?"

"Of course you're right, Shir, but it sure was fun and I'm having a real hard time growing up."

She went over to Pat and gave him a big kiss. "Please don't get caught. By the way, you didn't tell me about the Red Neck or Diamond number you called."

Pat and Eb looked at each other.

"She's getting scary, Eb! Can she read our minds?"

CHAPTER 11

Engine Out!

Saturday morning Pat went to Bellah Airfield while Shirley went back to her parent's house for more wedding planning. Pat was now a partner with John Beaver in an Eipper MX Quicksilver ultralight airplane that John had named *Gertrude*.

A new guy was at the airport and appeared to be interested in ultralight airplanes.

"Man, that thing sure is small," stated Pete.

"They can only have one seat and the total weight can't exceed around 260 pounds."

"What kind of motor does it have?"

"This one has a 42 HP Rotax engine and is a pusher type with the prop in the rear."

"It looks like a motorcycle with wings. How fast will it go?"

"Gertrude cruises at around 38 mph. I got to go fly now, but if you check with me or one of the guys later, we will be happy to tell you how to get started."

Pat flew for about two hours until the wind picked up as the day warmed up. Wind and ultralight airplanes do not go well together, because Gertrude was made of aluminum tubing and fabric. Anything less than a light wind would kick her all over the sky.

Pat sat in an unenclosed go-cart type seat, and because the wings were on top, he had an excellent view of everything below him. He had a 35-mm camera with auto-focus and auto-rewind strapped around his neck. This was an excellent aircraft for doing aerial photography.

After an early lunch, Pat called Shirley from a pay phone. He couldn't help laughing a little at Louie Lake shooting up those pay telephones. Thank goodness this one worked. Shirley told him she would be home about 7:00 when they could go out to supper. Pat would stay and fly again later in the day when the wind died down.

Later the wind did calm down and Pat got Gertrude out of her hanger, did a preflight inspection, and checked to make sure he remembered to fill up the gas tank. Some of the other guys were at the airport now and he went up with them, practicing emergency landings. He flew at various altitudes from 500 to 1000 feet, cut the engine and glided in for a landing. He almost crashed on his solo flight in Gertrude, so he practiced emergency landing religiously. In cool weather like this, Gertrude could glide about a mile from 1000 feet when the engine was shut down. With no engine noise, the silence was eerie.

After 30 minutes of this, Pat decided to fly to McDonough, which was about eight miles. On the way he would circle Elliot Fogelhorn's small farm and wiggle his wings. Elliot was a police officer who was shot by Skinny when protecting Skinny's ex-wife, Betty Johnson. Lucky for him, he had on a bullet-proof vest.

Pat followed Miller's Mill Road over to Hwy 155 and turned south toward the Fogelhorn's farm, flying at 1000 feet. He didn't go higher because he was within several miles of the Atlanta Airport, and he did not want to encounter one of Delta's 747s, or other large beasts of the air. Sometimes their holding patterns took them close to Bellah Airfield. Twenty-five miles is not very far when a large plane is circling Hartsfield Airport. He figured if one came within a half mile of him, he was a goner because of the vortexes created by the wings and the rest of the large plane as it punched a hole in the sky. Pat always was careful to keep an open field in sight when he flew and never went over heavily wooded areas unless he was sure he had enough altitude to glide over them to land in case of an emergency. Ultralight engines were not as reliable as regular airplane engines.

Boy, this is fun! I lucked out and caught a tail wind. I'll bet I have a ground speed of about 60 mph. I hope I don't have a problem getting back!

In a few minutes he arrived over Elliot's place, and circled, waiving his wings while Elliot waived back, and then headed for McDonough.

A few minutes later the engine sputtered and ran so erratic the vibration felt like it would shake the airplane apart!

I have to hit the engine kill switch in order to stop the violent vibration. There's a large field about ¾ of a mile ahead, so here we go.

As he got closer, Pat could see fence rows, which he had to clear, and then he saw cows, which he had to miss!

Lord, now I'm over a small subdivision and people are pointing up at me. I wonder how long it will take before they report a plane crash? Only a minute or two before touchdown and this one is for real! Okay. I cleared the fence. Now, Gertrude, please don't hit a cow!

He flew over some cows and touched down in the farmer's field. Pat got out quickly and reached for his spare set of spark plugs and wrench. Two-stroke engines sometimes fouled spark plugs, and the plane had acted like it had lost one of its two cylinders.

"Damn! What's going on here!" He watched as the cows were forming a circle around him and Gertrude. They had their heads down looking at him. "I don't need this!" He had read that cows liked to eat airplane fabric.

Pat kept working on changing plugs because he believed the police, fire trucks, and an ambulance would quickly show up looking for an airplane crash.

I gotta get out of here quick!

As he worked Pat noticed the cows still had him surrounded. Then, all at once, a cow which must have been the lead cow, let out a loud bellow and ran off, followed by the rest of the herd.

The new plugs were in now and Pat tried to start the engine. It fired right up but ran very rough, violently shaking Gertrude like earlier.

Well, nothing to do now but call John and have him bring his trailer to load her up. I also need to call Shirley, thought Pat as he trudged up to the farmer's house. *At least I'm in one piece.*

Apparently the farmer did not know anyone had landed in his field, or maybe he wasn't home. Pat found a gate, opened it, and went up on the back porch.

I hope he doesn't come out with a shotgun.

He knocked on the door, and as he waited, Pat looked over his shoulder at his plane and the cows, making sure they weren't eating Gertrude.

Suddenly the door opened and there stood the farmer! Pat need not have worried because Eugene, the owner of this farm, was a very friendly man. When Pat explained what had happened, Eugene smiled and showed him to the telephone.

Pat called John, who said, "I'll be there in about an hour. We'll have to tear her down and load Gertrude on the trailer."

This was a 30-minute job for two men who knew what they were doing.

They took her to John's place and then John took Pat back to Bellah Field to pick up his Mustang. He also called Shirley and explained what had happened, telling her he was fine and would be about an hour late.

The police, fire trucks, and ambulance never came.

"What a day, John! But at least I was able to put her down without breaking anything."

"You said it acted like a fouled plug?"

"Sure did. And once it was running on one cylinder, the engine vibrated the plane like it wanted to shake it to pieces! I was again reminded of what the *pucker factor* means."

"It doesn't sound like a fuel problem because it ran on one cylinder. Most likely an ignition problem."

"Most likely. Are you going to work on her tomorrow? If so, I can help you after church."

No, it's going to be later in the week. I'll call you if I need help."

* * *

Pat got into his Mustang and headed home. As he pulled the car into the garage, Shirley ran out and threw her arms around him. "I've been so worried about you, Honey! Your phone call scared me to death!"

"I'm fine, Shir, but it's nice to know someone cares," said Pat as he kissed her. He had known her only a few months but it seemed like forever. Neither one could imagine life without the other.

"Are you as starved as I am?" asked Pat.

"No wonder, it's 7:30, and, yes, I could eat a cow."

"Don't even mention cows to me today!" Pat had a big smile. "Let me take a quick shower and I'll be ready by 8:00. That is if you leave me alone and don't try to ravish me."

"I'll get you later, Buster. Now go take your shower."

CHAPTER 12

Sgt. Orris

"Where to, Shir?" asked Pat as he was getting dressed.

"How about the Brave Bull? You've got me hooked on that place." Then she looked up at him and let out a loud "Moooooooooo!"

"I never turn down a burrito, smart aleck!" laughed Pat. Let me make a quick phone call before we leave. Lt. Keller told me about retired police officer Sgt. Lorne Orris, who was one of the investigating officers of the shooting at Ed Edward's mobile home back in '55. I want to see when I can get together with him and pick his brain on this case."

"Hurry, Hon, 'cause I'm hungry."

Pat called the Sgt. and found out he, too, was about to leave for a late supper. Orris said he liked Mexican food and would meet them at the Brave Bull in about 15-20 minutes. Pat told him that all of the waitresses there knew him and they would be wearing white sweaters and black slacks. The weather had turned cold, so they grabbed their jackets and left.

* * *

Sgt. Orris already had a table and waived them over. Introductions were made and they sat down.

"I recognized you from the newspaper pictures when you were defending that Five-O'clock Traffic Bandit and Skinny was raising so much Hell. It was several weeks ago but it seems like yesterday. Especially now that I'm getting into a case that may have involved his brother, Jeb, and perhaps another brother and Skinny's little sister."

"You, young lady, look even better in person than in the newspapers." Then, looking at Pat, the Sgt. said, "And to think a beautiful young woman like this had the g _ _ _, ah, intestinal fortitude to face and shoot a cold-blooded killer like Skinny Anderson!"

"It wasn't quite like that. I had the drop on him and only did what I had to do. He was about to kill Pat!"

"You two sure got tied up with a completely dysfunctional family. The whole bunch was like a den of rattlesnakes, except for the daughter, Charlotte, who was a decent sort of person. Skinny's mother was also okay but the men and the boys in that family were trash!"

The waitress came and they placed their orders.

"So tell me, Sgt., what do you remember about the family and the shootout at the Edward's place?"

"Skinny's father was a liar, a bully, a thief, and a drunk. He beat the kids and his wife when he was drinking, which was most of the time. Finally, he picked on the wrong person. Somewhere around '53 or '54, he got into a fight with a guy at a poolroom and was beaten to death with a cue stick.

"After his death, Mrs. Anderson had to try to support the family. Skinny and Jeb quit high school but she somehow talked Jeffie into staying and he graduated."

"Jeffie, as you called him, is he still out there somewhere?"

"I'll get to that. After Jeffie graduated, he joined the Army and was in one of those outfits that jumped from planes."

"Airborne," helped Pat.

"I knew that. Anyway, he was in Germany, and from what I heard tell, he beat up a prostitute. Due to that and other trouble he got in, they kicked him out of the Army after a year or so. He came back and married a girl named Helen. I knew her family. She was formerly married to a wife abuser. When she hooked up with Jeffie, she got more of the same. They stayed together a few years, and then she divorced him."

"Jeffie sounds a lot like his brother, Skinny," commented Shirley.

"Worse, because he's even smarter."

"But is he still out there somewhere?" asked Pat. "Sergeant, I need to know if I need to be concerned about him because Skinny was more than enough to last a lifetime!"

"Two life times, mine and yours," added Shirley.

"I'm getting to that if you will just bear with me for a few more minutes. I need to give you the history of this creep. Since I was called to the scene of the Edward's shooting, I have kept up with Jeffie, and the rest of the family, through newspapers and my connections as a police officer."

"I'm sorry. Go ahead, Sergeant," said Pat as he ate more of his burrito.

"He has two years of college and made good grades even though he was a known party person and was often on a high from alcohol, drugs, or both.

"Jeffie went to A & P School to get a license to work on airplanes and was in the top ten percent of his class. How he did it is beyond me, as from what I hear, he was forever drinking, using drugs, and getting into fights. We suspected him of selling drugs, stealing cars, and of a number of burglaries, but could never get the goods on him. He has no doubt also murdered several people, but we can't prove that either. Anyway, that's the street talk I hear. Everyone is afraid of him and his Brotherhood friends because they're sort of like a mini Mafia. Some of my good snitches refused to talk about Jeffie. They told me that if they did, they were sure to wind up dead. One guy snitched on Skinny and was unbelievably mutilated. These guys don't play games."

"He has that kind of power over other criminals?" asked Shirley.

"You better believe it," said Sgt. Orris as he took a big bite of his burrito before it got cold. He was really enjoying this conversation - - retirement was boring. He felt like he was back in action again.

"Later, somewhere in the mid-sixties, Jeffie married a woman by the name of Renée. She was also previously married to a wife abuser. I don't understand why some women go from one abuser to another."

Shirley spoke up. "A lot of it has to do with their childhood and being abused at home. Mental abuse is often worse than physical abuse. The bruises go away, but mental scars often stay with a person for a much longer time. They have very low self-esteem after being told for years on end they are more worthless then whale crap. So, they psychologically gravitate to jerks like Jeffie because they think they're not good enough for a nice guy."

"Well spoken, Young Lady," complimented Sgt. Orris who was glad for the break so he could attack his food again. "Anyway, Renée had a daughter, who was around 12 or 13 at the time they got married. The word was he had his eye on the daughter, Cindy, who was a real looker even at that age. We, at the Police Department, strongly suspected incest, but, again, could not prove our suspicions. At that time he was working with Southern Airways as a mechanic, making big bucks. Later he was fired for punching out a supervisor.

"Again, the man refused to file criminal charges against Jeffie. Then a few years ago he disappeared. I have taken advantage of my many contacts but have found out nothing. So, to answer your initial question, I really don't know. I haven't heard he died, and he is not in a Georgia prison. Where he's at is anyone's guess."

"This whole thing is getting very scary again. We've been through one nightmare and survived it and don't need another one," said Shirley.

"I can always back off the Edwards' case," offered Pat.

"I know you mean well, Honey, but we both know it won't solve anything. If this Jeffie character is out there somewhere, the fact we killed his brother would be enough for him to come after us."

"You're probably right, Shir, but the Edwards' case will add fuel to the fire."

"Do you want to drop the case?"

"No," answered Pat with a light laugh.

"I didn't think so. What am I going to do with this guy, Sgt. Orris?"

"Marry him, I guess," said Orris with a laugh.

"What's the chances Jeffie is out there somewhere, planning revenge?" asked Pat with a very serious look on is face.

"You really don't want to know!"

* * *

Sunday morning Pat and Shirley got ready for church. Every Sunday they went to the Solid Rock Christian Church in Jonesboro with her parents.

"I guess you know Dad will be asking you about that airplane crash you were involved in yesterday," said Shirley with a smile.

"Airplane crash! What are you talking about?"

"And - - the ambulances, the fire department, police officers . . ."

"Wait a minute, Shir," interrupted Pat. "You know darn well that . . ."

"And all of those poor terrified cows that are now giving green milk!" continued Shirley.

"Green milk? Now I've heard of everything! You really are going to make a great prosecutor, you lovely little devil!" said Pat as he took her in his arms. "Are you sure you want to go to church?" whispered Pat into her ear.

"Yes, Handsome, but I won't let you off so easily tonight!"

They went out the front door and got into Shirley's car, because it was parked in the driveway and would have to be moved to get Pat's Mustang out. The house had only a single garage and it was part of the basement. He often wished for a double carport with a door leading into the house, plus the drive-in basement, of course.

The Solid Rock Christian Church building was a beautiful thing to see and was quite large for a city as small as Jonesboro. It sat 1000 people in the sanctuary, had a gym, a softball field, as well as a number of classrooms and a great room for social events. As everyone should know though, it's people who make a church, not a nice building.

This church was fortunate to have a very good group of people and strong leadership. There are always a few in any church who cause problems, but Solid Rock had only a few of the few.

"I see Daddy's car and they're waiting for us." Pat pulled into the parking place beside the O'Kelly's Mercedes and got out to open the door for Shirley.

"Hi, Momma, hi, Daddy," yelled Shirley as she gave them both hugs.

"You look lovely as usual, Grace," complemented Pat as he gave her a hug and reached out for Greg's hand. "Greg, it's always a pleasure to see you."

"Say, Pat, you'll have to tell us about the big plane crash when we eat after church," said Greg with a wink.

"Shir! You didn't!" exclaimed Pat.

"Guilty as charged, Sir. I couldn't help it. I called them when you were taking a shower."

"Pat, I have a question for you," said Grace with a dead-pan face. "What are they going to do with all of the green milk?" She held the dead-pan look for several seconds but then all broke out laughing.

When they went into the church building, none of them noticed a Camaro parked three rows in back of their cars. In it sat two men watching them.

* * *

After lunch they all went to the O'Kelly's house for the afternoon. Pat and Greg played pool, while Shirley and her mother worked on wedding plans. About 4:30 they returned home. Both felt some pent-up energy, so they went out for a three-mile jog.

Pat took a quick shower before going out for a late supper. When he was almost finished soaping down, he heard the shower door open a crack and saw an eyeball looking at him.

"Shir! What are you doing?" asked a laughing Pat.

"I just wanted to take a peek at it."

"You are a dirty girl."

"You know, it really is very cute!" said Shirley as she opened the door, exposing her naked body as she stepped into the shower with him.

"I'm s-o-o-o shocked at you!"

"Now give me the soap so I can wash that cute little thing, because he will soon have a very important job to do." At her touch there was an instant worm-to-snake transformation. That *cute little thing* performed its task flawlessly.

CHAPTER 13

Meeting with Louie Lake

On Jan. 12th, and Monday morning's first appointment was a meeting with client Louie Lake.

"Hi, Louie," welcomed Pat as they shook hands.

"Good morning, Mr. Patton. Have any news for me?"

"Of course. Here's the original Motion to Suppress and a copy of it for your file. I want you to look it over because I have an appointment with the Assistant DA on this case, Nancy Katman. Hopefully she will see the light, save the taxpayers some money, dismiss, dead docked, or nolle pross your case, so you go free and I make $1000. However, it doesn't always work that easily. Nancy is a practical person though, so hopefully she will not want to spend a lot of time on a losing case."

"One question, Mr. Patton. I know what dismissing my case is, but I'm not sure of the meaning of the other terms."

"Nolle pros basically means that although the case is not dismissed, the DA's Office elect not to prosecute. When dead docketed, it is kept semi-open for a period of time to see if anything else pops up, but then it is dismissed."

"When should I check with you?"

"Try about 4:30 today. I have an appointment with her this afternoon. She may want a day or two to think about it, so I might not have an answer for you."

"You're a good man, Mr. Patton. I have been around enough to know all an attorney can promise is that he will work diligently on your case. You certainly have done that and I will be more than happy to concede the $1000 retainer for any of the three results you mentioned.

"Thank you, Louie, and if I take your money, I will work for you. But – you're right; I can't guarantee the outcome."

"I'll check back later. Have a good weekend."

"You too, Louie. May you have a very good weekend."

"I intend to and I plan on making the $1000 retainer back that I spent on your services."

"How do you plan on doing that?" asked Pat, knowing the answer.

"Working for the telephone company," said Louie with a wink and a big smile.

Pat shook his head. "Careful, Louie!"

Louie left and Pat called Julie into his office.

"Julie, did you confirm my appointment with Nancy for this afternoon?"

"Jeez, Boss. You should know I'm *old reliable* by now. Of course I did! She said she would be there between 1:00 and 1:30. Best make it at 1:00 to be sure."

"Thanks, Julie. I'm going to file Louie's motion and take a copy stamped by the clerk to Nancy. Since I'm going to be there anyway, I told Shirley to meet me at the courthouse snack bar for lunch."

"Anything else, Boss?"

"No, Miss Efficiency" Although Pat was madly in love with Shirley, he could not help but notice Julie's figure. As she walked out of his office, he had trouble taking his eyes off her red sweater and black skirt, which were filled out in all of the right places. Her husband was a lucky man. Julie had both looks and personality. Pat would look, but it would never go further for three reasons: One, she was his secretary; two, she was married; and three, there was Shirley, who was every bit as luscious as Julie, and then some. He felt lucky to find two women with those qualities.

Pat did some work, filed his motion, and headed for the snack bar. He could not believe who was there and all sitting at the same table: Judge Musselman, Lt. Keller, Capt. Keefauver, Sgt. Orris, and his very own Shirley, who had a seat saved for him. They had shoved two tables together and were engaged in conversation.

Shirley motioned to him to get her lunch, too. He waived at her, went through the line, got them both ham and Swiss on rye, chips, and a Coke. He knew what Shirley liked, so he simply got two of each. Putting the food on the table, he greeted everyone.

"We have been discussing your favorite subject - - Skinny and his family," informed Lt. Keller.

"I found a copy of the original police report in our archives dated Aug. 25, 1955," said Sgt. Orris, as he handed it to Pat. "As you can see, the report has Edwards going out into the yard and blowing away an unarmed wounded man. Later the report says, 'Edwards stated the white man was armed and was going for his gun but he shot first.'"

"The police report said witnesses saw Edwards kill in cold blood, but there are no written statements to be found. The two witnesses were listed as Haddie Mae Dickerson and Jenel Freeman, neighbors of Edwards. If I remember right, he had the middle of three mobile homes parked on property owned by a black church. Back in those days blacks were not allowed to park at a commercial mobile home park. By the way, notice my name is not on the report!"

"Do you remember talking to them back then?" asked Judge Musselman."

"Yes, Sir. I remember. The next day they told me they didn't remember the white man having a gun when Ed shot him. But, I also remember something else. Both of the ladies were scared to death."

"I surely hope I can locate those two ladies and talk to them," said Pat.

"Assuming they're still alive," noted Lt. Keller. "After all it was 26 years ago."

"The Lt. and I can unofficially see if we can find an address on them. You don't mind, do you, Lt.?" asked Capt. Keefauver with a wink.

"Absolutely not, Capt. More and more this man Edwards seems to have received a raw deal and has lost 26 years of his life for something he is not guilty of doing."

"In the interest of justice," said the Judge, "if you find enough evidence to justify me looking into it, officially I mean, then please let me know and I will take a look. This is interesting, because we have sitting at these tables, a Superior Court Judge, a defense attorney, an Assistant DA, and members of the Clayton County Police Department. Shirley, please brief DA Colver of this meeting. I don't want anyone saying we were doing anything behind his back."

"Yes, Sir, I certainly will, and now that's out of the way, I have a question. Does anyone here have information on the whereabouts of any of Skinny's family?"

"Good question, Shir, complemented Pat. I know from talking to Sgt. Orris here, and my research of the old newspaper stories, Skinny had a brother named Jeb, who was killed by Edwards, another brother by the name of Jefferson, or Jeffie, and a sister named Charlotte. Jeffie had two ex-wives, Helen and Renée, and a stepdaughter named Cindy. Does anyone know of anyone I missed or have any idea where these people live?"

"I can help you with one of them," answered Capt. Keefauver. "Charlotte lives in a small house outside of town near Jimmy Cross's farm. You know, where they shot his prize registered Polchin cow back in 1955."

"Can you get me an address and phone number? Maybe she would be willing to talk to me."

"Sure, Pat. Call me tomorrow or I can leave a message with Julie."

"And speaking of relatives, would any of you gentlemen know where either of Jeffie's ex-wives live?" asked Shirley.

Everyone had a blank look.

"Well, how about the stepdaughter?"

More blank looks.

"Then I have to keep digging until something turns up," said Pat. Look at it this way, Honey, we now have a lead on Charlotte that we didn't have before. Perhaps she can shed some light on Jeffie and his two ex-wives."

"You're right, and let us hope she knows where Jeffie went because I'm getting very uncomfortable, to say the least, with him out there somewhere. His reputation worries me," said Shirley.

"Both of you have a right to be concerned. From what I know of Jeffie, he is probably a very unhappy camper because you two killed his brother. Self-defense would not matter to him," said Lt. Keller.

"What I find strange about a man like that is his not having a police record," interjected Capt. Keefauver. "We ran his name and came up empty. Hopefully it won't matter because Jeffie is most likely in another state, possibly even dead, or maybe he didn't like Skinny."

"I would like to know what this guy looks like, said Pat. Shoot, he could walk up to me today and I would have no idea who he is. I tried to get a high-school photo of him. When I called the school, I found out he graduated but his picture was not in the year book. Apparently he was absent the day the pictures were taken."

"You could try Southern Airways, one of his former employers, or maybe even the, ah, anyone sure of which branch of the military he was in?" asked Sgt. Orris.

"You probably aren't going to get too far with either of them, unless he's suspected of committing a crime. Am I right, Capt.?" asked Judge Musselman.

"Yes, Sir. While they might be good places to get a picture, the military would tell us to get lost unless we had a valid reason. Maybe later, but not now."

"Then we're back to Charlotte," said Shirley dejectedly.

"I guess so, Dear," replied Pat.

"Speaking of dear, I suspect some serious things are going on between my secretary and the Lt. here," said Judge Musselman with a smile. "Why, all she talks about is her Lt."

"Why, Lt. Keller. I do believe you're blushing," said Shirley with a smile.

"I have to say Dottie's more than a good friend," admitted Lt. Keller. "We'll keep you posted, Judge, as to any later developments."

"When I came in, I saw a beautiful 1957 Studebaker Golden Hawk. I thought Shirley's father had the only one around," said Pat.

Capt. Keefauver responded, "That jewel belongs to me, and believe it or not, before I got it, Greg O'Kelly had two Golden Hawks."

Pat knew Greg was a friend of Judge Musselman but did not know he was also a friend of the Captain. The present chief was rumored to be retiring soon and Capt. Keefauver was in line to take his place. Then, no doubt, Lt. Keller would be promoted to Capt. This was not a large force like in Atlanta and the Capt. did the duties of an Assistant Chief. *Old Greg does not miss a trick. I wonder how many speeding tickets he got in the last several years? Not only am I about to marry a beautiful and intelligent woman but I'm also going to be a member of a socially connected family.*

"I wonder how it would do against my '67 Mustang?"

"Who knows? Maybe we could find out some night," replied Capt. Keefauver with a big smile.

Everyone laughed and rose to get back to work.

CHAPTER 14

Pat Meets Sam

"I'll walk you up to the DA's Office since I have an appointment with Nancy," said Pat to Shirley.

Thelma, the receptionist, told Pat that Nancy requested he come as soon as he walked in the door, so they walked to Nancy's office. She had a visitor, but they were waived in anyway.

There sat a very strange-looking individual talking to Nancy. Pat was not sure if it was a man or a woman. The person had on black slacks, a black shirt, and wore a Harley hat. It must have weighed between 350 and 400 pounds, had dark short haircut like a man's, thin eyebrows, long lashes, sparkling eyes, a big smile, and soft pinkish skin.

"Pat, Shirley, I want you to meet a friend of mine - - Sam.

Sam, thought Pat. *So, it's a man.*

Pleased to meet you, Sam," said Shirley as she shook hands.

"And pleased to meet you, Shirley," said Sam in a low feminine voice.

"Sam," said Pat as he felt a strong manly handshake.

"Likewise," said Sam.

Pat and Shirley were both confused.

"Sam is a very old friend of mine. In fact I've known her from back in the '60's. We were sitting here talking motorcycles.

So, it's a woman. "What do you ride, Sam?" asked Pat with a smile, because he knew it had to be big to handle all her weight.

"Just got my Harley last week. Say, you don't happen to know of anyone who would be interested in a Kawasaki KZ1000, do you?"

"Pat has talked about getting one ever since I've known him," answered Shirley.

"She's right. I have loved those things clear back to 1973 when they first came out with the KZ900."

"I'll make you a deal on it that you can't refuse. It's only a year old, has 3,000 miles on it, and has always been kept in a garage."

"I can't believe I'm saying this but when can I see it?"

"Is tonight soon enough?" answered Sam with a grin.

Smiling, Nancy said, "Did you hear about the big festival in St. Augustine, FL, this coming weekend? Bikes from all over the U. S. will be there and way above-average temperatures are forecast clear from New York to Florida. Sam and I are riding down Friday afternoon. I'm only going to work until noon and will pack everything up the night before. Why don't you and Shirley come with us on your new KZ1000?"

"You already have me buying her bike, huh?"

"When you see it, believe me, you will have to have it. Sam would clean it up, even if there was only a speck of dust on it."

"I can't go this weekend because of wedding plans. We're picking out the matching dresses for my court, but, Pat, why don't you go with them? It would do you good to get away for a few days," said Shirley.

"That would be a rough trip on my 450."

"But not on a KZ1000," said Sam.

"Talk about high pressure!"

"So, here's my address where you can pick up the bike tonight. I told you I would make a deal you can't refuse. I will lend it to you for the trip, no strings attached, because, once you get back here, there is no way you will part with it."

"Damn, Shir! I've been blindsided! How can I say no?"

Sam handed him a slip of paper with her address and directions to her house, and they said their goodbyes.

"And now for the Lake case," said Nancy.

Pat handed her the Motion to Suppress, which she read with care. If granted by the judge, it would prohibit the use of the illegally seized evidence against Louie.

"Very good, Pat. This is the excuse I need to place this case on the Dead Docket. The Jonesboro police, and I'm glad it was not our Clayton County Police Department, really screwed up this stop. From what I can see, there is no doubt in my mind that he did it, but they pushed this stop beyond the limits. I'm sure they saw your boy, got excited, and decided to bust him no matter what. But we'll get him sooner or later. He really thinks he's smart, but one day he'll make a big mistake and we will nail him. Louie does have a few prior arrests, but no convictions."

"Then I can tell my client you will dismiss this case?"

"No, Pat, you sly fox. I said I will place it on the Dead Docket, not dismiss it. As you know, this way I have a little time to see what might develop. Tell him it will be placed on the Dead Docket and I will send you a copy."

"Mr. Lake will be happy to hear this."

"Yes, and I'm sure you made enough off of this case to buy at least half of Sam's bike. Huh?"

"What a way to make a living," laughed Pat as he got up to leave.

"I guess I had better make plans to take you to Sam's tonight to pick up the motorcycle," said Shirley with a fake sigh.

Shirley left for her office, while Pat went across the street to his office. There he found three reporters waiting for him: Vivienne Cove from The Clayton News Daily, Sandi Desanto from WHIT radio, and Zel Murray from TV News Channel 3.

"Mr. Patton! Is it true you are now taking on a case defending the man who killed Skinny's brother back in 1955?" asked Sandi.

'Yes, but how did you find out?"

"A little snack bar bird overheard some interesting bits of conversation," replied Zel.

"Right, and then made each one of us promise to pay him for the tip without telling us he also made the same deal with two other reporters," said Vivienne, trying to hide her irritation.

"Who told you about this?" asked Pat.

"You know we can't tell you, Mr. Patton, but maybe we can get you to defend us when we beat him to death," said Vivienne with a smile.

"How about a statement?" asked Zel with her cameraman at her side on ready.

"Okay, ladies. And – please call me Pat."

About that time Steve Futo of TV13 showed up with his cameraman.

"Thank you, Pat. Go ahead when you're ready," requested Sandi.

"Mr. Ed Edwards, a black man, came into my office asking for help. He claimed he was convicted of murder in 1955 by an all-white jury and served 26 years in prison for defending his wife and home. I am finished with a preliminary investigation and have decided to take his case.

"Who was he accused of killing?" asked Zel.

"According to Mr. Edwards, three members of an organization called *The Brotherhood* went to his mobile home and shot it up, wounding his wife in the process. Mr. Edwards shot and killed three white men, Jeb Anderson, Bubba Hawkins, and Bo Cain."

"What are you planning to do?" asked Vivienne.

"Once my investigation is completed, I plan on filing a Habeas Corpus action on his behalf."

"Why file something now? He's out of jail isn't he?" asked Sandi.

"That's correct, but a habeas could do two things for him. One, exonerate him of the crime, and two, when you are paroled on a life sentence, you never get off parole. We need to get rid of that because, as long as he is on parole, he not only is subject to going back to prison for life for any violation of the rules but this man has lost most of his rights. He can't vote or own fire arms and is not free to move without permission from his parole officer. He needs his record cleared, and a habeas is the way to do it."

"When he came to see you, did you know he had killed Skinny's brother?" asked Vivienne.

"No, that came out later when I did my preliminary research."

"Why were they, whoever they were, after him?" asked Sandi.

"You have to understand - - this was back in 1955, and Mr. Edwards was a successful manager of a store, which was an unheard-of position for a black man back then. And – he was married to a white woman."

"That certainly would raise some eyebrows! Wow! What a story. Thank you, Pat," said Vivienne.

They practically ran to phone in their stories. Pat had already been on local, state, and national news a few months earlier when he defended Sammy Joe Washington, one of the Five-O'Clock Traffic Bandits, while Skinny was harassing Pat and making plans to kill him. This made him familiar with the reporters and the routine.

Futo was still talking into a mike while his cameraman continued to take pictures.

* * *

That evening Pat and Ed were front-page news in the newspapers, on the Six-O'clock and Eleven-O'clock News on Channel 3, on WHIT Radio, TV 13, and now the networks were picking up the story. Pat's friends were calling him, and a wave of calls came into his office the next day from reporters. Most importantly of all, people who wanted to hire this high-profile attorney kept Julie busy with the appointment book.

* * *

Jeffie heard about it the next afternoon at a bar and just happened to catch the news on Channel 3. He flew into a rage and almost swallowed his toothpick. Reb could hardly control him, and was afraid they'd call the cops.

Finally, when Reb got him under control, Jeffie got very calm. He pointed his finger at the TV when it showed Pat's picture for the second time and quietly said: "He's a walking dead man! You hear me, Reb? A walking dead man! If I had reason to get him before, I now have twice as much reason. Two brothers' worth, Reb! Two brothers' worth of reason!"

Mary Ann, the head waitress, came up to him and told him to tone it down. Jeffie backhanded her and she fell over a table and onto the floor.

"Don't tell me what to do, you stupid broad!"

"Yeah, ah, you don't tell Jeffie what to do!" repeated Reb.

She lay on the floor in a daze, with blood coming from her nose and cut lip.

They slowly walked out of the bar, both smoking cigars. "Come on, Reb, we got some work to do. Patton and Little Miss Tight-Ass are going to regret the day they were born!"

No one in the bar attempted to help the waitress, because they knew trouble when they saw it.

CHAPTER 15

The Drag Race

Pat had one more appointment on Monday afternoon and Louie called right at 4:30.

"Good news, Louie. Nancy has agreed to put your case on the dead docket. She really does not want to prosecute it and said our motion was the icing on the cake, so to speak, and gave her a reason to dead docket your case."

"Great, Pat! Then we both win. I'll have to thank the telephone company when they pay your fee," said Louie with a laugh.

"Careful, Louie! If you remember, I told you to be careful before. Number one, you're talking on the phone, and number two, I do not want to hear anything about any plans for a future crime, because I could be under an obligation to give the information to the police so they could try to prevent it. Attorney-client privilege applies only to past crimes. Please keep this in mind when talking to me in the future."

"Thanks for the warning, Mr. Patton. I didn't know that and will be very careful from now on. By the way, could I redeem my check with $1,000.00 in change?" said Louie while laughing very hard.

"What a clown. See you, Louie.

"Have a good weekend, Mr. Patton."

"And, Louie?

"Yes, Mr. Patton."
"You paid me in cash. Bye."

* * *

Pat and Shirley agreed to meet Eb and Kathy, his blind date and Shirley's best friend, at Jerome and Mickey's Steak House. Afterward they would go to Sam's to pick up the bike. This was turning out to be one busy day.

He loved the food at their restaurant. Two guys owned it, a really odd couple. Jerome heard voices, which advised him how to run the business. He was very intelligent and had many good ideas, but some were way off in left field. Mickey was extremely hyper and an excellent cook, so he ran the kitchen. They spent half their time running the restaurant and the other half trying to strangle each other. But, somehow the partnership worked. The restaurant seated 250 people and was always full on weekends, so Pat had Julie phone ahead for reservations.

Pat and Shirley were seated and about ten minutes later Kathy came in followed by Eb. Unknown to them, Eb and Kathy had been eyeing one another in the waiting area. They had no idea that the persons they were immediately attracted to were going to be their dates. Kathy looked over Eb's face, build, and butt, then quickly looked away when he caught her looking at him. Eb, in turn, admired her face and figure, and was watching her butt as she walked in front of him to their table.

Kathy was an attractive tall and trim woman, with blue eyes and long light brown hair. She went jogging and attended an aerobics class. Eb got his exercise by jumping into and out of cars all day long working as an auto-body repairman and painter. He also got exercise by lifting beer cans, but his metabolism was such that he was still a trim and good-looking man.

The two of them hit it off right away and Pat was left to talk to Shirley most of the meal. By dessert, though, they settled down and all four were engaged in conversation. Somehow, the subject came up about a new drive-in restaurant called Hot Rod Heaven, which actively promoted drag racing and old car clubs, and gave discounts to guys who drove an antique automobile or hot rod.

"Eb, let's go check the place out when we finish here. We could get a milkshake or something," suggested Kathy.

"Great idea, how about it, Pat?"

"It's okay with me if it's okay with Shirley, but I have to pick up a motorcycle from here. We could meet you two there later, or we could all meet back at the house and go in my Mustang. It's not quite an antique yet, but it is different."

"Fine with me," said Shirley. "Where do we meet?"

"At the house, if it's okay with Kathy," said Eb. "That way we can all go together."

As Kathy shook her head yes, Pat was thinking: *Right, Eb, and then you have Kathy all to yourself in that small back seat of my car. But, hey, I don't blame you a bit.*

Shirley drove Pat to Sam's. They couldn't believe her house - - a tiny frame place painted three different shades of blue. The front third a dark blue, the middle third a medium shade of blue, and the back third a light blue. They both shook their heads in wonder. A small two-car garage had the same paint scheme. The garage was old and made for small pre-WWII cars, so you would not be able to get two modern cars in it and be able to open the doors.

Sam came out and took them to the garage which had two locks on the door. She opened the door and turned on the light. There sat two beautiful bikes, one the new Harley, the other the Kawasaki, which looked as good as the new Harley.

"I took good care of it, Pat."

"All it took was a quick look and I could tell that."

"Shirley said you need to meet some people, so I won't keep you. Here is a letter signed by me giving you permission to ride my bike, the insurance card and registration. We leave Friday at 1:00 and meet at the Burger Doodle, right?"

"You got it, Sam, and thanks."

"Don't thank me. You got the fever already, don't you? Well, wait until you fire that baby up and hear those four pipes. You will buy that bike. Believe me!"

Pat put on his helmet and heavy jacket because the day was starting to cool down. He was glad Sam had put a windshield on the bike - - the wind would not blow right through him. He started it up. Music to his ears!

Boy, does this bike sound good! "I'll see you at the house, Shirley. By the way, did you notice Eb didn't even acknowledge my picking up a motorcycle?"

"I did, but I don't think they noticed anything but each other all evening. You don't think they'll be in bed when we get there, do you?" said Shirley with a wink.

"You're a dirty girl, Shir, but I wouldn't have you any other way."

At home, Pat put the Kawasaki to bed beside his Honda 450.

I love my Honda, but there is no comparison between the two. The good-looking Kawasaki has the largest displacement of any Japanese motorcycle and so many technical advances, such as dual overhead cams, four cylinders and dual disk brakes up front. It was smooth, fast, good looking, and got around 55 mpg, two up, at a steady 60 mph.

They had heard him coming and met him in the garage.

"Say, Eb, I like that shade of lipstick on you," said Shirley with a smile.

"Eb accidently touched my lips with his," answered Kathy with a laugh.

Eb had a sheepish grin on his face.

* * *

Hot Rod Heaven was a neat place, and busy even on a cool Monday night. Since it was new, lots of people were checking it out. The weather was also warmer than usual for this time of the year.

They ordered some shakes and admired the cars.

85

"Look at that gorgeous '57 Chevy Convertible. I wonder what he has under the hood," asked Pat.

"And that '34 Ford coupe. He probably has a Chevy engine in it. What do you think, Pat?" asked Eb.

"Only one way to find out."

The two of them got out while the girls stayed in the car and talked. They walked over to the '57 Chevy.

"Very nice set of wheels," complemented Eb.

"It not only looks good, but I'll bet it's a real runner, too!" said Pat.

"Thanks, guys. I replaced the 283 with a 327, put in a roller tappet cam, and two fours," said the owner, who looked to be around 35 years old.

"Not bad, 327 cubic inches, a hot cam, and two four-barrel carbs," nodded Pat.

Next they walked over to the '34 Ford Coupe.

"Very nice set of wheels," said Eb.

"It not only looks good, but I'll bet it's a real runner, too!" said Pat.

"It will go," said the owner, a younger man.

"What do you have in it?" asked Eb.

"Ford flathead, dual carbs, and a ¾ cam."

"Thanks, Man," said Pat.

"That will never do; it wouldn't even be a race," said Eb. "The Chevy would eat the coupe alive!"

"Right, old great one. We need to find something faster."

Just then a 1950 Mercury in gray primer came pulling in and did it sound good.

"You thinking what I'm thinking, Old Bean?" asked Eb.

"Right. That sounds like a big inch V8 to me. Shall we?"

"Oh, indubitably so!"

Off they went to the Mercury.

"Say, Mister, your car sure sounds good. What do you have under the hood?" asked Eb.

"That's a secret, fellows, smiled a young guy in his early twentys.

"Come on, Man, you can tell us," said Pat in a trustworthy voice.

"Stock '50 Merc flathead," said the owner.

"Stock, my foot," answered Pat as he eyed the very large tires on the rear.

"Seriously, will it run?" whispered Eb.

"Seriously?"

"Right."

"There ain't a thing here that will touch it!"

"I told you this car was a real runner," said Eb to Pat.

"Yeah, that guy in the Chevy is out of his mind."

"What are you guys talking about?"

"Should I tell him, Pat?"

"I don't know, Eb, the Chevy guy really said some bad things about this man's car."

"What did he say?" asked the agitated owner.

"Go ahead, Eb. Tell him."

"Well, to be plain honest, he said your car was a dog."

"And not only that," cut in Pat, "it was the ugliest excuse for a car he ever saw."

"And don't forget when he said it looked like an ugly upside down bathtub," said Eb.

"Well, I can blow the doors off that stupid Chevy - starting out in 2nd gear!" said a pissed off Merc owner. "And you can tell that creep I'd be willing to spot his bucket of bolts two car lengths and still whip his butt in a quarter mile!"

"Okay, Man, we'll be back in a minute," said Pat as they started walking over to the Chevy.

"I say, Old Bean, fun, say what?" said Pat.

"Oh, indubitably so!"

"Say, Man," said EB, "I'm afraid we heard some bad news about your car."

"What's that?" asked the Chevy owner.

"Pat, shall we tell him?"

"I'm afraid we have to. Mister, do you see that '50 Merc over there?" asked Pat.

"Ugly, isn't it?"

"Well, the owner said some very unpleasant things about your car."

87

"What did he say?"

"Well, for starters, he said you didn't keep your car in a garage. You kept it in a big dog house."

"Oh!"

"That's not all," said Pat. "The guy told us you had to keep it on a leash at home, and fed it Bow Wow dog biscuits!"

"Then he said he'd be willing to spot you two car lengths if you weren't afraid to run your piece of junk against his Merc."

"I've heard enough! I'm ready now. Tell him to be over at Churchtown Road at the Spotted Crow Store in 30 minutes!"

With that, he cranked it up, and squealed tires when he left. Pat & Eb slowly walked over to the Merc with smiles on their faces.

"Okay, what did he say?"

"He said you were just plain chicken if you didn't show up at the Spotted Crow Store on Churchtown Road in 30 minutes," answered Eb.

"That's right. And he also said he doubted your bucket of bolts would make it that far," added Pat.

"The jerk! Here comes my food. I'll be there in 30 minutes, and then we'll see if his car is as fast as his mouth is big!" said the Merc owner.

The guys hurried back to their car. Their food was already there and the girls were halfway done with theirs.

"Eat quick, girls. We got to go in a few minutes," ordered Pat.

"Go? Go where?" asked Shirley.

"To see a drag race."

Pat started laughing, almost uncontrollably. "He keeps his car in a big dog house!"

That got Eb going. "He feeds it Bow Wow dog biscuits."

They laughed until tears were rolling down their faces. Then the girls started laughing but had no idea why. It was just contagious. They ate quickly and headed for the store on Churchtown Road, a road that went from nowhere to nowhere but was four lanes wide and straight as an arrow. This is where most of the drag races took place. It was open and had very few places for a cop to hide. Someone had even painted white lines on the road at the start and finish of a quarter mile. Apparently some high-placed politician had it built for himself and his friends or for the benefit of a contractor buddy.

When they got there, they saw the Chevy in the parking lot, its owner standing outside of his car drinking a beer.

"Hi, guy!" greeted Pat.

"Hi. Is that creep going to show, or was he all mouth?"

"His food arrived as we talked to him, but he said he'd be here."

Just then the Merc pulled into the parking lot. Eb went over to talk to the owner. He wanted Pat to drive down the road past the drag area and check for bubble gum machines (slang for the shape of the light on the roof of a police car.)

"Good idea," said Eb.

Eb talked to Pat and the Chevy owner, who also thought it was a good idea. Off they went to check out the area, and even the girls were getting excited. Eight cars from Hot Rod Heaven showed up to watch the race. This was a really big show! No head lights in sight, and Pat saw no cops and told the guys so. The two cars lined up side by side with Pat and his three passengers behind them. They had agreed to start when Pat blew his horn.

Engines revved up and Pat hit the horn button. They took off in a cloud of squealing tires and smoke. Right off the line, the Merc jumped to a two-car lead.

Pat's Mustang had a bored and stroked Ford engine, highly modified, which sported close to 400 cubic inches and at least 350 HP. He jumped right into the race in back of them. By the time he was in second gear, he had pulled up beside the Chevy, but the Merc had pulled up another two car lengths. At the end of the quarter mile, Pat was about three car lengths in front of the Chevy, but the Merc was about four car lengths in front of him.

All of them backed off and headed to another store about three miles down the road where it was customary for drag race contestants to meet and talk.

"Man, talk about fast! Even if I didn't have passengers and had started even with him, he would have blown the doors off my Mustang!"

"Come on, Pat, open the doors! We've got to see what he has under the hood of that ugly Merc!" cried Eb.

By now the other eight cars had arrived and soon there was a crowd around the Merc.

"Open the hood!" was the cry of the crowd.

The Merc owner relented to the pressure and popped the hood latch. There sat a modified Chrysler Hemi engine with 426 cubic inches of brute horsepower. Soon the Chevy owner was telling him what an awesome car he had, and the Merc owner was in turn telling him he had a great looking Chevy.

"I couldn't believe the guy in the Mustang passed me while I was dragging you! And he had four people in the car!"

The next thing you knew, everyone was circled around Pat's car.

"Want to run it against my Merc?"

"Maybe another day."

"Hey, I know who you are!" interrupted the guy in the '34 Ford Coupe. "I couldn't place it at the drive-in. This is the attorney who was on TV! You know, the one who blew away Skinny!"

Pat talked to them for a few minutes, and then said his good buys, but not before he passed out several business cards.

Everyone was in good spirits, except for two guys sitting in a Camaro. No, they weren't laughing at all. Jeffie cranked up his car and headed for home, an intense anger building in him.

"We'll get him, Reb! And soon! Miss Tight-Ass, too! Tomorrow we visit the auto parts store and do some experimenting."

CHAPTER 16

The Booby Trap

Tuesday morning Brian Brown, the Court Administrator, called Pat to say he had been appointed to represent a woman charged with bringing a suitcase full of drugs into the Hartsfield Atlanta Airport from Jamaica. Pat walked over to Brian's office.

"The concourse where she was arrested is located in Clayton County, so we got the case," said Brian. "LaShandra Tidwell is being held without bond, so you need to see her ASAP. But first, let me tell you what I know about her case."

"Fire away, Mr. Helpful Court Administrator."

"They caught her at the airport with a very large suitcase lined with marijuana. Somehow, it was pressed into sheets about a half-inch thick and put between the suitcase and the liner. She had it under the liner on both sides. The Narcs are calling this the *Dope Fairy Case* because she claims she didn't put it there."

"Who's got her case?"

"Assistant DA Shirley O'Kelly was originally assigned to it, but since you were appointed before we caught the connection, DA Colver reassigned it to Nancy Katman. The judge is none other than your friend and mine, Judge Harold 'Chain Gang' Musselman," said Brian with exaggerated voice and hand gestures.

"I thought Mark Kimbrough prosecuted all of Chain Gang's cases?"

"You're right, but Mark has a conflict. Ms. LaShandra Tidwell lived in Clayton County for a short time a few years ago and Mark did some legal work for her when he was in private practice."

"So, no bond yet?"

"No, she came in last night. I really don't think she will get out on bond. If one is set, it's going to be high because the only contact she has with Georgia is her job. She has family in New York and California and could flee to them."

"When's the preliminary hearing?"

"January 14th. The day after tomorrow at 2:00 PM.

"Okay," said Pat with relief. "I was afraid of a Friday court date because I'm planning on going out of town."

"I know, with Katman and that strange character she hangs out with. I was in the DA's Office yesterday and everybody thought she was a guy. Anyway, Nancy told me you were going, but don't be surprised if your relationship with her also results in it being a conflict."

"Right. I kind of expect it. I'm planning on buying a motorcycle from the person you describe as a strange character. Her name is Sam and she is very strange but also very likeable."

"If you say so."

"I'm off to meet with Nancy, so I'll see my new client either late this afternoon or first thing in the morning."

"I see you're in the news again. The Edwards case this time."

"Sometimes stuff just happens. Bye."

"Bye, Pat."

Pat went to see Nancy who told him, "I know little about the case; it was dumped on me this morning. I will be happy to discuss it with you when I get more information."

Since Pat had some work to do at the office, and a few clients to see, the Tidwell visit at the jail would have to wait until tomorrow. There was not enough information to recommend a bond amount.

"How do you like the Kawasaki?"

"I got to ride it from Sam's house home last night, but that was it. I've been pretty busy."

"I know, promoting drag races at Hotrod Heaven." Nancy winked.

"Has Shirley . . .?"

"Don't worry," interrupted Nancy, "your secret is safe with me. Bye, Pat. You take good care of Shirley. She's a real sweetheart!"

"Don't I know it? See you Friday, if not sooner."

* * *

That morning, Jeffie had made a run to an auto parts store and a hardware store. As soon as he got home, he headed for his garage. He lived in a modest rundown house with an attached garage. Jeffie was busy working on his project when Reb walked in.

"Ah, you think it's going to work, Jeffie? Do you really think it will?"

"We'll find out soon enough, Reb. Soon enough."

Jeffie had a piece of plastic ½-inch wide, ¼-inch thick, and two inches long, with two wires taped to it, so the bare wire ends were about ¼-inch from each other on opposite sides of the plastic. One wire had an alligator clip attached to it and the other one was a long spark plug wire with a nipple end that fit into the distributor. He took this rig over to his Camaro, which was parked in the garage with the hood open.

"Reb, hook this alligator clip to a good ground, or just put it on the negative terminal of the battery."

After explaining it two more times, Reb half-way understood.

Jeffie pulled out a spark plug wire from the distributor cap and put the wire in the empty socket. The igniter was simply the small piece of plastic with the wire from the distributor and a ground wire taped to side by side.

"This is the igniter, Reb," said Jeffie as he taped a fire cracker fuse between the two exposed wires on the plastic block.

"Now, go crank the car!"

Reb hit the starter and in a fraction of a second the car started and was running rough on seven cylinders, but not before a spark jumped between the two bare wires, instantly igniting the fuse.

Bammmmm! Reb jumped when it went off even though he was expecting the explosion.

"It works! It works!" yelled a jubilant Jeffie as he grabbed Reb and danced around the car. He was ecstatic!

"Wait until my igniter is connected to a stick of dynamite instead of a fire cracker!"

"Where are we gonna do that, ah, Jeffie?"

"Under the hood of a certain Mustang!" informed Jeffie, and they both broke out laughing.

CHAPTER 17

The Dope Fairy

Wednesday morning Pat went to see his new court-appointed client, LaShandra Tidwell.

Deputy George Lincoln, the jailer in charge, signed him in. George was a graduate of Morris Brown College and was going to law school at night. He used the job at the jail to work his way through. He and Pat had that in common and often talked with each other before Pat saw a client. George was a religious man and his father had the honor of preaching with Martin Luther King at the Ebenezer Baptist Church in Atlanta.

"So you're appointed to represent LaShandra, huh?"

"Why the frown, George?"

"Look, Pat, she is a real looker, but you'll see soon enough why I'm not a fan."

George was right. She was a very attractive light-skinned black woman about 28 years old. She did not look very happy but the orange jump suit looked great on her, particularly with her long black straight hair. However, LaShandra was not a nice person.

Female clients were not seen in the library. He had to talk to her in the hall outside of the cellblock housing female prisoners. Pat introduced himself and asked her to explain what happened, cautioning her that if she lied to him, it could hurt her, not him.

"I was taking a vacation in Jamaica and met what I thought was a real kool dude. I ended up movin' into his hotel room," said LaShandra in a monotone voice.

"Go on."

"When it was time for me to leave, he was staying another day or two; I was running late and my suitcase strap broke. Carlos, that's his name, told me he would pack my things for me in his suitcase while I took a shower."

"How about your suitcase?"

"Carlos said he would have it fixed and use it. We would trade suitcases temporarily. I got out of the shower and dressed. He closed the suitcase and took it down to his rental car. As I got into the car, he was putting it into the trunk. When we got to the airport, he parked outside the place where you buy your ticket and check your bags. Anyway, Carlos took out the suitcase from the trunk and gave it to the man at the ticket counter. He gave me a kiss and left. I bought . . ."

"Did you ever touch that suitcase?" interrupted Pat.

"I don't think so. No, I know so."

"From what you told me so far, Carlos, and we'll get back to him in a few minutes, packed his suitcase with your things, took it to the car, drove you to the airport, took it out of the car, and gave it to the man at the ticket counter when you checked in. Is that right?"

"Yeah."

"Okay, then what happened?"

"I got on the plane, flew to Atlanta, and when I got here, they searched my bags and told me they found a whole bunch of marijuana."

"Where was it?"

"All I know is they said it was in the suitcase."

"And you claim you never touched it?" reiterated Pat as he took notes on a legal pad.

"That's right. I never touched it."

Something didn't jell. She was too calm, her story too pat, and her demeanor showed little or no outrage for being unjustly accused. In short, he did not believe her, but his job was to represent her to the best of his ability, whether he believed her or not. It was a good story, and there was always the possibility she was telling the truth. She came across as an educated well-spoken woman.

"May I call you LaShandra?"

"Sure."

"Okay, LaShandra, and please call me Pat. We have a preliminary hearing tomorrow. At the hearing, I can ask the judge to set a bond for you."

"It don't matter none, as I don't have anyone to go a bond for me."

"I'll try to get one set anyway, but I understand you have no one, family that is, here. I believe your people are in New York and California."

"Right. How did you know?"

"We defense attorney have our ways. Can one of them make bond for you?"

"We don't get along too well."

"Did you make a statement to the police?"

"What I told you."

"No confession?"

"Heavens no!"

"If they come to talk to you, tell them you want your attorney present during any questioning, and they will normally back off. In other words, don't talk to them without me present. I mean don't even talk about the weather. They have some slick dudes working at the police department and they will be real nice and try to get you talking about anything. Then they skillfully feed you questions about the crime. Before you realize it, you've made a confession. So, don't talk to them period, except to advise them you want your lawyer present."

"I got you, Mr. Patton."

"At the preliminary hearing tomorrow, I don't want you to say anything more than the story you told me today. Anything else can be answered with, 'I don't remember', or 'I don't know.' But don't outright lie. Say nothing instead. Is that clear?"

"Yes, Sir."

"At this hearing, the judge cannot find you guilty of anything. He can only dismiss your case or bind it over to the Grand Jury. He also can set a bond, but will defer to the Superior Court if the charge is serious enough. Any questions?"

"No, Sir."

"If there are no questions, I'll see you tomorrow at 2:00 PM. I'll plan on getting there a little early to talk to you again. You might think of something between now and then. If so, I'll be happy to talk to you about it."

Pat got up and put his legal pad in his briefcase. "Bye, LaShandra. Oh, and you don't have to say anything at the hearing tomorrow if you don't want to, but I'd like to see you in action on the witness stand."

"Bye, Mr. Patton."

"Clang, clang!" went the big steel door as it opened, and then shut to let him out. The noise was loud and echoed. "Click!" went the lock as George twisted the large key.

Pat thought back to the first time he had come into the jail. *What a strange feeling being locked in this place. And, the smell! Nothing smells quite like a jail. The strong odor of disinfectant, bleach, sweat, and urine is very noticeable. It's gloomy and a feeling of helplessness could take over anybody after only a short time.*

"All done, Pat?"

"Yeah, George. She didn't seem bad at all," commented Pat as he was escorted to the entrance.

"Wait until you get to know her."

"By the way, after you pass the Bar, Herb and I will be glad to help you find a job in the legal community, and answer questions you might have."

"I appreciate that. Until next time?" said George as they shook hands.

As Pat walked from the jail to his office, he saw Judge Musselman get out of a young lady's car and give her a good-bye kiss. She was very good looking and at least 20 years his junior. Probably his daughter.

* * *

Ed Edwards had gone back to drinking again. He worked at a gas station that did light auto repairs, and when he was off work he would hang out at a bus stop with some of the other guys, drinking and looking at the women. Unknown to him, he was being watched. Two men in a Camaro were parked about half a block away, watching.

They had a pair of binoculars, comparing him to a picture in the newspaper. Vivienne Cove of the Clayton County Daily News somehow had found Ed and interviewed him. His picture was taken by her news photographer.

"Look at that damn nigger stumble around there. Why, he might get run over crossing the street when he walks home. That would really be a shame, now wouldn't it, Reb?"

"It would? I thought we didn't like him." Reb had a puzzled look on his face. Jeffie shook his head. He liked old Reb, even though he sure wasn't very smart. He always did what Jeffie told him to do and that's what counted.

"Reb, we don't like him. Okay?"

"Okay, Jeffie."

"We got a couple of things to get," said Jeffie, deep in thought.

"What's that?"

"We have to find some dynamite and steal us an old car. Better yet, an old truck. Something bigger than a car, but not so big someone could easily get out of the way if it was comin' at 'em. Maybe even get a new truck."

"Dynamite! ! We gonna, ah, get us a Mustang?"

"Right! But first we gonna get us a truck that's gonna get us a nigger."

"That one over there?" said Reb pointing toward Ed.

"That's right, Dumbass. That one over there."

* * *

Pat was working in his office in the afternoon when Herb, his mentor and landlord, came in.

"Hey, Pat, have you heard the rumor about old 'Chain Gang'?"

"No, what's going on?"

"He's seeing a good-looking young lady and the word is she moved in with him."

"Then that wasn't his daughter."

"What are you talking about?"

"A little while ago, I saw him get out of a real looker's car. He went around to the driver's side and gave her a big goodbye kiss. I thought she was his daughter. Chain Gang's outdoing Hollywood."

"Speaking of Hollywood, next week Reagan will be sworn in as President. I wonder how a movie actor will do in that office."

"No worse than the rest of them."

Just then Julie came in.

"Sorry to disturb you, Boss, but Capt. Keefauver is on line one. He has Charlotte's address for you."

"Excuse me, Herb. I need to talk to him. Stay if you want."

"Thanks, but I've got a client waiting for me."

"Hi, Capt."

"It's always good to talk to you, my good man. As you know, our men in blue are out there to serve you, and serve you we did. Not only do I have Charlotte's address and phone number . . . I gave it to Julie . . . but she has agreed to meet you tomorrow night, if you can make it."

"Great, Capt. I'm leaving for Florida Friday morning but I'll pack up most of my stuff tonight. If I cancel, she may change her mind. What time?"

"She said anywhere, anytime. I'm to let her know when and where. She knows what you look like. The newspapers, I guess.

"Tell her Jerome and Mickey's at 7:00. I'm going to bring Shirley along unless she objects."

"I'll tell her."

"And Capt. . . . ."

"Yes?"

"Tell her I appreciate this and dinner is on me."

"You got it."

He felt like he didn't have time to turn around. Things were happening so fast, it was almost like he was on a roller coaster.

"Julie buzzed Pat.

"Jeez, Boss. It's Ed on the phone and he sounds like he's been drinking again."

"I'll talk to him. Line 2?"

"Right."

"Hi, Ed. What can I do for you?"

"I jus, ah, jus wanted to, ah, know what you, ah, found out." Ed was slurring his words.

"I tracked down Jeffie's sister, Charlotte. We're having supper tomorrow night. So things are coming right along."

"And I jus, ah, wants to let you know, ah, that I 'preciates what you're doing fer me."

"Thank you, Ed. I'll keep you posted. After I talk to Charlotte, I need to locate those witnesses. That is, if they're still alive. Believe it or not, the police are helping me."

"Ah, okay. Thank you, Mr. Patton."

"And, Ed. You need to lay off the booze. It could send you right back to prison."

"Ah, yes, sir. Bye."

Just then, Herb popped back in.

"Quick appointment, huh, Herb?"

"The jerk had stolen a car and wanted to sue the owner because the brakes were bad and he got hurt when they failed and he hit another car."

"What's he doing out of jail?"

"He got probation. First offender because he had no prior record. If you ask me, it's only because he never got caught before, not that he hasn't broken the law. He came to the wrong attorney. He needs to go to Dewey, Cheatem, and Howe."

"You're probably right. Say, I have been meaning to ask you how they are coming with your house."

"Great. It's been dried in and they're working on the interior. We lost a lot, Pat. Much of what didn't get burned up had smoke damage, or water damage from the fire hoses. The worst thing is the loss of pictures and personal papers, which can never be replaced. Seems like yesterday Skinny planted the fire bomb."

"I can only imagine. Poor Bonnie. I'll bet she and the kids can hardly wait until this ordeal is finally over."

"Right. How do you like being a lawyer so far?"

"I love it, except I never seem to have enough time to do the things I want to do."

"Don't worry, it'll only get worse! By the time you have ten years under your belt, you'll have learned to hate this job."

"I hope not. Here I am, the first year in law practice, semi-famous, pulling in big bucks, when the minimum wage is, what? I think $3.10 per hour? I was reading in the paper last night that the average factory worker makes $6.56 per hour. Herb, I'm living in a dream world!"

"You lucked out, okay, but you're more than lucky Skinny didn't kill you."

"I know, Herbie, I owe my life to Shir. But, I'm having fun in spite of the work and the danger. I'll have to admit, though, I'm very uneasy wondering what might be out there ready to bite me. Like Skinny's little brother, Jeffie."

"It would be nice if you only knew for sure."

"Well, I'm still researching. Maybe Charlotte, Skinny's sister, can tell me something. I'm having supper with her tomorrow night."

"I hope so." Herb looked at his watch. "I need to get going."

"I need to get to work, too, and do something, even if it's wrong!"

They both laughed and Herb left as Julie stuck her head in the door.

"Hey, Boss! Is this a zoo or something? What a day!"

"What is it?"

"Jeez, Boss, since you were in the news a-g-a-i-n, the phone has been ringing constantly. Speaking of the phone, Lt. Keller wants you to call him."

The phone rang and Julie answered it from Pat's office.

"You don't have to call Lt. Keller back, Boss. That's him on the phone."

"Hi, Lt., what's the good word?"

"I really do have a good word, or maybe even two. One, I have reason to believe the trial judge, now deceased, in Ed's case, had ties to the Brotherhood."

"Boy! Now if we could only prove it!"

"We're working on it. And two, the witnesses are still living and are believed to be in this area. We're working on that, too!"

Finally the working day came to a close and Pat headed home to pack up for his weekend trip. Sam recently had the KZ1000 serviced, so it was ready to go. It had a large luggage rack on the back, and Pat would pack his things in a waterproof bag about the size of a five-gallon can. A rain suit was a must, as were gloves, and sunglasses. He had two face shields for his helmet - - one clear for night riding, and the other a dark smoke for daytime use. He was getting excited about the trip.

When he got home, the house seemed empty because Shirley had gone to her parents' house for a few hours. Then Eb came in.

CHAPTER 18

Doctor Calhoon

"What' up, Great One?" asked Pat

"Got about two hours to kill and then it's off to see Kathy."

"Got it bad, huh?"

"No worse than with you and Shirley. Speaking of Shirley, where is she?"

"Went to see her momma for a few hours. She'll be back later. It's going to be hard going on this long weekend trip without her. We've been together every day since our second date. Oh, how I love that girl!"

"So how about a Redneck or a Diamond number? Then get a Burger Doodle, and I'll leave to see my sweet, sweet Kathy."

"I'll humor you, Eb, because I'll only be a single man for a little more than a month, and will have to kick you out then. What do you have in mind? But - - no nasty stuff."

"Who knows? The Great Eb makes it up as he goes. Find me a name and number in the phone book, kind sir, and I will put the old brain in gear! I will practice my excellent redneck and black dialects while you be lookin'.'"

"A Claude Hoofer lives in a redneck trailer park called Bubba's Estates."

Eb dialed the number while Pat waited to pick up the phone.

"Whatsyawant?" said a deep voice.

"Hoss, I'm from the Red Warrior Chewing Tobacco Company. This is your lucky day. You do use our product, don't you?"

"Sure."

"Do you own a hound dog?"

"Sure."

"Well, Hoss, we developed a chewing tobacco for dogs. Our tests found that coon dogs, rabbit dogs, and hound dogs love it. We are prepared to give you a free t-shirt, a hat, and a bumper sticker for agreeing to let your dog try it. What do you think of that?"

"Ma huntin' dog, Moonshine, would love a good chew. And I get a shirt, hat, and a bumper sticker?"

"And that ain't all, Claude. If you win our contest, we gonna do an article on you and feature it in Mud Car Today Magazine. Then we gonna truck you to Mississippi to judge the Miss Trailer Trash beauty contest with none other than 'Cooter' of WBBQ Radio."

"Me and my son, little Glock, would like nothin' more then to meet Cooter and see all them gals. You know, dependin' on what them gals offered me, I could be bought," laughed Claude. "WhatsIgottado to win?"

"Nothin' ole Hoss. All we ask is that you let your dog give it a try. Then you enter him in a spittin' contest. Fair enough?"

"I can't wait to tell ole Moonshine. He out chasin' coons right now."

"Only fair to warn ya, last year's winner was a basset hound what done spit 22 feet 7 inches. Bye, Claude. You be hearin' from us real soon."

Pat was choking from laughing so much.

"Eb, your brain must have come from outer space! Where do you get this stuff?

"Here you are, Eb. DeOmni Jones," said Pat when he was able to talk again.

Eb dialed the number and when the number began ringing, gave Pat the sign to pick up.

"Hello," said a black female voice.

"Say, dis be DeOmni Jones?"

"Dis be her."

"Well, dis here be Alawishes Worthington, III, from your doctor's office. You knows who dat is, don't you?"

"Sure, dat be Dr. Calhoon."

"Well Dr. Calhoon be concerned wif somethin' he done saw on de X-rays dat you had taken."

"But, I didn't have no X-rays taken."

"Sure you did. Dat Dr. Calhoon, he be's real sneaky and took 'em so quick dat you really didn't know he done did it!"

"Wow! He be dat good, huh?"

"Sure, Honey. Now fer de questions. When was de last time you had sex?"

"What? I thought dat dis was about de X-rays!"

"It is, and I be tyin' it in in jus' one minute. Now, please jus answer de questions dat de doctor himself ax me to ax you."

"Ah, okay. Let's see. It be three nights ago."

"You be married?"

"You ought to knows dat if you gots my file."

"I jus has de short file. De long file be kept by de doctor himself in a big vault underground. It be under his office and he allow only himself, me, and de FBI in der. He change de code to de vault every week and if you punch in de wrong code, do you know what happens?"

"No, I don't" said DeOmni in awe of Dr. Calhoon.

"You won't tell anyone will you?"

"No, Mr. Worthington, I won't."

"You're sure dat you won't tell even one little teensy-weensy little bit of dis to anyone?"

"Honest, I won't tell."

"Now, you understands dat I'm not supposed to tell you this, don't you?"

"But tell me, tell me!" she demanded with irritation.

"Okay, but understands dat dis makes us, ah, sorta real close, don't you? You see dat, don't you?"

"Well, I guess so."

"Now don't breathe a word of dis to anyone, but when you presses de wrong code in de vault, a mechanical arm comes shooting out of de wall and grabs you, and den another one, it shoots out wif a hypodermic needle which gets jabbed in your arm. It puts you to sleep and den when you wakes up, you done believes you was abducted by spacemen and taken aboard their space ship."

"Really?" said an excited DeOmni.

"Sure. Now you knows where all dem people comes from dat says dat dey was abducted by space men."

"I never knowed dat. And - - I won't tell no one. I promise."

"Now you knows why I don't got dat long file."

". . I understands now."

By now Pat was putting his hand over his mouth trying to control himself and not laugh.

"Okay, Honey. Who'd you have sex wif?"

"I be wif Brother LeRoy from de church. You won't tell nobody, will you?"

"Baby, you knows I won't."

"My ole man, he be away most of de time drivin' dem big ole trucks, and I jus' gets lonely."

"I understands, Honey. What kind of sex was it?"

"What's you mean?"

"Well, was it on de ironing board, or . . . ."

"On de ironing board?" interrupted DeOmni. "How you do it on de ironing board?"

"Very carefully, Honey. Ver-r-y, ver-r-r-y carefully! Or, BLAMM! Den it goes down on de floor! You times it jus' right and BLAMM! Right at de end."

"Oh, dat sounds exciting!" said DeOmni with emotion.

"Say, Honey, you want ole Alawishes to show you how sometime?"

"But I doesn't even know you!"

"Sure you does, Honey. We be very close. Tell me, how many people know about de underground vault?"

"Uh, not many, I guess."

"How 'bout dem super-fast X-rays?"

"Uh, not many, I guess."

"And how 'bout dat arm what comes out of de wall and gets you when you punch in de wrong code?"

"I now sees what you be talkin' 'bout. We be very close, don't we?"

"How 'bout me showin' you dat ironing board thing?"

"Well - - okay. When?"

"Is you're ole man out of town tomorrow night?"

"He not be coming home until next week."

"Okay, Baby, be ready 'bout 8:00 tomorrow and I be der wif my own special ironing board."

"Oh, it sounds so exciting!"

"Now, 'bout dat X-ray. Dr. Calhoon thinks dat you might has an inflamed gizzard."

"Dat be serious?"

"Not if you goes on dis special diet dat I's gonna tell you 'bout."

"What's dat?"

"Well, Honey. You get a pen and paper and ole Alawishes gonna tell you all about it."

"Yes, Alawishes, Honey. I gots it."

"First you has to go out and find a grasshopper."

"A grasshopper? Dis be January!"

"Dey be around. Dey jus puts on little coats, dat's all."

"I didn't know dat. You be so smart,"

"Anyway, if he has a little coat on, take it off first. Den get you some hot sauce and put it on him. If he's cold, dat will warm him up. Den get one ounce of milk and put it in your blender. Next one ounce of cabbage juice, two ounces of Ripple, and three ounces of mineral oil. Den throw dat sucker in der and turn on de blender. Now I be tellin' you right off dat he ain't gonna like it none too much, but dat be his problem. Anyway, drink down dat stuff and it will put out de flame in your inflamed gizzard."

"Oh, thank you so much, Alawishes, Honey. I be gettin' my boys to find me a grasshopper first thing in de morning."

"How many boys you be got? Remember, I don't have de long file."

"I be got seven boys and five girls."

"Well, I guess you don' wasted no time when your old man comes home!"

"What?"

"I said, I guess you spend a lot of time at home alone."

"I do."

"See you tomorrow night, Honey."

"Oh, I can't wait, Alawishes, Honey. Bye."

Pat was almost on the floor laughing.

"That poor woman will be driving her kids nuts looking for a grasshopper and her heart will be broken when Mr. Wonderful doesn't show up. You are not a very nice man!"

* * *

A black 1967 Camaro was parked outside a trailer in a rundown mobile home park. Two men got out and one knocked at the door. A big ugly-looking bearded man answered.

"What the hell do you . . . Jeffie! Man, I didn't know you was back in town," exclaimed the big man as he gave Jeffie a bear hug.

"John Quincy! If you ain't a sight for sore eyes! Just like the old days, except we don't have no burning cross."

"Whose your friend?"

"J. Q. , meet Reb. He's a little slow, but a hell-of-a-good guy. Reb's my right-hand man."

"When did you get back in town?"

"I came for brother Skinny's funeral. My shack has been boarded up, but it's a safe place to be because it's in my other name."

"I heard about old Skinny. Wanted to go to the funeral, too, but the word was out that the cops were watchin' it. I'm out on parole and don't need to go back."

"I understand. I stayed back in the shadows myself, but didn't see no cops." Jeffie lit up a cigar.

"Hey, Ida! Get these two friends of mine a beer! Now!" yelled J. Q.

A haggard, beaten-down woman brought two beers.

"Damn, Woman! Don't you know nothin'? I'm ready for another one, too! Get your ass in there and get me another cold one!"

"You got your ole lady trained real good," complemented Jeffie with a smile.

"Hey, if you guys want some of it, I can tell her to go back in the bedroom with you."

"Thanks, J. Q., but not right now 'cause I need to talk to you about something.

"Can I?" asked Reb.

"Huh?" responded J. Q.

"Can I go back there with her?"

"Ida, old what's his name here has something he wants to talk to you about, back in the bedroom," said J. Q. with a grin.

Reb got up and went to the bedroom with a very sad-looking woman who knew better than to cross J. Q., or he would beat her again. She felt she had nowhere else to go. If she did leave, she was afraid he would kill her.

"Look, J. Q., I need a big favor. Can you get me a few sticks of dynamite?"

"Man, I only got one stick, but I can let you have it. The cops been keeping their eyes on that stuff and the quarries are making it harder to get where it's stored."

Sounds were coming from the bedroom.

"I guess one will have to do, but I'd love to have something even stronger."

"Well, why don't you tape a soft drink bottle to it what's filled with gasoline?"

"Good thinkin'. I'll do that!"

"You need to anyway, as I don't know how good my stick is. It's been under my trailer for several months and it's damp under there. Pipes leaking, you know. Sit here and I'll get it."

J. Q. left and when he came back a few minutes later, Reb was sitting there and Jeffie was missing.

"Where'd Jeffie get off to?"

"Ah, he said he'd take his turn before we left and all."

"I hear the bed springs singing now. That's about all women are good for. That and cookin' and doin' house work."

A little while later Jeffie came out zipping up his pants.

"You got the bang, J. Q.?"

"I got it while you was getting your wick dipped. Not very good, was it?"

"Well, you know what they say? Any old port in a storm."

Neither one of them had an ounce of compassion for Ida, and Reb didn't know how to have it. All three were dirt bags.

"Here it is. I found one stick but it has been damp, actually a little wet. I don't know how good it is, so you better tape that soft drink bottle of gas to it. Just to be sure. When they get wet, they get weak."

"I owe you, my brother of the Brotherhood. We'll put this stick to good use."

"It's that attorney, isn't it?"

"I'll just say this, my friend. Stay away from Mustang convertibles!"

CHAPTER 19

Jerome and Mickey's

That night Pat met with Eb at Jerome and Mickey's Steakhouse, had supper and then packed for the trip. As Pat was telling the waiter that two women would be joining them and they would wait to order, he recognized the waiter. He was the little guy in pink pants who was Pick'em-Up-Man's girlfriend, or whatever. Of course he was dressed in black slacks and a white shirt.

"Sir-r-r, my name is Willie-e-e, and I will be your server-r-r tonight. When your party has all-l-l arrived, I'll be back here in a twinkle. You can be sure I will be lo-o-o-king to see if they have arrived every time I'm out on the flo-o-o-r," said Willie with a stutter and very noticeable lisp.

"Thank you, Willie, but that won't be necessary because here they come now."

Shirley and Kathy came in and both turned a lot of heads. When Shirley got to the table, she stifled a laugh and raised her eyebrows at Pat, who acknowledged her with a big smile and a wink. As they ordered, neither Eb nor Kathy knew what was going on but were both wondering why they were acting strange.

"Okay, you two, what's so funny," questioned Eb when Willie left.

"You won't believe this, Eb, but you remember talking, or rather Brown Sugar talking, to Pick'em-Up-Man?"

"Wait a minute. You aren't trying to tell me . . ."

First Pat, then Shirley, then Eb started laughing. Finally Kathy did too, although she didn't really know what was going on. They explained the situation to her and she joined them. People started to look, so they tried, rather unsuccessfully, to tone down their voices.

"Eb, this is too good to be true! The next time we get on the radio with Pick'em-Up-Man, we can really have fun with this. Now we got his or her name - - Willie," said Pat. "However, Willie does seem to be a very good waiter in spite of his relationship to Pick'em-Up-Man."

"I've got to hear you two on the radio. It must be a hoot!" said Kathy.

After they ate, Pat said he had to go, and pack for his trip. The girls, as girls will do, went to the restroom together. When they were gone, Pat asked Eb how things were going with Kathy.

"Using your words, Pat, Kathy is a keeper! I like everything about her. She is such a nice, sweet, good-looking thing!"

"All true, Old Great One, but what about her judgment?"

"What are you . . . ! Was that inference about my character?"

Pat just grinned.

While in the restroom, Shirley was asking similar questions of Kathy, and got much the same response.

* * *

At home Pat packed his bag. He checked over the bike, his helmet, sunglasses, gloves, leather jacket, snowsuit, and rain gear. He had Chap Stick, some aspirin, and a couple of spare spark plugs Sam had given him. She also had put a new type chain on the Kawasaki, which had special links impregnated with lubricant and did not need to be oiled. He wiped the chain down with an oil-soaked rag anyway, to prevent surface rust. Watching TV with Shirley, Pat worked on his boots and leather jacket with special grease made to soften and waterproof leather. Finally finished, they went to bed, but not before Shirley played some light classical pieces on Pat's old upright piano.

* * *

They decided Shirley would keep her job as an Assistant DA for a year or two to get trial experience. Later they could form a law partnership, possibly with Herb, if he wanted to come on board.

Just watching Shirley get dressed turned Pat on. They arose a little early and went out for a 30-minute jog. When they got back, Pat lifted weights for 20 minutes, took a quick shower and joined Shirley for cereal, coffee, and orange juice.

* * *

"Good morning, Boss," said Julie as Pat walked into the office. "I want you to know that the phones have not stopped ringing since your radio and TV interview last Monday. There are so many calls that I am only setting up appointments for the ones I think are the best, and as you told me to do, I'm sending the overflow to Herb.

"Julie, you surely are doing a great job!"

"Thanks, Boss. I need to tell you something, but I'm almost afraid to, because I don't know what you'll do."

"Come on, Julie, tell old Pat all about it."

"It's the Insurance Guy in his pickup truck. He started parking me in again," said Julie in a very soft voice.

"He hasn't learned his lesson yet, huh?"

"Jeez, Boss, I guess not, but please don't get into any trouble over me."

"Don't worry, Julie. I'll take care of it before I leave tomorrow, and boy am I looking forward to that trip."

Pat went out to the parking lot and looked around. Sure enough, the jerk, who worked a few doors down, parked his older 1971 Chevy work truck so close to Julie's car that she would have to get in the passenger's side door to go home. What a creep. The last time he did it a talk did not help, so Pat gave him a couple of flat tires, which stopped him until this week.

Well, just don't switch to your new truck at lunch time, Brother. On second thought, why not now.

He stuck his head in the door and yelled to Julie, "I'm going out for about 15 minutes." He knew The Insurance Guy usually went out for lunch. Pat went to a key shop about five minutes away and asked for a key blank for a 1971 Chevy pick-up truck. Joe, who owned the shop, was a client of his and Joe agreed to forget Pat bought the key blank if anyone asked about it.

"Now, Joe, please break it in half for me, but I want both halves."

"That's a pretty mean trick to play on someone, Son.

"No trick, Joe. It's a lesson in life."

He told Joe about what this jerk was doing to his secretary, and Joe was very sympathetic.

"Be prepared, because he may call you."

Pat went back to the office and saw no one around the parking lot. He put the front half of the key into the driver's side door lock and then shoved it all the way in with the other half of the key.

Now let this jerk see what it's like to have to get in the passenger's side, which is impossible because he was too close to Julie's car to open the door.

"Julie, I want you to leave for lunch before the Insurance Guy. I have a feeling he is going to have trouble getting into his truck and I don't want him screwing up your car door trying to get in his passenger's side door."

"What did you do, Boss?" asked Julie in a resigned quiet little voice.

"Why nothing. Nothing at all. I'm just psychic. Take your lunch hour a little early today. Okay?"

"Sure, Boss. I don't know what you did, but I'd really like to look out the window and watch."

"You are something else. You certainly are! Just move your car about 11:30 and then, if you want to sneak back in and peek out the window while you eat lunch, be my guest."

A few minutes later she buzzed him and said Eb was holding for him.

"Hi, Old Great One."

"I called the U. S. Army number like you asked me."

"And?"

"Well, I told them I was a member of the Class of 1959 at Griffin High School, and I was doing a story on what our fellow classmates were doing now. I told him I thought Jefferson Davis Anderson went into the Army, and could he confirm that and perhaps give me some information on his job and rank, and if we could get a picture."

"What did he say?"

"Sorry. I can't give out that information. Against regulations. But I did succeed in tricking him into admitting Jeffie had been in the Army."

"Well, that's something. I had a feeling they were not going to cooperate."

"He was very nice, but very firm, even when I told him we had lost track of Jeffie and wanted to send him a notice of an upcoming class reunion."

"But his 20-year reunion would have been back in 1979, and assuming they have one every five years, the next one would not be due until 1984."

"You're right, Old Sharp Legal Brain, but the guy never caught that."

"Who knows, maybe when I meet with Charlotte tonight, she can give me more information on him."

"Where are you meeting?"

"Jerome and Mickey's at 7:00. Why?"

"Because you don't know her, there is no way to know if you can trust Charlotte. I was thinking of taking Kathy out to eat tonight anyway, so what if we sit somewhere we can watch her and anyone else who may be watching you?"

"Great idea, Old Great One, but something not so great is the fact people there know you and will wonder why we didn't speak."

"True, but I can stop at Geleta's Costume Shop on the way home from work. I saw a program on TV where a simple mustache, hat, and dark glasses will change your appearance so much that 90% of your friends would not recognize you, unless they were looking for a disguise."

"Sounds good to me. As far as I know, Kathy has only been there once with us, so no one should make the connection."

"I'll see you there at 7:00, or, should I say, I'll look for you there, but I hope you don't spot me. Kathy now is another story. How could any male miss her? "

"I could never guess."

"I am lucky, aren't I?"

"We both are."

"At 7:00 then."

"Boss, Ms. Grey, of The Department of Family and Children's Services Adoption Unit, called about sending you a client. She asks that you work them in now, if possible."

"What's the rush?"

"Geez, Boss, I don't know, but I think they're here already. Let me check."

Julie left and was back in a few minutes.

"What did you find out?"

"Mr. and Mrs. Vernon Jones are a distinguished-looking black couple, who want to adopt a black male child. Mr. Jones is a manager of a Home Depot store and she is a school teacher."

"Now I understand the rush. Black male children are the hardest to place. The Department puts a couple willing to adopt a black male child at the head of the list and bends over backwards to help them. I'll do everything I can to expedite this adoption because every child needs a mom and a dad."

"Boss, Ralph and I have talked about adopting. I can't have any more children but we both love kids and Mindy has been asking about our having a brother or sister."

"Do you have to have a baby? They're the hardest to obtain. At present there is a two-year waiting list."

"No, Boss. Wouldn't want one. I like working and don't believe in child care unless it's a family member, and my parents are deceased. Ralph's are also gone. I would consider one school age up to ten, since Mindy is ten. That way I could still work."

"That's great because school age white children and young siblings are hard to place. Older children are even harder. Everyone wants a baby. Think about it and we'll talk some more."

"You and Shirley should think about having children before you get too old. I know you like kids and Mindy really enjoyed the time when the two of you took her to the circus. I'll show Mr. & Mrs. Jones in now."

When they came in, Mr. Jones handed Pat a large sealed envelope from Mr. Gray. Pat looked over the paperwork shaking his head *yes*.

"Mr. and Mrs. Jones, this case should fly through the system because the Department has finished your background checks, you have completed their adoption classes, and they have consented to the adoption of Justavious. Because he is only two years old, you can change his first name and the new name, with the last name of Jones, will appear on his birth certificate. At his age, he is unlikely to remember his old name.

"Julie will type up the legal forms, they will be filed with the Clerk of the Court, and the Clerk will set a date for us to go before the judge."

Pat thought they would make fine adoptive parents. Julie let him know she was moving her car out front and then would eat at the office, as a friend had dropped off a sub and chips for her. She quickly moved her car and came back in.

Pat was on his way to tell her he was going to lunch with Shirley when Julie yelled, "Shirley called and is on her way over here." Then she peeked out the window and excitedly yelled, "Hey, Boss, Boss! Here he comes."

Julie pointed excitedly between the blinds and Pat witnessed a beautiful sight. The Insurance Guy had apparently broken his key off trying to get the door open. He started jerking on the handle, and when that didn't work, he started jerking on the handle again, and when that didn't work, he started kicking the door. Finally he limped away. Julie kept pointing and could not talk for laughing.

Shirley walked in and Rhonda came back to see what was going on.

"Look! He's coming back," said Julie, after she explained the situation. Rhonda, Shirley, and Julie fought for space to look out the window between the blinds. Pat could see above their heads.

"Now he has a clothes hanger, but still can't get it open," commented Rhonda. Finally he left, and so did Pat and Shirley.

"We need to eat quick, Shir, as I have a 2:00 preliminary hearing at the jail courtroom, and I really need to get there 15 minutes early so I can talk to her some more."

"I guess you know all the people in the DA's Office are referring to it as the 'Dope Fairy Case.'"

"That's what I've heard, and in fact that's how I now think of it. Even though I tend not to believe her, she really may have been set up."

"Could be, Sweetie, but not very likely."

They walked about a block down the street and went into a small mom-and-pop restaurant featuring home-cooked meals which had opened up and they found the food to be reasonably priced and good.

"Just think, Hon, in only about six weeks, on Saturday, March 7th, you will be Mrs. Patrick Patton."

"Oh, Pat! I can hardly wait. You have been the man I have searched for all of these years."

"And you are the woman I've always wanted. I still can't believe you feel the same way about me," said Pat as he took her hand.

"Are we still on for visiting your parents next week?"

"Sure are. They are looking forward to seeing you. I know we visited them over the Christmas holidays, but those few weeks seem like a few months ago."

Pat walked back to his office for his briefcase, and Shirley went back to the DA's Office.

CHAPTER 20

The Preliminary Hearing

After reading about Pat and Shirley's wedding announcement in the newspaper, Jeffie turned to Reb and said, "Are the trucks still there? How about the one at Smiths?"

"Ah, it's still there."

"How 'bout the one on the 10th Street lot?"

"That one is still there, too."

"And the one at Pruitt's Used Cars?"

"Nope. That one's gone."

A week earlier, Jeffie test drove three black full-size pickup trucks at three different lots. He talked the sales people into letting him go for a test drive by himself, and then had the keys duplicated at three different places. He threw away the keys to the truck that was at Pruitt's lot.

"Hopefully at least one of the two trucks will still be there this weekend," said Jeffie.

"Jeffie, I, ah, can't wait!" said Reb with a big grin. "When we gonna use the dynamite. I like blowing people up!"

Looking back at the newspaper, Jeffie said, "I think we'll wait and give little Miss Tight-Ass a wedding present she will never forget in her whole short life. But first we take care of that damn nigger. If only the South had won the war, we wouldn't have to go through all this."

Pat went to talk to LaShandra Tidwell through the cell bars before the hearing started and explained the process again. She had no questions, so he went from her holding cell to the courtroom. They were almost ready to start. Normally, unless it's a notable crime, the DA lets the arresting police officer make out, or prosecute, the case. Usually only enough evidence is presented to get the case bound over to the Superior Court so the defense doesn't get too much to work with.

"Next, we will hear the State vs Tidwell."

Pat went over to the counsel table and told LaShandra to sit next to him.

"Are you ready for the State, Officer Sgt. Holden?" asked Judge Wheeler. The judge was in his late sixties, gray-headed, looked distinguished, and sat in a wheelchair due to an automobile accident some years earlier.

"Yes, Your Honor."

"Mr. Patton, are you ready for Ms. Tidwell?"

"Yes, Sir."

"Sgt. Holden, call your first witness."

"I call Mr. Bob Hare, who is employed by the GBI in the crime lab."

Pat turned on his tape recorder and placed it on the witness stand in front of the officer.

Mr. Hare took the stand and testified he worked for the Georgia Bureau of Investigation and was qualified as an expert in identifying drugs. For the last 10 years he had analyzed drugs and had run several hundred tests for marijuana. He was given a suitcase that was in the possession of the defendant and said it did contain marijuana. He gave the weight, which was more than enough for a felony charge of trafficking in marijuana.

Pat asked him several questions about his background and education, as well as the chain of places the marijuana was kept. Sgt. Holden covered only what he had to, so Pat tried to fill in the missing pieces. Mr. Hare said he got the substance from the GBI property room, which was kept under lock and key, but he did not know where it had been before that. He and Lab Technician

Supervisor Eleanor Loveless had previously examined it and it tested positive for marijuana.

Sgt. Holden took the stand next and testified he was called by the airport narcotics unit to talk to a person who was detained for possession of a large quantity of marijuana. He identified Ms. Tidwell as that person. She was arrested and taken to the Clayton County Jail. Pat cross-examined the witness and tried to find out how and why Tidwell was found with the marijuana, but he had little success. Pat came to believe the officer really didn't know a whole lot more about the case than what he testified to on the stand. He said a random search of a number of suitcases uncovered the drugs.

With that, Sgt. Holden rested his case and Pat called LaShandra to testify. There are pros and cons about putting your client on the stand at a preliminary hearing. In most cases, Pat did not have his client testify, because the client could easily say something at the hearing that could later cook his or her goose. In this case he was very concerned about the way she might testify. Pat wanted to see how she did under the gun of being in a courtroom, within the parameters of the story she told him. He cautioned her not to deviate from that story when cross-examined by Officer Sgt. Holden.

Pat watched as he questioned her on the stand and paid close attention when she was cross-examined by Officer Sgt. Holden. Just as he suspected, she came across like a wooden Indian. No emotion at all! LaShandra was as believable as a used-car salesman. Her testimony was okay, it was the ho-hum way she delivered it. On cross-examination, she also came across as evasive. He and LaShandra would have a lot of work to do if this case went to trial.

When they were done, Judge Wheeler bound the case over to the Superior Court, as Pat thought he would.

"Mr. Patton, the amount of marijuana involved precludes me from setting a bond. It will have to be taken up with a superior court judge."

LaShandra told Pat to forget it. She had no one to put up money or property, and even if she did, she had nowhere to go.

"At least I've got three meals a day, a place to sleep and a semblance of medical treatment while I'm in here."

"Okay, LaShandra, but I would be happy to file a motion for bond for you."

"No, it's a waste of time. These suckers are out to get me."

"Then please sign this." Pat handed her a hastily drawn Waiver of Bond Hearing. As Herb had taught him, half of what you do is covering your tail, and he didn't want her coming back later saying he was a terrible attorney because he wouldn't petition the court for a bond hearing.

She signed the waiver and went back to jail, while he went back to his office. He found out what he wanted to know, but hoped he would not have to go to trial. She would make a terrible defense witness.

What was a well-spoken, attractive, and apparently well-educated woman doing in this mess? She had the ability to be a successful person in work and life.

Nothing surprised him anymore. A female Louie Lake.

CHAPTER 21

Ten Pay Telephones

Pat got to Jerome and Mickey's early and bought a newspaper from the machine outside the restaurant. As he read, his eyes focused on an article in the lower left-hand corner of the front page. It said the police were mystified that no one heard or saw anything when several pay telephones were found shot with a high-powered rifle and the coin boxes removed. Ten phones had been shot up at a fairly busy intersection with a grocery store, gas station, shopping center, and package store on its four corners. The thief or thieves got between $300 and $500 worth of change. Police questioned one person of interest, one Louie Lake, but he had an alibi for the entire night.

Louie said the cops had suspected him for some time. It was probably him pushing the envelope. I guess Louie will never change, but he is a fool for messing with Nancy, because he will eventually screw up. Next time there will be no deals. She will throw the book at him and with the judge's blessing.

Willie the Waiter escorted a once very attractive woman to his table. Charlotte was 35 and, although she had a great figure, she wore lines of a hard life on her face.

"Mr. Patton, this young lady said she was meeting you and another lady here," said Willie with a heavy lisp.

"Thank you, Willie."

"I gather you're Charlotte. I'm Pat Patton," said Pat, as she sat down at the table.

"Nice to meet you, Mr. Patton. I thought Shirley O'Kelly also was going to be here."

"That's correct, but she will be a little late."

Willie came by to ask, "Can I get you anything to drink while you're waiting for your other party?"

"Willie, you're like a magnet, because here she comes now."

The two girls were introduced.

"I wasn't sure you would talk to us, ah, because of what happened between Skinny and us." Pat cautiously eyed Charlotte.

"If I can be blunt, Mr. Patton, under the circumstances I would have shot the bastard myself!"

Both Pat and Shirley were surprised - - this was certainly not what they expected. Hostile, yes, but with Skinny!

"I can see by the look on your faces you were shocked at what I just said. Before I go on, though, I want both of your assurances that what I say will be kept private. I don't mind giving you information, but I know you're in the newspapers a lot and I don't need publicity."

"Fair enough," agreed Pat.

"With me, too," echoed Shirley.

"Okay. My father and all three of my brothers were trash. I guess *is* trash would be the word for Jeffie, because he's probably still out there somewhere. I don't really know, though, because we haven't spoken in years."

"Here are your drinks." Willie took their order and said, "We'll have your food out in a jiffy."

"Thank you, Willie. Then you have no idea where Jeffie is?" asked Shirley.

"Not the slightest. Now I don't want this to go any farther for obvious reasons and it is very hard to talk about, but all three of my brothers sexually abused me. They also mentally and physically abused me. They knew I would never tell. I was the youngest by four years and the only girl. They were evil and bad to the bone, Mr. Patton. Believe me, you saw how bad Skinny was, but Jeffie is every bit as bad, if not worse! Oh, the things they did to me, and the things they made me do to them! I was so afraid. And my dad? He was an equal-opportunity abuser, who abused the whole family!"

Charlotte had to stop for a minute to collect herself as tears came to her eyes and she softly sobbed for a short time. Shirley took her hand and held it while Pat gave her his handkerchief.

"I'm so sorry you have to go through all of this," comforted Shirley.

"I know it's very painful for you but please go on," urged Pat.

While Charlotte was composing herself, Willie brought their order.

"I guess you're most interested in Jeffie, huh? 'Cause the other two are taking dirt naps."

"Right. If he's out there, I'd like to know what to expect, especially now that I agreed to represent Ed Edwards."

"I know what you must think, what with me talking about my brothers like this, but I can't stop being bitter toward them. Anyway, expect the worst, if he's alive. He is evil, brutal, but worst of all, he is smart. Jeffie probably won't come at you head on, man to man. He is the type to have someone else get you, or shoot you from a hiding place. Ambush, I guess you would call it. Or maybe a bomb, or poison, or a fire like Skinny did. He's a long-time Brotherhood member, was taught every dirty trick there is, and would not hesitate to use any of them. However, if he does decide to go one-on-one, he will be a very formidable adversary.

"Not a very pretty picture that you're painting," nodded Pat.

"Assuming he is out there, would he try to get you for killing Skinny and helping this black guy? Damn right he would! My brother is an animal, and if he found out I was talking to you, my life wouldn't be worth a Confederate dollar bill."

"Please tell us what you can about him," asked Shirley with compassion.

"Sure. He would be about, let's see, ah, 40 now. He's about six feet tall, and always had a good build because he lifted weights. He worked for Southern Airways, but I heard he got fired. A toothpick is sometimes hanging out of his mouth, as well as a cigar. Doesn't smoke cigarettes, but chews tobacco. He's not too bad looking . . ."

"Do you have a picture of him?" cut in Pat.

"No. I don't think I do. Oh, he's a smart ass, a bully, and does drugs. What kind I don't know, and he's also a big beer drinker. All of his life he's owned Camaros, so he probably still has one, and he always had a Harley and rode with a gang. Some kind of club he belonged to. Brotherhood members were always doing dirty work for each other. That's what makes them so dangerous. You put one away and all he has to do is give the word and one of the members will put a real hurt on you. They will even kill for each other."

"Another pretty picture," commented Shirley.

"Can you think of anything else?" asked Pat.

"Well, he was in the Army for a while, and he was married a couple of times. Have you talked to them? His ex-wives? They could probably give you an earful because he beat the hell out of both of them. There was one strange thing though - - he was overly protective of his step-daughter, Cindy, by his second wife, Renée. I haven't seen either of them in years. Even at age 13 she was a good-looking young woman, filled out early, if you know what I mean. That made me believe he had something going with her, too. Why, he wouldn't even let her have a boyfriend and threatened to kick the ass of any young boy she brought around the house. Finally she stopped bringing them."

"You didn't go over to their house much?" asked Shirley.

"Absolutely not! I stayed away from my creep-of-a-brother all I could. Cindy, and both of his ex-wives, seemed okay though. In fact, I pitied them, because I knew what a devious, dia bolical person he was and I'm sure still is."

At this time Willie again appeared asking if they would like dessert or coffee. All declined dessert but some wanted coffee.

"Charlotte, I really need a picture of him, and some idea where he might be now. Through the back door, I tried to get information and a picture from the Army, but they wouldn't let me get to first base. He doesn't have a criminal record, so I'm out there. I tried the high school, but apparently he was out the day the pictures were taken. I can't find his ex-wives, so I'm striking out all over. Dixie Airlines, another one of his employers, won't cooperate either - - because so far, he hasn't done anything against the law. The same for Southern Airways. I know your father is deceased, but is your mother still alive? She may have a picture."

"Sorry, Momma died a few years ago, in a shelter. She was a hopeless alcoholic. I hate to say this, but she led a terrible life, not eating right, living on the street, drinking alcohol, and taking drugs. Momma died of pneumonia. She had lost everything, but we never did have many pictures anyway. I'm afraid that if there was one, it's long gone."

"Just my luck. It surely is," said Pat as he happened to glance at the customers and noticed a strange man looking at him. He couldn't believe his eyes. It was Eb! If it were not for Kathy sitting with him, he never would have recognized him. Then Eb winked at him.

The check came and Willie got a good tip. He really was a nice little guy, and Pat wondered what he was doing with a jerk like Pick'em-Up-Man. Love sure is strange. They left with Charlotte's promise to check around for the possible locations of Jeffie's ex-wives, especially Renée, as she was the last.

Charlotte left after a thank you from both of them, and Pat paid the bill. As Pat and Shirley left to meet Eb and Kathy at the house, a group of motorcycle riders came in. Pat couldn't help noticing their cutoff blue-denim jackets, which read Confederate M/C Club.

What a group of rough-looking misfits.

Something about the name rang a bell, but Pat was so busy thinking about his conversation with Charlotte, he couldn't put his finger on it.

"Hey, Reb! Look at the broad getting in the grey Ford over there. She looks like my little sister," exclaimed Jeffie, parking his Harley chopper at the restaurant.

"Well, ah, isn't that, ah, Piss-Ant Patton over there with Little Miss Tight-Ass?"

"It sure is, and I'd bet the fact they're both here at the same time is no coincidence."

"Hey, Snake, Yanker! We'll be back a little later. Save us a seat," yelled Jeffie.

Snake was a big vicious man with tattoos, an earring, shaved head, pot-marked face and, although very strong, a beer gut. Yanker was average size, but crazy. He carried around a pair of rusty pliers and had yanked a couple of his own teeth out. Enemies of the Club would be held down while Yanker pulled out at least one tooth. These were the kind of men Jeffie called his friends.

Eb spotted them watching Charlotte and following her. He and Kathy took off behind them in his pickup. He hoped Pat had his CB radio turned on.

"Blade, Blade, dis here be Brown Sugar," yelled Eb into the mike.

Pat had pulled out of the restaurant last and drove into a gas station next door when Eb called him on the radio.

"You got the Blade, come on Sugar."

"Two two-wheelers are following the crying lady's 4-wheeler and I be following them. Mean-looking dudes!"

"Which way are they headed?"

"North on the main drag, come on."

"Stay on Channel 6 and give the location often. I'm getting on a land line and will try to get a bubble-gum machine to follow them. Maybe it will make those boys break off."

"Ten-four, Blade."

Pat lucked out and got Lt. Keller on the third ring. He hurriedly explained what was going on. Lt. Keller told him all of their police cars were equipped with CB radios and he had a car in the area. Lt. Keller had Dispatcher Evette Franklin relay the info to Sgt. Ricky Siniard, who was patrolling in the area, and was told to turn on his CB and tune to Channel 6. He was instructed to follow the motorcycles until they decided to pull in somewhere. About five minutes later a cruiser pulled in front of Eb, who radioed Pat that a bubble-gum machine was on the tail of the two bikers.

"Hey, Blade. After a few minutes of the dudes lookin' over der shoulders, dose boys be pullin' into a liquor store. I be pullin' into de hardware store next to it. Da machine done kept goin'."

"Ten-four, Sugar."

A few minutes later, Eb leaned his face down close to the seat and said, "Dey jus turned around and headed back toward de restaurant."

"Mission accomplished. I gots de ladies number and will call her later tonight. I wonder who dey was and why dey followed her?"

"Who knows, but I done forgot to get de license number. Sorry 'bout dat. Sugar out and will meets ya at home base."

"Ten-four, Blade out."

"I wonder what that was all about," questioned Shirley.

"Probably two horney guys looking and then following an attractive girl. It's done all the time, Honey."

"I guess you're right, but I sure wouldn't want those two creeps following me!"

* * *

Jeffie and Reb pulled into Jerome and Mickey's Steak House.

"Bad luck that cop car being behind us. I still believe the broad in the car was my baby sister, but I'm not positive as I haven't seen her in years."

They got off their bikes and went into the restaurant. The gang was terrorizing the customers, so Mickey called the police. Two uniformed officers came in and Mickey seated them at a table close to the Confederates, who then calmed down, ate and left. The officers loved that assignment - - Mickey took care of the bill.

CHAPTER 22

The House

About two miles from the house, Shirley told Pat to turn off and go into the Sunrise Lake Subdivision. The houses were selling for twice what his was worth. Pat's was valued at $40,000 to $50,000, but these were much bigger, had double garages with electric door openers, 2 ½ baths, full basements and acre lots. The subdivision also had a small lake, a community swimming pool, four tennis courts, a club house, bicycle paths and jogging trails. All in all, a really nice place to live.

"Hey, Blade, where it is ye be? Dis here be Brown Sugar, come on."

"Tell him we'll be there in about 30 minutes," said Shirley with a smile.

"We be's der in about 30 minutes, Sugar."

"Ten-four, Sugar out."

"Blade, out."

"Now do you mind telling me what this is all about?"

"I will in a minute. Turn right here on Twilight Lane and stop at the end of the cul-de-sac."

They stopped in front of a very nice all-brick new home that had an Under Contract sign in the front sodded yard.

"Okay, I give up. What's going on?"

"How would you like to live there?" asked Shirley, pointing to the house.

"Does a bear . . .,"said Pat with a smile.

133

"Well, I know the new owners very well and they gave me the keys to look around. Come on!" Shirley excitedly jumped out of the car, after handing Pat the keys.

They went in and Pat was very impressed. A very large garage, modern kitchen, great room with a real brick fireplace, three bedrooms, with the master bedroom having its own full bath, another full bath adjoining the other two bedrooms, and a half bath next to the great room. Then there was a laundry room and a large dining area, which overlooked a large screened porch through a bay window and had double doors with glass from top to bottom, which led out to the screened porch.

Pat opened the kitchen door and went out on the porch. The yard was beautiful. He could see everything from there because the porch was up one story over of the full basement. They opened the screen door, walked down the outside stairs and Pat immediately noticed the new owners were putting in a swimming pool.

Shirley excitedly opened a lower back door, which led into the basement. It was really huge. He could see the furnace and central A/C unit were located together with the hot water heater. A garage door was located at the back left side of the basement and had a paved driveway leading up to it. A bath with a shower was already finished.

"Shir, your friend's husband is really going to have a super workshop if he's into that. Look at the size of this place! It's twice as big as my little 1250 sq. ft. house."

"You like, huh?'

"Of course, I love it. You have some lucky friends."

They went back upstairs using the inside staircase.

"Now for the upstairs."

"What upstairs?"

"Over here," said Shirley as she opened a door to the left of the basement door.

"I had no idea it had a 2nd floor."

Pat noticed the door to an overhead set of disappearing folding stairs in the ceiling. He pulled them down and climbed up. When he got to the top, he found a light switch, turned it on, and felt cold because there was no heat.

"Shir, look at this! You wouldn't believe the storage space up here and the floor is put in! But – it doesn't seem to be near as big as the house."

She was up the stairs far enough to stick her head up and look. Pat came back down and closed up the stairs.

"Boy, this sure is some house!"

A door beside the basement door, led to a second floor. Upstairs, she showed him two fairly large rooms and another bath; this one had a commode, wash bowl, and a shower. It was compact and well laid out. The upstairs rooms explained the attic seeming smaller than it was.

"My friends thought this would be a quiet place for a study for the man and a sewing room/office for his wife-to-be.

The two rooms were fairly large with the ceiling angled part way because of the slope of the roof. Both rooms had dormers with windows facing the rear of the house, which let light into the room but were deceptive because they could not be seen from the front of the house.

"You mean they're not married yet?"

"No, we're not, Honey. It's a wedding present from Momma and Daddy!"

Pat stopped short and felt dizzy. He leaned against a wall feeling numb. *This is going to be my house.*

"I – I – I'm speechless," said Pat with noticeable disbelief in his voice.

She went over and gave him a hug and a kiss.

"This is going to take a while to . . . to sink in. How long have you known about it?"

"About a week now and I just couldn't hold off telling you any longer. Momma and Daddy were trying to keep it a secret."

"What a wedding present! Your parents are just too good to us. If it's okay with you, I don't want to sell my old house. It would make a fine rental property."

"That's fine, Hon. Maybe we could rent it to Eb and Kathy. After all, she is still my best friend and Eb yours."

"Eb told me she was a keeper, so who knows. I still can't believe this is happening to me! Now I wish I didn't agree to go on the trip."

"Don't be silly, you need the break, and Momma and I have a lot of things to wrap up for our wedding. With the names you gave me, the invitation list is now up to around 200 and growing. I hope I'm not so nervous I fall in the aisle."

"And I hope my knees don't buckle," laughed Pat. "You did invite Gloria, didn't you?"

"What? I'm not believing you!" laughed Shirley. "I keep wondering when they will fire her. The word is she is giving free samples to all the Asst. DA's who are interested - - which includes all of the males."

"Let's get out of here before Eb has a heart attack. Our 30 minutes has turned into almost an hour. Here's your keys back."

"They're yours, Sweetie. I have another set."

"Wake me when this is over. I need to call your Momma and Daddy and thank them when we get home. I also need to pick up a nice thank you card for our wedding presents. Hon, your parents have only known me for a few months. Are they sure they want to do this? Tell them to put the house in your name."

"No, Pat. We're not going to do that. You trust us and we have to trust you. It's in their name now but it will be changed on our wedding day."

When they got home, did they ever have a story to tell Eb and Kathy. They called both sets of parents and finally got to bed late. They were both very tired. But – not too tired.

CHAPTER 23

St. Augustine

Pat did not go to the office the next day, because he needed the time to get ready for his motorcycle trip. He did not have time to ride since he brought the Kawasaki 1000 home. It would go right back to Sam's place, because that's where they finally decided to meet. The engine was a duel overhead cam masterpiece and the four exhaust pipes sounded like a Grand Prix race car. With power to spare, it would still get 55 mpg with two people on it at 60 mph.

"Shir, I've had breakfast and I'm going so I can swing by the new house and see it in full daylight."

"We need to pack stuff up and move some things to the new house as soon as we can. Daddy said we could use his pickup truck and Eb has one, too," commented Shirley.

"Good idea."

Boy it feels good to ride this bike. He dressed in layers of clothing so he could remove a sweat shirt or whatever as he went from cold mornings to warm afternoons. Also, the farther south, the warmer it would get. His left shoulder still bothered him from where Skinny had shot him, but not enough for Pat to call off this trip. It tended to hurt some when he twisted his body to the left.

At the house, a crew was already working on the pool. He pulled around to the garage and parked. A man with a white safety hat came over. "Can I help you?" He looked at Pat suspiciously.

"Just looking around, thank you."

"I'm sorry, Sir, but this house has been sold, or at least is under contract to be sold, and the new owners may not care to have the public looking through their house."

"I'm glad to see you're on duty, Sir, because I'll rest easier." Pat smiled. "I'm Pat Patton, one of the new owners."

"Yes, now I remember. Dr. O'Kelly mentioned you. What a nice fellow he is."

"I know. The motorcycle threw you, but I'm on my way to Florida."

"Now I know where I've seen you. On TV, of course. The Five-O'Clock Traffic Bandits and that Skinny fellow."

"That's me."

"Tillison, Ray Tillison." The man held out his hand. He had a shaved head and a strange looking beard.

Pat looked around for about an hour. The place looked even better in daylight. He was told the pool would be ready next week and then the fence man would be by to fence it in, while the pool company put in a bath house with a small screened-in porch. Pat did not want to leave, but he said goodbye and headed for Sam's place.

Sam had her Harley out, was finished loading it when Nancy pulled in behind Pat.

"I thought you were working until noon," said Sam to Nancy.

"The Boss felt sorry for little old me and told me to go back home almost as soon as I got to the office. By the way, speaking of my boss - - Pat, your client, Ms. Tidwell, has been shooting off her mouth at the jail and has pissed off everyone, including Mr. Colver. He told me to offer ten serve five and not to come off it. If she goes to trial, I have been told to ask for ten to serve. I don't know what she has done but even Chain Gang is ticked at her. I do know she has been yelling false arrest, the cops are on the take, the judge has been bought, I am stupid, and the DA hates black people."

"Well, Nancy, you have to admit she is an equal opportunity bad-mouther."

"I'll give her that, but if she goes to trial, all bets are off. I can't let our friendship stand in the way of my job."

"I wouldn't expect it to be any other way."

"I think we need to talk about something much more interesting, namely motorcycles," interrupted Sam.

"I guess she told us," said Pat to Nancy.

"No more shoptalk until we get back off of this trip," said Nancy.

"Step right over here, my good man, and feast your peepers on this lovely piece of art work. We have one 1980 Harley Tour Glide FLT, 80 cubic inches, that's 1340 cc for your information, 65 HP, a three-point rubber-mounted engine to reduce vibration, a five-gallon gas tank, saddle bags, trunk, fairing, all color-matched, dual headlights, triple disc brakes, a five-speed transmission, and 781 pounds at a bargain price of only $6,961. Of course, I got a little better deal than that."

"She ought to be selling those things," said Pat, while looking at Nancy.

"She sure should. Hey, it's almost noon. Let's get a quick bite and get down the road. After dark, it's going to be a little cold to ride. So, if it's the same to y'all, I'd rather do most of the riding in the daytime.

Nancy also had a Harley, and off they went for a quick cheeseburger and then headed south on I75. They planned to stop for a break, get gas and use the restroom, at least every two hours, or less if one of them needed to stop. Nancy's 1978 Harley Sportster had a small gas tank, so she filled up at each stop, rather than chance running out.

They stopped the first time on the other side of Macon. It was a beautiful day, and Pat soon fell in love with his KZ1000. He would have to buy this machine. They decided to ride a little after dark as Sam wanted to make Jacksonville, FL, that night. She had lived there and knew a lot of people, many were motorcycle riders. They road at 70 MPH, but gas and rest stops ate up time. Even though they took only 45 minutes to eat, they hit Jacksonville at almost 8:00. Their motel was located down the road and on the other side of the street from The Seaweed Tavern, a bar Sam wanted them to visit.

They checked in, used the bathroom and rode over to the Seaweed. Two years earlier, Sam had worked as a cabdriver and bouncer at a nightclub in Jacksonville. Pat immediately got bad vibes when they pulled into the parking lot and saw it was full of Harley choppers, the kind outlaws ride. A large Harley would be stripped of its large fenders, gas tank, seat, and the minimum required parts installed. That made the bike lighter, faster, and different-looking.

They locked their bikes and went inside.

Pat could not believe his eyes! It was full of outlaw bikers from a club that called themselves Hitler's Henchmen. Even their girlfriends looked like they could chew nails and whip his butt with one hand tied behind them. The leader of the group, Der Fuhrer, was so big that, as he bent over the bar, he was able to reach one of the shelves on the bartender's side. He had on a Harley hat with the bill cut off, black gloves with cut-out fingers, blue jeans, and motorcycle boots. His head was shaved, but he had grown a beard, and had an earring in one ear.

Sam went over and goosed him! Der Fuhrer very slowly straightened up to his full 6' 6", his massive chest bulging out of his T-shirt and cut-off blue denim jacket, and equally as slowly he turned around to see who dared to goose him. Der Fuhrer stared at Sam through ice blue eyes. Then a smile broke out on his face, showing two broken teeth.

"Sam, Baby," cried out Der Fuhrer, as he put his arms around her and actually picked her up.

They all talked a few minutes and had a beer, as Sam introduced everyone.

Pat got Nancy aside and said, "Sam knows these people, but they don't know us from Adam. I'm feeling very uncomfortable. How about you?"

"Ditto here. I was about to tell Sam this is not my kind of place. Maybe you didn't hear about it, but about two years ago, these nice people crucified a girl by nailing her to a tree. I can imagine the headlines now - - 'Georgia Assistant DA busted in drug raid on a Jacksonville biker bar!'"

Nancy said something to Sam, and in a few minutes she told everyone they needed to be going. They hopped back on their bikes and rode back to the motel, but not before Sam showed Der Fuhrer, and the gang, her new Harley FLT.

Pat had a beer in the room the girls were sharing, and then he went to his room, took a shower, and went to bed.

Early Saturday morning the trio was on the road again. The KZ1000 felt good under him and, although it did not sound as good as a Harley, it would pull away from them with ease. The dual overhead cam engine was a masterpiece of engineering and full of power.

After breakfast they decided to take the coast road, A1A, to St. Augustine, so they could see the ocean along the way. What a ride! Water as far as one could see, whitecaps breaking as they hit the shore, seagulls and pelicans flying effortlessly over the waves, and the sun reflecting off of the white sand beaches. Occasionally a boat could be seen plowing through the water, fishing off shore, or going on a pleasure cruise. They took their time and enjoyed the incredible scenery, arriving at St. Augustine about 10:30. Sam showed them the sites - - The Fountain of Youth, the old Spanish fort, and especially a back street with trees growing on both sides of the road with branches forming an arch over the road, giving the sensation of going through a tunnel. Motorcycles were everywhere!

Traffic was a mess as people came from miles around for the festival. As they waited in line to eat, Sam lit up a cigar, walked out into the middle of the intersection and started directing traffic. She used hand signals like a cop. Being she was so big, nobody wanted to mess with her. Soon she had traffic flowing fairly well, and Pat and Nancy held her place in line, watching in disbelief, which soon turned into tearful laughter. What a sight!

After lunch, they rode across the historic Bridge of Lions to the beach area. Pat wanted to go exploring for another five miles or so, and they even thought about riding down to Marineland, but that would be pushing it. Nancy led the way, this time on two-lane A1A, with Pat following, and Sam in the rear.

Sam had made a sign out of white cardboard and a magic marker that read 'Caution, Wide Load', and taped it on the back of the box on her luggage rack. She constantly got attention from the rear, but now Pat saw a car, which came from the opposite direction, run off the road while apparently looking at them. He glanced back and understood why the guy almost lost control. There was 360-pound Sam riding side-saddle and smoking a corn-cob pipe! He almost ran off the road himself!

Remarkably warm for this time of year, they all hoped it would hold for the entire trip, especially the ride back to Atlanta. Before they knew it, the sun was starting to go down. They headed for the main part of town, or Old Town, where most of the action would be taking place. Motorcycles outnumbered cars in town and the roar of exhaust pipes could be heard all over town. Luck was with them as they found one of the few very valuable parking places and got all three motorcycles in it. Venders were all around selling food, so

they got hotdogs, chips, and a Coke. Pat and Nancy got two each, but Sam ate four and two bags of chips.

Sam had a handout that gave the location of most of the venders, along with a map and description of what they sold. A booth which made hand-rolled cigars caught her eye, so they locked up the bikes and headed there.

Sam took the lead, and they walked in her wake as she made her way through the crowd. They found the booth, and all of them bought some freshly made hand-rolled cigars. By this time it was dark and cold enough for long-sleeve sweatshirts.

CHAPTER 24

Hit and Run

While Pat, Nancy, and Sam were having fun in Florida, two men in a Camaro drove to Smith's Used Car Lot in Jonesboro.

"Damn our luck," said Jeffie, "it's gone!"

"That's right, Jeffie, first it was Pruitt's, and, ah, and now Smith's. Both of them had nice trucks."

"Well, we still got the lot at 10th Street. If that one is not there, we'll have to steal one the hard way."

It was there but now a chain was across the driveway. They both saw it at the same time. This was new because they never had a chain up before.

"Look, Reb, here's the plan. I'm going to pull up in the drive when there are no cars coming. You jump out and use our bolt cutters on the lock, but do it quick. Throw the cutters back in the car, and use this key to get the truck. I'll meet you at the shopping center. I'll park next to the end where we planned. You got that?"

"Ah, go over it again, okay, Jeffie?"

"Sure, 'cause we need to get this right."

"Right, Jeffie, I know 'cause we gonna have fun tonight! Gonna get us a nigger!"

Jeffie went over the plan not one but two more times. Reb finally understood it, and Jeffie pulled up to the drive where his car covered the view from the road of the chain and the lock. Reb jumped out and quickly cut the lock, threw the bolt cutters back in the Camaro, and headed for the Ford F-250 pickup truck. The key fit a little tight, but worked. As soon as Reb had it started, Jeffie took off for the shopping center.

He pulled into a space at the end and Reb came in beside him a few minutes later. Jeffie got out of the Camaro and told Reb, "Go around the 250 and get in the passenger's seat. I'll drive."

Reb was clearly disappointed, but Jeffie did not trust him with the job he had in mind for tonight. He went to South Atlanta and checked out the bus stop at Main and Pinecrest. No one was there, which was good. He drove around the block and parked the truck. Then they waited. He was glad he was able to get a truck with tinted windows all around.

* * *

Pat, Nancy, and Sam were puffing away on the hand-rolled cigars when Sam said, "Down the street at the end, if you turn right, they have a neat place beside the waterwheel, where we can get a beer."

It was, as usual, a very busy place. At the top of a flight of stairs was a huge screened porch with large tables, which sat six or eight people each.

"This place is packed, Sam. We won't be able to sit down."

"Tell ya what, Pat. You buy me a beer and I'll have us a table by the time you come back," answered Sam, as she blew out a cloud of smoke.

"You're on!"

Pat and Nancy went in a door that led to a small bar. He ordered three drafts, gave one to Nancy, and tried to keep the other two from spilling as he went through the crowd to the porch. There was Sam sitting all by herself at a table for at least six people.

"Sam, how did you get a table so quickly?" asked Pat.

She took a big drag on her cigar and said, "I moofed their hoof!"

Pat and Nancy burst out laughing, as they could only imagine what had transpired. It was so nice to relax and leave the office behind. They had another beer, and talked about anything except the law. Of course, Pat had to talk about his new house. From their perch on the porch, they could see the street and the water, as well as Castillo De San Marcos, the old Spanish Fort, which dated back to 1672 and guarded the harbor. But mostly they watched the motorcycles go by and talked about them. After the beers, all of them had to use the restroom.

"I know where there's a public restroom down the street," said Sam. "This place has a mile-long line."

She led the way and they found the public restrooms. Nancy headed for the ladies room, but Sam started to follow Pat into the men's room.

"Hey, you're going in the wrong place," yelled Pat.

"I know," smiled Sam, "but whenever I go to the ladies, room, I cause a riot."

She continued into the men's room, not paying attention to the men standing at the urinals, or them to her - - as they thought she was a man. She found an empty stall and went inside.

Pat never ceased to be surprised by this character. He met Nancy outside and they both laughed when Sam came out of the men's room.

They had a good time going into different shops and getting things to snack on. All kinds and makes of motorcycles lined the streets - - new, old, foreign, two-wheel and three-wheelers. Sam had to be especially watchful over her new Harley; it was a known fact that thieves would rent a large U-Hall truck, equip it with a generator and air tools, then steal a Harley and have it completely dismantled in less than an hour. They could get more for the parts, with less chance of getting caught, than they could for the whole bike. After Sam had a conversation with two guys on Harley choppers, they headed back to the motel.

When Pat got to his room, he noticed a red light blinking on the phone. He called the desk and was told a Capt. Keefauver of some police department wanted him to call back as soon as he got in. Since it was now 11:00, he called the Capt. at home. *Shirley must have given this number to him.*

"What could be wrong?" asked Pat to an empty room.

"Hello," said a male voice.

"Captain, this is Pat returning your call. I hope I didn't wake you up, but I got a message at my motel to call you as soon as I got in."

"Right. Thanks for returning my call, and no, I wasn't asleep yet. I've got some good news and some bad news. I'll tell you the worst first. Ed Edwards was the victim of a hit-and-run accident; however, we're not so sure it was an accident."

"I'm sorry to hear that. Was he hurt bad?"

"Very bad, but he's still alive. He lost a leg, a lung, and a kidney. He was hit by a full-size pickup truck, a Ford F-250."

"Do the doctors think he will make it?"

"Touch and go but he's a tough bird. He made it through 26 years of prison, so he should be able to get through this, too."

"Did they get the person who did it?"

"Not yet but what raises our eyebrows in this case is that, according to Atlanta PD, a home owner said a strange pickup had been parked in front of her house for about 30 minutes. She was suspicious and looked out her window several times and could see Ford F-250 written on the side of it. The last time she looked, she saw Ed walking down the street with a bottle in his hand. About that time, she heard the truck start up, and when Ed crossed the street, it pulled out very fast, hit him and kept going. How much do you want to bet it was stolen?"

"I won't take that bet but I sure do hope you catch him, or whoever it is."

"Them," corrected the Capt. "There were two of them, according to the witness. She said the windows appeared to be dark colored, but when a car went by, its headlights shined in the truck and she could make out two figures sitting in it."

"Thanks, Capt. Now what's the good news?"

"Lt. Keller has located both witnesses from the 1955 shooting at Ed's place. They are sisters, with different last names, but living together."

"Will they talk to me?"

"I don't know. We found out they went to Tampa, FL, for a short winter vacation at a relative's house but should be back within the next week or two. Lt. Keller is trying to get an address and phone number of the place where they went, but their home address is right here in Jonesboro. After the shootout with Ed, they got scared and moved from Griffin to Jonesboro. This was back in the 1950's."

"I assume Shirley knows about this because you must have gotten this phone number from her."

"That's right, and she wants to talk to you. She said you would be calling her every night."

"I'll do it. Anything else, Capt.?"

"If I were you, I would watch myself, and look out for Shirley, too! I don't like the timing or smell of the hit-and-run on Ed. Shirley gave me Charlotte's phone number and I called and told her about it. She said that information coupled with your call Thursday night, makes her feel she needs to leave town for a few weeks. She has three weeks' vacation built up and is leaving in the morning. She left a personal message for you on your office answering machine, but I don't know what it said. She'll call you some time this next week at the office."

"Thanks, Capt., and please thank the Lt. for me. I'll be back tomorrow night. See you."

"Be careful. Bye."

Pat called Shirley and they talked for about 15 minutes before he finally got to bed. The 400-mile ride home would come too soon. They planned to get up early and be home Sunday night.

CHAPTER 25

How Much Is Enough?

The gang got up at 6:00 and was ready to leave by 7:00. They ate a quick breakfast at a fast-food place and stopped to top off their gas tanks before heading north on a beautiful day. Many motorcycle riders had the same idea. The station was crowded; then they couldn't believe what pulled in beside them.

A 400-pound man, named Bubba, who looked to be in his 30's, wearing bib overalls, and a long flowing red beard, came in riding a one-of-a-kind three-wheeler, a homemade red-neck work of art. They talked to him a few minutes and found out the crude machine had a Chevy car frame and rear end. A Chevy 350-cubic-inch engine with an automatic transmission powered it. A Harley 74 motorcycle front fork, wheel, and handlebars, welded to the front of the Chevy frame, made up the front end. He sat on some kind of car seat, which had worn and ripped upholstery, and it was obvious the engine and transmission had not been cleaned or degreased before or after it was installed. Bubba and Sam from becoming instant friends who exchanged address and phone numbers.

To start it, he had to touch together two bare hanging wires. The dual exhaust pipes emitted a cloud of blue smoke. Basically, it was a shortened Chevy frame and drive train with a Harley front end grafted to it.

Pat examined the welds on the contraption and they looked like all were done with an oxygen-acetylene torch, which were not half as strong as ones done with an electric welder. The welds were terrible. Pat shook his head when the Bubba left for Tennessee in a cloud of smoke and two bald rear tires. What a hoot!

At 8:00 they got on the road and did not arrive home until 6:00 that evening. In spite of the terrific weather, they were all tired and saddle-sore. The Kawasaki was a joy to ride on a trip, especially with the custom seat Sam had put on it, and he got 60 MPG on the trip. Pat and Nancy talked Sam out of a stop at the Seaweed Biker Bar in Jacksonville, which would have cost them another hour and possibly their lives.

They stopped at Sam's house first and took a short break, before Pat and Nancy split up and headed their own ways. He gave Sam a check for the bike and asked to use her phone to call Shirley before he left. As Pat started the Kawasaki, Bubba arrived in his Red Neck Cadillac. They made a fine-looking 760- pound couple.

Shirley had the garage door opened and was standing waiting for him. She looked beautiful!

As soon as he got the bike parked, they were in each other's arms.

"Oh, Honey, I missed you so. I'm so glad you're back safe and sound!" Shirley kissed him repeatedly.

"It's what happened to Ed, isn't it?"

"I guess that's a lot of it but, now that I have found you, I don't know what life would be like without you!"

"I feel the same way, Honey, but you couldn't have expressed how I feel any better than what you said and the way you acted."

Pat unloaded the motorcycle and they went upstairs. He sat down and told her about the trip while drinking a big glass of ice tea. He told Shirley that he doubted Bubba would be heading for home tonight.

"Has Eb been around?"

"Are you kidding? It's been all Kathy. He's over at her apartment all the time now."

"What did he say about renting this house?"

"He's all for it and Kathy is going to move in with him. Her roommate already has someone who is interested in taking Kathy's place. And, before you ask, the apartment complex is going to waive my rent for the two months left on the lease after we get married. I'll have to pay for all of March, but they will waive April and May."

"Good! Let me take a quick shower so we can go get something to eat and take another look at our new house. You don't mind, do you?"

"Your wish is my command, Ole Master. Say, do you want me to hop in the shower with you and wash your back?" teased Shirley.

"You do and we'll never get out of here. However, I'll gladly take a rain check."

"You better! Here it is, only two nights away from you, and I'm already horny."

"Keep your motor running, Baby," yelled Pat as he headed for the shower. "And please call the hospital and ask about Ed's condition."

Shirley said Ed had improved and they left. They went to Palumbo's Little Italy, and Penny, a co-owner, greeted them warmly, as Pat had been coming there for quite some time. They were seated at a good table beside a window and both ordered the ravioli.

"Shir, I'm glad he is going to pull through but he's a tough old bird."

"Old bird? He's only 47."

"You know what I mean. Tomorrow I need to call the hospital and find out when he will be allowed to have visitors, and I'll schedule some time to see him."

"Pat? You don't think this is Skinny all over again, do you?" asked Shirley with concern in her voice.

"Gosh, Honey, I hope not, but it's got me wondering again. Life is always harder when you don't know who or what you're facing. With Skinny, it was a mixed bag. On the one hand we knew he was after us, what with the phone calls, Herb's house being burnt down, and my car being destroyed. Then on the other hand we never knew how he was going to disguise himself. Here, we don't know if Jeffie is behind Ed's injuries, or even if there is a Jeffie. He may be dead."

"Maybe it's someone out of Ed's past, or maybe it was just an accident."

"You really don't believe that, do you?"

"No," said Shirley very slowly.

About that time Lt. Keller and Dottie Albert walked in. They saw Pat and Shirley and came over to join them.

"What a coincidence seeing you two here."

"It was no coincidence, Shirley. I called Jerome & Mickey's, and a few of your other hangouts when I couldn't get you at home. Penny told me you were here."

"Something important?"

"You might say so, Pat. The two witnesses are back and have agreed to see you. Sgt. Orris was right - - they were threatened back in 1955. Both Haddie Mae Dickerson and Jenel Freeman were told they would be burned out and killed if they said anything against the white guys who did the shooting. They were scared, and now it's starting all over again with Ed's hit-and-run. You had better talk to them tomorrow, while you can, because they're nervous as a pair of jackrabbits."

"I talked to them on the phone, and they don't believe Ed being run down was an accident," added Dottie.

Lt. Keller told Pat he had a lead he was checking about the whereabouts of Renée, Jeffie's last known wife. He gave Pat the address and phone number of the sisters, and told Pat he had a meeting set up for 7:00 tomorrow night at their house. Pat was welcome to join him.

"I'll be there, Lt. The sooner this case is resolved the better for everyone. If I can dot my I's and cross my T's, I'm sure Judge Musselman will grant a habeas corpus petition, and when the facts are heard, Ed will have his name cleared and be off parole.

"And your inside track to the judge is sitting there talking about wedding dresses."

"I know but we can't do without them, can we? You know, Lt., how important it is for me to get Ed cleared and off parole. The general public has no idea that when a man has been given a life sentence, and is released, he is on parole for the rest of his life. Most anything can get his parole revoked. They don't understand he doesn't have to get convicted of a new crime to be sent back to prison. Just being accused of wrongdoing is enough. All a woman needs to say is she's afraid of him and he could be sent back for the rest of his life. Boy, what a way to live. All I can say is, after all this work, if he dies on me, I'll kill him!" said Pat as they all laughed.

"Right. It might seem funny for a cop to say this, but how much punishment for committing a crime is enough? The trend is to put criminals in prison for longer and longer periods of time. But is that reducing crime? Absolutely not. And the longer a person spends in prison, the harder it is to rehabilitate them."

"I agree, Lt. People who commit crimes need to be punished, but these long prison sentences are counter-productive and are nothing but a feel-good measure for the public. 'I'll get tough on crime if elected' is just a vote-getting ploy for politicians."

"Maybe you didn't know it, but I was a prison guard before I joined the police department."

"No, I sure didn't."

"Men in prison are much the same as people out on the street, only they got caught, or a few minutes of anger or pleasure got them there. Oh, you have the ones with a criminal mind, always thinking up new ways to rob, kill or whatever, and when they get out will do it again. But, believe it or not, murderers were some of the nicest people I dealt with."

"You've got to be kidding."

"Not at all. Now, I'm not talking about the guy with no conscience who made a little Korean store owner kneel down while he shot him in the back of the head. Those are the small minority of murder cases. Most of them are in for things like a DUI where they kill someone in a wreck, neighbors who get angry and one shoots the other, a fight and one of the combatants dies. Or maybe a mother gets mad and shakes her child too hard and the child dies, or a man gets mad at the spouse and blows her away. Things like that. I believe only the violent criminals or the repeaters should receive long sentences."

"I see what you're talking about. And the average criminals are nice people for the most part?"

"Sure, just like Sammy Joe Washington, your Five-O'Clock Traffic Bandit. He's a nice guy, isn't he?"

"Very much so, as are his mother and aunt."

"Well, most of the murderers, if left out of prison, would never do it again. A moment of anger can ruin one's life. Do they need punishment? Sure, but how much is enough?"

"I'm not sure since I have never worked in a prison," said Pat, "but take my secretary, Julie, for instance. She is not a criminally minded person but spent time in prison for causing a death in an accident."

"Did you know there is even talk about registering sex offenders? As I understand it, anyone committing a sex offense would be prohibited from living in certain places, like near school bus stops, schools, or things of that nature. The problem is that in over 90% of sex cases the victim knew the offender. So, what good does a law like that do when it really applies to less than 10% of the sex crimes?"

"Gets politicians votes?" answered Pat with a question.

"Precisely. And it is a proven fact that when a person is over punished, it is much harder to rehabilitate them because they are bitter at the system.

"After a period of five years I believe every offender should come up to be evaluated for parole. Should all of them make it? Of course not. It should depend upon the person as well as the crime they committed. As it is now, about all the court looks at is the crime and the legislature is hung up on minimum sentences. The legislature should only make laws concerning maximum sentences. Let the judge in the case decide how much time is enough. They should be automatically reviewed after a few years, as after a man is in prison for a couple of years, he has either learned his lesson or he hasn't. We have a horrible system that looks basically at what a person did, and not at the person himself. We need people, trained people, to talk to these inmates personally, interview guards, the warden, counselors, etc., and then make a recommendation to the Parole Board.

"What have they been like in prison? Are they trouble makers, have they learned to read and write, gotten their G. E. D., learned a skill or gotten a degree. All of these things need to be taken into consideration. Also, all of them need help by trained counselors, particularly for drug and alcohol problems, by people who do not work for the Department of Corrections. They need to be under another agency."

"Why is that?" asked Shirley.

"That's because they need to be an advocate for the inmate, to try to help him or her, and not be under the thumb of the warden or other officials. You could look at it like the Department Of Corrections was the DA and the Counselor was the Defense Attorney. Can you imagine what it would be like if defendants were both prosecuted and defended by the DA's office:"

"Hey, I heard that," said Shirley. "But it really is the truth. Pat, there is no way you could do a good defense job if your boss wanted to put the guy away. A defense attorney needs to be able to do his job without worrying about losing it. Also I think every prison should have a licensed psychiatrist available at least one day per week to take care of the many emotionally troubled people in prison. Give them the help they need and get them treated for their addictions, or psychological problems, before they get out. And one of the things stopping that is money."

"Sure it would cost a lot, but do you know what the rate of recidivism is?"

"Yes," interrupted Pat. "It was in the paper last week - - the article said 65% go back to prison within the first year of release. Something is very wrong. Multiply 65% of our prison population by the cost of housing each inmate and see what could be saved."

"We have about 8,500 inmates coming back the first year," said the Lt., as he figured with his pen and napkin. "And I read the cost is between $10,000 to $15,000 per year to house an inmate. Let's take the lower amount of $10,000."

"That's $55,250,000!" answered Dottie.

"And if we only decreased the amount of men who go to prison by one half, we still would save over $27,000,000 per year."

"Gosh, Lt., we could spend $8,000,000 on professional help for these guys, and still save $47,000,000 per year," said Shirley.

"Not only that, but you have to take into account the saving to the taxpayers by the DA not having to handle these 5,000 plus extra cases each year.

"And from a police standpoint, that's many less arrests, and a much less-crowded court calendar. The only drawback would be a higher caseload on parole and probation officers, but because men on parole and probation are charged a monthly fee, they pretty well pay that extra cost themselves.

"I would like to see a hospital with doctors, psychiatrists, and counselors, with a barbed wire fence around it where a judge could send mentally disturbed criminals for treatment."

"If we could do a really good job of counseling, we could reduce the prison population, but we would also reduce jobs, and the control the Department of Corrections has. No one wants to lose a job or have a smaller department to run. Politics and money!" said an exasperated Pat.

"Exactly, Pat! They think if my prison system is reduced, then my budget will be reduced and the amount of people who work for me will be cut. Instead of being a big frog in a little pond, I'll now be a little frog in a big pond."

"You're both right," Shirley jumped in. "What do politicians do when they end up with extra money? Do they give it back? Heavens no, they find other ways to spend it or their budget will be cut the next year."

"So politics, power, and money are keeping men in prison who could otherwise contribute to society," concluded Pat.

"That's my opinion anyway," said the Lt.

"Fellows, this conversation is going to change the way I think about sentence recommendations. However, anything I recommend must be approved by the judge," stated Shirley.

"And I believe that's where this whole idea will go up in smoke. In this state, the district attorney and the judges are elected positions, are they not? DAs and judges are politicians in that they run for office. And what does a politician want more than anything else? Why, to get reelected, of course. And what does the public want? Put those crooks in jail and throw away the key! So, what are they going to do when it comes to doing the right thing, or the politically expedient thing? It is the rare person who will not give in and do what it takes to stay in office," said Pat.

"I hate to admit this but I believe you're all right," said Dottie, "but don't tell the judge I said that."

The food came and during an excellent supper they talked about Ed Edwards and Sam. Pat told Lt. Keller he would let him know if, for some reason, he couldn't make it tomorrow night. They laughed again about Pat's Sam stories, her 400 pound boyfriend, and then headed home. Pat needed a good night's sleep after that long ride. He would not get it until after he took care of Shirley's request.

When they got home, Pat called the hospital and found out Ed most likely would not be allowed to have visitors until Wednesday. He made a note to call back Tuesday for an update. That's when Shirley grabbed him.

* * *

Jeffie was at Reb's old rented dump of a trailer, which was like most in that park. Reb stayed there most of the time, but sometimes he would go back to his ex-wife and four kids. She put up with him only because he sometimes brought her money, and the kids loved their daddy, even if he was a 100% loser. They sat on a cluttered couch and talked.

"You say when you followed old Piss-Ant that he usually went to the Jamestown Plaza to shop?" asked Jeffie.

"Ah, Jeffie. He went to lots of other places, too, and you know what?"

"No, I don't know what! You think I'm some kind of a mind reader?" snapped Jeffie.

"No, ah, I got that feeling again."

"Okay, Reb. What feeling?"

"Like I was being watched."

"Of course you were being watched, Dumbass, you were in a shopping center full of people!"

"Not that kind of watched."

"Aw, drop it, man. We got work to do. One down, although I don't know how he lived. I nailed him real good, and two more to go."

"Did you see his face? Huh, Jeffie? I was a lookin' right at it when we hit him. His black face turned white. It was so funny," said Reb laughing.

"No, I didn't see his face but I can still hear the *thud* when we hit that nigger!" said Jeffie, laughing, and coming out of his blue mood. "But nothing will bring back the brother that he shot and killed!"

"I, ah, wish we could have backed up and ran over him again."

"So do I, but we couldn't take that chance. Now what we gotta do is find us a '67 Mustang somewhere, maybe in a junk yard, or car lot, it don't matter, and see exactly how the hood is opened and where the battery and distributor are located. Then we need to practice opening the hood and putting our little present in the engine compartment as quickly as possible. Then we get the hell away from there just as quick," said Jeffie chewing on a toothpick.

"Jeffie, ah, you are so smart! You think of everything."

"I just thought of something else. You saw how fast his Mustang was at the drag race we watched. He must have an expensive souped up engine in his car, which costs a lot of money. I'd be willing to bet that the hood opens from inside the car to prevent someone from messing with the engine. So, what that means is we have to also practice getting into the car, without leaving marks and making him suspicious."

"Can we watch him blow up? Can we?"

"Sure, we'll park several aisles away," replied Jeffie with a crooked smile.

CHAPTER 26

The Salvage Yard

Monday morning Pat went to the office and met with a man and his elderly mother. The son wanted Pat to draw up a General Power Of Attorney, so he could handle her affairs. She agreed that was her wish.

Pat had a series of questions he asked all elderly persons before he made out a will or power of attorney to make sure they knew what they were doing before a document was executed. He asked for their name and address, if they knew where they were, what city they were in, who Pat was, and several other questions. He had the questions typed out, wrote the answers the client gave him on the sheet, had them sign it, and had his secretary notarize it. That sheet was kept in the client's file in case questions of competence came up later.

Mrs. Simmons did really well with the questions, and had Pat fooled, until he asked her, " What year is it?" and "Who is the president of the United States?"

"Why it's 1942 and Roosevelt is our President. A real good man he is, too! Doing a fine job!"

Pat explained to her son, "I cannot draw up a General Power Of Attorney because she is not competent. I can execute a Special Power Of Attorney that would cover you handling her business affairs, like writing checks for her everyday expenses, but you would not be able to transfer any of her assets, such as her house, no matter how she might answer those questions in the future."

I have nothing against the son, but she could be coached into giving the right answers.

When they left, Pat told Julie he was going to walk over to the jail and talk with LaShandra Tidwell. Going to the jail was old stuff now. He knew all the deputies and joked with them. He and George always had a stimulating conversation. The deputy would make a fine attorney.

He told LaShandra the recommended sentence for a plea was ten years, serve five, or five years in prison followed by five years' probation. If she went to trial and lost, the DA would ask for ten years to serve. He also told her he did not know what she had been doing but whatever it was stirred up a hornet's nest.

"They haven't been treating me right! They don't like me because I'm black! All I been doin' is demanding my rights and tellin' it like it is!"

"Well, you are buying yourself a lot of grief by tellin' it like it is. You have pissed off both the DA and the judge, which is not the smart thing to do."

"I ain't takin' no five years. I want a jury trial!"

"I will be happy to try this case, but you might not like the outcome. And, by the way, why didn't you put a little of that emotion into your testimony when we were in court? You need to put some feeling into it."

"Normally I'm not an emotional person. I can't help it. But I got to try to get out of this place!"

"Look, I'll try again, but I doubt if they come off the ten do five, because it came from DA Colver himself."

"Just get me out of this place!"

"Is there anything else you need to tell me before I leave?"

"No, just get me out of here," said LaShandra in her usual limp-rag voice. I ain't takin' no time. I want probation!"

Boy, do I have my work cut out for me, thought Pat.

"I'll get back to you in a few days."

* * *

While Pat was talking to his client, Jeffie was on the phone talking to a salvage yard worker.

"So you do have a '67 Mustang. Very good! Now, does it have a good hood?"

He was told it had no hood, so Jeffie continued to call auto salvage yards until he found a '67 Mustang in a yard about 30 miles from Jonesboro. He told them he would be there right after lunch to take a look at it.

"Reb, old boy, we are going to look over a '67 Mustang real good right after lunch," said Jeffie with a big grin.

"Then we gonna give that Piss-Ant Patton a present! Ain't that right, Jeffie?" exclaimed a very excited Reb.

"Right. One he'll get a big bang out of!" laughed Jeffie.

At the salvage yard, they went through a drill of opening the door with a coat hanger, opening the hood, pulling a distributor wire and playing like they hooked a ground clip to the non-existent battery.

"Now, all we got to do is find his car parked in the shopping center. Then we'll sit back and watch the fireworks!"

Jeffie looked around and then hit the hood a good lick with a big rock, putting a large dent in it.

* * *

Julie, Rhonda, and Herb were going to try to make it to the Brave Bull. As Pat and Shirley pulled in, he couldn't believe Herb's car was already there. Pat would know that yellow Fiat 124 Convertible anywhere. They found Herb and Rhonda sitting at a large table eating chips and dip.

"Hello, Herbie! I thought Shirley and I would be here first."

"Have a seat, Hot Shot!" As they were sitting down, Julie came in.

"It's sure nice to be able to get into your own car from the driver's side," commented Julie.

"What's she talking about?" asked Shirley.

"You hadn't told her?"

"I forgot."

With that, Julie proceeded to tell the story, adding a few embellishments as she went along, and they were cracking up laughing.

"Well, Herb, we have a new President of the USA being sworn in tomorrow," commented Pat "A movie star at that. I liked him as an actor but wonder how he'll do as President. I want him to fix these high taxes and interest rates. He says he will do something about it, so we'll just have to wait and see."

Julie agreed. "Give Reagan a chance and let's see what he will do, 'cause he sure won't do no worse than high-interest-rates Jimmy the Peanut."

They talked about the election, the Dope Fairy Case, Ed's condition and his Habeas Corpus, Pat's trip and Sam. The girls had a side conversation about the wedding and the guys talked about their houses.

Shirley announced, "I have to tell you something, Pat. The DA thinks you and Nancy are a little too close for her to try the Dope Fairy Case. If it goes to trial, he will prosecute the case himself."

Pat had to admit the move was appropriate. Even though he and Nancy would fight each other to the best of their ability, their friendship was bound to cause talk.

* * *

Jeffie and Reb walked to the salvage yard office.

"Find what you need?"

"I'd have liked to have had the hood off that '67 Mustang but the damn thing has a big dent in it!"

"What? It was okay a few days ago."

"I don't know what happened but I can't use it."

161

"How about if I knock a little off of the price?"

"No. I need a good one," answered Jeffie as they walked out.

* * *

Pat saw a few clients that afternoon, then called Nancy to see if they would back off the 10-to-serve-5 on the Dope Fairy Case. Just as he was afraid would happen, it was a no go. She also confirmed that Colver would prosecute Tidwell if this case went to trial.

Since they were living together, Pat sometimes rode to the office with Shirley. Tired from the trip, he had Shirley drive that morning. He called her and asked if she could get off work a little early so he could take a nap, as he still was tired from the trip.

"I can be at your office at 4:00. Eb and Kathy will be at our house at 6:30 for a dinner date."

"But, Honey, I have to be at the witnesses house at 7:00," protested Pat.

"Not to worry, Big Boy. Lt. Keller called and said they can't make it until about 8:30. Some kind of church function."

"I wonder why he didn't call me?"

"He did but you were with a client."

"Must be in the stack of phone messages Julie gave me that I haven't had time to read," said Pat with a sigh. "Okay, see you at 4:00, Good Looking."

"Bye, Handsome."

As he hung up the phone, he heard a scream - - loud and piercing! He reached into a desk drawer and took out a pistol he had kept there since Skinny was after him. When he ran into the secretarial area, he saw Rhonda standing on top of a chair and Julie beating a mouse to death with a broom handle. Herb was standing there laughing. He finally laughed with Herb but the strain he was under made him jumpy. When he heard the scream, Pat didn't know what to expect and went into survival mode.

"You going to shoot the mouse with a .357 Magnum?" asked a smiling Herb.

"Not hardly, but with Skinny and now possibly Jeffie, I didn't know what to expect." He picked up the dead mouse with a tissue and headed for the bathroom.

Shirley came in and could see the strain on Pat's face.

On the way home, Pat was quiet.

In less than two weeks we'll move into our new house, we have to pack for the move, the trial is coming up soon, and we're going to Charlestown this coming weekend.

He was tired thinking about it but he had to be on constant guard for his life and that of Shirley.

When Pat put his head on the pillow, he instantly fell asleep.

He woke up to the ring of the doorbell. It was Eb and Kathy.

"I left my Mustang parked out in the front yard, so let's take it."

"Turn the CB to Channel 3," asked Kathy. "I just love it when you two get on the radio, but I have to admit those bikers were a little scary."

"Okay, get ready, Boys," said Shirley, as she turned on the CB radio.

Sure enough the gang was on the air talking about race cars and drivers. Pick'em-Up-Man was there, and Shirley wondered if Willie the Waiter was with him.

"Sa-a-y-y, Pick'em-Up-Man, guess who this is, Sweetie," said Pat with his Gay Blade lisp.

"Oh, no! Blade, what do you want now? Haven't you caused enough misery in my life?"

"You got it all wrong, Honey. It's spelled p-l-e-a-s-u-r-e, and you know it!"

"Listen to that, Boys. Old Pick'em-Up-Man has the 14th Street Fairy after him again!" interjected Sheet-Metal King.

"That's right you c-u-t-e Sheet-Metal King, but its 14th and Greenwood Way to be exact," corrected the Blade.

"How did you find out where I live?" yelled Pick'em-Up-Man.

"How did you know where my little baby Pick'em-Up-Man lives? You got a lot of explainin' to do to your little Brown Sugar!" agitated Eb in his gay black lisp. Eb had to lean over the back of the front seat to reach the mike.

"I don't know what the hell – cut that out – is going – stop it right now – ow!" cried Pick'em-Up-Man.

"He must have Willie the Waiter with him," said a laughing Kathy.

"Hey, this here be Diamond Jim. Boys, it sounds like Pick'em-Up-Man has his hands full again, and now he's got them going to his house!"

"Ten-four. This be the Mopar Man. With all the pansies Pick'em-Up-Man has, he could start a flower shop. How 'bout it Eighteen-Wheel Willie?"

"Right, that's a big ten-four. And don't think we missed the Blade calling the Sheet-Metal King cute."

"Why, Honey, you ain't so b-a-d yourself, except your beard tickles," commented the Blade, taking a guess he was a truck driver and had a beard.

"Now wait a damn minute, you damn limp-wristed fruit basket. I'll punch your lights out!" said Eighteen-Wheel Willie, who now had his dander up.

"Yes, and I'll scratch your eyes out!" promised the Blade with an angry lisp.

"See, Willie, you can't take it when it gets thrown your way, can you?" said Pick'em-Up-Man with a laugh, but just before he un-keyed the mike they heard, "I said take me home! Now!" It was Willie the Waiter's voice.

"Boy, did we stir up a mess that time!" commented Pat, as he turned off the radio.

CHAPTER 27

Haddie Mae and Jenel

The foursome went to the Chinese Lullaby Restaurant, which featured a good all-you-can-eat buffet and soft Chinese music. The hostess seated them, took drink orders, and away they went to dig in to the feast. While loading up on steamed rice and several crab rangoon, Pat bumped into John Beaver and they talked about Gertrude for a few minutes. John had fixed the ignition problem. The distributor had a faulty contact point and the engine must have been running on only one cylinder.

"John, I really feel bad about this, especially since I was flying her when the trouble happened. I won't be able to help you get her to the airport this weekend because I'm going to Charleston."

"I'm just glad it was you and not me because I don't need that kind of excitement in my life. If I can find some help, I'll do it this weekend. If not, we'll do it in two weeks."

"Okay, John, see you then."

* * *

Two men sat in a Camaro at the small strip shopping center where Pat and his friends were eating. A grocery store was beside the restaurant and bag boys were playing around, taking their time collecting the shopping carts. About the time they rounded-up the carts to take them into the store, Pat was seen in the window paying the bill. That's all that saved them.

"Damn bag boys, Jeffie! We could'a got to see four of them blow up. Why did they have to screw around like that? Huh, Jeffie?" said a very disappointed Reb.

"Don't worry, Reb. We'll watch for that car, and we'll get him. I'd rather not blow-up Little Miss Tight-Ass yet, as I have other plans for her. Know what I mean?" asked Jeffie with a leer.

"Ah, Jeffie, can I have my turn when you're done with her?"

"Sure, Reb. I'd like to watch her face while you have fun with her."

* * *

When they got back home about 8:00, there was a message from Lt. Keller to meet him at the witnesses' house at 8:30.

Pat got out a city map, located the address, got a good- bye kiss from Shirley, then left.

The women lived in a small wooden house in a predominantly black section of town. The yard was clean and the grass mowed. The house was freshly painted, and two elderly black ladies stood on the porch talking to Lt. Keller, who was dressed in civilian clothes. Pat was so used to seeing the Lt. in uniform that he almost didn't recognize him. Pat pulled in beside Lt. Keller's car. When he went up to the porch, the Lt. introduced Pat to the women and they went inside to a small spotless living room. The night was too cool to talk outside.

"I understands dat you gonna be tryin' to help dat black man what shot those white boys so long ago. Is dat right?" asked Haddie Mae, a very thin white-haired woman in her 70's.

"That's right, Ms. Dickerson. We have reason to believe Ed Edwards may have been sent to prison unjustly," replied Pat.

"Probably so, and everyone calls me Haddie Mae."

"No probably 'bout it," said Jenel, a heavy-set grey-headed woman also in her 70's. "Dat white man had one of dem big ole long guns and was tryin' to point it at him when Ed shot him first."

"Why didn't you tell that to the court?"

"First, you gots to understand dat we be talkin' 'bout 1955 when dat Brotherhood was real powerful. We was afraid to say much because dey told us dat if we says anything bad about them white men, dat we would be burned out, killed, and our families burned out and killed," said Haddie Mae. "And dey was not foolin' neither. I knowed of two families who were burned out and one man disappeared and never was found to dis day. So, I didn't say nothin'. I'm ashamed to say it, but I was scared and dat nice Ed went to prison. I didn't approve of him being wif dat white woman, 'cause it made it look like us black ladies ain't good enough fer him. But — he be a nice man and never caused no trouble. We both be old now and don't wants to go to our graves wif dis curse on us.

"Lookie here, Mr. Patton, we willing to say de truth in court, but we still scared," said Jenel in a very weak squeaking voice. "Now Mr. Ed, he's been hit by a car, and de police don't think it be no accident according to dat TV news lady on Channel 3. We be leavin' in de morning, but I be givin' Lt. Keller a telephone number where we can be reached. I knowed him a long time and I trust him."

"Where are you going?" asked Pat.

"We take de bus to Jacksonville where we gots a niece dat we can stays wif for a few weeks."

"Well, Pat, I'm convinced more than ever Ed should not have been convicted," said Lt. Keller.

"Haddie Mae, did you see the white man point, or try to point a big old long gun at Ed when Ed shot him?" asked Pat.

"Yes, Sir. I sure enough did."

"And you would be willing to tell the judge that?"

"Yes, Sir. I sure enough would."

"Lt., I have enough to go ahead with a habeas now but I surely would like to talk to either of Jeffie's ex-wives. They may remember Jeffie saying something that can help

Ed. Something that might point to a crooked DA or judge. Also I would like to talk to Renée especially, about Jeffie's whereabouts and who he might be staying with. He's out there somewhere - - I can feel it, and I won't feel safe until we know where he is."

"And also if he had a hand in Ed's hit-and-run," said Lt. Keller. "I forgot to tell you we found the truck. Stolen and wrecked."

"Wow! You're absolutely right! This situation is very scary, and I'm especially concerned for Shirley's safety. If I only knew for sure that Jeffie were out there *and*, if so, does he intend to go after Shirley and me. Of course, if we knew for sure Jeffie was behind the attacks on Ed, we could assume he is after us, too. But – think about it. Who else would steal a truck to run down Ed?"

"Yes, and the moment Jeffie is tied in with Ed's hit-and-run, if he is at all, we can pull all stops in trying to track him down. I can assure you that our police department will be working hard to do that, if we ever reach that point."

"Ladies, I can't thank you enough. I believe we can clear Ed's name, thanks to the two of you. I know it's late, but could you spare another 30 minutes? What I would like to do is call my secretary to come over and notarize your statements and have Lt. Keller witness them. Would that be okay with you?"

"I guess so, but then we gots to get us some beauty sleep," said Haddie Mae, with a big smile on her face.

"We gotta get up early and catch a bus in de mornin'," said Jenel.

Pat called Julie, who had been told ahead of time he might need her. She was given directions and Pat sat down at the kitchen table and began to write out the statements. Julie got there about 20 minutes later. The ladies and Pat went over their statements, they signed, Lt. Keller witnessed, and Julie acted as the notary. It was almost 10:00 when they left.

Outside, Pat said, "I can't thank both of you enough. I didn't want to take a chance of something happening to those two ladies on their trip without getting a written notarized statement from them. I still want them in court, but I feel better with those statements on paper. I'll be sure DA Colver and Judge Musselman get copies, but I'll hold off filing the habeas until I return from Charleston. I'm still hoping to talk to the ex-wives. I'll give it until, let's see, this is the 19th, to the end of the month. If we can't find them by then, I'll file it anyway."

"You attorneys! Always dotting the I's and crossing the T's, but I guess you have to."

"No, Lt., I'm the one he has doing the dotting and the crossing," corrected Julie with a laugh. "See you in the morning, Boss."

"Right, and I want you to plan on taking off a half day when we're, ha-ha, not too busy, to make up for this time, or I can pay you. It's your call."

She smiled and stuck out her hand, palm up. Pat put a $20 bill in it, and she was thrilled to death.

"Thank you, Boss."

"Where's mine?" said Lt. Keller.

"Are you telling me to bribe a police officer?"

"I'm on my own time now, fellow."

"Well, how about lunch, 12:00 noon, at Jerome and Mickey's?"

"You're on! I presume you mean tomorrow?"

"Right. Call Julie to confirm. She'll make sure I'm there."

CHAPTER 28

Tidwell Case Unravels

"Good morning, Boss. I've got two appointments lined up for this morning, with the first one at 9:30, and two for this afternoon. I know you will be gone all day tomorrow to a bankruptcy seminar, and you have two uncontested divorce cases on Judge Cody's 8:30 Thursday morning calendar, and three criminal pleas in Judge Starwell's courtroom at 10:00. And – don't forget lunch today with the former Lt. Keller and 7:00 supper with your wife-to-be at her parents' house. And - -Nancy Katman called and said no deals on Tidwell. It's ten do five on a plea or go to trial. Her choice. I have a feeling they're out to get her."

"Thanks, Julie, but the way she's been acting, she is out to get herself. I have several phone calls to make first thing today. I can't believe I have all of this work lined up when I'm going out of town Friday, moving in ten days, and getting married in 18 days. Hey! What did you mean by the former Lt. Keller?"

"I was wondering when that comment would dawn on you. You see, we secretaries have our own network. The courthouse, Police Department, Probation Department, and, well you get the idea, Boss. My contact told me that as of 8 o'clock this morning, Lt. Keller was promoted to Capt. Keller by, you guessed it, Chief Keefauver and the city fathers. Also Officer Siniard is now Sgt. Siniard, Lt. Tomble made Capt., and my very own husband is now Lt. Ralph."

"Wow! That couldn't happen to two nicer people! And Siniard deserves something for what Skinny did to him. Tomble has become a good boss, and lastly, Ralph deserves a promotion for putting up with you!"

"What! I'll sic the whole Atlanta PD on you for that!"

"Seriously, they all deserve their promotions."

"I'll add them to my 'need to call list' for this morning and please get me four congratulations cards when you go to lunch."

"They're already on my list."

"I might have known, Julie - - the wonder secretary."

"You got it, Boss, and, speaking of promotions, Lt. Tomble did make Capt., and did recommend my very own husband for promotion to Lieutenant, but he's not one yet. You know, there are tests and all, but he could pass them in his sleep."

"Ralph will make a very fine Lt. on the Atlanta Police force. You married a good man. When he gets the promotion, I would like to take you both out to dinner. Shoot, even if he doesn't get it, I still want to take the two of you out to dinner. And if it is okay, I'd like to bring my new wife along," said Pat with a smile. "Ralph and the former Lt. Tomble seem like a team now."

"Ever since you conned him into throwing that big lunch party!" exclaimed Julie.

The phone rang and Julie answered it. "Forget trying to call anyone. First client, a divorce, is here, and your second client, a personal injury case, should be right on his heels."

"I take it that was Rhonda?"

"Give that man a cigar, or... a Hershey bar," smiled Julie.

"Look, Julie, see if you can arrange for me to take both the Capt. and the Chief out to lunch today. Call Capt. Keller first though, because my lunch date is with him. I'm sure he will not mind, but check with him first anyway. And do it now, because, as soon as the news breaks, both are going to be in big demand for lunches."

"Got you, Boss. I'll give you a few minutes and then bring back your first client."

What a secretary, and to think that she spent time in jail for manslaughter due to a traffic accident that was her fault.

* * *

While Pat was meeting with his clients, Jeffie and Reb were looking for Enchanted Lake Estates Subdivision because Jeffie wanted to get *the lay of the land* at the O'Kelly's house. Jeffie was about to turn into the subdivision when he saw a guardhouse and gate across the road.

"Reb, how did you get in there?"

"Ah, the guard, he was busy on the other side, and this Mercedes that was in front of me put a card in the slot, and when the gate opened up, I just followed him in."

"You dumbass! That was taking a big chance. What if the guard had questioned you and had taken your tag number? And what if it was all connected somehow to the demise of their little Tight-Ass daughter? Huh? Dumbass!"

"Sorry, Jeffie, but you, ah, told me to check out their house."

"Oh, forget it. It worked out okay in the end."

" Jeffie, what's a demise?"

"Death, Dumbass. Death."

Jeffie turned around and headed back to town.

Two gay men were walking along the side of the road and holding hands. Jeffie and Reb agreed it was not only disgusting but super disgusting as one was black and one was white.

"Those two queers will have to pass the road we went by a minute ago. Let's have some fun with them!"

"Yeah, Jeffie. What are we going to do? Huh? What are we going to do, Jeffie?" said Reb in an excited voice.

"You'll see."

They drove back past the gay guys and around a long bend in the road. They turned left on a dirt road and Jeffie pulled in. About 100 feet on the left was a place he could hide his Camaro.

"Quick! Put on the coveralls, and then put one of those stockings over your head. Quick!"

Jeffie took a couple of 2½-foot lengths of heater hose and the shotgun out of the trunk.

"Here they come. Don't talk at all! I'll disguise my voice!"

"Are we going to kill them? Do I get to kill one? Huh, Jeffie?"

"No, but after we get through with them, they're going to wish they were dead."

* * *

Julie was able to set up a lunch date with both Keller and Keefauver for 12:30. Pat arrived at Jerome and Mickey's around 12:15 and Willie the Waiter got Pat a choice window table where he could look for them. Finally, they both came at the same time.

Pat stood and shook hands. "Congratulations, Capt. You too, Chief!" He put emphasis on the Chief and on Capt.

"Sorry we were running late. The first morning on our new jobs, we get two guys severely beaten for no apparent reason," said new Chief Keefauver.

"What happened?"

"The Capt. interviewed them at the hospital, so I'll defer to him."

"Weird! Apparently, two homosexuals were walking down the road and, as near as we can find out, two men were waiting in the bushes and grabbed them as they walked by. The victims said they were both big guys, but one was very big."

"Any witnesses?"

"No, not to the beatings, but the victims were seen holding hands. The traffic was light. Apparently the attackers had on white coveralls, stockings over their heads which covered their faces, and gloves. They made them go back into the woods and pull down their pants. Then they were beaten with rubber hoses on the buttocks and the genitalia area. The doctor said that, given time, they most likely will be able to have sex, but they probably will never be able to father children. Pat, it was a very brutal beating," exclaimed Capt. Keller with disgust on his face.

"And senseless at that!" said Chief Keefauver.

"I hope I don't get those two to defend," said Pat.

Willie the Waiter came to take their order.

"How's the love life, Willie?" asked Pat with a smile.

"W-e-l-l, not too good," said Willie with the heavy lisp. "My boyfriend denies it but I think he's cheating on me!"

"Really! What makes you think that?"

"W-e-l-l, he's a-l-w-a-y-s on that CB radio, and two hussies keep calling and talking to him."

"What's wrong with that?" asked Capt. Keller.

"W-e-l-l, that, that, that, ugh, Gay Blade, even knows where he lives. Now I ask you, how would that hussy know where my boyfriend lives if she hasn't been over to his house? And that, that hussy that calls herself Brown Sugar is so disgusting! Oh, I'm getting upset, and don't even want to talk about it!"

"Did you ever think it might be a big joke, Willie? Some guys on the radio playing a joke on him and you."

"W-e-l-l, I don't happen to think it's funny. In fact, I slapped the hell out of him and tried to hit him where it hurts!"

"Careful, Willie, look who you're talking to. You know, the blue uniforms?"

"Oh, well, ah, okay."

"We didn't hear anything, did we, Capt.?" said the chief.

"No sir, we sure didn't."

"Well, thanks guys. The next time I hear them on the radio, I'm going to take the mike and tell them I'm going to scratch their eyes out!"

"That's the spirit, Willie!" encouraged Pat.

"I feel better already," smiled Willie.

"Why do I have this gut instinct that you know more about this than you're letting on?" said Chief Keefauver.

When Pat told them the story, Capt. Keller started laughing so hard he excused himself to go outside.

"Poor old Willie and especially Pick'em-Up-Man. You should be ashamed of yourself."

"I am, I am." Pat sheepishly grinned. "But you know, Pick'em-Up-Man isn't some innocent victim. He tried to pick me up as the Gay Blade. He was waiting for me behind the bowling alley on two different occasions."

"How do you know he wasn't there to beat the hell out of you?"

"If he were straight, that might be an option, but he's a fag and I know why he was there, and believe me, it was to love and not to fight. The only one I feel for is Willie. He really is a nice guy, and a very good waiter."

Willie came in with the food.

"Oh, thank you, thank you! I couldn't help overhearing the last part of that conversation. I really appreciate your vote of confidence."

"You're welcome, Willie, but I bet you'd rather have me vote with a nice tip, wouldn't you?"

"W-e-l-l, that would be n-i-c-e." Willie just grinned.

"Nothing new on Jeffie and company?" asked Pat.

Chief Keefauver answered. "Afraid not much but I did find an address on Renée. A real fresh address. She moved two weeks ago. No neighbors seem to know where she went. I asked Officer Ethel Felix, because she's a female, to nose around a bit, but Renée moved once again. One of Renée's neighbors thought she was moving to another place in town but they were not close friends, so she doesn't know where. She believes Renée is hiding from bill collectors."

"But ve haf vays of finding her, don't ve, Mein Fuhrer?" asked Capt. Keller.

"Yes, ve do!" said the Chief with a laugh.

* * *

When Pat got back to the office, Julie had Nancy holding for him.

"Hi, Nancy."

"Pat, the DA asked me to call you. Will The Dope

Fairy cop a plea?"

"Afraid not, Nancy, unless it's for probation."

"That's out of the question."

"Then I guess we'll have to go to trial."

"You mean, you will have to go to trial. Look, the DA is going out of town on a ski trip to Colorado in less than two weeks. Yesterday your client filed a motion for a speedy trial."

"What!" exclaimed Pat. "Without even consulting me?"

"I have it here in front of me in my hot little hands. Also seems word has gotten back to Mr. Colver and Judge Musselman that she has been saying – how should I put this – that neither of their parents had been married, and therefore they are illegitimate. You know the word for that."

"This case is going to hell fast!"

"That's not all. DA Colver says that if it's a speedy trial she wants, then it's a speedy trial she will get. Arraignment will be on Thursday at 11:00 AM, which has been specially set, by the way. Of course you know all specially set hearings or trials are number one out and take priority over all other cases or trials."

"Oh, great," responded Pat in a voice completely lacking enthusiasm.

"But that's still not all. I informed DA Colver you were going out of town this weekend and would be moving on the weekend of Jan. 31st, so he has graciously consulted with Judge Musselman and specially set this trial for Wed., Jan 28th. He says that will give you a few days to prepare, and because he expects this trial to be over in a day or two, then you have a day or two to rest before your move and he has the same amount of time to prepare for his ski trip."

"Nancy, this is too much! I go out of town this weekend, move next weekend, and now have a jury trial sandwiched in between. Plus I have two uncontested divorce cases with Judge Cody and three criminal pleas with Judge Starwell. I'm sorry but I can't do it. I'm being beamed up to a space ship!"

"Today has not been a total loss. Look, we have a new President sworn in today. Smile. See you, Pat."

"Bye, Nancy," said Pat with an expressionless voice.

Pat was tired thinking about his schedule, but he knew Nancy wasn't telling stories, and he also knew Ms. Tidwell was getting exactly what she wanted. He also knew if he lost this trial, one Dope Fairy would be going bye-bye for ten years. They were not playing games. It was tempting to do the least he had to do for her, but that was not Pat. He would give the trial all he had.

Julie buzzed him that Shirley was on the phone, so he talked to her.

"You poor Baby," consoled Shirley with conviction. "I just heard what was going on. I really feel for you, but she is at war with the establishment and you are caught in the middle."

"I know, Honey, however I feel like I'm a victim of time. Tonight is supper at your parent's house, tomorrow a bankruptcy seminar, Thursday the Dope Ferry arraignment, Friday we leave for Charleston, a jury trial next Wednesday, we move next Sat, and get married in six weeks! My life is out of control! I also have a habeas to file for Ed, the Chief is hot on Renée's trail, and I can't even find time to help John with Gertrude on a problem I had with the plane."

"Take two aspirins and call me in the morning, because I was about to ask you to go shopping for furniture. You know. The new house?"

"Shir, you really know how to break a guy up." Pat finally was able to laugh about it. "I'm going to use what's left of the day to work on the trial. And — now I have to go back to the jail and let Ms. Tidwell know about the latest developments in her case, and how displeased I am with her filing things without my knowledge. And - - I don't even want to think about furniture. I'll leave that up to you."

"Go get 'em, Tiger. It will all work out. You can practice your opening statements and closing arguments to me on the way to Charleston."

"Bye, Hon. Oh, I need to work until at least 5:00. That should give us plenty of time to get ready and be at your parents' house by 7:00."

"I'll be there at 5:00. I've got some things to work on, too. Several of my cases could end up in trial, so I may have a jury trial of my own soon. One for sure will go to trial."

"What's it about?"

"The Bus Stop case. Remember? I told you about the lookout on an armed robbery, standing at a MARTA bus stop. When the bus came along, he didn't know what to do, so he got on it and rode to downtown Atlanta. Well, as I thought, he has a smart attorney who thinks he can beat the case, but the guy's two buddies, who got caught because of him, are pissed. We will knock a few years off their sentences in exchange for their testimony. They both signed statements saying he was a lookout and did not get on the bus until after the robbery was in progress."

"Let me guess. The attorney is going to argue that his client abandoned the crime before it started and the other two, so-called buddies, are ratting on him to get some time knocked off their sentences. In other words, you bought them. Right?"

"Yes, O' Great Defense Attorney. You hit the nail on the head. He's claiming I'm knocking time off as a reward -- that I started high and then took off several years for their testimony."

"Well, didn't you?"

"Of course, but he's making it sound like we're setting up an innocent man, which we're not doing. I never would be a part of something like that."

"I'm sure if you found out he really did abandon the case, you would move to dismiss it."

"In a heart beat."

"You're my kind of prosecutor. How about marrying me in about six weeks?"

"I already said yes, Silly."

"Say it again. I love you and can't believe you're about to become my wife. How lucky can a guy get?"

"Yes! Yes! Yes! I will marry you. I love you, too, and you really know how to make a girl feel good!"

"I'll see you at 5:00. And – Shir - thank you for calling and getting me out of that flustered mood."

"Buy. I love you."

* * *

They both forgot about Jeffie, which was a big mistake.

* * *

Pat told Julie what was going on. "I won't be able to accept any new cases, not until the trial is over. If they can't wait, refer them to Herb. I'm on the way to see Tidwell." Pat grabbed his briefcase and her file and headed for the jail.

On the way, Pat saw a blind man helping a legless man by pushing him down the sidewalk in a wheelchair. The legless man was giving him instructions about where to turn. He also would also tell him when he was about to go off the sidewalk.

And here I was feeling sorry for myself! Why, I have it all!

He went in to see Tidwell and told her what had transpired. He also told her he did not appreciate her filing that motion without even talking to him. She got smart with him, but Pat refused to get upset, and told her he would see her Thursday in Judge Musselman's courtroom for arraignment. He had a feeling her same attitude would come across to the jury at trial and she would cook her own goose. She was the opposite of Sammy Joe Washington. He would do his best, even if he did not like her.

Back at the office, Julie said Louie Lake was on the phone and urgently needed to talk to him.

"Hi, Louie."

"I'm glad I got you because it sure is hard to get to use the phone here."

"Where's here, Louie?"

"Fulton County Jail. It will be all over the news tonight. Watch Channel 3, or listen to the WHIT radio news. All the newspapers also will have a story in tonight's paper."

"You lost me, Louie. What's going on?"

"You've read about the series of warehouse burglaries over the last several months, right?"

"Sure, everyone has, the press calls the burglars the Warehouse Weasels."

"Well, they think I'm part of the gang doing those burglaries, that I'm one of the Weasels."

"If you are, sure don't say anything over the phone."

"I ain't that dumb, Mr. Patton, but it doesn't matter. Anyway, me and two other guys were in this warehouse last night. We were on the loading dock getting ready to put the safe in a truck when one of the guys goes out and starts backing our 2 ½-ton rental truck into the loading dock. He came in too fast, nervous energy I guess, and hit the overhead door before I could get it completely open. As luck would have it, a police car was going by and the cops heard the truck crash into the door. They blocked the driveway with their patrol car and the truck driver got out and ran into the building with us."

"You're saying too much over the phone. This conversation could very well be recorded."

"It don't matter, Mr. Patton, as you shall see in a moment. As I was saying, there we were, trapped in that warehouse. I was in back looking for a way out when I overheard two cops talking outside the window. One told the other, the *word* has been passed that the only way these burglaries will be stopped is by killing the guys doing them. They planned on shooting us by making it look like we were trying to escape or trying to kill them!"

"What did you do? How did you get out alive?"

"I found an office telephone and phone book. While one of the guys was looking up numbers, I was calling Channel 3 news, WHIT radio, the Clayton newspaper, and the Atlanta Journal. Also any more we could find. I told all of them the same thing - - where we were, what we were doing, and to get over there quick, preferably with news trucks with lots of lights and cameras, or we were dead men. Well, they all came, and since they saved our lives, we gave them a story. These cops were pissed and were planning on killing us."

"And what do you want me to do?" asked Pat.

"I want you to work out the best deal you can for me, that's all. No trial, just a good deal."

Pat told him about the booked-up next week to ten days, but Louie said okay since he wasn't going anywhere and would not be able to make bond - - it was sure to be extremely high. Pat agreed to see Louie as soon as he could the first week of February, and told him to have as much information with him about his case as possible.

The Drug Fairy case and his two afternoon appointments took up the rest of the day. At 5:00, Shirley came in. Pat gave her a tight hug and a long kiss.

On the way home, he told her about Louie, and they also turned on the CB to see if Pick'em-Up-Man was on, but had no luck.

Before leaving home, Shirley talked Pat into taking his sweat suit, tennis shoes, and tennis racket along, because they might get a game in before supper. They could shower and change clothes later. The evening was cool but not freezing cold.

When she called to say they were on their way, her father said he would be glad to turn on the court lights for them to play.

CHAPTER 29

Renée

Pat grabbed the newspaper from the driveway and tossed it to Shirley. He drove while she searched for the Louie Lake story. She went through the paper only to realize it was on the front page. Vivienne Cove's byline told the story Louie told to Pat. Of course the police denied any thoughts of violence against Louie or his friends.

They pulled into the entrance of Enchanted Lakes Estates and stopped at the guardhouse. The guard told them that Greg had given a blanket clearance for Pat, as he had previously given for Shirley, and waved them in. Shirley knew all the guards, and Pat knew most of them by now.

The O'Kelly's large brick house was at the end of North Lake Drive on a cul-de-sac. Pat pulled in and parked the Mustang in back at the downstairs basement garage. Greg already had the tennis court lights turned on. They got out and Shirley used her key to let herself in the back door and went upstairs.

Mr. and Mrs. O'Kelly greeted them warmly. Greg shook Pat's hand and Grace gave him a hug. He hoped Shirley would look like her mother when she got older because her mother was a striking woman. You would never guess she had a 30-year-old daughter. Also, Dr. Greg did not look 55 years old except for a balding high forehead. He kept very active as a specialist in plastic surgery, and physical workouts three times per week at the gym with his doctor friends kept his frame a trim 190 pounds. Both Greg and Grace swam often in their pool when the weather permitted and played tennis on a regular basis.

Greg had a handsome round face, which always contained a smile. He was a hunter and a pilot who owned a Cessna 172 airplane. His classic car collection consisted of a 1939 Ford coupe, a 1957 Studebaker Golden Hawk, a 1957 Thunderbird, and a 1931 Ford Model A roadster with a rumble seat.

Grace was an older Shirley, at 5'3", 120 pounds, green eyes, a good figure, blonde hair with a little gray mixed in made people question her being 52. She was a registered nurse, and both she and Greg were active in the Solid Rock Christian Church. Grace often filled in for Robin West, the church administrator.

Pat could never get over the size of the house. He could put two of his new houses in it, and it had a full basement to boot. A pool and pool house was in back, a two-car garage in the basement, and a six-car garage in back for his classic cars, with an attached drive-through shelter for his motorhome. Also in the basement was a dream workshop with every tool known to man. Then there was the tennis court and the lake with a dock and boathouse.

They had all this, but were very down-to-earth people. When Pat first met Shirley, he told her, "Had I known you were from a well-to-do family, I never would have asked you out." She told him she was tired of the rich guys who pestered her, because most of them were self-centered and false. Pat was what she had been looking for all her life. She could not conceive of life without him.

They changed into sweat-suits in time for the Six O'clock News with Zel on Channel 3. She told much the same story that Louie had told Pat with clips of the warehouse as the police were leading them away. Sandi went on the air with her report of the arrest, also telling her listening audience that Louie Lake had called her by name on the phone, and said she should get to the warehouse before the police killed him and his friends.

Louie really did it this time. The telephone company would be very happy to see him put away.

"Shir, I found out how reporter Futo is getting inside information."

"How?"

"He was seen coming out of a motel with Gloria."

Pat's shoulder still bothered him a little from the buckshot wound, but it was his left shoulder, and he used his right arm to play tennis. Pat and Shirley went down to the tennis court to play while Grace worked on supper. Shirley would help as soon as it was ready. Greg put on his coat and hat and went to watch the game.

Shirley had a challenge playing tennis with Pat. She had to look like she was really losing. Pat was a better-than-average athlete and could play all sports and do most things better than average. However, he was never the star on any team. Shirley, on the other hand, was very good at tennis and was the captain of her college tennis team. She was smart enough to know the guys did not like to be beaten by women, so she did not play up to her potential against him. Pat could sense it, but said nothing, although he knew in his heart she could whip his tail if she really wanted to. As it was, he won two out of three, and they both got some good exercise.

"Race you to the house," yelled Greg when he was halfway there.

They took off running and came close to catching him by the time they got to the house, with all of them laughing.

"All of you might be interested in this. I got a court-appointed case today that I had to turn down," announced, Pat.

"You know our mild-mannered church administrator, Robin West? Well, she was leaving the church last night when a man accosted her. He demanded money, but she could sense he was after more than money. Only three weeks ago she had completed a self-defense course and learned that the average woman is physically no match for the average man; however, surprise can be an equalizer, but only if she had reason to believe she was in danger of serious physical injury or death."

"What happened?" asked Shirley.

"She played like she was terrified, which wasn't hard, because she was scared. The man got in close and she brought her knee up hard and hit him between his legs where it really hurts. When he doubled over, she grabbed him by the hair, pulled his head down and brought up her knee in his face as hard as she could. He went down hard and had a broken nose with blood all over the place. Two big men had come out of the church as it was happening. They watched over the guy while she called the cops."

"I had to turn down the case as I am a member of the church and a friend of hers."

"Wow. One never knows," said Grace.

"I know DA Colver will take a dim view of this guy," explained Shirley.

"Shirley, please go on up to the house and help your mother. I have something to show Pat in the classic car garage."

"Okay, Daddy, but don't be too long."

"I won't."

Greg punched a security code into an alarm keypad, unlocked the door, stepped inside, and then hit the light switch. Pat liked the way Greg had this place set up. The main light switch turned on single florescent lights in all six bays, giving off plenty of light to move around. Then each bay had a separate light switch which turned on three double-tube florescent lights, one in front, one in the middle, and another in the rear of the bay. Greg took him to the end bay on the left.

"It is my latest acquisition, Pat. What I think will be the most collected car, American that is, of the future." Greg turned on the bay lights and pointed to a beautiful 1957 Chevrolet convertible, red with a white top.

"Greg, it's beautiful!"

"A rare fuelie. That's fuel injection in case you didn't know. The top horsepower in 1957 came from a duel four-barrel carb set-up, which was rated at 270 HP, until Chevy released the fuelie. This baby has all of that and more. It's rated at 283 HP."

"Mind if I sit in the driver seat?" asked Pat, as he opened the door.

"Not at all, and that's part of the reason I brought you out here. As you know, I have some very nice cars, although none are show quality. I believe these cars are made to be driven, as well as for people to look at. So, I keep full coverage insurance on all of them at their appraised value and I drive them. One problem though, I don't get to drive them as much as they need to be driven, and, until now, I didn't know anyone who I trusted enough to take them out for a spin now and then. Would you be willing to drive one for a day or two every once in a while, just to keep the batteries charged, and the oil flowing so the seals don't dry out?"

Pat was sitting in the driver seat of the Chevy and was flabbergasted by the offer.

"Would I? Does a bear – – –, ah, I would love to. Wow! I'm so pleased you have that much trust in me. I surely am."

"I do, Pat, and I also know what a bear does in the woods." They both laughed.

"I had these keys made for you." Greg handed Pat two keys. "This bigger one fits the main door, and the smaller one fits the key safe, which I'm about to show you. I also had this wallet card printed up and signed by me, giving you express permission to drive all of these cars, which are listed on the back of the card, with the tag number and manufacturers' ID numbers. You will find my cars with the tanks full of gas to prevent condensation buildup. Please return them with a full tank of gas."

"I surely will, Greg, and I know that all of your cars, with the exception of the Model A, have high-performance engines in them, so I will use premium gas."

"If you drive to a shopping center, please park somewhere out-of-the-way where there is less likelihood of someone slamming a car door into the side of the car, or ramming it with a shopping cart."

"Will do. I can't believe this!"

"I have watched how you treat your cars and motorcycles, and you take very good care of them. Now, come with me, as we're running out of time. It's almost time to eat."

A buzzer sounded from an intercom box by the main door, followed by Shirley's voice.

"Daddy, Pat, it's time to eat. Come and get it."

Greg pressed a button and said, "Coming right up, Honey."

He took Pat to the back of the bay that the main entrance door was in and pulled on a perforated board holding some tools, while pushing down on an empty tool clip. A panel opened up exposing a safe. The other key that Pat held fit it. "Open it up, Pat." In it were two sets of keys, neatly labeled, for each car. Pat closed and locked the door, then practiced opening the panel.

"Here on this hanger is a clipboard with the sheet for each of these cars. On each line is a place for the date, start and stop mileage, two lines for notes, such as problems observed, and a place for either your or my initials. Of course, Grace and Shirley are also welcome to drive them, but their interest is low. Grace and Shirley have been known to drive the T-Bird, but only occasionally. And lastly, the keypad code to both unlock and lock the security system is 1957 followed by an asterisk. A garage door opener is in each car's glove compartment. When you drive in or out, you have 120 seconds, which starts when the door begins to open, to punch the security code into the keypad. If you don't, all hell will break loose. Lights, bells, sirens and a recorded call to the police will take place, so don't forget the code or to punch it in. That's why I park the T-Bird in the same bay as the main door, so Grace and Shirley don't have to rush."

"Thank you, Greg. I especially want to drive your 1939 Ford Coupe. As you already know, I had one that I put a Cadillac engine in right out of high school."

"Take it tonight, as it needs to be driven. By the way, Shirley loves to ride in all of these cars. Take one any time and you don't have to ask me first. I'll see your car parked in its place, or outside of the garage, and know that you

187

took one. Just fill out the log, so I'll know which cars need to be driven. I don't care if you put 10 miles, or 1000, on the car. I just need to know how much it is driven so I can keep it up."

As Pat was closing the door and resetting the alarm system, the buzzer went off and when Grace's voice came over the intercom, they both scooted toward the house.

"Well, it's about time you two got up here," chastised Shirley.

"Do I have time to change clothes?" asked Pat sheepishly.

"No way, Buster. Go wash up and get right back here before I box your ears."

"Yes, Ma'am!" Pat saluted and took off for a conveniently located half-bath.

Only gone a few minutes, he was surprised to see a steak, baked potato, ear of corn and spinach on each plate and everyone seated. Greg said the blessing, and they started eating.

Pat excitedly told Shirley about being able to drive her father's cars.

"You boys and your toys," laughed Grace. "I don't think either one of you will grow up! At least I hope not."

"You're right, Mama. I like the little boy in them, too, even if they were late for supper."

When finished with the delicious meal, Pat called the hospital to check on Ed. The report was good, but visitors who were not immediate family members were not allowed for the next few days. He asked if there was an exception for a patient's attorney, and the answer was yes. Pat could see him anytime.

"Sorry you kids won't be able to go to church with us this Sunday, because Grace and I really look forward to it, and having lunch afterward, don't we, Grace?"

"He's right, we will miss the two of you, but I know it's important to visit with your parents, Pat, before the wedding. We're looking forward to having them over here when they come in. Shirley, your brother insisted on getting the plane tickets and hotel reservations for your trip to Hawaii, as a wedding present. You need to firm up the date at least two weeks in advance and they are good for a year," said Grace.

"This is a dream come true! I'm going to Hawaii on my honeymoon with the most wonderful girl in the world. That is except for you, Mrs. O'Kelly," said Pat with a wink at Grace.

"Oh, Shirley, you do have a charmer."

"And, Momma, I've got the most wonderful man in the world. Except for you, Daddy," said Shirley with a big wink at her father.

They all had a laugh at that and all winked at each other. Finally it was time to go.

I always hate to leave the O'Kelly's. What a great mother-in-law Grace will make, and Greg is already like a second father. I'll have to make time to go flying with him.

Arrangements were made for Pat to drive Shirley's Oldsmobile in the morning because he was going to pick up the 1939 Ford on his way to the bankruptcy seminar, and Shirley wanted to drive the Mustang for a change.

"Mama, your cleaning lady does a great job. Is she the same one you have had for the last few years?" asked Shirley.

"Yes. You met her. She has worked for us going on four years. She is a very good worker, and honest. Although from what I gather, she cannot handle her finances. I understand she was forced to move again. Renée works for me Monday, Wednesday, and Friday, but she has another job working Tuesday and Thursday, so she works fulltime, but still can't seem to pay her bills. From the way she talks, I think she has a bunch of credit cards."

"And that is in spite of us helping her financially a few years ago. You would think Mrs. Anderson would have learned by now," said Greg.

"Did I understand you to say Renée and Anderson? Renée Anderson?" asked Pat.

"It can't be, Honey. How could it be?" asked Shirley.

"I don't know what's going on, but, yes, her name is Renée Anderson." Grace answered with a questioning look.

"This wouldn't have anything to do with Skinny Anderson, would it?" asked Greg with a look of incredibility.

"I don't know, Greg, but the names the same."

"She wouldn't be here to spy on us, would she?" asked Grace fearfully.

"I wouldn't think so, because we hired her years before any of this came up," commented Greg.

"To think I've known her for years, but just as Renée, and never made the connection," said Shirley.

"We need to talk to her. What hours does she work tomorrow?" asked Pat.

"Normally, from around 10 to four o'clock," said Grace.

"Can you keep her here another hour? I can cut out of the seminar a little early and be here before five."

"I guess so."

"I'll be here too, Momma."

"Okay, I know it's time to go, but I want Shirley to play my favorite piece on the piano for me," said Grace. "Just one song?"

"Okay, Momma, but then we need to go." Shirley walked over to the Baldwin grand piano.

She had over 10 years of piano lessons and was an accomplished piano player. Shirley sat down and played Tchaikovsky's First Piano Concerto almost perfectly. It gave Pat goose-bumps when he heard his wife-to-be play so well. She was light years ahead of him at piano playing.

* * *

At home, it was time to take a shower and go to bed. Pat was still in his sweat-suit.

"Since you're so filthy dirty, you can have a shower first." Shirley laughed as she gave him a shove toward the bathroom.

"To show you that I'm not a greedy person, I'm willing to share it with you," said Pat with a gleam in his eye.

"Well, why didn't you say so in the first place," said Shirley as she started to strip.

Pat could not help looking as she took off her clothes. Her body was a sight to behold! He watched her, and she watched him, as he had a very nice body, too! And while they were both undressed, Shirley walked over to Pat and rubbed her tail over his manhood.

"Well, look what I did!" announced Shirley with fake surprise. "It's rising to the occasion!"

They did more than take a shower.

CHAPTER 30

A Present from Jeffie

The next morning Pat and Shirley got up early for a jog together, and then he lifted weights while she made breakfast. Pat glanced through the newspaper while he was eating.

"Shir, look at this! On the front page of the Atlanta Journal - - a picture of Robin and a featured story of her knock-out of a 220 lb. male attacker."

"Let me see!" Shirley grabbed the newspaper. "Gosh! This man is a serial rapist and takes pleasure out of severely beating his victims. The police have been after him for almost two years. Robin stated: 'I said a quick silent prayer asking Jesus for help as soon as I realized this guy was serious trouble.'"

"Shir, look at the sidebar. Women's groups are asking her to speak to them and several associations are giving her awards for bravery. She has also been asked to lead women's self-defense classes. That's our Robin. Got to go. Love you!"

He got in Shirley's Olds to pick up the 1939 Ford coupe. She took Pat's Mustang and went to the DA's office.

When he arrived at the O'Kelly's, no one was home, so he went to the classic car garage. Pat parked the Olds, opened the entrance door, and quickly went to the keypad, punched in 1957 followed with an asterisk. The little red light on the keypad went off and a little green light came on. Greg had installed motion detectors in the rear of each bay, as well as sensors on the doors and windows. He also had a battery backup in case someone cut the power, but that would be difficult because the lines were run underground. He took his other key and after opening the panel, opened the lockbox and found the keys to the 1939 Ford. Pat closed the key door and panel, and made his way to the coupe.

Pat was like a little kid when he got into the car. He took out the garage door opener from the glove box and pushed the button. As the door opened up, he pumped the accelerator pedal one time to set the choke, and then hit the starter.

The 350 Chevy engine sounded awesome! Pat pushed in the clutch pedal, eased it out, added a little gas, and drove out of the garage. He let it idle while he backed the Olds into the space that the coupe previously occupied. On the way out, he closed the garage door by pushing a button beside it, and set the alarm again as he went out. This was going to be a ball.

He caught weekday commuting traffic but made his way the expressway. About 45 minutes later, he arrived at the Skyland Hotel for the bankruptcy seminar. Pat was lucky there was not the usual morning wreck to hold up the traffic. The coupe drove flawlessly, and Pat got a few thumbs-up from some of the other drivers.

* * *

The seminar was very good and he took a lot of notes. When they had a break at 3:00, he left and only missed the question-and-answer session. He called Shirley on his way out and was told to go ahead and talk to Renée when he got there and she would see him later. She had to do some shopping, which had been put off for several days.

Pat called Grace and confirmed that Renée was there. He cranked up the coupe and took off, doing his best to suppress the urge to mash down on the accelerator pedal. This car might be a good match for his Mustang in a

193

drag race. It may not have quite as much horsepower, but it did not weigh as much either.

Traffic was backed up some, so it took him about an hour to get back to the O'Kelly's, not including a gas stop.

He went through the reverse routine to exchange the Olds for the Ford coupe, filling out Greg's log, locking up, and setting the alarm. Then he went up to the house to confront Renée.

* * *

While Pat was at the O'Kelly's, Shirley went to the Jamestown shopping center. She parked Pat's Mustang near the end of the parking lot as was Pats habit to avoid dings in his doors. Several minutes after Shirley went into the store, Confederate Motorcycle Club members, Snake and Yanker, were making a routine ride through the parking lot looking for Pat's Mustang.

"Damn, Yanker, I can't believe it! There sits Piss-Ant's car."

"Hell, Snake, you're right. Park several rows back of it, and watch the damn thing while I call Jeffie on that payphone across the street."

Snake pulled his Harley into a parking space about 20 spaces closer to the store than the Mustang.

"Phone for you, Jeffie," announced Reb.

"What! . . . Good going! I won't forget this. We'll be there in a few minutes! I'm going to give them a present they'll never forget!"

After being told where to find Pat's car, he almost swallowed his toothpick.

"What's going on, Jeffie?"

"Get the coveralls quick, Reb, and the hats, shades and wigs. The boys spotted Piss-Ant Patton's car at the Jamestown shopping center. Get the hidden box with the dynamite and wire now, Dumbass!"

Reb drove the pickup, with mud covering the tailgate and license plate. They both put on coveralls saying John's Auto Repairs. They had an old Brotherhood friend make the jumpsuits for this occasion.

Jeffie grabbed the stick of dynamite that was taped to a small soft-drink bottle filled with gasoline and corked. Paper was wrapped around the dynamite and the bottle to hide what it was and secured by tape. He laid it on his lap along with the wires, and they put on long wigs, hats, and large dark sunglasses.

They found the Mustang. It took Jeffie only a few minutes to get into it and rig the bomb. They pulled over several rows and waited. No one seemed to pay one bit of attention to them.

"Damn, Reb, there's gonna be a hot time in the old town tonight!"

"And, ah, I get to watch him get blown up, don't I, Jeffie?"

CHAPTER 31

The Explosion

Right after Pat got to the O'Kelly's house, Greg came home, as he wanted to hear what was said between Pat and Renée. Mrs. O'Kelly asked Renée to come into the den where Pat and Greg were waiting. She introduced Pat, and Renée just looked at them and started crying.

"I knew you would find out! I knew it, I knew it! And now you're here to fire me!" said Renée sobbing.

"We're going to do nothing of the sort," consoled Grace, as she went over to comfort Renée.

"You're not? Then why are you bringing me in here with all of you? I recognize Mr. Patton from the newspapers." She was sobbing a little less now.

"I can assure you we are quite happy with your work, and you will continue to be employed by Grace and me," stated Greg.

"Oh, thank you! Thank you! I was so worried I would lose my job because I used to be married to Jeffie and was Skinny's sister-in-law." Renée started sobbing once again.

"You're right. I'm Pat Patton, but all I want is to ask you some questions about Jeffie, and see if you know anything about the shooting back in 1955. Also, the police believe Jeffie was sexually and physically abusing your daughter, Cindy, as well as you."

Renée took a few minutes to calm down, and then blew her nose. She was in her late 30's by his calculations. Her hair was cut unevenly short. She had large, tired eyes, and unattractive skin. Renée had led a hard life and her body showed it.

"Mr. Patton, I'll talk with you, but first I just got to go out and smoke a cigarette. I'm so nervous I just gotta have one!" said Renée with a pleading look at Greg and Grace.

"Of course, Renée," said Grace.

Renée hurriedly went outside to smoke her cigarette as the O'Kelly's did not allow smoking in their house.

"That must have been on her mind for some time," said Pat.

"I guess so," said Greg, "because you can see how pitiful she is. Her work is good, she doesn't steal, and she needs the job. We wouldn't have the heart to let her go."

"Renée is a real help to me with this big house, and in a way, she has become a friend. By-the-way, how long has it been since she had a raise, Greg?"

"I really don't know. Too long would be my guess, but I'll let you take care of that. Say, Pat, what is the minimum wage now?"

"Sir, I think it's $3.10 per hour. I know the average hourly figure for a production worker is $6.56 per hour, because I looked it up when trying to figure out what to pay my secretary."

"Here it is," said Grace while looking in her checkbook. "We are paying her $4.50 per hour."

"Why don't we raise it to $5.00 per hour?"

"Done," replied Grace.

About that time Renée came back in and when told she was being given a raise, started to cry all over again. But, this time, with tears of joy.

"I can't believe this! Domestic help usually gets a 10, or 20 cent per hour raise, but you gave me 50 cents! Thank you, Dr. Greg and Ms. Grace!"

Pat changed the subject. "Renée, what was it like living with Jeffie?"

Renée thought for a minute. "About like living with Adolph Hitler, or the devil himself, I guess. He is a very bad man. He beat me and my Cindy a lot, usually when he was drinking. He even forced me to do sexual things with his friends from the Confederate Motorcycle Club."

At that Renée started to sob again.

"How about your daughter. What did he do to her?"

"When she was about 14, he forced her to have sex with him. She told me about it later and wanted me to get him to stop. Cindy said he took her little puppy and hung it right in front of her and made her watch while it wiggled and struggled and then got still. Then – then he told her he would kill both of us, just like he did her puppy, if she didn't have sex with him and keep her mouth shut about it." Renée stared into space with a defeated blank look.

"I'm sorry to ask you all of these questions, Renée, but, as you know, Skinny tried to kill me and Shirley. We killed him in self-defense. Now, I have reason to believe Jeffie may be out there somewhere waiting to kill us."

"It's okay, Mr. Patton."

"To make matters worse, sometime later, about 1955, a black man by the name of Ed Edwards, killed Jeffie's brother, Jeb, when he was shooting up the black man's trailer. Ed recently came to me for help and then became a victim of a hit-and-run. The doctors believe he will live but he was seriously injured. I'm concerned for the safety of my fiancée, Shirley, as well as myself. I don't know if Jeffie is alive or what he might do. We don't even know what he looks like. Do you have a picture?"

"I hear you, Mr. Patton. If he's out there, he's mean enough to do a hit-and-run and a heap more. The man is an animal. Oh, my poor baby, Cindy. She won't forgive me for not stopping him! But I was afraid if I stood up to him, he'd kill the two of us. He also told me if I ever did anything to put him away for anything, the world wasn't big enough to hide in. I could kiss my butt goodbye! The Brotherhood or the Confederate Motorcycle Club would find me and kill Cindy, too. I was scared to tell!"

"Cindy left home how long ago?"

"She was 16 when she ran away. My baby never came back, Mr. Patton. Never came back. Cindy was a very, very, angry girl, at Jeffie, me, and at the world in general."

"Did she ever mention where she was going, or do you know where she lives?"

"I don't even know if she's still alive. If only she would contact me!" replied an obviously grief-stricken Renée.

The phone rang.

"I'll get it," said Greg. "Hi, Chief. What's up?"

As he listened, Greg turned ashen white.

"Oh, no! Where? How is she? At Clayton General? We'll be right there! Pat's here."

"Grace, Pat! Shirley's been in an accident and is at Clayton General Hospital. Let's go! That was Chief Keefauver and all he can tell us is that she is alive!"

"My God! She just has to be alright!" Pat tried to fight the despair in his voice. "Come on, I have Shirley's Olds parked out back!"

They grabbed their coats, thanked Renée and hurried out of the house as Greg yelled, "Lock up when you leave, Renée."

Pat drove as fast as he safely could and was at the hospital in less than 15 minutes. They went in and Greg, as an M. D., took charge of their group. Even then 20 minutes passed before he found out what happened. After talking to a doctor, Greg came back to the waiting room with tears in his eyes. He looked from Grace to Pat.

"From what I can find out, she was at the Jamestown Shopping Center. When she came out of the store and started up the car, it – it blew up!"

"This can't be! Not our Shirley! How is she?" asked Grace and Pat almost simultaneously.

"She will live and be pretty much okay, but the doctors are mostly worried about her facial burns and her eyes. My little girl is blind!" sobbed Greg.

"Oh, no!" cried Grace and Pat again and again.

All three held each other, their grief pouring out tears. After a few minutes, they tried to compose themselves and were able to talk again.

"It's my fault! If only I hadn't got involved with Skinny, and now Jeffie!" blurted out Pat.

"But Pat, how could you have known?" said Grace, as she put her arms around him.

Capt. Keller walked in with a somber expression on his face.

"I can't tell you how sorry I am. How is she?"

"Shirley will live, Capt., but my little girl is blind!" said Grace, crying again.

Greg held Grace and Pat put his arms around both of them and said nothing. What could he say? He wanted to comfort these two good friends and parents of his future wife. They in turn comforted him.

"What can you tell us, Capt.?" asked Pat.

"I was at the scene and talked to Detective Sgt. Ricky Siniard, who is in charge of the investigation, the fire chief, and even an expert from the bomb squad. They all believe it was some type of homemade bomb but have to run several tests to be sure. One thing was strange. There was an abnormal fire in the engine compartment, almost like a small gas tank exploded. They think something placed in the engine compartment burnt Shirley's eyes and face. It was a cool day and she was wearing a coat, gloves, and a hat when they found her. Sgt. Siniard thinks she was wearing her sunglasses, but they were laying beside her and were cracked. Apparently she put her hands in front of her face at the time of the explosion. Somehow most of the glass from the windshield missed her and her hands protected most of her face. But Shirley's eyes and face still got burned from the intense heat of the explosion. Two men got her out of the car and a woman ran into the store and 911 was called."

Greg interrupted. "Excuse me Capt., but in my grief I failed to mention something. One of the nurses, Bernice Ahrens, who works at Clayton General, happened to be coming out of the store with two bags of ice and saw the explosion. She was one of the first on the scene and immediately applied ice to Shirley's face and eyes. Then she sent a bystander into the store to get a bottle of saline solution and began irrigating Shirley's eyes. A store employee, Pat Farmer, donated a towel and the nurse kept ice in the towel, which was placed over Shirley's face. She has a few glass cuts, but not too bad. The doctor from the burn unit thinks the nurse saved her face from scarring and may have helped prevent more serious eye damage."

"Greg, will she regain her sight?" asked a shaken Pat. "You're a plastic surgeon.

"They don't know yet, but if the eye damage is limited to a burn of the cornea, a transplant is possible. The cornea is the outer clear part of the eye. Corneal transplants are highly successful because the cornea normally does not have blood vessels in it. This means the rejection rate is low and a blood type match is unnecessary. It is not a complicated operation, but if it is done, I want the best doctor we can get.

"As a plastic surgeon, I took a careful look at her face, while she was still unconscious and before it was bandaged, and don't believe a skin graft will be necessary."

"She sure was lucky Nurse Ahrens was there," sympathized Capt. Keller.

"I don't think so, Capt.," contradicted Greg. "I believe it was much more than luck. I believe He was watching out for her."

"I do, too," agreed Pat.

"Maybe you guys have a point," replied the Capt. "In fact, I'm sure you do."

"When will we be able to see her, Greg?" asked Pat.

"As a doctor, I'm sure I can get to see her very shortly, but visitors? Who knows? Perhaps tomorrow, or Friday."

"I need to call Julie and cancel my appointments for - - Oh! I forgot! Court tomorrow morning. Two different judges and the Tidwell arraignment, too. I also have to call Mom and Dad."

"Excuse me, Honey, Pat, Capt. Let me see what I can find out now."

Greg was gone about 20 minutes while Capt. Keller made a phone call.

"Shirley will not be able to have visitors and then only immediate family until tomorrow evening at the very earliest. Pat, I told them you two were to be married next month and got them to make an exception. She is going to make it okay but needs rest. Shirley has a mild concussion from the explosion."

"Speaking of explosions," said Capt. Keller, "if that was a bomb, somebody screwed up. Although the Mustang is a total loss, the bomb squad boys from Atlanta told me, over the phone, that this was the mildest car bomb they ever saw. They said it was the equivalent of less than a stick of dynamite. More like a half of a stick, plus whatever caused the fire. Most likely gasoline, but they're not sure yet."

"He was with her," said Grace.

"Amen," said Greg, Pat, and the Capt.

"Look, Pat, stay around for a while tonight if you like, but go on to court tomorrow and get those cases finished. Believe me, there is nothing you can do here. I know. I'm a doctor. Also try to get some sleep tonight. When you're allowed to see her tomorrow night, you'll not be worn out."

"You're probably right, but I feel so helpless. That should have been me in there you know. It was meant for me!"

"I'll concede that but think, man, think! Was there anything, anything at all you could have done about it? Absolutely not. So, get that out of your head. There is someone you can see, though. I checked and Mr. Edwards can see you. Room 404. By the way, when you talk with your parents, tell them they are welcome to come and stay with us."

"Thanks, Greg. You're right as usual except for one thing."

"What's that?"

"You said we were to be married next month. Greg, I don't know how, but we will be married next month!" said Pat very firmly.

"Darned if I don't think you will!"

"I'll go see Ed now, but I'll be back within an hour."

"Pat, be very careful. I don't have to tell you that Ed's accident and now Shirley's are too much of a coincidence. Skinny's brother, or an unknown friend, probably is behind this," said Capt. Keller.

"One good thing has come out of it. You will now be able to list him as an official suspect and then maybe twist some arms at the airlines and the Army."

"You're right! I'll get the new Lt. on it right away. Pat, we need a picture of this guy, although we need to remember he is what? About 35 to 40 years old now?"

"More like 40, Capt. I'll be very careful. I need to call Mom and Dad, see Ed for a few minutes, and then I'll be back to take us to get a bite to eat. Mom and Dad will just have to come here if they want to see us. I can't get there this weekend, that's for sure. I know they will come as soon as they learn about Shirley."

Pat led them in prayer, and left.

"Quite a guy, huh Greg?" commented Capt. Keller.

"I'll be proud to have him as a son-in-law."

* * *

Jeffie, Reb, Snake, and Yanker were at the Silver Slipper, having a beer at a back table.

"So, you did it! Good going!" said Snake.

"We did it okay. Not only did we get the wrong person, but from what I heard on the news, we didn't even kill Little Miss Tight-Ass!" Jeffie blew out some cigar smoke. "J. Q. warned me the stick had been wet and might be weak."

"But we blew up Piss-Ant's car, Jeffie." Reb was overjoyed.

"Look, Dumbass. At this very minute Piss-Ant Patton should be dead – dead – dead!" yelled a very angry Jeffie. "But where is he? Out running around caring for his girlfriend and that damn jungle bunny. I tell you, he should be dead! Some explosion! Hell, it should have blown that car into so many pieces some of it should have been found in California. Once Piss-Ant and the cops catch their breath, what do you think is going to happen, huh, Dumbass? They're going to put two and two together and come looking for us, that's what!"

"I, ah, never thought of that, Jeffie."

"That's the trouble with you. You don't think!"

"I'm sorry, Jeffie."

"Boys, Reb and I are going to put our bikes in the back of his truck and go on a Florida vacation for a few weeks. When everything has blown over, we'll come back and kill Piss-Ant, Tight-Ass, and that damn coon!"

"Whatever you say, Jeffie," agreed Reb.

CHAPTER 32

The Hospital

"Ed - - - Ed, it's me, Pat Patton."

"Hi, ah, Mr. Patton," said Ed with a half-smile and a weak voice. "They took ma leg off from de knee down. All I's gots left is a stub from ma knee up. Dey gots a lung, and a kidney, too."

"I'm sorry, Ed."

"It was no - - no accident, Mr. Patton. Dat truck was, ah, parked, den when I crossed de street, it came after me. Almost – almost like it was alive! I was drinkin', but not drunk. I'm, I'm, very tired."

"Okay, Ed. I'll let you go for now but will come back later."

"Thank you, Mr. Patton. How's Miss Shirley and Miss Julie?"

"They're fine. Now you get some rest." Pat did not want to tell him about Shirley yet.

"Dat's good. Thanks fer comin' to see me. Dey tell me I'm gonna be here another week," Ed seemed to regain some of his strength.

"I'll be sure to come back again. Is there anything I can get for you?"

"How 'bouts a pint of liquor?" said Ed with a grin.

"Glad to see you're feeling better. But – no dice! How about a Hershey Bar instead? See ya."

"Bye. Ah, Mr. Patton?"

"Ed?"

"A can of beer," said Ed, trying to laugh, but not succeeding.

Pat waived goodbye. He called his parents, and with tears in his eyes, told them about Shirley. His father said they would be at Pat's house Friday afternoon. Because they had a key, they would let themselves in.

"That's not going to work. Movers are coming Saturday morning to move the guest bedroom, and really everything except the living room and master bedroom. The rest will be moved next weekend. We also packed a lot of stuff at Shirley's apartment for them to move. We were lucky to have Eb and Kathy help with the packing."

"What should we do?"

"Greg O'Kelly has invited you to stay with them. You have their phone number, so call them first. If you can't get them, try again because they will be spending much of their time at the hospital. I'll ask if they can have Renée, their domestic help, be available to answer the phone and let you in. They also need to inform the gate guard that you are coming."

"Okay, Son, will do." His father was still finding it hard to believe what happened to Shirley.

"I'll let Greg know you're planning to be here Friday."

"Thanks, Son. We'll see you then and will pray for Shirley. And - - please take care of yourself and be careful!"

"I will, Dad. I love you and tell Mom I love her. Bye."

Pat went back to the waiting room where Greg, Grace, and Lt. Keller waited.

Greg had a smile on his face when he said, "She woke up for a short time and asked for you, and us, in that order."

"Gosh, that's good news! I know she will be okay in time and will get her sight back."

"They will not allow you in until tomorrow after 6:00 PM. After that, we can all go in as a group, but we are asked to leave if she gets tired or weak. That will be left up to me since I'm an M. D."

"I talked to Ed and he does not think the truck hitting him was an accident. He said it came after him like it was alive."

"That doesn't surprise me," said Capt. Keller.

"This whole thing scares the hell out of me!" blurted out Grace, with an uncustomary burst of profanity.

"Out of all of us, Honey."

"I talked to Mom and Dad, who will be here Friday evening. Since the movers are coming on Saturday, they would like to take you up on your offer to stay at your place."

"Certainly," said Grace.

"They'll be in sometime Friday evening but will try to call first. They know you will be at the hospital much of the time, as will I. There will not be a day go by that I don't come to see her." Pat wiped a tear from his eye.

Greg and Grace both gave him a hug but said nothing.

"So, you actually saw her?" asked Pat.

"Yes, but just for a very short time."

"How does she look?"

"It was hard to tell, because unlike before, she was bandaged this time. Her hair got a little singed, the part not under her hat, and her eye brows are also singed. She is being treated with wet bandages soaked with silver nitrate solution, but the earlier application of ice to her face and eyes being irrigated were extremely important. Shirley was under heavy medication but her being able to talk this soon shows the concussion is not too severe. Richard is also coming Friday night, so she'll be glad to see, ah, talk, with the young doctor." A tear flowed down Greg's face.

"I'll bet she will. I'm looking forward to meeting your son."

"I told Grace I left a message for a friend of mine from medical school, Dr. Orhan, who is now one of the leading eye surgeons in New York City. I will want the opinion of our local doctors, but I trust Dr. Orhan with my life and want him to operate."

"Capt., I just thought of something. When I talked with Renée earlier this evening . . ."

"Renée?" interrupted Capt. Keller. "Renée Anderson? How? You never told me!"

"This is hard to believe, but she's the O'Kelly's housekeeper, at least for three days per week."

"Unbelievable! And we were looking everywhere else for her!"

"What I was going to say, she mentioned the Brotherhood and the Confederate Motorcycle Club as being linked to Jeffie. She said if he was locked up because of her, one of them would get her. All I know is Skinny was somehow associated with them. What do you know about them?"

"As you may know, the Brotherhood was mixed up in the 1955 Edwards' shooting. A mixture of a mini KKK and a mini Mafia. They're still around, but a few years ago they went underground. The Confederate M/C Club was started back in the '50's by men who were also members or friends of the Brotherhood. They are anti-black, anti-Jew, anti-homosexual, and anti about everything else except rednecks, beer drinking, and Harley riding. They copy some of the older clubs, like the California Hell's Angels. Some of them caused a disturbance at Jerome & Mickey's Steak House last Thursday evening."

"Hey, that's when I talked to Charlotte. You mean that was the Confederate M/C Club?"

"That's right. Are you thinking what I'm thinking?"

"That Jeffie or his friends were there. Yes, I am, and I'll get someone on it first thing in the morning."

"They had those blue denim jackets with the sleeves cut off and writing on the back. Colors they call them, the name of the club and artwork. It was night and hard to read."

"Like I said, I'll put a man on it in the morning, but it sure looks like someone is out to get you, Shirley, and Ed."

"Well, not me yet, although now it's obvious the car bomb was meant for me."

"Probably was, but not necessarily because Shirley was the first to shoot Skinny, and his brother may have been deliberately gunning for her."

"Thinking like a cop, Capt., but of course you're right. They could have been after my daughter all of the time," agreed Greg, who really didn't believe it, but was trying to take some of the guilt off of Pat.

"Good try." Pat put his arm on Greg's shoulder. "But I don't think so."

Pat and Greg were bonding very fast now that a person they both deeply loved was lying in a hospital, hurt and blinded by a cowardly car bomber.

"We need to get something to eat," said Grace.

"Right. Everyone ready? How about the new Flying Buzzard Restaurant around the corner? Wouldn't a delicious buzzard fillet sandwich, fries, and a Coke be good about now?" asked Pat.

"That's okay with me, Son, but I hope that 'buzzard' part is a joke!" said Greg.

He called me, Son! Sometimes good things come out of bad things. It gave Pat a warm feeling inside.

They all went to The Flying Buzzard for real tasty chicken. The restaurant was busy, but a table was found in a few minutes.

If we had 360 pound Sam with us, she could have got any table they wanted.

"The good food and catchy name is really drawing people to this place," commented Capt. Keller.

"I'm glad it really wasn't buzzard," said Grace trying to smile, but still numb. "Pat, there is something on a serious side I want to say to you. What does a woman really want from a man? The Bible answers that question. It is love. Of course romantic love, but it goes much deeper than that. It is an unconditional love. Pat, by your unselfish devotion to our daughter, you have given her that love."

They hugged with tears flowing down their cheeks.

* * *

After they ate, Pat took the O'Kelly's home, and finally got home himself. It was almost 10:00 and he would have court in the morning.

His answering machine had several messages, most asking how Shirley was doing. Pat called Julie, Herb, Eb, and Judge Musselman. He told them what he knew, and the judge that he would be in court in the morning. He was glad he had previously arranged his calendar with Judge Starwell and Judge Cody. Normally criminal cases take precedence over civil cases, but the judges had agreed to let Pat present his two divorce cases in Judge Cody's courtroom at 9:00, and his two criminal pleas would be heard by Judge Starwell at 10:00. Then finally, the one he dreaded - - the arraignment of the Tidwell Dope Fairy case - - in Judge Musselman's courtroom at 11:00.

Pat took a shower and went to bed exhausted. But sleep came slowly because Shirley was not there beside him.

CHAPTER 33

Jeffie Goes To Daytona

Jeffie and Reb woke up the next morning yawning, having had only a few hours' sleep because they drove most of the night. They were at a biker friend's rundown shack on the outskirts of Daytona Beach, FL. He was called The Scorpion or Scorpie for short.

"Man, I'm tired! That was a hell of a long drive!" commented Jeffie.

"Me, too, but at least you got the couch. I had to, ah, take the recliner."

"Well, it's free, but we got to get a room somewhere. Maybe we can find some gals to stay with."

"Yeah, I'd like that!"

"You know, Reb, our car bomb has been bugging me. I talked to Scorpie last night and he said he could get me a couple of sticks of good stuff for a reasonable price. He thinks for $100 I could get four or five sticks, but he wasn't sure what the guy would take."

"What's we gonna do? Huh, Jeffie, huh?"

"How about if we experiment with two sticks and take the other three back with us?"

"Who we gonna blow up?"

"Does it matter? Some niggers, some Jews, rich guys, queers? Who cares?"

"Ah, Jeffie. Watching Tight-Ass get blown up was fun, but I want to see Piss-Ant really, really, get blown up!"

They got up and told Scorpie they would take their bikes and look around. The first stop was breakfast; the second was an auto parts store. Jeffie bought a long spark plug wire and things to make an igniter. He bought a Coke in a plastic bottle, a roll of plastic tape and a tool to open car doors. He drank the Coke as he wanted to fill the bottle with gasoline.

Jeffie strapped the bag of goodies on his bike and they went to see Scorpie's buddy, who had the dynamite. The address turned out to be a dingy apartment. Jeffie knocked on the door and waited.

"Who the hell is it?" yelled a man with a deep base voice from inside.

"Jeffie for Seal. Scorpie sent me."

"Okay, man, just a second." Seal got his name because he was an ex-Navy Seal.

When the door opened, they saw a huge man.

Damn, he's a few inches taller than Reb, who stands 6' 3". This sucker must weigh at least 350 pounds. I wonder how he got that five-inch scar on his face?

"Come on in. Wan'a beer? Of course you do! Sit!" He went in the kitchen and had to bend down under the doorway.

"Scorpie said you could get us half a dozen sticks of bang for a hundred. I got the hundred; you got the sticks?"

Seal smiled. "Man, truth is I only got four sticks and that stuff is gettin' hard to find, but since you're a friend of my good buddy, Scorpie, I'll let you have 'em for the hundred."

"How about $75?"

"Look, man, they're worth the hundred, but since you look like a good man, and like I said, a friend of my good buddy Scorpie, I'll throw in four caps and ten feet of fuse. But that's it. Take it or leave it."

"You drive a hard bargain, Seal." Jeffie pulled out a $100 bill from his wallet, which was chained to his belt. He showed it to Seal while chewing on a toothpick.

Seal looked at the hundred. "Be right back."

"No wet stuff!" yelled Jeffie.

"Jeffie, ah, I ain't used to lookin' up at nobody." Reb had a look of awe on his face.

"I know, but we'll get the stuff and get the hell out of here. He's a big sucker and he's too nice. Probably has a whole room full of dynamite and wants to make as much as he can off of us," whispered Jeffie.

Seal came into the room with four sticks of dry dynamite, fuse and caps, sealed in a large Zip-lock bag that was sealed in a second Zip-lock bag. Jeffie was genuinely pleased, took the bag and gave Seal the hundred.

"Good doing business with you, Seal."

As they were putting on their helmets, Reb asked, "Jeffie, ah, could we get us a nigger, a Jew, a queer, and a rich guy, and put 'em all in the car when we blow it up?"

"You know, for a Dumbass, you come up with some good ideas sometimes. However, the answer is no, because there is too much chance of getting caught."

After some investigation, Jeffie stumbled on a gay bar that catered to both black and white upper class homosexual men.

"Reb, this is perfect! We'll stake out the place and watch for salt and pepper couples in expensive cars. After they go into the bar, we look for a time when no one is in the parking lot, and then we'll go to work. Love it!"

"Yeah! Yeah!" exclaimed Reb as he clapped his hands.

"After we get them fairies, we got to case some places to get some money. You still got them magnetic signs that say Jones Construction Company?"

"The ones that goes on the doors?"

"Yes, Dumbass, the ones that goes on the doors."

"I got 'em back of the seat."

"Good, now let's get us some hardhats. A white one for me and a green one for you."

"Why don't you get a colored one, too?"

"Because I'm no dumbass, that's why! White is generally accepted as a supervisor, or foreman, and green for a worker. If anyone notices, I'm a supervisor for Jones Construction Company, and you're one of my men. We also got to get me a clipboard and some tablet paper."

"I'm glad you're my friend, Jeffie, 'cause you're so smart," idolized Reb.

"As much as I hate to think about it, I really need to buy a pair of black pants, a white shirt, and a tie. Damn, I hate to wear those things."

"Do I have to wear a tie, too?"

"No, Dumbass, just me."

That seemed to make Reb happy.

"What do we do now?"

"Scorpie told me about a restaurant where chicks go for lunch who seem to like bikers. Maybe we'll get lucky. I'd like to stay with them while we're here, but with what we got goin' on, it won't work."

"Why not, Jeffie?"

"'Cause they're too damn nosey, that's why! We got to stake out the queer joint tonight, and tomorrow case some places to make a score. We'll need a cover for the back of your pickup to store goodies in. We'll also need to steal a truck for the job, a Chevy 'cause their easier to jump the ignition and break the steering-wheel lock. And always remember this: Never, never, never tell a broad what we're doin', 'cause that's a sure way to go to jail. Now repeat what I said back to me," said Jeffie, while chewing on a toothpick.

"Ah, we gonna steal a Chevy 'cause . . ."

"Stop right there, Dumbass! About the broads! What did I tell you about the broads?"

"That, ah, there was some eatin' place. . ."

"Damn! Damn! Damn! Now listen good! If we pick up some broads, you're not to tell them about the queers or the job we're gonna pull! Got that! In fact, you don't talk about nothin' but takin' a Florida vacation and havin' a good time. Now what did I say about the broads?"

"Not to tell 'em nothin'."

"What did you come to Florida for?"

"To get away from Piss-Ant . . ."

"No! No! No! Vacation! Vacation! Vacation!"

"To go on vacation and, ah, to have fun."

"Good! Now make sure you remember it."

Jeffie and Reb met a couple of low-class girls, but did not get lucky, because the girls had to go back to work. They did get phone numbers and told them to expect a call. Hell yes, they would like to ride on Harley choppers.

The guys went back to Scorpies and crashed for a few hours, as they already had a big day, and it was far from over.

CHAPTER 34

The Arrow

Pat got up and went for a 30-minute jog to relax. When he got back, he called the hospital waiting room and talked to Grace. Greg had gone to work but would be at the hospital sometime after lunch. Shirley was sleeping and was doing as good as could be expected. Pat said he would be in about three or four o'clock. She asked him to make it four of five and to bring a takeout order from the Flying Buzzard so they wouldn't have to worry about eating out or eating hospital food.

Judge Cody was very understanding and knew what Pat was going through. In 30 minutes, Pat had two happily divorced clients, a man from one marriage and a woman from another, who planned to marry each other! He walked down to the Clerk's Office with his clients to get a copy of their final decrees. Judge Cody allowed attorneys to walk the clerk's original file to the Clerk's Office, but Heaven help an attorney who lost the file. As he headed to Judge Starwell's court, Pat noticed the two who were not planning to get married hitting on each other and walking out the door holding hands. Pat thought, *Go figure. Half of my divorce clients are getting a divorce so they can marry someone else.*

It was close to 10:00 when Pat entered Judge Starwell's courtroom. The judge heard Pat's criminal plea cases, where his clients pled guilty to serve a previously agreed-to sentence. He was out of the courtroom by 10:45.

Pat had a Coke at the snack bar and then headed for Judge Musselman's courtroom. Tidwell was in a holding cell.

"Good morning, Ms. Tidwell."

"Hi," said Tidwell in a monotone.

"Let me explain the procedure again. This is the arraignment stage where you plead Guilty, and receive a sentence recommended by the DA's office and approved by the judge, or plead Not Guilty, as you indicated you will do. You will be put on the judge's trial calendar for a jury trial. Your trial date has been specially set for next Wednesday, Jan. 28th. Do you understand?"

"Just get me probation."

"Look, Ms. Tidwell. We are way past that point and I'm tired of playing games with you. Now, do you or don't you want to go to trial?" asked Pat in a stern voice.

"Yeah."

"Yeah, what?"

"Yeah, I want to go to trial."

"Now, do you understand the process? When we go up before the judge, I will tell him you are entering a plea of Not Guilty and he will announce the trial date, which will be next Wednesday. You will sign your name on the indictment and check the Not Guilty box.

"Yeah."

"Yeah, what?" Pat was exasperated and disgusted with this very arrogant woman. She was lucky she had him, because some attorneys would do as little as possible for her. He could not stand her, but he had tried to do his best in spite of her. Fortunately, he had done a lot of work on this case because he felt it would go to trial.

"Yeah. I walk up with you in front of that damn goofball wearing a woman's robe and stand there looking dumb, while you do all the talking."

Pat shook his head and motioned for the deputy to let him out. A few minutes later the deputy brought her to the jury box and sat her with the other defendants awaiting arraignment. Jurors would occupy these seats during a jury trial. When Judge Musselman finished the case in front of him, he called the State vs. Tidwell. Pat went to the lectern and waited for the deputy to instruct her to stand beside Pat at the lectern. He heard *Dope Fairy* being muttered after the case was called.

"What is your announcement to this Court, Mr. Patton? Guilty, or Not Guilty?"

"Your Honor, Ms. Tidwell wishes to plead Not Guilty and I wish to be released from representing her."

This statement caused a buzzing in the courtroom and reporter Vivienne Cove began taking notes. Radio and TV personalities Sandi Desanto, Zel Murray, and Steve Futo were standing in back of the courtroom waiting for Pat to leave, hoping for a statement from him, because they did not get one earlier. They all wanted to talk to him about Shirley when he was at the hospital, but Dr. O'Kelly snuck them out the back way. Now they had even more questions.

"Very well, Mr. Patton, but first things first."

DA Colver put the indictment on the lectern and checked the Not Guilty box. Tidwell glared at Pat, but signed it without a word.

"Now, Mr. Patton, we will hear your motion," directed Judge Musselman.

"Your Honor, I would like to make a motion to withdraw from this case. Ms. Tidwell has been very uncooperative, and there seems to be a personality conflict."

"What do you say, Ms. Tidwell?" asked the Judge.

"Yeah, get me a new one. This one sucks!"

"Ms. Tidwell, if you do not show more respect for this Court, I will have you removed from the courtroom and continue without you!" warned Judge Musselman in a very firm manner. He was plainly agitated with her.

"Mr. Colver, we will now hear from you. As you know, this case is specially set for next Wednesday at 9:00 AM because Ms. Tidwell petitioned this court for a speedy trial, which is the Defendant's right under the 6th Amendment to the Constitution of the United States."

"Your Honor, I oppose the motion. If you release Mr. Patton and appoint another attorney, he would not have proper time to prepare a defense. I understand Mr.

Patton is going through emotional stress right now with his fiancée in the hospital, but as they say, *the show must go on*. I think Mr. Patton is a very capable attorney and will be able to overlook his and Ms. Tidwell's differences. Thank you, Your Honor."

"Some questions, Mr. Patton. First, in spite of your fiancée being in the hospital, can you be ready to defend your client next week?"

"Yes, Your Honor."

"Second question. In spite of your personality conflict, can you, and will you, defend this woman to the best of your ability?"

"Yes, Your Honor."

"To both parts of my question?"

"Yes Sir, to both parts of your question."

"Very well, motion denied. This case will be called for trial at 9:00 on January 28, 1981. Thank you, gentlemen."

Pat got up and headed out the door, with people talking and the judge calling for order. All three reporters were waiting for him, and they could sense a good story brewing. "The only comment about the trial I can make is that I'll do my best to show the jury why Ms. Tidwell is not guilty.

"How about Ms. O'Kelly?" asked Steve Futo.

"I am dealing with another coward. Bombing a woman when I was the target. She has some major surgery coming up, so please pray for her."

With that, he smiled and left, as they continued to fire questions at him, even on the Louie Lake case, which Pat had not thought of since Shirley's injury. Apparently word was out that he would be representing Mr. Lake again. The press was referring to him as The Telephone Man.

Pat went to his office and talked with Julie for a few minutes about Tidwell before he went to lunch. A quick call to the hospital told him Shirley was awake more often and wanted to see him, but they were sticking by their rules and said "No visitors before six."

"Let me know when she can have outside visitors, Boss, and I'll be there. Jeeez, life ain't fair."

Shirley and Julie had become good friends.

"I will, Julie, and thank you. Want to come along to lunch?"

"Does a bear . . .," said Julie . . . with a smile. "I'll tell Rhonda to cover for me. Herb's at his house and says it will be finished within two to three weeks . . . if the weather holds."

They went to the Brave Bull in Julie's car and never noticed the Ford pickup truck following them. They ordered the special of the day.

"Ralph got his promotion. I'm now the wife of Lt. Crawford. How about that?"

"I'm really happy for you, Julie. If I don't seem too excited, it's just that I'm thinking about Shirley."

"I understand, Boss. Hey, look! There you are on TV."

Zel Murray of Channel 3 News was telling about the latest development in the Dope Fairy Case and then commenting on the Telephone Man. She reported that Pat called the bomber a coward, and how he did the same thing with Skinny before the shootout at Pat's house. People in the restaurant were looking and pointing at him. She closed with a cute comment, "When the Telephone Man turned to warehouses, he almost got his line disconnected."

The next story was about an apparent serial killer in the Atlanta area who struck for the 2nd time. The police found the body of a black male laying next to a white female in an alley. They had been killed by a small caliber weapon and sprayed with disinfectant. Two weeks earlier, police found bodies of a gay couple murdered in a similar fashion and sprayed with disinfectant.

Pat shook his head. "Just what Atlanta needs, after the Atlanta Missing and Murdered Children case last year, had everyone nervous.

"Ralph and the Atlanta PD have their work cut out for them on this one. Sounds like a real weirdo," said Pat. "Wayne Williams was suspected in as many as 21 murders and disappearances but I understand the FBI doesn't think he did all of them."

"You got that right, Boss. Here comes our food!"

About that time Capt. Keller and Dottie, Judge Musselman's secretary, came in and were asked to join Pat and Julie. Capt. Keller asked about Shirley, and then told them the latest news on trying to find out who placed the bomb in Pat's car.

"We found a witness who saw two big men, with coveralls on, with the name of some garage on the back, open the door with what looked like a piece of wire. They had a truck with some of those stick-on magnetic signs on the doors, but she does not remember the name of the place. One guy was big, but the other one was even bigger, and both were white. She thought someone was having car trouble and didn't pay much attention."

"I wish she would have got a good look at the tag number, but then the truck they had was probably stolen." Pat's voice indicated a tired and exasperated man."

"It probably was."

"Can she identify either of them?"

"No. Only that they both had long hair, wore coveralls, and were both big men. She went onto a store and did not see them again."

"Anything else?"

"Mostly routine stuff this morning. We had two officers call in sick, so I took a call to a trailer park. Someone was mad at the owner of a trailer and burned it down. A Chevy Camaro, which was sitting there, was worked over pretty good with a baseball bat. All of the windows and lights were smashed and dents all over it. The fire department was there, and a uniform worked it, but he was new so I checked it out," said the Capt. as he finished his food. "If you will excuse me, I need to check in with the dispatcher. Dottie drove, so I don't have my car radio to check in."

Capt. Keller returned about ten minutes later.

"Pat, I have some interesting news. The trailer was rented by one Johnny Carter, who goes by the name of Reb and is a known member of the Confederate M/C Club. We don't know who the Camaro belongs to, presumably to Carter, because it is still registered to a man who said he sold it over three years ago. Apparently the new owner never had the registration changed. Evette, our dispatcher, told me the trailer was owned by the park."

"It's a wonder someone didn't hear the Camaro getting beat up," commented Pat.

People in that park have learned to mind their own business and didn't want trouble with the Confederates or their enemies. I doubt if anyone would talk even if they saw what happened," said Capt. Keller. "So, now there is no way to tell if someone was after Carter or the park, but if I were a betting man, I would say Carter, because of the damage to the Camaro."

"Probably some other biker mad at him," suggested Julie.

"Maybe, but most of them wouldn't want to mess with the Confederates."

"More puzzles, when my brain is tired and overwhelmed." Pat closed his eyes and threw his head back.

"We've got to go," said Capt. Keller.

"Right. Julie and I need to get out of here, too."

"We're still looking for Carter. A neighbor said she saw him and another guy put their Harleys in his pickup truck and leave yesterday, or the day before. She wasn't sure and didn't know where they went."

"See you later, Capt. and Dottie," said Pat as he and Julie waved goodbye and headed for her car.

"It looks like the Capt. and Dottie are a couple now."

"Yeah, Boss, it sure looks that way."

* * *

"Julie, I need to stop by Saunder's Jewelers for a few minutes. You know where it is, don't you?"

"I'm a woman, aren't I? Of course I know where it is. One whole block away, and about sixty seconds to get there."

As they pulled out, a Ford P/U truck, with one man driving and another in the bed, pulled out behind them.

Snake and Yanker were caught by surprise when Julie turned into Saunder's Jewelry Store. They went by and pulled into the first available parking spot and waited.

David Saunders, the owner, was a big man with a big smile. He was known for his honesty and fine merchandise. Greg O'Kelly talked highly of Mr. Saunders and had done business with him for years.

"Good afternoon, Mr. Patton. Welcome to my store. What can I show you? I'm not sure I know this young lady, but she is not Shirley O'Kelly."

Pat was flabbergasted!

How did Saunders know who I am? I've never seen Mr. Saunders before, let alone met him or visited his store.

"Good afternoon. This is my secretary, Julie Crawford. How did you know. . ."

"TV, Mr. Patton," interrupted the jeweler. "You were on the news again. I know Greg and his daughter Shirley, because they have done business with me for years. I also know you're engaged to her. A pity you didn't buy her engagement ring here."

"I gave her my grandmother's ring. I'm sure you're aware that Shirley has been hospitalized. What would you suggest for an appropriate gift at a time like this?"

"How about a diamond pendant? We have them from an eighth carat up to three." He walked over to the pendants.

While Julie looked around, Pat picked out a half-carat pendant and had Mr. Saunder's assistant, a beautiful young woman, wrap it for him. They left in Julie's car.

The street was fairly wide and Julie was in the left-hand lane. She drove a few blocks when a pickup truck pulled up beside them in the right lane, and a little ahead of them. A man, in the bed of the truck, drew back on a bow and let loose an arrow.

"Look out, Julie!" yelled Pat, as he thought he saw a man throw something.

The passenger's side front window shattered as the arrow hit it and then exited through the driver's side rear window. Yanker had miscalculated only a little, but it was enough for the arrow to miss Pat by a few inches and Julie by a foot. She almost lost control of her car but managed to safely come to a stop. She was shaking and turned toward Pat as he was trying to get to his revolver.

"They turned down the side street. Damn! Now I've endangered you!" exclaimed Pat.

Neither one of them had realized it at the time, but, after the arrow exited the rear window, it hit the rear door of a car going in the opposite direction. The driver, a young man, got a good look at the man in the pickup truck.

Julie did not receive a scratch, but Pat had cuts on his head and face from the flying glass. He was lucky he was wearing sunglasses, because they were cracked on one side, indicating some glass would have hit him in his right eye.

Soon the police arrived, and Pat asked the officer to call Capt. Keller, who arrived several minutes later. Pat explained what happened.

The witness was interviewed and gave his statement. "I'm sorry, Capt., but the guy had a stocking or something over his face. As I was coming toward the car and the truck, I saw someone almost stand up in the bed of the truck. With a bow and arrow! I got a good look at him but his features were, like, distorted. You know? Gross looking. Not real. I was only going about 30 mph but in the opposite direction."

"Did you notice anything else?"

"Not really."

A driver behind Pat stopped and was questioned.

"Mr. Morrow, I understand you saw what happened."

"Yes, sir! I even got the tag number. It was, like, a Georgia plate, FORDPU2. I saw this figure in the back of the pickup pull back on a bow and he shot an arrow at the car almost beside him. The pickup driver got a little ahead of the car, I guess so the guy in the pickup bed, he looked like a freak, could get a good shot at the car. They couldn't have been more than a car length apart. I'm glad the people in the car didn't get hit."

Capt. Keller ordered frequent drive-by visual checks by patrol cars of Pat's house and office. This was attempted murder.

"Who else could it be but Jeffie and his buddies?" asked Pat.

"I'll double-check, but we're still observing what's left of Reb's trailer and the Confederates are still out of town."

CHAPTER 35

You Still Want Me?

After the EMS treated his cuts, they went to Gator's Glass Shop. Although Julie was quite a woman in the no-tears category, she let Pat drive. He arranged for her to get a rental car while hers was being repaired. Julie called her husband and Pat called the hospital. They let their loved ones know what had happened.

"Julie, it looks like the lead on the two Confederates who got their trailer burnt down is going nowhere. The Capt. said they were still out of town when the attempt was made on my life."

"Maybe they came back."

"Possible, but I don't think so." The phone rang.

"Anything new, Capt.?" asked Pat.

"We found the truck parked at the Jamestown Shopping Center. Stolen, of course. No prints. Nothing else, yet."

"Great, Capt.! Shirley and I, and now Julie, not to mention Ed, are targets of some unseen, unknown force, and we can't fight them because we can't see them. We don't even know for sure who they are!" Pat was frustrated.

"We're doing all we can. We're now trying to get Jeffie's picture from the airlines and the military. If we get them, they will be several years old, but still could help. I will not rest until we nail these creeps."

"I know, Capt., and I don't mean to take my irritation out on you. Have a good day. Bye. "

Pat told Julie to hold all phone calls for about 15 minutes, as he did not want to be disturbed except for an emergency. Julie closed his office door and Pat got down on his knees and prayed.

"Father, please listen to me. I know I'm a sinner, and not worthy, but please help Shirley. Father, she is laying in the hospital and has lost her sight. Please be with her, love her, take care of her, and heal her. She is a good woman, and I love her very much. Lord, please guide the minds and the hands of the doctors who work on her. Give them the wisdom and skills to restore her sight. With Your Devine help, I know all things are possible. I believe, with all of my heart, you can do it! Thank you, Lord, for listening to me, and Father, thank you for your son, Jesus Christ. I ask this in His name. Amen."

Pat got up with tears in his eyes and sat for several minutes. Life was getting so complicated. As he was about to leave, Julie said he had two phone calls holding - - one from the insurance company on his Mustang, and Chief Keefauver, who said he would hold while Pat talked to the insurance man.

"Pat Patton, speaking."

"Good afternoon, sir. First, my condolences concerning the young lady who was injured. My name is Artis McDuffy from Georgia Metro Auto Insurance Company. As you are aware, your policy has an agreed-upon total loss value of $8,000, the appraised value of your automobile. I put a check for that amount in the mail to you this morning."

"Thank you for acting so quickly."

"That's the good news. The bad news is that since this was the second automobile we have had to cover in less than three months, the company is reviewing your file. Your premiums will either go up substantially or we may have to refuse to renew your policy. I'm not sure which."

"I understand, Mr. McDuffy. Thank you for calling."

"You are a gentleman, Mr. Patton, as most of our policy holders cuss me out at this point. I will do all in my power at this end to help you, sir. Have a good day."

"You, too, sir."

"Hi, Chief. Sorry to keep you holding, but a check is on its way for my Mustang."

"I wanted you to know I got a call from Lt. Ralph Crawford, of the Atlanta PD."

"Julie's husband?"

"Right. Well, we now have the resources of the Atlanta PD to help us. He went ballistic when he heard about the arrow being shot through her window. She could have been killed. How are you doing?"

"Fine, except for a few cuts here and there. The EMS boys patched me up, but I'll admit it scared the hell out of me."

"Me, too, and I wasn't even in the car. I also wanted to warn you that the reporters were all over Julie's car at Gator's Glass Shoppe. Old Gator figured he could use the free publicity, so he let them look over the car as long as they gave him a free plug."

"Chief, I used to think it would be neat to be well-known, but now I'm not so sure."

"You have a point. I know you're on your way to the hospital, so don't let me hold you up. And – Pat, if you don't have that .357 magnum on you, go get it now."

"I had it on me, inside my suit coat, but they were gone before I could get it out. See you, Chief."

"Bye, and keep on your toes."

Now 4:30, Pat said goodbye to a mostly recovered Julie.

At the hospital, Greg and Grace were waiting for him, worried even more as the arrow shooting incident had been on the Ch. 3 News at Five, with Zel. Giving a short review of the day's headlines, a warm up to the News at Six show. It was very clever how Zel kept telling her viewers to tune in at Six for more of the story.

"Oh, Pat, your face!" exclaimed Grace as he gave him a hug. "They tried to kill you!"

"It's nothing. Just a few small glass cuts," said Pat as he shook Greg's hand.

Greg said, "I saw her about two hours ago and she's looking much better. She keeps asking for you, and Grace, but I told her she had to wait until six. I also told her what you said about the wedding going on as planned, and she just beamed, even though the bandages. I kept quiet about the arrow."

At last 6:00 came and they were told to go in. Shirley wore a clean gown and a nurse had fixed her hair for the visit. The smell of a hospital was in the air as Greg and Grace gave her a hug, being careful not to touch Shirley's bandaged face. Then Pat got his turn and gave her a very careful kiss on the lips. She held him and cried, while the rest of them joined her with their tears.

"I love you, Shirley. I'll see you and call you every day."

"I love you, too, Pat," whispered Shirley.

"Your eyes are going to be fine. You're daddy has you set up to see Dr. Orhan in three weeks. The doctors say an operation could be done a lot sooner than three weeks, but his schedule is full. That is if they find a suitable donor. Hopefully, a cornea transplant will be in order. You have an excellent chance of getting your sight back."

"Listen to him talking like a doctor," smiled Greg.

"I feel small Band-Aids on your face." as Shirley, as she ran her hands over his face. She had trouble talking.

"It's nothing. I just cut myself shaving."

"Pat, are you sure you want me, like - - like this? I have to know for sure. I've had time to think and know there's the possibility I will not regain my sight." Shirley talked with difficulty, trying to refrain from crying.

"Want you? Why that's all I can think of."

Shirley smiled and squeezed his hand.

"Daddy, the truth now. What can you tell me about my eyes?"

Dr. Greg had seen her eyes only once and quickly. They were milkfish white when the bandages were off.

"Honey, the truth is we don't know. We assume your sight was lost to burns of the corneas, but we don't know how badly burned, or if there is other damage, such as a detached retina or damage to the optic nerve. Sure, there is a chance you won't regain your sight, but the chances are on your side that you will. I have arranged for a doctor from Emory University Hospital to examine you in the morning. She is a widely respected ophthalmologist, and when she is finished with her examination, we will know more. Dr. Judy Stangl is known state-wide."

Pat noticed the IV tubes and a bottle of fluid hanging from a metal stand. The needle was placed in her left wrist, so she had to be very careful when using her left arm, such as giving someone a hug. Greg had arranged for a private room and she had her own telephone and remote control TV.

A lot of good that's doing her.

She also had a window with a view of the hospital grounds. *She can't see that either.* All of these thoughts brought a tear to his eyes. He was glad that was one thing she couldn't see.

Oh, how I love this woman!

"Shir, I will be with you always! A day won't go by that I don't come and visit," whispered Pat.

"You have to talk a little louder. They said I could expect to have trouble hearing for several days, or longer, and I have a ringing in my ears. Pat? Please check on Braille and other blind services. Just in case. Okay?"

"Let's not be pessimistic. And let's not rush. You have plenty of time for that. I love you, love you, love you!"

He held her close and repeated those words to her, with his mouth close to her ear. Small talk went on for about 15 minutes, then Greg saw her noticeably tiring. They all said their goodbyes and left.

Out in the hall, Grace burst into tears. Greg put his arms around her and consoled her. Pat said sternly, "I'm going to find out who did this to her, and when I do, I'll get him!"

"Son, be careful about vengeance. It can destroy you. The Bible speaks of it in several places. But, I know how you feel. I'm her father, you know, and have to fight the same feelings."

"I'm a Christian lady, but I'm afraid to tell you what I would do to him!" said Grace to an astonished Pat and Greg.

Now about 7:00, Pat decided to go back to the office to work on the Tidwell case for a few hours, because things really would be hectic, with his parents and Shirley's brother coming into town.

CHAPTER 36

Fireworks At A Gay Bar

Earlier in the day, at a nearby town, Jeffie had two signs made that said MAXIE MARKET. They staked out Daytona's high roller, gay nightclub in a stolen pickup truck. It was 8:00 PM, and people were starting to come in.

A big crowd is not expected on a Thursday night, but two perverts is all we need.

As they were sitting across the street listening to the truck radio, the news came on. Even in Florida, the attempt on Pat's life with a bow and arrow was big news. The story built upon the bomb blinding Shirley, the Skinny Anderson case, which was still fresh on people's minds, and Ed's hit and run. The press believed these events were tied together.

As Jeffie listened to the story, he shouted, "What the hell? Damn! Damn! Damn! Who could have done a stupid thing like that?"

"Why you mad, Jeffie? Huh? Whoever it was, ah, almost got Piss-Ant Patton."

"You really are a Dumbass! Now he'll be on alert, and the cops will be watching him like a hawk! Damn! That's one reason we left town. We needed to let things cool down! Now it will be twice as hard to get at him and

Little Miss Tight-Ass," Jeffie angrily chewed up a tooth pick and then lit up a cigar.

"We gonna get her again?"

"Again? Man, I hope she gets her eyesight back so she can see what I'm going to do to her!"

"Me, too?" asked a leering Reb.

"Sure, Reb, but not until I'm done with her!"

A Mercedes pulled up in the parking lot and a well-dressed black man in his 30's got out. A BMW pulled in beside him. A well-dressed, feminine-looking white man got out, and the two of them walked up to the club holding hands.

"Did you see those two disgusting queers?" Jeffie started up the truck and pulled in beside the BMW. The tag attached to the license plate displayed a medical symbol that read MD.

With Reb as the lookout, Jeffie took only a few minutes to get the BMW's hood open and plant two sticks of dynamite. He took two sealed soft-drink bottles, filled with gasoline and taped them to the dynamite. Again, he used a long, spark plug wire, which had one end placed in one of the receptacles in the distributor cap and the other end attached to his homemade igniter, which had the other end grounded. It would ignite a very short fuse attached to a cap, which was placed in one of the sticks of dynamite. Starting the car would instantly set off the dynamite. He closed the hood and they left to get rid of the stolen truck and get back in Reb's pickup.

Thank you for parking beside a light pole, you dumb queers. 'cause it will be easy to spot you.

Jeffie stopped to get a dozen donuts and some drinks for what might be a long wait. They drove back to the club and found a parking space across the street approximately 50 yards away on higher ground so they could see the BMW in the club parking lot. They waited and waited.

At 11:00 the two lovers came out of the club and stood by the BMW for a few minutes and talked. There were several other men in the parking lot now, standing beside their cars and talking. At last the guy with the Mercedes opened the door for the doctor, who got in his

BMW and rolled down the window. The guy outside, leaned over and kissed the doctor, who then closed the window, and turned the ignition key to the start position.

Jeffie and Reb were totally unprepared for what happened next! First, the whole area lit up like a giant flashbulb went off, and then the light was followed by the noise of a dozen freight trains! After that came a shock-wave and wind that rocked their pickup! What seemed like minutes later, pieces of debris came down, some landing on their truck! Finally there was the fire!

"Damn! I ain't believing this!" Jeffie started Reb's pickup and left. "Boy, did we ever give them hell! We gotta get the hell out of here before the cops come. Man, I can't wait to read about it in the paper!"

"Can we do it again sometime, Jeffie? Huh? Can we?" asked Reb happily clapping his hands.

* * *

Friday was a big day for Pat. He spent the morning at his office, finishing up his defense of Tidwell, and then had lunch with Capt. Keller and Chief Keefauver at Palombo's Little Italy Restaurant. Penny and Carl welcomed him as usual.

Penny was there to take their order, when Herb came in and sat with them. Pat had told him where they would be.

"I'm ready for the Tidwell Dope Fairy case, Herb, but we both know we never are really ready no matter how much time we spent on it."

"Found that out early on, didn't you?"

The Chief said, "You might be interested to know Dixie Airlines is sending us a three-year-old picture of Jeffie. I sure hope it's not like a passport picture, because if people actually look like their passport pictures, they really need a vacation." Everyone laughed and shook their heads in agreement.

"That sounds like a step in the right direction," smiled Herb.

"It sure does," responded Pat. "Any other news?"

"Not really. Atlanta found two more victims of what the police believe is the work of the serial killer that the press is calling Mr. Clean. The bodies were two lesbian women, who appear to have been murdered over two weeks ago. The apartment manager had a report from a neighbor that a strange odor was coming from their apartment and she had not seen them lately."

"Let me guess," said Pat. "They were killed by a small caliber gun and sprayed with disinfectant."

"How did you know?" stated the Chief, rhetorically.

"Something else happened that I just can't get out of my mind since I first heard about it this morning," said Capt. Keller.

"Well, spit it out," said the Chief.

"It's the Daytona Beach bombing incident. I just can't stop thinking about it. Have you heard about it on the news, Pat?"

"No, I surely haven't. My nose has been stuck in the Tidwell file."

"It happened in Daytona Beach last night and has been all over the news. A doctor was going from a night club to the parking lot with his, uh, lover. It was an upscale gay bar. Anyway, as he is saying good night to him or her, or whatever the other one was, he apparently turned on his car's ignition switch and quickly became part of the landscape, along with his lover. Both were killed instantly as well as two others who were standing beside a car two parking spaces away. Four more men were injured, and one other may not make it. Bomb experts from Miami were flown in and estimate the equivalent of two to four sticks of dynamite were used. Even broke windows and started a fire in the clubhouse. Some adjoining businesses were also damaged."

"What's bothering you about it, Capt.?" asked Herb.

"Two things, actually. One is the car bomb itself, which was very similar to the one used that hurt Shirley, except on a much grander scale. The other is the similarity between the gay couple in Daytona and the Mr. Clean murders here. I know there is no way to tell if a small caliber weapon was involved, or if disinfectant was used, as there is not much left of either one of them. Neither one of the crimes up here exactly fits the one down there, but something about it is nagging me."

"Thinking like a cop, Capt. Which is very good," said the Chief. "Maybe, because homosexuals were involved in both cases?"

"Thank you, Capt. I need to make sure I read about it tonight.

"I'd also like to see what kind of take my media buddies have on it. If y'all will please excuse me for a few minutes, I want to call the hospital to check on Shirley. She was scheduled to have an Emory doctor look at her eyes this morning, so I want to touch base with Greg. He also may have heard from my parents and future brother-in-law."

Shirley was doing much better and the eye examination was positive in that Doctor Stangl did not find reason to believe the bomb caused serious eye damage, other than burns to the cornea. There was no word from either his parents or Richie, which was good, as it meant they would be at the hospital on time. Greg saw Ed, who was also improving. Shirley could be released Sunday or Monday. Ed would take much longer because of the lung removal.

That man has been through hell.

When he went back to the table, he had a question for Capt. Keller. "Do you really think Mr. Clean had something to do with Shirley's explosion and the one in Daytona?"

"No, I don't, but something – call it years being a cop, if you want, but something about Daytona bothers me."

They talked for about 15 minutes and left. As Pat drove home to pack a few more boxes for the move, he could not help thinking of all the things he had to do in the next few days. He felt overwhelmed, but when he got home, he felt a little better. His $8,000 check had come in the mail. He had been so busy he almost forgot that his 31st birthday was the following week, on the 9th of February.

I'll listen to Sandi on the radio. Maybe I'll hear about the Daytona bombing. She's covering it now. It was similar to Shirley's bombing, but so much more powerful. I can't help thinking about Capt. Keller's words, but other than both of them being car bombs, I can't see any similarities. Willie Lake's new case! How am I ever going to get to all of these things? Shirley asked about Braille, but I ignored her. I don't want to think about her being permanently blind, but I guess I'll have to check on it anyway. What do I know about Braille? Nothing, except it's a bunch of raised dots blind people read with their fingers.

Pat called Eb at work.

"Body and paint, Eb speaking."

"My good man, this is Mr. Mockturtle. Do you paint all kinds of bodies?" asked Pat in a disguised voice.

"Huh?"

"You see, sir, I have a yellow cat that just passed away, and I need his body to be painted – let's say – red. I simply never did like yellow and red would look good at his funeral."

"Look, Mr., we paint cars, not dead cats. My suggestion would be for you to see a good shrink. Bye!"

Eb hung up. Pat glanced at the phone with a surprised look on his face, and then redialed.

"Paint and body shop, Eb speaking."

"Why did you hang up on my friend, Mr. Mockturtle?"

"I should have known it was you! I guess you know I'm going to have to get revenge for that, don't you?"

"Fine, Eb, but first I need a favor. A very big one! Are you busy tomorrow?"

"The Great Eb stays busy, but you know I can always break loose for you, Buddy."

"Thanks, Eb. I needed that. The movers are coming tomorrow and going to pick up most of the things from my house and some of the things from Shirley's apartment. They will finish next weekend. We had it planned so we wouldn't be overwhelmed with all of the furniture from both places at the same time, but now that Shirley is in the hospital, and with my parents and Richie coming in tonight, and the Tidwell trial, all on top of the move, I'm lost! Could you supervise the move tomorrow? You know as much as I do where everything will go. I could leave a key on the kitchen table for you and you still have a key to this house, don't you?"

"It'll cost you, Buddy. Have a cold six-pack in the frig and we got a deal. I can get Kathy to help and she knows Shirley's style pretty good."

"I don't know how to thank you, Eb. They are supposed to be here at 9:00. The things downstairs and the shop will be moved next week, along with my bedroom furniture."

"Make that two six-packs. I'll give each of the movers a cold one. Never hurts to have them on your side."

"Thanks again. It's a deal!"

Pat headed to the Flying Buzzard and then to the hospital. First he stopped and bought two six-packs, which he would put in the frig before he went to bed.

As he drove, Pat thought about a telephone conversation he had with Greg earlier that day. Greg told him the immediate application of ice to Shirley's face saved scarring, and her bandaged face with a wet silver nitrate solution was precautionary to prevent infection. The bandages would be off within a day or two. But − Pat still felt scared for her.

CHAPTER 37

The Grocery Store

"Okay, Reb, let's double check our list. We got the hard hats, white for me and green for you. I got this stupid white shirt and tie. You got your coveralls. I got the clipboard, a flashlight and a penlight, yeah – and paper for the clipboard, those quickie printed business cards for Jones Construction Company, Bob Hardy - Foreman, and we got the Maxie Market signs for the sides of the truck. We also need a good place to transfer the cigarettes from the stolen truck to your truck. We need a cover for the back of your pick up so no one can see what we've got. Maybe we should steal a van this time - - easier to hide our loot. And we also need a sledge hammer, chisel, eye protection, and a ladder. One where you can go up on either side. We already have rubber gloves, and rubber masks for when we're inside where cameras could see us. And, yeah, my .357 Magnum and sawed-off shotgun.

"Ah, Jeffie, how much we gonna get for this job?"

"Our old buddy, Seal, said he could get us $3,500 per 1000 cartons of cigarettes. First we go shopping at the Maxie Market. Then we put on the hard hats and case the back of the store. They close at 11:00, so about midnight, or a little after, we hit it. Scorpie had his boys check on police patrols and they hardly ever cover this place. We owe him 25 cartons for that work. Say, I just got an idea!"

Jeffie called Seal, who happened to be home.

"Hello," said a deep voice.

"Seal, this is Jeffie. Look man, Scorpie talked to you about a certain business transaction."

"Yeah?"

"Well, what if we leave the container with the merchandise in it with you. Could you dispose of the container, too?"

"Yeah, and if it is a nice container, I could sell it for a few extra bucks. Give you 25%."

"We'll get a very nice one."

"Make sure you do. When can I expect it?"

"Sometime after midnight – tonight."

"Any change, call me. I got a machine. Bye."

Real pleasant fellow, that Seal, thought Jeffie sarcastically.

They went to the Maxie Market to shop and look for security cameras and burglar alarms. Reb was not very bright, but he had been involved in several large grocery store burglaries in the Atlanta area and knew what to expect.

"Ah, Jeffie, there's the cigarettes, like before in Atlanta."

"Right. Most stores are laid out pretty much the same. Over there," pointing down the aisle, "is the alarm beam that we got to go over tonight," said Jeffie as he pushed his buggy.

I calculate about 1500 cartons, plus several hundred loose packs at the cashier's checkout counters. Some would be sold today, but it would be quite a haul!

Next he threw a newspaper in the cart so he could read about the explosion last night. They went past the beer and a six-pack went into the buggy. They bought a few things, because they wanted to be seen as shoppers. Jeffie also threw in a loaf of bread but had no idea what he would do with it. He also bought a box of toothpicks and some cigars.

"There – between those two Coke machines! Another beam covering the meat department. Let's mosey on over to the meat department real slow. Yeah! I can see through the glass in the doors that it goes clear back to the outer wall of the stock room. The refrigeration room must be outside t on the other side of that wall."

"Jeffie! Look! A wallet on the floor!"

"Grab it quick, Dumbass, and give it to me."

Less than a minute later an old woman came by asking everyone if they saw her wallet.

"I had it in my buggy and it must have slipped out."

"No, lady, we ain't seen one, but if we do, we'll be sure to tell you."

"Oh, thank you! I just cashed my Social Security check and won't get any more money until after the fifth of next month."

After she left, Jeffie looked through the wallet and said, "Tough stuff, lady. We need it more than you. Man, there's about $750 here." He put the money in his pocket and threw the wallet behind some canned goods.

"Finders keepers, losers weepers," chanted a grinning Reb.

"Okay, let's get some donuts and check out where they keep the pantyhose. We gotta get something to give the girls when we celebrate pulling off this job."

They found the nylons, went through the checkout, and out to Reb's truck to eat the donuts, drink a beer, and look at the newspaper.

"Well, Reb, you can cross off a few more queers. We really did some damage last night!"

"I, ah, wanna do it again! Ah, Jeffie, don't let me forget to get some good chewing tobacco tonight."

When they were done, the boys drove around the back of the store and parked the truck so no one could see the Georgia plates. Jones Construction signs were quickly put on the truck doors. They changed into a suit and coveralls. On went the hard hats and Reb carried a large pair of bolt cutters and a new lock. While Jeffie played lookout, Reb cut the lock on the door to the refrigeration room, and then quickly put the bolt cutters back in the truck. Jeffie had on his white hardhat and clipboard, so when a car came around the corner, the man waived at them. He parked about a hundred feet away and went in the back door of one of the row of stores beside Maxie Market. Jeffie shined his flashlight in the refrigeration room, saw the cement block wall, and nodded to Reb. They went back out, and Reb locked the door with his new lock, to which Jeffie had the key. They got into the truck and left, with smiles on both of their faces. Now, to find a nice new van.

* * *

Pat got to the hospital at about 5:15. He grabbed a six-pack of Hershey Bars, and went up to the waiting room.

I could never be a doctor because I could never get past the foreboding smell of a hospital. But then, I guess, jail smells are no better.

He gave Greg and Grace a big hug, and then hugged Eb and Kathy, who had just arrived.

It was time to see Shirley. There were flowers and get- well cards everywhere in her room.

Her face looked much better, although if you looked closely, you could see some bruises. Her eyes were still bandaged. She acted tired but gave them each a hug. When Pat's turn came, she wouldn't let him go. Neither of them wanted to let the other go, but finally they had to separate.

"Richie and my parents aren't here yet?" asked Pat.

"No, not yet," answered Greg.

"Listen, y'all! I got some good news from my doctors today. Because of the quick application of ice to my face by Nurse Bernice, they don't believe I'll have facial scarring!" said Shirley with a low strained voice. "Also, only a small chance of permanent eye damage.

"Great news, Honey," said Pat, and the others joined in with their congratulations.

"Now for some even better news! The Emory eye doctor thinks a cornea transplant will be successful. It could be done in about ten days, but I don't think Dr. Orhan will be available that quickly. Will he, Daddy?"

The whole room was lit up with excitement by that last announcement, and Greg had a hard time being heard. Finally they quieted down enough so that he could answer her.

"After talking with your doctors and with Dr. Orhan, your cornea transplant is scheduled for Friday, Feb. 20, pending available corneas at the eye bank. All of the doctors agree an extra two weeks won't hurt anything and most likely will benefit you by letting your burns heal a little longer. You are recovering much quicker than normal because of the quick action by Nurse Bernice."

Just then Richie and Pat's parents walked in laughing.

"What's so funny?" asked Shirley.

"As I was about to ask the Patton's where the room was, they were asking me the same thing. We both thought the other one knew the way around the hospital and did not realize who the other party was at the time. Anyway, we're old friends now, and the operation sounds good, Sis."

"How did you know?"

"We were standing outside the door and heard you, but didn't want to interrupt your little speech." Richie gave his sister a hug. Adam and Ethel were right behind him and introductions were made.

Richie was shaking hands with everyone. He looked like a younger copy of Greg.

"We ran a little late because we went to your house first. Renée let us in and was very helpful," said Adam.

The joyful visit went on until a nurse announced that Shirley needed to get some rest.

"How long will I be in here, Daddy?"

"If you keep this up, you can expect to go home Monday. Infection is something they are watching carefully. But you seem to be fine in that department. You also seem to be able to hear much better than last night."

"I never thought about it but I guess I can hear better."

Kathy spoke up. "Dr. Greg, can you explain what the cornea is and what we can expect? As Shirley's best friend for years now, you know how concerned I am, but not being a doctor like you, there's much I don't understand."

"Okay. Let's see if I can put my daughter's situation in layman's terms. The severity of the eye injury depends on the type of burn, duration of the burn, and the elapsed time before the initial treatment. Thank God for Nurse

Ahrens. Normally thermal burns are mild and when the eye is exposed to extreme heat, it reacts by blinking to protect the eye. In Shirley's case the extreme sudden impact of the bright light and heat, combined with the fact that somehow her eyes apparently stayed open too long, caused an unusual amount of trauma to the corneas. As a result, both eyes are opaque.

"The outside of the cornea has cells that regenerate but the inside has a finite number of cells that maintain clarity and do not regenerate. That is why she needs a cornea transplant.

"Because the cornea usually has no blood vessels in it, as contrasted to kidneys and lungs, there is little chance of the body rejecting it."

"Thank you, Dr. Greg, but how does she get new corneas? How long can they keep them in storage? How long does it take to recuperate?"

"Kathy, that's a lot of questions. In this country we are lucky to have an ample supply of people willing to donate to the Eye Bank. The donor corneas have to be harvested within 12 hours after death, and then they are examined under a powerful microscope. Also, blood from the donor is tested to see if the person had diseases, such as hepatitis. If okay, the cornea can be kept in cold storage for about a week and still be used. Donor age does not seem to make any difference so long as the corneas are healthy."

"What is the surgery like and how long will it take Shir to recover?" asked Pat .

"The patient is sedated and the eye and lids anesthetized locally. She will feel no pain.

"As far as rehabilitation is concerned, vision returns in incremental steps and it can take up to a year for complete recovery. Some recover much sooner, depending upon the patient and the circumstances."

"Wow. What an explanation," said Pat. "Now that I'm aware of the facts, I'm going to sign up to be a donor."

"Me, too!" echoed Kathy, as the rest of the group nodded their heads.

Everyone said their goodbyes and headed for the parking lot. Pat told them he would catch them in a few minutes as he wanted to stop to see Ed.

He was doing much better, but told Pat he wouldn't be released for another week because of his lung removal. He thanked Pat for stopping to see him, and Pat gave him a Hershey Bar and left.

They all went to the O'Kelly's house and talked for two hours, when everyone realized how tired they were. Greg told them that tonight was the end of the immediate family restrictions, and tomorrow would be a mad house as Judge Musselman, Chief Keefauver, Capt. Keller, Julie and Ralph, Rhonda, and a host of others would be headed for the hospital. Pat gave Greg his check from the insurance company and asked him to find a replacement for the Mustang.

Pat looked at Eb. "How did you and Kathy get in to see Shirley?"

"You didn't know I was Shirley's step-brother?" said Eb with a big smile.

"And I was Shirley's sister," said Kathy.

"I wouldn't put anything past you, Buddy! You're a bad influence on Kathy."

Pat got home late with plans to return to Greg's and visit with his parents and the O'Kelly's in the morning. Cold beer awaited Eb and the movers.

* * *

At 11:30, Jeffie, in a recently stolen Chevy van, watched the employees of the Maxie Market leave. After 15 minutes the manager and assistant manager left. A few minutes after midnight, Jeffie drove the van around back and parked with the back doors facing the refrigeration room. They put on masks for the benefit of possible security cameras. Reb placed the magnetic Maxie Market signs on the van doors.

The refrigeration room door was unlocked, and they threw the sledgehammer, chisel, and ladder inside. This place was always noisy due to several compressors and at least one running all the time to supply coolant to the many freezers throughout the store. The room reeked of compressor oil, which had a strange smell. Jeffie used a small penlight instead of the large flashlight. When a compressor ran, the fan opened up exhaust louvers in the outside wall and Jeffie was afraid the light might be seen from the outside.

"Reb, you start knocking out the wall, while I keep a lookout through the louvers." When they were open, ample light came in the room from an outside security light. Reb could see the wall well enough to pound on it with the sledgehammer. With each hit, cement blocks crumbled, and pieces flew everywhere. With the compressors cycling on and off, and Reb hitting the wall, Jeffie was sure everyone in Daytona could hear them.

"Reb! Headlights coming! Stop now!"

Slowly the headlights came around the corner and the beam from a five-cell flashlight searched the buildings. The light was coming from – a police car!

"Damn!" whispered Jeffie. "It's the cops."

He pulled out his .357 magnum and watched out the louvers. Jeffie had to duck once as the beam of light searched him out.

Officer Freddy Merritt drove very slowly in back of the stores while Officer Henry 'Big Dog' Mayes shined the light around. Mayes immediately became suspicious when he saw the van.

"Freddy, drive close to that van parked over by the market, but be careful 'cause I don't like the looks of this." He pulled the shotgun loose from its holder between the seats. They slowly approached the van when Officer Merritt let out a sigh of relief.

"It belongs to the Maxie Market! See the signs. Boy, am I glad, because I really don't need any trouble this close to getting out of the hospital," exclaimed Merritt with a sigh of relief.

"I'm not exactly ready for a shoot-out myself, but that's part of the job, too."

The police car went on down the row of back entrances and disappeared.

Reb was urinating in the corner of the refrigeration room. "Man, when that flashlight beam came in the louvers, ah, I about wet my pants, what with me armed with a sledgehammer. Ah, Jeffie, a gun next time?"

"We'll see. Now get back to work on the wall. You almost got the hole big enough for us to go through, but make sure you give us plenty of room to get the cigarettes out!" said Jeffie, who was not about to give a mental midget like Reb a gun.

A gun? Hell, he might just shoot himself, or worse — me!

Finally, the hole was large enough for them to pass through carrying large boxes. Jeffie went first and had to use his pen light to penetrate the eerie darkness of the stockroom. A faint light could be seen coming through the windows of the swinging doors leading into the meat department. The glow of the night light seemed to light the store up almost like a bright sunshiny day. The place was spooky! No people, no noise, and a feeling they were being watched by at least a hundred people who were outside, looking in the large windows.

"Let's hustle." Jeffie carried a six-foot aluminum stepladder with steps on both sides.

They quickly went through the meat department to the far right of the store, walking as close to the meat coolers as possible. He located the alarm beam sending unit between the vending machines and carefully put the ladder legs down so they straddled the beam. Up and over it they went, each steadying the ladder for the other. Jeffie carefully picked up the ladder and they moved down the long isle to the cigarettes. They dumped boxes of food to make empty boxes. While Reb packed cigarette cartons into the boxes, then boxes into shopping carts, Jeffie carefully placed the ladder over the second beam and quickly went over it. They were working as a precise team now, having done this several times in the Atlanta area. They both wore thin rubber gloves.

"Ah, Jeffie, ah, why are we just taking cigarettes?"

"Look, Dumbass, I told you before that for the size of the load, they bring more money than anything else we could steal. They are easy to sell and can't be traced."

"Jeffie, you're so smart!"

After loading all the unopened cartons, Jeffie grabbed two shopping carts and hurriedly took all of the loose cigarettes from the cashier's booths and threw them into the boxes in the shopping carts. He pushed carts back to the ladder and lifted the boxes over the ladder and into the arms of a waiting Reb, then quickly did the same with several more. He wanted to be away from those windows in the worst way!

After putting the loose packs of cigarettes in boxes, they loaded the boxes, and boxes containing cartons of cigarettes Reb had packed up into the shopping carts. Off they went down the aisle, pushing carts, and Jeffie also carrying the ladder under one arm. Again the ladder was placed over the meat counter alarm beam. Reb went over the ladder and received the boxes Jeffie handed him. Then Reb came back over the ladder and they raced down the aisle for another load. This process was repeated until they had over 1500 carton of cigarettes and a few hundred loose packs in boxes.

When all of the boxes were moved over the beam, Jeffie handed the carts to Reb. As Jeffie started back over the ladder, he told Reb he was going to get some nylon panty hose. Because he had previously checked out the location, Jeffie found them in short order, grabbed several dozen pair, and took off back to the ladder. Then it happened! He dropped one of the packs of nylons and it went through the alarm beam.

"Damn, damn, damn!" yelled Jeffie. "Quick, Reb, we gotta load this stuff and get the hell out of here."

All of the boxes were taken through the hole in the refrigeration room. Jeffie looked through the louvers, then went out and opened up the back of the van. Boxes of cigarettes went flying into the van. Then Jeffie quickly went back to the meat counter, grabbed a few boxes of T-Bone steaks, ran back, closed the doors, took off the Maxie Market signs from the van and quickly, but carefully, drove away. A few blocks away two police cars passed them going in the opposite direction, lights flashing, but no sirens. One contained Officer Freddy Merritt and Big Dog Mays.

"The silent alarm! We did trip it!" exclaimed Jeffie.

"Yeah, but, ah, we sure fooled 'em. Didn't we, Jeffie. Huh? Didn't we?"

"Yeah, we sure did!" laughed Jeffie, now that the pressure was off. "I shouldn't have gone back after those steaks. That could have gotten us caught. I'll know better next time! I would have liked to have seen the faces of the two cops we just passed? I'll bet they was the same cops that checked out the store."

"But you're so smart - - you got the steaks and we got away!" said Reb while clapping his hands.

When they got to Seal's place, he was waiting with another man. Twenty-five cartons were put into a box to pay for the worthless information they provided as to police rounds at the market. The remaining cartons were counted and the boys walked out with $5,825.00, plus a future share of the van sale. Jeffie threw in several T-Bone steaks, and a dozen pair of nylon panty hose. Seal was very pleased with that.

"Thanks for the steaks and hose. I'll settle up with you on the van as soon as I sell it. As I said, I'll give you 25%, and here's that magic white powder you wanted."

They shook hands and left in Reb's truck.

"Reb, not bad for one night's work.

"Now to a club and see if we can get us some poontang. With a little booze and what I got in my pocket, we're going to fly high tonight! Ah, hell, we gotta stop and get us some coolers and ice for them steaks or they'll thaw out."

They cut it close but managed to get to a club seven minutes before it closed at 2:00. Once in, the doors were locked they bought six beers each because the law prohibited all sales after 2:00. After a few beers and some magic white powder, they didn't care if the women were painted up and worn out.

CHAPTER 38

Burn, Baby, Burn

On Saturday, the 24th, Pat got up early, went jogging, lifted weights, took a shower and ate breakfast. Oh, how he missed Shirley being with him! Without her, he felt he was just going through the motions of life. At 9:00, Eb and the movers were to be there. Maybe he had a few minutes to call a blind client of his named Vera and ask about Braille. She answered on the third ring and they talked for about ten minutes when Eb and Kathy arrived. Vera only lived a block away from his route to get to the O'Kelly's house. Although Vera would not be home, she was going to leave an 8 ½ x 11 envelope packed with Braille information for Shirley on her porch. He thanked her and hung up.

Eb and Kathy arrived and they exchanged greetings. Pat saw Eb popping a top on one of the six packs. Pat showed him what had to be moved. Eb's bedroom would stay 'as is' because he and Kathy were moving in right after Pat moved completely out. Pat left them playing house, going from room to room planning where they would put the furniture from her apartment. As he was leaving, the phone rang.

"Hello."

"Good morning, this is the Chief."

"You working on a Saturday morning?"

"What do you mean? We public servants work all the time. Pat, Dixie Airlines sent us a picture of Jeffie. It's dated three years ago, but at least we now have an idea of what he looks like. I'll bring you a copy tonight when I visit

Shirley in the hospital. Jeffie worries me because I don't want to bury another one of my officers like I had to when we were trying to apprehend his brother, Skinny. I also don't want to bury you or Shirley."

"I agree, and thank you. Chief, getting the picture is a break."

"Just a second, Capt. Keller wants to talk to you."

"Hi, Pat!"

"What? Another public servant working on a Saturday?"

"Just keep it up and I'll withhold the information I was going, past tense, was going to give you!"

"You win, Capt. With the huge salary you're receiving from the county, I guess I should have expected you to be working today."

"I'm not sure that was what I wanted to hear, but – being the great public servant that I am, plus a nice guy, I will go on."

"Thank you, oh great protector of the people.

"Seriously now, there was something bothering me about the two car bombs. I told you that."

"Yes," said Pat, with sudden interest.

"I found out from a call to Daytona, that, here in Jonesboro with Shirley and with the doctor in Daytona, witnesses are giving the same general description of the bombers! They were two big white men wearing coveralls, both big, but one much bigger than the other."

"But, Capt., the distance?"

"I know, but it bothers me. Something else. Early this morning the Maxie Market in Daytona was hit to the tune of 1,500 to 2,000 cartons of cigarettes, a bunch of steaks, and they are not sure what else. Yesterday afternoon, one of the store owners of a shop four doors down from Maxie, saw two guys going into the refrigeration room. That's where they broke through the wall. Anyway, he saw two men in hard hats. One looked like a boss with a white hard hat and a clip board. The other one also wore a hard hat, but he couldn't be sure of the color. When Daytona Beach PD asked him to describe them, guess what he said."

"Two big men, one even bigger than the other one."

"Bingo! See why all of this is bothering me? Just little things, but they add up. Daytona never has had a car bombing, and it has been over a year since a grocery store has been burglarized. It was professionally done. The doctor, except for being gay, was known as a good guy. No known enemies. Looks like an indiscriminate act aimed at homosexuals in general, rather than the doctor himself. Lt. Crawford tells me Atlanta had several similar grocery store robberies where cigarettes were taken."

"Is it possible the guys who bombed Shirley were pissed off at the results, go to Daytona and bomb somebody else for practice, to perfect their art of car bombing? Could anyone be that cold?" asked Pat with disgust and bewilderment in his voice.

"Now you're thinking like a cop. There are people out there like that, you know, people who have no respect for other people's property, or life. The type, who has no conscience, would murder a human being, and then make a sandwich in the victim's kitchen."

"Sounds like you're talking about brother Skinny. How can you catch them?"

"Right now we have no proof, but fingers are pointing to the two confederates who left town a few days ago. I don't understand why their trailer and car were destroyed, or who could have done it. I'm also wondering if Jeffie was one of them."

"I can't figure out that one either. So, what do you do now, especially if Jeffie is one of them?"

"We watch them when they come back. We also watch the Confederates. Right now we're getting all the info we can on the club, and I have my men calling in all markers from their snitches. Lt. Crawford is also helping us, with the blessing of his boss, Capt. Tomble."

"I guess Daytona wants these guys as bad as we do."

"You guessed right, and the Chief has sent Daytona PD all information he thinks might help them catch these guys. But, even if one of them were Jeffie, we can't prove a thing. If what we suspect is true, we have some real bad boys on our hands!"

"What else could you expect from one of Skinny's brothers?"

"Not much else, I guess."

"Be careful, Pat. Remember, they were out of town when that arrow was shot at you!"

"More Confederates?"

"Could be."

"Anything else on Mr. Clean? You know, the disinfectant killer?"

"No, he must be laying low for awhile, but that is exactly the kind of mentality I'm talking about. Our shrinks think this guy is having fun killing people. A real sicko. I got to go. Again, be careful!"

"Bye, Capt., and – thanks!"

As he was getting off of the phone, Eb tried to talk Pat into a quick diamond number.

"Eb, how about another time? I have a lot on my mind right now."

"Then a Diamond or redneck number is what you need to take your mind off things."

Pat caved to Eb's wishes. Kathy had never seen this so Eb had her pick a number with a female name. She chose Bertha Lincoln, and Eb dialed the number. She stayed right beside Eb while Pat went to the extension phone. Eb signaled for Pat to pick up the phone.

"Hello, dis here be Bertha speaking," said a black female voice, with the sound of a big woman.

"Bertha, honey, dis here be your very lucky day," said Eb in his best black voice. "I knows dat you received yo complimentary copy of 'Black Beauty Today' dat we has sent you, what has all of de latest beauty tips, and what de brothers is sayin' 'bout de sisters and what de sisters be sayin' 'bout de brothers. Dis be de one and only Tyrone Thesbit Torpedo, calling you from Hollywood, California!"

"Ah, ah, I don't knows what to say. I ain't never talked to no real live Hollywood magazine man before."

'Well, Bertha, honey, dis really be your lucky day! Say, baby, how would you like to be winnin' a all-expense-paid trip to Hollywood, wa-a-a-y out here in California?"

"Sure, well, ah, yeah, I'd like dat!"

"See, it works like dis. We be taken a sex survey from our readers. We be talkin' to 25 women from 'round de country, and one of dem is gonna win dis trip. And since I really likes yo voice, I can puts you on de inside track. Get me, Honey?"

"Well, well, y-e-s," said Bertha.

"Now just fer answering my questions, you be gettin' a year's subscription to 'Black Beauty Today', and yo name gonna be in it as one of de coolest sisters in Atlanta! We be puttin' yo picture on de front cover and all, when you win! Also, you be gettin' a year's supply of Tyrone's Treacherous Taxidermy Beauty Cream. One application and you be a trophy fer any man! How 'bout it, Bertha? Is you ready fer de questions?"

"Ah, ah, I guess so. I's so excited I's don't know what to say. Do I really has a chance to go way out der to Hollywood."

"If I can get you out here, Honey, is you willing to stay in old Tyrone's pad?"

"Why, sure, Tyrone."

"And do whatever old Tyrone tells you to do?"

"Anything?"

"Like I said, Baby, you'se gots de inside track!"

"I's so excited! I's do anything what you wants."

"First question. How many sex partners has you had in de past year?"

"Well, let's me see. Der was de meter reader. I's don't knows his name. My mechanic, Tyrell, de post man, Spook, den der was dat cop so's I wouldn't get no ticket. Den de school principal, my very own Preacher Gustavious, and, of course, Brother Turnipseed. Ah, ah, does I has to tell de last one?"

"Bertha, Honey, you knows dat you has to."

"Ah, ah, okay, it – it be sister Freeman."

"So you'se likes de ladies, too?"

"Well, not like I'd like you, Tyrone, but I guess I does."

"Second and last question. What would get you turned on de most? Doing it in bed, on de sofa, in de car, at de drive-in, in an elevator, in an airplane, on de boss's desk, or on an ironing board?"

"Ironing board! What! I gots a friend named DeOmni who told me dat some Alawishis dude was supposed to do her on an ironing board and he never showed up. She done called Dr. Calhoon's office and der not be no Alawishis, and she didn't have no gizzard trouble neither!" said Bertha, getting louder and louder. "And I don't think you be from no magazine no how, and if you show up here, I'll tie dat thing in knots so's it be lookin' like a pretzel! Bye!" said Bertha as she slammed down the phone.

They all broke out in uncontrolled laughter.

"Well, Eb, I guess you sure told her, didn't you?"

"A pretzel? You poor thing! You have to take better care of it than that!" said Kathy, still laughing.

"I'll never look at a pretzel the same way again!" said Eb with a big sheepish grin.

"Eb, you're nuts!" said Kathy.

"Look, here come the movers! I've got to move my car and get out of here, but I have to admit I had to laugh when Bertha told you off."

Pat left, stopped by Vera's house to pick up the Braille information, and then headed for the O'Kelly's. He spent the morning with them and his parents. Everyone got along fine, and Richie turned out to be a very likeable person. They joked and told stories and everyone had a great time. Grace fixed a wonderful lunch, with the help of Ethel, Pat's mother. Pat's father, Adam, and Greg talked fishing, and after lunch the guys walked down to see Greg's classic car collection, while the ladies talked about the upcoming wedding, and got to do the dishes.

They decided to have an early supper at Jerome and Mickeys and then spend the evening at the hospital with Shirley. Pat called home several times to check on the move, and the hospital to check on Shirley. He was not able to reach Eb until after lunch. He and Kathy had been back and forth between the two houses and were just leaving for the second time. Pat invited them to meet him at Jerome and Mickey's, and he would pick up the tab. Then they would have to go over to Shirley's apartment to load up there. Her apartment probably would also take two trips. Shirley would be out of the hospital soon, and they could supervise the rest of the move. Company would be gone by then, too. The trial would also be over, and hopefully the press would leave him alone, although he knew they would be swarming around the Dope Fairy Trial.

The older folks took a half-hour nap, while Pat and Richie looked over the Braille packet Vera had given Pat. They discovered that a Frenchman, Louie Braille, invented the system around 1824 when he was only 16 years old, and then he developed it into the form used today. Louie had an accident and was blinded at age 3.

Pat learned it uses *cells*, which can consist of up to six raised dots in a vertical rectangle, with a row of three dots beside another row of three dots, like two traffic lights side by side. The alphabet consists of using one or more raised dots in a cell to stand for each letter of the alphabet. Writing in Braille takes up a lot of room on paper, so to reduce the amount of paper used, and time to type out a sentence in Braille, short cuts are used. Some letters stand for whole words. Some cells have meanings totally unknown in English, like a symbol that means the first letter in the next word is capitalized. Even more confusing is the use of cells that are not letters, but stand for certain commonly used words, like *for, and, of, the,* and *with.*

"In addition to that, Richie, symbols or cells signify punctuation - - a period, apostrophe, comma, and so on," stated Pat.

"I never knew this stuff was so complicated. Try to read the raised dots with your finger on this sample. In theory it sounds simple, but, in practice, I find it extremely difficult," said Richie, as he passed Pat a sheet of thick Braille paper with a message typed in Braille.

"I see what you mean. This must take hundreds of hours of practice to learn. I'll never look at Braille the same way again, and pray Shirley won't have to depend on this stuff to read."

"Me, too. Sis has been through a lot."

"Look at what a Braille typewriter looks like." Pat showed him a picture of one with arrows pointing to various parts of it, along with an explanation of what that part does. Only six keys correspond to the six dots in a cell. They do what the 26 letter keys do on a regular typewriter, plus a whole lot more. Then there is a line space key, backspace key, space bar, and carriage return. And – that's it! Amazing! You punch up to six keys at one time."

Before they knew it, everyone was up and getting ready to go to supper. Greg drove his van so they could all go together.

They got to Jerome and Mickey's before the big Saturday night crowd, but it was still busy. They were greeted by both Jerome, who walked with a cane and talked everyone's leg off, and Mickey who talked, and then flew back and forth from the customers to the kitchen, which he supervised. Mickey was thin, had boundless energy, and considered the kitchen to be his kingdom.

Everyone was seated and soon Willie the Waiter came prissing over to their table.

"Good evening, Mr. Patton, and Mr. and Mrs. O'Kelly. Let me s-a-y how s-o-r-r-y I was to hear about poor Miss Shirley," said a very sincere and animated Willie as he put both of his hands to his face to hide a tear in his eye. Shirley had received flowers from him.

Pat introduced his parents and Richie. They thanked him for his concern and, as he took their order, Eb and Kathy came in. They were invited to sit with the O'Kelly group so Willie quickly slid another table beside theirs.

"Hey, Willie. I talked to a friend of yours who said to say hello when I saw you. Do you know a person by the name of Brown Sugar?" asked Eb.

That threw Willie for a few seconds. He recovered and said, "What did this – this – this – Brown Sugar s-a-a-y?"

"Something about a man and a pickup at a bowling alley, or wait a minute," said Eb playing like he was thinking. "It was behind the bowling alley."

""Oh! Thank you," said Willie in a huff, muttering to himself, as he hurried away.

"Eb, you should be ashamed of yourself," chastised Pat.

The meal was good as always, Willie's service was excellent, and everyone enjoyed the company. Then they headed for the hospital. They got there right at six and the place was crawling with visitors to see Shirley. Judge Musselman, Dottie, Capt. Keller, Chief Keefauver and wife Pat, the four reporters Sandi, Zel, Steve and Viv, Herb, Julie and Ralph, Rhonda, and many more, including strangers who had read about her injury in the newspaper. Then DA Colver came in with Nancy Katman and several members of the district attorney's office and the police department. What a zoo, but a very nice zoo! Soon there was no place to sit down.

The head nurse on duty, Bernice Ahrens, and the one at the scene of the accident, made sure the family got in first. Pat and Shirley held on to each other as long as they could, then it was time for Pat to go. Shirley was looking much better and expected to go home on Monday. Pat agreed with Greg and Grace that Shirley needed to stay with them for a few days, because Pat would be busy with the Dope Fairy Case.

Capt. Keller and Chief Keefauver were going in to see Shirley as Pat was coming out. The Chief stopped him for a minute and handed him a picture of Jeffie, along with a description sheet.

Pat sat down to absorb the information. Jeffie would now be 40 years old. The sheet said he weighed 185 pounds and was 5' 11". In the picture he had a smirk on his average face. His teeth seemed stained from smoking, chewing, or both. He was a weight lifter, had a 120 IQ, and there were no visible facial hair or scars. He had worked at Dixie Airlines and Southern Airways as a mechanic.

After seeing Shirley, the Chief said he had talked to a supervisor who described Jeffie as a know-it-all, and a few days after he was fired for fighting, the supervisor's car tires were slashed. Jeffie was the prime suspect but there were no witnesses.

"That's your copy," said the Chief, as Pat started to hand it back. "I have a feeling Jeffie is even bigger than the airline ID stated."

"I really appreciate this. I'll show it to Sh . . ." Pat stopped when he realized what he said. A tear was in his eye.

"I know, but in a few weeks she will see again. By the way, Mr. Clean is at it again in Atlanta. Last night they found a rich Jewish couple, shot to death in their Mercedes, which was parked on a side street. Their bodies were sprayed with disinfectant, so it's either him or a copycat."

"Small caliber gun?"

"You got it. A .22 caliber bullet did the job. We also suspect a silencer is being used."

"If that's so, it precludes a revolver, as silencers don't work well on them. A .22 automatic with a silencer then?" That's an assassin's weapon of choice. Quiet, yet very deadly."

"Very good! You know your firearms. The Atlanta Police Department is coming to the same conclusion. The murder count is now up to six, with four in two days. By the way, Ralph got his promotion."

"Speaking of Ralph, here he is with my favorite secretary, Julie." She gave him a big hug.

"Congratulations, Lt. Ralph!"

"Thanks, Pat. How is she?"

"Looking much better, thank you. Check this out you two." Pat showed them the picture of Jeffie along with the description. "She's up and walking now with help, not because she is weak, but because she can't see."

"Can you get me one of these, Chief?" asked Ralph.

"Already in the mail."

They talked a few minutes and then Pat left to find his father talking to Greg, and his mother talking to Grace at the far end of the waiting room. As he was making his way over to them, Pat got stopped by his favorite four reporters, Sandi, Zel, Steve, and Viv.

"Mr. Patton, a few questions, please?" asked Sandi.

"No questions, but Shirley has agreed to see all of you for a few minutes at the end, so sit tight. Nurse Ahrens is in charge and will see to it that you get the last five minutes or so without being interrupted." The cameras rolled anyway.

Pat said his goodbyes and went home to a very lonely house.

* * *

Sunday morning was the 24th and they all gathered in the O'Kelly's kitchen and ate blueberry pancakes and sausage prepared by Grace. Then it was off to church, which helped all of them. After lunch at the Happy Hog BBQ, they met Eb and Kathy at the new house, where they had done a great job putting furniture in place. Pat felt the arrangement would be fine while they got settled.

"This place is beautiful," complemented Ethel, "especially the kitchen."

"I prefer a shady spot by the pool with lots of bikinis!" winked Adam.

"Why you old buzzard!" said Greg, "You're a man after my own heart!"

Both Grace and Ethel gave them pretended dirty looks and snickered.

Soon, they were off to see Shirley again.

* * *

"You're looking really good, Honey! I know you want to get out of here!" comforted Pat.

"The doctors here and the Emery doctor confirmed I would leave tomorrow. "Honey, I want you to prepare for that trial. Momma and I have been talking on the phone and they want you to spend the next week at their house with me while I get used to walking around. We can move into our new house next week when everything is moved there. Daddy said you can use his study for trial preparation."

"Wow! What gracious people you have for parents. It sounds good to me. I'll load everything up tomorrow and take it to your parent's house and prepare for the trial there. I love you, Shir!"

"And I love you, too, Honey."

* * *

Sunday afternoon Jeffie and Reb got back to Scorpie's house. They were both happy, but hung over.

"Hey, man," said Scorpie with a beer in his hand, "I've been looking for you since yesterday. A guy called Yanker says you need to call him about something very important."

Jeffie went right to the phone and luck was with him - - he got Yanker on the first try.

"Yeah, whatdoyawant?" answered Yanker.

"Hey, this is Jeffie. You have some important news for me?"

"Right, man. Look, I can't believe this myself, except I seen it with my own eyeballs!"

"Come on, Yanker, spit it out."

"Man, like, Reb's place got burned to the ground. Nothing left, man, just ashes! I heard the cops don't think it was no accident."

"Damn, that's terrible! I had some of my stuff stashed there. Who did it? The Ringtails?"

"They don't know, man, but no, not them Ringtails. That club wouldn't have the guts to do something like that. They jus' ride their scooters around acting bad, but they don't bother any of the other clubs. We talked to members of the Iron Fist, and the Copperheads, but nobody don't know nothin'. The news reported a slight built man dressed in black was seen leaving after the fire was started. Don't sound like no biker."

"Look, man, how about you checking on my place and make sure it's okay? We'll leave for home in the morning."

"Ah, Jeffie, that ain't all. That pretty Camaro you parked there. Well, ah, someone broke out all of the windows and put big dents in almost all of the body panels. And – it rained that night."

"Damn! Damn! Damn! I'll find 'em and I'll kill 'em! They ain't gonna get away with this! See you tomorrow night. Bye!" Jeffie's face was red with rage.

"Damn, I'll kill 'em! I'll find out who they are and I'll kill 'em!" reiterated Jeffie, pounding his hand on the table.

"What, ah, happened, Jeffie? Huh, Jeffie?"

"Reb, some low-life S.O.B. smashed up my Camaro and burnt down your trailer!"

"Jeffie, I'll help you find 'em and kill 'em! We'll get 'em, won't we, Jeffie. Kill 'em good, too!"

"Damn right we will!"

He told Scorpie what happened and had Reb get the steaks out of the truck. He also gave Scorpie a few pair of nylon panty hose, and $100. They would leave the next morning and find out who did it. In the meantime they would enjoy a steak dinner, feeling great knowing they had their wicks dipped last night and had $5,452 in their pockets.

CHAPTER 39

The Drug Fairy Trial

Pat got up feeling very excited. Shirley was getting out of the hospital today. Out of respect for the O'Kelly's, he would not sleep with her. If he could get Shirley situated, the trial and the move over, maybe he would have time to think about who was after them and why. Pat had been in the news enough that there was a possibility it was not Jeffie. He had to be able to think clearly, but with everything going on, how could he? Who burnt down the trailer, beat up the car? Who ran down Ed? Why? His brain was numb! Would Shirley see again? How would the Dope Fairy trial come out?

If I can somehow get through this next week without ....

Then it dawned on him! Without getting himself killed! This was most likely Skinny's brother, Jeffie. Skinny, all over again. Somebody was out there somewhere, waiting for him to make a mistake. He would be sure to be armed at all times. And Shirley, what could she do, with no eyesight, if someone came after her? He just wanted to get Shirley, find a cave somewhere, and hide!

He called Julie and told her he was going to the O'Kelly's house to see his parents and Richie off. After that he would come into the office if time permitted. He was due at the hospital at 2:00, as Shirley would be released then. This day would be semi-wasted as far as his law office was concerned, but he would spend all day Tuesday on the trial. He was almost ready, but needed to go over some loose ends. Pat had no witnesses, except for his own client. He had to see Louie Lake, and do the habeas for Ed. His mind was swimming and his head pounding.

Grace said breakfast would be served at 9:00 and it was now 8:30. He had packed a suitcase and suit bag the night before, so he put them into the trunk of Shirley's car, and took three aspirins. He had to think straight because his very life depended upon it.

I sure do miss both of my Mustangs.

Pat pulled around back of the O'Kelly's house and used a key they had given him to let himself in. He felt like a real member of the family now. Pat greeted everyone and sat down at the table. Again, Grace outdid herself. What a breakfast! The aroma of the omelets and bacon was overwhelming good. The Texas Toast was brown with honey and butter melted on top. Also included was a large glass of fresh-squeezed orange juice and coffee. His head felt better already.

There were the usual sad good-byes, come-again-soons, and calls of drive safely, with lots of hugs and kisses. His mother and father left about 11:00 for Charleston and Richie left soon thereafter. Pat called Julie to tell her he wouldn't be in at all, or tomorrow either because he was spending the day at the O'Kelly's working on the Tidwell trial, then Wednesday he would be gone all day at the trial, which would be a real circus with all of the news media. He never had given them a story on the arrow, so that was bound to come up, too. Julie had told them she was driving along and an arrow came flying through the window. That was all she knew. Ralph had told her to downplay it so the story would blow over quickly. He didn't want her exposed to the forces out to get Pat. It's a wonder he didn't put pressure on her to quit her job. After all, it was attempted murder. Pat got organized at Greg's desk and started working on the trial.

Pat felt much better as he could see things getting done, such as seeing his parents and Richie off. He was about to get Shirley home, and Wednesday afternoon the trial should be over. With Tidwell as his only witness, the trial shouldn't last over a day. He expected the DA to grandstand, because of the media exposure, which could make it last a little longer.

They left for the hospital in Greg's van because it had more room for Shirley to stretch out.

"Son, I got a deal working on another car for you. I understand Feb. 9th is your birthday and I told them I had to have it by then. It's a little different, but I think you're going to like it."

"Different? How?"

"Can't tell you. It's a surprise."

It was good to see Greg smile. They all were in good moods now that Shirley was coming home. Grace was visibly excited as they went up the elevator to Shirley's room. When they got there, she was already dressed, radiating beauty and charm even here, and her suitcase was packed. Grace and Greg gave her hugs, but she clung to Pat and never wanted to let go. Except for the eye bandages, she really looked good.

"I missed you so! I love you so! I want you so! Did you ever do it with a blind girl?" whispered Shirley in Pat's ear.

That cracked him up. "I'm not believing you said that."

"What did she say that was so funny?" asked Grace.

"I'll never tell," said Pat, "but you sure did raise a naughty girl." That broke all of them up.

"Bye the way, I love you, too," Pat gave her a big kiss and two nurses standing in the doorway began to clap.

Shirley was given a pair of dark glasses to wear over her bandages, which were coming off soon. They gave her eye drops and ointment to take along and directions for their use.

On the way home, they went through the drive-in lane of the Flying Buzzard to get a takeout order. Shirley had heard all of them talking about the buzzard sandwiches, so she had to try one.

"Hospital food, ugh, buzzard sandwich, yum!" Then after thinking for a few seconds, she said, "I sure hope the buzzard part was a joke!"

"Hey, Pat, see any in the sky," asked Greg.

"Not a one."

"Me neither," said Grace. They all felt good to laugh again.

When they got home, Shirley spent about an hour, lying on the couch with her head on Pat's lap. They talked about a lot of things, including the Braille packet Pat got for her.

"When I get my sight back, I want to study Braille and volunteer to help blind people. I can now relate to how they feel. I know I'm not helpless, but I could easily feel that way."

"That's fine with me, Shir." Pat rubbed the back of her neck, and whispered, "I could really get turned on, seeing you laying there helpless and all."

"Wait until Momma and Daddy leave and I'll use my female radar to seek you out."

That's the way the rest of the day went except Greg and Grace joined them and did not leave.

* * *

Jeffie and Reb got up at 6:00 and loaded the bikes onto the truck. They said goodbye to Scorpie, and Jeffie decided to give him another hundred in case they needed a place to hide out in the future. Several times, Scorpie told them to come back anytime.

Not bad, thought Scorpie. *Five nights, and them hardly ever here. I got $200, T-bone steaks, and enough panty hose to make all my girlfriends smile.*

They ate breakfast at McDonalds, gassed up, and took off up A1A as far as Jacksonville, because they liked the ocean drive. The sea had a bluish-green cast, and the sun glistened on the ocean's white caps. Seagulls and pelicans seemed to float through the blue sky with outstretched wings, while distant boats bobbed on the water.

By going this picturesque route, they reached Jacksonville at lunch time. Then they stopped for a beer at the Seaweed, where they could fellowship with members of the Hitler's Henchmen M/C Club. This was the same bar

Pat, Sam, and Nancy had stopped at ten days earlier. Der Fuhrer had a day off, but most of them were at work.

Der Fuhrer worked for a collection agency and was very successful at collecting debts. He would simply grab the persons by the shirt, lift him or her up to his eye level, tell them they needed to pay up, and let them down with an evil smile. You better believe they paid up.

They hit the Georgia line at 8:30, tired and half-drunk from their stop at the Seaweed and the six-pack they got to go. They decided to stop at Valdosta for supper, a good night's rest, and get to the Atlanta area during daylight hours, when they could survey the damage to their property.

"Reb, we're going to find them! And when we do, they will beg us to kill them to stop the pain!"

"Yeah, ah, Jeffie. I wanna help! I wanna hurt them, too!"

* * *

Tuesday morning, Pat woke at 6:00 feeling disoriented until he realized he was in one of the O'Kelly's guest rooms. He put on a sweatsuit, used the bathroom, and brushed his teeth. No one appeared to be up, so he left a note on the kitchen table and went for a 30-minute jog. It was cool, so he had put on a 3rd sweatshirt and wore a hat and gloves. After a few minutes of jogging, he felt comfortable.

Pat felt so alive when he was out on the road jogging on a cool crisp morning! The sun was coming up, the birds were, and he didn't have a care in the ... "Then it hit him! I just left a completely defenseless lady who I dearly love to go out on a dark morning for a jog! Unarmed!"

How could I do something that stupid! I need to be aware of every person in every yard and every car on the road. I know this is a gated community, but it's possible Jeffie or one of his men could find a way past the guard. In the future, I need to be more careful and make sure I'm armed. I need to step up my speed and get back to the house!

Grace had breakfast ready and Shirley was up and sitting at the table. Shirley always looked good to him. She refused to have the loss of her eyesight get her depressed and her upbeat personality and radiant smile made her all the more beautiful. Each day her face looked better, fairly normal now, and there would be no scarring.

After breakfast he told her about the arrow and what the police were thinking about her bomb and the car bombing in Daytona. He needed her to be aware of the ever-present danger. That's when she decided to keep her .38 with her at all times. They took the cylinder out of it so she couldn't possibly shoot anyone, and Shirley practiced pointing it at sounds Pat deliberately made in the room. When she was pointing it wrong, he would correct her with a "little to your right or left."

Pat also informed Greg and Grace of all developments so they could protect themselves. Greg started to carry his 9mm automatic. The rest of the day was spent working on the Dope Fairy Case.

Julie called and told him Charlotte had left a message that she would be in Orlando taking in the Disney attractions for the next week. She left Pat her motel phone number.

"Well, at least someone's having fun," said Pat.

"I'm glad, Boss, but you and Shirley will be in Hawaii in no time flat, taking in all the sights. And I do mean sights, because I know the good Lord will restore Shirley's vision."

"Thank you, Julie. If I can get this trial behind me tomorrow, maybe I can concentrate on Jeffie and the rest of our move. Please be careful, because whoever is after me could go after the office."

"Geez, Boss, that's a comforting thought. Ralph insisted on getting me a pistol permit, and I got a snub-nose .38 Colt Cobra in my pocketbook. If a .38 is good enough for Shirley, it's good enough for me."

"You might want to put it on your desk and cover it with a magazine."

"Good idea, Boss."

"Did you practice?"

"Sure. Ralph took me to the range and I can do pretty good up to about two car lengths away, but after that, forget it!"

"Don't feel bad, because that is all that type of gun is designed for anyway. If you can hit a target the size of a man across a room, you're doing fine."

"That's what Ralph says, but I guess I'm expecting too much. Too many westerns under my belt. How about you? I sure hope you're packing that .357 Magnum. Ralph has been teaching me gun lingo. Anyway, are you packing?"

"Sure am, and the judges are letting me take it into the courthouse, but I have to check it with security and pick it up when I leave. At least I'm not unarmed when I go to the parking lot. Before I forget, if Rhonda is able to cover for you after 11:00 tomorrow, you can go over to the courthouse and watch the trial. You may catch jury selection being finalized, but what would interest you most would be the start of the trial."

"Thanks, Boss, I'd like that. I'll talk to Rhonda. Got to go catch the other line. Bye."

"See you tomorrow."

That evening Pat and Shirley relaxed on the sofa watching an early movie which Greg had raved about. It had come out the previous year and neither had seen it. Raging Bull, starring Robert DeNiro, was the story of boxing's middle-weight champ, Jake LaMotta. Pat cuddled Shirley who could only listen to the soundtrack, while, much to his surprise, Greg did the same thing with Grace on the other sofa. When the movie was over, he went to bed in the guest room, but pre-trial jitters prevented him from immediate sleep.

* * *

Pat had set his clock for 5:30. He ate breakfast, and got ready for trial by going over his opening statements and closing arguments with Shirley as his audience. She wanted so much to be in the courtroom with him, but only a week had passed since she was admitted to the hospital.

"Take care, Shir." Pat kissed her goodbye. He gave Grace a hug and shook Greg's hand as he, too, was leaving to get back to his office.

Doctors make a lot of money, but they work hard and put in a lot of hours, not to mention the cost and time for medical school.

He arrived at the courthouse at 7:30. Not only were Sandi, Zel, Viv and Steve waiting in the parking lot, but also two other Atlanta TV trucks as well as Brian Sistrunk, a new reporter from the major Atlanta newspaper. They swarmed him and all started talking at once. Two uniformed police officers were present.

"Ladies! Ladies! Gentlemen! Please. Quiet.

"The only thing I have to say about today's proceeding is I am here to get my client a fair trial. I will do all I can to show the jury Ms. Tidwell is a victim and not a criminal. As you are all aware, I am very limited as to what I say until after this trial is over, as I, in no way, wish to jeopardize my client's case."

"Do you have a comment about the recent attempt on your life, namely the arrow that barely missed you?" asked Sandi of WHIT radio.

"We are dealing with a coward, or cowards, who sneak around planting bombs. Last Wednesday, someone put a bomb in my car and got Shirley O'Kelly instead. They blinded a beautiful girl and my future wife. The very next day some coward, maybe the same one, took a shot at me with a bow and arrow. It just missed me, but, in addition, put my secretary in grave danger because she was driving. The arrow also hit another car. What if it had hit some innocent person or child? Whoever is doing this needs to be put away for a long time! The Police Department, under the able leadership of Chief Keefauver, is doing all they can, but if someone out there knows something which might help catch this monster or monsters, please notify the police. I have to go now to talk to my client. Thank you."

Pat made his way into the courthouse, checked his .357 Magnum, and went up to Judge Musselman's courtroom. He set up his briefcase and trial folders on the defense table and then made his way to the holding cell to see Tidwell. She was stone-faced while he went over things she could expect to hear at the trial and the order of events as they would take place. He also reminded her to show feelings of outrage when she testified and never to volunteer information under cross-examination. She was clearly not happy to see him, so he left and went back to the courtroom.

Shortly the judge came in and the case was called for trial. DA Colver was shaking everyone's hand, with a big smile on his face, trying to line up votes for the next election.

Pat and the DA had a jury picked in about 2½ hours - - seven women and five men. The judge called for a 15-minute recess before the start of the trial. Both Pat and DA Colver left to stretch their legs and returned at the appointed time.

"Are you ready for the State, Mr. Colver?"

"Yes, Sir."

"And, Mr. Patton, are you ready for the defense?"

"Yes, Sir."

The judge explained to the jury that opening statements were not evidence and were used so each side could tell what they expected to prove during the trial.

"Very well, Mr. Colver, you may proceed with your opening statements."

"Ladies and gentlemen of the jury, Judge Musselman, and Mr. Patton. My name is Dean Colver and I am the District Attorney of Clayton County and will be prosecuting this case. I know you are all busy people, so I will be as brief as possible so you can return back to your families. We expect to show you that the defendant, Ms. LaShandra Tidwell, blatantly brought into this country over 20 pounds of high-grade marijuana from Jamaica on Jan. 8, 1981. This happened in the part of the Atlanta airport that is located in Clayton, County.

"Now, I promise you will hear a clever story from the defense, but the fact remains that we found sheets of marijuana fitted between the liner and the outside walls of a suitcase with her name on it. We will show you this was not someone else's suitcase as the defense might lead you to believe. It was checked in at Jamaica, picked up in

Atlanta, and it had her personal belongings in it! Her name tag was on it, her baggage claim slip was on it, her finger prints were on it, and a toothbrush bag with her name on it was found in the suitcase!

"Ladies and gentlemen, this is not a complicated case. I contend she was caught with her hand in the cookie jar! The dope was there and it certainly was not put there by the Dope Fairy!"

This last statement received the positive reaction from the jury that Colver wanted, as some of the jurors were nodding their heads *yes*.

"You will hear from Agent Jeffrey Griffin of the Drug Enforcement Administration, or DEA if you will, who will testify as to the procedures they used to find these drugs. You will also hear from Officer Greg Crumbly, who was the arresting officer, and last, but not least, Ms. Tootsie Upchurch, a long-time lab technician at the Georgia Bureau of Investigation, or GBI if you will, who will testify that, according to her analysis, the substance was indeed marijuana."

DA Colver went on for a few more minutes about how the State would prove Ms. Tidwell was guilty. As he sat down, Dottie came in behind the judge's chair and whispered something in his ear.

"Ladies and Gentlemen, something has come up that we need to take care of, so there will be a short recess. Bailiff, please show the jurors to the jury holding room. Let me caution you not to discuss this case among yourselves or anyone else until instructed by this court."

When they were gone, he called Pat and Dean up to his bench.

"Pat, I don't want to alarm you, but I think someone has taken a page out of Skinny's playbook. Dottie received a call from someone claiming to be a paramedic from the Jonesboro Ambulance Company saying Shirley fell down some stairs and is on the way to the hospital and not expected to live. Dottie called the O'Kelly's house, but the line was busy. Later it rang, and rang, but no one answered. She is having a patrol car sent to the house to check it out."

"Judge, I can't believe this is happening again!" exclaimed an exasperated and worried Pat. "I wish I knew who and why they are doing this to me."

"I'm sorry, Pat," said a sincere Dean Colver. "What a rotten thing to do! I'm sure it is a hoax, but I don't blame you for worrying because this announcement has had an effect on me, too. Shirley is a member of my staff."

"Thank you, Dean. I just want to hear that she is okay. Someone should be home."

Tidwell was taken to a holding cell while the judge, Pat and Dean went to the judge's chambers.

Pat paced back and forth for ten minutes until a call came in from the police, who were at the O'Kelly's. Dottie put him on the phone with Shirley.

"Honey, I'm fine. It's happening all over again, isn't it?" said a very disturbed Shirley.

"Shir, thank God you're okay! What happened? Why didn't you answer the phone?"

"We got a call from someone who said he was from the telephone company and they were working on some line trouble. He told us not to answer the phone for 30 minutes so he could make some test calls. The man told us if we picked up the phone, it would ruin their trouble-shooting procedure and they would have to start over again. We heard the phone ring and ring, but that's why we wouldn't answer it."

"Colver is right. We are dealing with someone very cruel, but very smart. It has to be Jeffie!"

Pat told her how the trial was interrupted by the call.

"I love you, Honey!"

"I love you, too, Shir, and I'll see you as soon as this trial is over. Please be careful and ask Grace to lock the doors and windows."

"Both the subdivision security people and the Clayton County PD are regularly running patrol cars by here. We have a signal set up to let them know if we are in trouble. Since part of the lake is in Henry County, they also have been notified. The police departments have been told to watch conversations on the radio as the bad guys could have scanners."

"I'll be home as soon as I can. Again, I love you, and please be careful. Bye."

"I love you, too. Bye."

"Are you able to continue, Pat?" asked Judge Musselman.

"Yes, Sir. But please give me another 10 minutes. This phone call leaves no doubt in my mind Jeffie is behind everything. I'm getting sick and tired of being a sitting duck in a shooting gallery. Somehow I have to nail him before he gets to Shirley, her family, or me! Something that bothers me, Judge, is his sister saying he is evil, brutal, and smart. She mentioned he would try to ambush me, maybe even plant a bomb. It's all coming together now. She said the Brotherhood taught him every dirty trick there was! I can't let him get to Shirley again."

Capt. Keller came in and greeted Pat and Judge Musselman.

"Pat, all officers on the Clayton County PD now have a description and picture of Jeffie, and although there is not enough evidence to charge him with a crime, we do have enough to bring him in for questioning. Automobile, motorcycle, and deed records are being checked, but he could easily have these in someone else's name. We will also give you as much police protection as our manpower can provide."

"Good work, Capt.," complemented the Judge.

"As a side note, you both may be interested in knowing Mr. Clean hit again, or at least the Atlanta PD thinks it was him. Another gay couple was shot and killed with a .22, but this time from a distance of 40 to 50 yards, and therefore no disinfectant on them. Both were shot in the head. This change in M. O. has the Atlanta PD confused. There is talk about getting the FBI profilers back. As you know, they are trained to look at a crime scene, and then tell you what kind of person did it. I have no idea how, but they were very close on the Atlanta Missing and Murdered Children case last year. Got to go. See you Judge, Pat."

"Gentlemen, take a ten minute break, then I will resume the trial."

Pat and Dean talked until Judge Musselman called them into his chambers.

"Gentlemen, it is approaching noon, so I have decided to break for lunch. We will continue the trial at 1:00. Mr. Patton will give his opening statement at that time."

The judge called the jury back in and explained there had been a telephone hoax involving both the prosecution and the defense, and all were excused for lunch until 1:00.

CHAPTER 40

The Trial Concludes

Four men were gathered around the kitchen table in Jeffie's house. Reb, Yanker, and Snake were all laughing along with Jeffie at what they had pulled off.

"Snake, you really did a job with the phone call," said Jeffie while still laughing. "I'd have loved to have done it myself, but they are bound to be looking for me, at least for questioning, and I didn't want to chance them recording my voice."

"I'll bet Piss-Ant thought your brother, Skinny, done came back to life, all over again."

Reb sat there with a dumb look on his face and laughed whenever they did. He was still numb from the burning of his dump of a trailer. It wasn't much but it was all he had.

"Maybe you ought to move out of this place until the heat is off," suggested Snake.

"Not to worry, Snake old buddy, 'cause my other self owns this house, and what's left of my car. Several of us Brotherhood members established IDs in another name years ago, in case we needed to get out of Dodge. Mr. Robert Ellsworth Lee owns this house, the car and scooter. He has a birth certificate, Social Security card and driver's license. And I grew a beard."

"I get it, Robert E. Lee! That sure was smart, Jeffie!" said Yanker.

"What are you gonna do now, Jeffie?" asked Snake.

"I'm gonna cool it for a few days, or maybe even a week. By then, according to the newspapers, Piss-Ant and Tight-Ass should be in their new house, and that tar baby should be out of the hospital. Then me and Reb are going to kill all three of them! If only the South would have won the war, I wouldn't be going through this. That coon never would have been able to marry a white woman."

"Yeah, and I'm gonna help kill 'em," said Reb with a big smile. "And, ah, I get Tight-Ass when you're done with her, ain't that right, huh, Jeffie?"

"That's right, Reb."

* * *

Judge Musselman called for the jury to be brought in.

"Mr. Patton, you may now give your opening statement.

"Thank you, Your Honor. Ladies and gentlemen of the jury, and Mr. Colver. As you know, my name is Patrick Patton and I represent the defendant, LaShandra Tidwell. I really appreciate this chance to speak to you on my client's behalf."

How dumb can you get, LaShandra? The jury saw you frown and roll your eyeballs at my statement!

"You heard Mr. Colver tell you LaShandra's case is a simple one - - she had marijuana in her suitcase, and her personal things were in it with her name on one of them. It is true she had a suitcase, and some of her things were in it. But — ladies and gentlemen, it was not, I repeat, was not her suitcase! Not only that, but at no time did she have control of it.

"Can things seem one way, but be another way? Certainly. Suppose you were driving down the road, had an upset stomach and had to pull over to the side of the road. Now suppose a police officer came along about that time, pulled in behind you, and low and behold, there at the very spot you stopped were several empty beer cans and whisky bottles. And there you are emptying your stomach. What would he think? What would it look like to him? DUI, of course, but was it? Absolutely not!

"Suppose you are walking down the street and see a wallet laying on the sidewalk. You pick it up and open it to see who it belongs to, and all at once a man in front of you looks around, sees you, and yells, stop thief! The police come and take you away! Did you have the wallet in your possession? Yes. Did you steal it, or for that matter have the intent to keep it? Of course not! But – what did it look like?

"Ladies and gentlemen of the jury, we will show you something similar happened to LaShandra. We will show you that, although her things were in it, the suitcase was not hers.

"Fingerprints? Where were they found? On the suitcase? No – on her toothbrush bag ID tag inside of the suitcase. We will show you not only was the suitcase not hers, but she ... never ... even ... touched ... it!

"Please listen carefully to the witnesses and weigh all of the evidence. When you do, you will see LaShandra is not guilty. Remember, it is not enough to think someone is guilty in a criminal trial, but the State has to prove it beyond a reasonable doubt. So, what is a reasonable doubt?"

Pat walked to his briefcase and pulled out an empty can, which was approved beforehand by the judge.

"Suppose this can is our evidence can. How far would it have to be filled to get a conviction? Halfway? Not in a criminal trial. How about ¾ of the way? Not in a criminal trial. Ladies and gentlemen, it has to be filled almost clear up to the top," said Pat, pointing to the top of the can and slowly walking the length of the jury box. "Please remember that. Almost to the top. Thank you."

As Pat was sitting down, he noticed jurors shaking their heads up and down. Then another good sign - - Court Reporter Margie Loftin was giving him a big smile.

"Mr. Colver, you may call your first witness."

"Your Honor, the State calls Agent Jeffrey Griffin."

DA Colver had him give his background and experience in law enforcement. He was a tall distinguished-looking black man.

"Mr. Griffin, on Thursday, Jan. 8, 1981, did you have reason to search a suitcase belonging to the defendant?"

"Objection, Your Honor! Ms. Tidwell adamantly denies the suitcase in question was hers, and there has been no proof to show otherwise."

"Objection sustained. Mr. Colver, the suitcase has not yet been shown to belong to the defendant. Please continue."

I know the DA will establish at least constructive possession, with the name tag and the baggage claim check, but I want the jury to get in their heads from the very start of this trial that she was denying ownership.

Mr. Colver did that in short order.

"Mr. Griffin, why did you pick this particular suitcase to search?"

"We didn't. 'We' being Sgt. Crumbley of the Clayton County Police Department and me. We work as a team. A tip was received that drugs were coming in from Jamaica in a large suitcase, so we pulled all large suitcases before they went up to baggage claim and searched them. Later, with the aid of a drug-sniffing dog, we homed right in on the suitcase with Tidwell's name on it, as well as two others with lesser amounts of drugs in them. The tip may have been on one of the other suitcases, I don't know, but we pulled all of them, and hers was a hit."

Agent Griffin proceeded to show the jury how he established there were drugs between the suitcase itself and the linings. He opened it up and placed the palm of his left hand against the outside part of the lid, then ran the fingernail of his right hand over the inside part of the lid. When there was insulation, like a sheet of marijuana between the lining and the lid, no vibration could be felt on the palm of his left hand as he ran the fingernail of his right hand over the area covered by the palm of his left hand. Normally he could feel a vibration when doing this.

Very interesting, but this still does not prove this was her suitcase, only that there was dope in that suitcase.

During cross, Pat had few question for Agent Griffin. Pat was not there to contest the dope, but rather to show it was not her dope.

The next witness DA Colver called was Sgt. Crumbley, who testified that, based upon what he saw, her arrest was justified, and he proceeded to take her in. Also, DA Colver established the crime occurred in Clayton County, Ga, on Thursday, Jan. 8, 1981.

Pat had few questions for him. The suitcase and the dope were admitted into evidence.

Pat continued. "Sergeant, when did you see LaShandra with the suitcase?"

"Ah, I didn't. It came off of Dixie Airways flight 116 from Jamaica to Atlanta, the same flight Ms. Tidwell was on. It was routed to baggage claim where we intercepted and searched it."

"Did anyone see her with . . . ."

At that point, Judge Musselman stepped in and severely admonished Tidwell for, of all things, sticking out her tongue at Sgt. Crumbley as he was testifying. Pat was told to continue after the judge told Tidwell he would remove her from the courtroom if she continued with childish behavior. Pat could not believe she had done that! The jury was noticeably turned off by that act.

"Sgt. Crumbley, did anyone actually see her with the suitcase?"

"Well, no, but . . ."

"You answered my question," interrupted Pat. "Thank you, Mr. Crumbley."

"Oh, one more question. It is possible then that her things could be in someone else's suitcase, isn't it?"

"Well, I – ah – suppose so."

"Thank you, Sgt. Crumbley." Pat headed for the defense table.

"Oh, I almost forgot, there is one more thing. Did you find her finger prints on the outside of the suitcase?"

"No."

"I have no more questions of this witness, Your Honor."

This trial was moving along fast.

DA Colver called his last witness, Lab Technician Supervisor Tootsie Upchurch. Colver qualified her as an expert and Pat did not object. Her credentials were credible. She had a Master's Degree in Chemistry, had written a book on drug testing, published several articles, and had 15 years' experience working in labs. It's hard to argue with that background, so he didn't.

Ms. Upchurch went into a detailed explanation of how she determined the sheets under the liner of the suitcase were marijuana, which bored the jury. She went into the weight, which put this case under the trafficking in marijuana statute, and the fact that a proper chain of custody procedure was followed and the marijuana tested was a sample of the same marijuana that was in the suitcase.

When Pat was told Ms. Upchurch was his witness, he stood and said, "Thank you Your Honor, but I have no questions for this witness," and sat down.

The prosecution rested, and, after a short recess, Pat was to have his turn. He called LaShandra Tidwell to the witness stand. You could feel the excitement in the courtroom and hear an unmistakable murmuring of Dope Fairy. The reporters sat up in their seats now with pens and notebooks ready. An artist busied himself with a drawing, as the judge would not allow cameras into his courtroom - - he said they would turn this trial into a circus, as attorneys, witnesses, and even judges were tempted to put on a show, especially for TV cameras. Pat agreed with him. The courtroom quieted as she took the stand.

"Please state your name and address for the record," asked Pat.

"LaShandra Tidwell, presently of the Clayton County Jail," replied LaShandra in a sarcastic way.

"Ms. Tidwell, were you in Jamaica on Jan. 8, 1981?"

"Yes," responded LaShandra, with a smirk and in a monotone voice.

"When did you get there?"

"Let's see, about the 2nd, I think. I was on vacation."

"Did you meet a man there?"

"Yes, and he was a real kool dude."

"What was his name?"

"Carlos. I never did know his last name and he didn't know mine. That's the way we both wanted it."

"Did he stay with you?"

"No, I moved in with him."

"Okay, now it's the morning of Jan 8th and you're getting ready to come home. Did you pack your suitcase?"

"Yeah. I packed it, but I never got to use it," said LaShandra, still in a monotone, but getting a little more emotion into her testimony.

"Why not?"

"Well, I was running close to flight time and needed to get my shower. I had my suitcase packed, lying on the bed open. I yelled to Carlos to close it up, 'cause it had straps on it that was hard for me to buckle up. It was a big old suitcase that I could hardly lift, but when you're a young, good-looking female, you can always get some dude to carry it around for you."

"What happened next?"

"Carlos said the strap broke, but he would let me use his suitcase which was similar. He could get mine fixed and use it 'cause he was staying another three days. We agreed to swap suitcases."

"Pardon me, LaShandra, but why was the suitcase being closed up before you finished your shower?"

"Like I said, I was running close to flight time, and I already got my clothes out of it, and was working out of my carry-on bag."

"Tell the judge and jury what happened next."

"The dude, Carlos, he took my things out of my suitcase and packed them in his. I hurried and got dressed. Carlos took his big old heavy suitcase off of the bed, while I grabbed my pocketbook and carry-on bag. We went out to his rental car, and he put his big old suitcase in the trunk while I got in the car."

"Did Carlos's suitcase have an identification tag on it?"

Yeah, he took it off of my suitcase and put it on his. You know, one of them leather strap things you put around the handle and buckle up like a belt." LaShandra was starting to get into it now.

I just hope it's not too little, too late.

"When you got to the airport, what happened to the suitcase?"

"Carlos, he got his big old suitcase out of the trunk, and he took it into the baggage check-in counter for me."

"He checked it in?"

"Yes, for me. I didn't then but now I smell a rat. That kool dude, he done set me up!"

Good! That will make the jury think. "Then what happened?"

"Well, by then it was only 15 minutes or so until flight time, so the little man behind the counter did whatever they do to the tickets and I hurried to my departure gate. Five minutes after I got there, they started boarding the plane."

"When you got to Atlanta, what happened?"

"I got off of the plane and went to baggage claim. You know, they have those neat underground trains that just swish-h-h you away to the next stop. I was waiting for my luggage to come when this ugly Sgt., the one who testified earlier, grabbed me and took me to an underground room and told me I was under arrest."

When she said *ugly Sgt.*, Pat groaned.

"Now I want you to think carefully about my next question. Did you ever, even one time, put your hands on or touch in any way, the suitcase labeled State's Exhibit #1?"

"No! I sure didn't," said LaShandra with a little more feeling.

"Now, LaShandra, I want you to look the jury right in the eye. Is that your suitcase?"

"No!"

"Is that your marijuana?"

"No! No! No!" she said with much more conviction.

They had gone over this last question several times, and again this morning, and she did much better this time, when it counted.

"Thank you, Miss Tidwell. No more questions of this witness, Your Honor.

"And him," she said pointing to Sgt. Crumbley, as Pat was walking away, "I should have kicked him right between the legs for grabbin' my arm like that!"

Oh no! She just can't keep her mouth shut.

"Young lady," admonished the judge, "you have been warned before! One more outburst from you and . . ."

"What the hell you gonna do with me, Judge? Put me in jail? I'm already there, Dude!"

Pat couldn't believe what he was hearing. Chain Gang was livid! The people in the courtroom were stunned. The reporters were writing away at high speed.

"I find you in contempt of this court! Ten days in jail and a $100 fine! Mr. Colver, you may cross-examine this witness, and at the conclusion, she will be removed from this courtroom until the jury comes back with their verdict."

DA Colver got up and, as he started to ask her some questions, she blurted out, "I don't have nothin' to say to this creep! He's the one who's tryin' to put me in prison!"

"Twenty days and a $200 fine. Bailiff, take her away!" said a very angry judge.

Pat shook his head and sat down.

DA Colver made his closing argument, stressing it was her suitcase with her name tag and her dope in it. He pointed out her outrageous behavior on the stand and asked she be convicted. He argued we need to get drugs and people like her who deal in drugs off of the street.

Then it was Pat's turn. Since the only witness he put up was his own client, he got the last say with the jury. He asked the jury to please separate her behavior in the courtroom from the crime itself, as they were two separate things. He told them that this was the anger of an innocent woman who is outraged at being arrested and grabbed by the arm by a police officer. Next, Pat zeroed in on the suitcase belonging to Carlos, his packing it, putting it in the car, and checking it in. He pointed out that at no time did she have control of the suitcase. She was a victim and not a criminal.

"The State had not met its burden of proof. Remember the evidence can! If you say to yourself, I think she is guilty, but I guess it could have happened the way she said it did, then it is your duty to vote Not Guilty. Thinking she is guilty is not reason enough to convict this woman of a crime. The state must prove, beyond a reasonable doubt, that LaShandra committed the crime of Trafficking in Marijuana. Please remember, she is on trial for drugs, not for her behavior in court."

Pat rehashed a few more points and sat down at an empty table.

The judge charged the jury, that is, he told them what the law was concerning this case, and they retired to deliberate. In Georgia the jury decides the facts, but the judge gives them the law that applies to the case. The jury decides whether or not the defendant is guilty, but the judge hands out the sentence. If the jury comes back with a Not Guilty verdict, the defendant is free to go home. If the defendant is found to be guilty, it is within the judge's discretion to hold the person in jail until sentencing, let them out on bond until sentencing, or be sentenced immediately.

"Mr. Colver and Mr. Patton, please approach the bench."

Both of them dropped what they were doing and walked up to talk to the judge.

"It is now almost 5:00. I will allow the jury to deliberate until around 6:00, and unless they reach a verdict by then, which is very unlikely, I will allow them to go home and start again in the morning. Both of you be back here by 6:00, and if you leave, please let the bailiff know where you went. Something could come up and I may have to call you back to the courtroom. And Mr. Patton . . .your client had better hope she is not found Guilty!"

They both thanked the judge, and he thanked them for a clean trial. As Pat headed out the door to use the restroom, the press was all over him, and DA Colver, too, but to a much lesser extent. Pat was clearly the one they wanted to interview.

"Mr. Patton, you did a great job for Ms. Tidwell, but do you think her bad behavior in the courtroom will help to get her convicted?" asked Sandi of Whit Radio.

"Thank you for the compliment, Ms. Desanto. I would hope they would put that aside when deliberating this case."

"Do you really think the Dope Fairy put that stuff in her suitcase?" asked a laughing Zel from Channel 3 News.

"No, Ms. Murray, I don't believe in the Dope Fairy, but I also don't believe it was her suitcase that the dope was in," answered Pat without a lot of conviction.

"Is Shirley O'Kelly recovering okay, and what are you doing to protect yourself from these attempts and threats on your life?" asked Vivienne Cove of the Clayton Daily News.

"I understand a false alarm was phoned into the judge's office, claiming Ms. O'Kelly was seriously injured," jumped in Steve Futo.

"She is recovering from her injuries just fine, but still can't see. We are praying the operation to be performed, by noted surgeon Dr. Orhan in a few weeks, will be successful. As for the second part of your question, there are some very sick people out there."

"Are you still planning on getting married?" asked Zel.

"Absolutely!"

"Any comment on the attempts on your lives?" asked Vivienne again.

"Only that the police, under the able leadership of Chief Keefauver, are doing everything they can to bring those cowards to justice."

"Mr. Patton . . ."

"Please ladies and gentlemen, no more questions for now. I'll be glad to talk with you again after the verdict comes in."

Back in the courtroom, Pat talked to both the court reporter and the bailiff about their take on what the verdict would be. They both thought there was reasonable doubt, but LaShandra really did her best to screw up her chances with the jury. The court reporter gave him an 80% chance of winning, but the bailiff gave him only a 70% chance. Both agreed it could end up in a hung jury, in which case the DA would have to decide if he wanted to retry it or let it go. They also agreed they wouldn't want to be in her shoes if the verdict were Guilty. The sentencing by Chain Gang wouldn't be pretty.

At 6:00 Colver walked into the courtroom. Then the judge entered and called for the jury to be brought in.

"Ladies and gentlemen of the jury, have you selected a foreman?"

"Yes, Sir, we have," said Ken White, a retired Army Captain and foreman of this jury.

"Have you reached a verdict?"

"No, Your Honor."

"Very well. I am excusing you until tomorrow morning. You are all cautioned not to discuss this case with anyone, not even among yourselves, until after you have reached a verdict. You are excused until 8:00 tomorrow morning."

Pat left by the back door, drove to the O'Kelly's house and laid down on the couch with his head on Shirley's lap. He was very tired and went to sleep right there, and then went to bed early. When he got out of the shower, he found a naked blind girl in his bed. He was tired, but – not too tired.

CHAPTER 41

The Louie Lake Deal

Thursday morning had the promise of being a very beautiful day. The sun was coming up, painting the sky brilliant colors, and winter would be over in a month. Pat's birthday was less than two weeks away, and Shirley would be able to see again. He felt better now that the Tidwell trial was almost over, and he and Shirley were about to move into their new house. In less than five weeks he would be married to the most wonderful woman in the whole world. He had a lot to thank God for giving him.

Then his thoughts turned to Jeffie.

Where is he? What does he look like now? He is sure to have changed his appearance. Grown a beard? Let his hair grow long? That was about all a man could do. But, wait a minute; he could also dye his hair, put on sunglasses, and a hat, couldn't he?

Pat ran to the phone and called Capt. Keller at home. Several rings later, the Capt. answered.

"Capt., I'm sorry to bother you at home. Do you have a police artist on your staff?"

"Sorry, Pat," answered the sleepy Capt., but we are too small for that, but I'm sure Lt. Tomble could help you."

"Good idea! Thanks, Capt."

He immediately dialed Julie's number.

"Julie, is Ralph there?"

"That you, Boss? This early in the morning? It's only 6:30 and we were just getting up." Julie yawned. "Here he is. Ralph, Pat wants you on the phone . . . I don't know, but it must be important because the Boss hardly ever calls here at the house."

"Hi, Pat, what can I do for you?"

"Look, I'm sorry to call this time of the morning, but I have to be back in court in an hour and a half and just got an idea."

"Okay, what is it?"

"You guys, you and Capt. Tomble, have access to a police artist, right?"

"Sure, but why? In fact he's going to be in my office this morning."

"Jeffie's picture has been spread around, but he almost surely has changed his appearance. So, how many ways can a man do that, without going to Geleta's Costume Shop like his brother Skinny? What if we got an artist to do an 8½" x 11" drawing, split in four panels? The upper left quarter would have a picture of him like we got from the airlines, the next one to the right would show him with long hair, the bottom left quarter with a mustache and beard, and the last quarter with long hair, a mustache, and a beard. I say mustache and a beard because if a guy were going to try to change his appearance, he would most likely do both."

"Great idea! I'll talk to Capt. Tomble today, but I know he will buy it. When they're done, I'll send Chief Keefauver 100 copies to spread around, and I'll give Julie several copies for you. Then I'll spread them all over Atlanta!"

"Make that several dozen for me, if you can, as I want to nail this guy!"

"Me, too! Remember, it was my car with my wife in it that got its windows shot out by an arrow. What? Okay. Julie says it was her car, and I'm not going to argue the point with that wild woman. I'll try to have them for you tomorrow. In fact, you will have the pictures by 2:00 tomorrow afternoon, even if we have to work all night."

"Thanks, Ralph, and as soon as I get my copies, I'm going to provide one each to three beautiful news ladies and a news guy."

"Another good idea. Maybe we can put some heat on Jeffie and make him panic, or run him out of town."

"Ralph, I know in my heart he is back of all this. The arrow, Shirley, Ed, and maybe even the bombing in Daytona."

"I do, too, but so far we don't have any proof."

"See you, Buddy."

"You, too, Pat."

"I love that idea," commented Shirley after listening to his side of the conversation.

"Sneaking in my room again, huh?"

"I missed you, and since I met you, I sure don't like sleeping alone. I want a masculine chest up against my back and strong arms wrapped around me. I feel so content and safe when you hold me. For awhile, I can forget all the Skinnys and Jeffies of the world."

Pat pulled her into his arms and held her tight. "Shir, I know exactly how you feel. I miss you, too! Things have been happening so fast, my head is spinning. But, you know, everything is starting to come together. The jury should issue their verdict today, Ed gets out of the hospital day after tomorrow, and we move Saturday. Three more days and we'll be together at our new house."

"I can't wait!"

"Me neither. Trial! I have to be in court in one hour and five minutes. I haven't even had my shower or breakfast." Pat rushed to get his clothes together and headed for a very quick shower. He looked out the window and saw a police car sitting there. Good old Capt. Keller or maybe the Chief.

Grace gave him an egg, cheese, and ham sandwich to go, along with a glass of orange juice. She greeted him with the bag as he came into the kitchen with his briefcase

"Grace, you don't how much I appreciate this! Good morning, Greg."

"Same to you, Son. Look, I don't wish to seem presumptuous, but I took it upon myself to hire a lady to be with Shirley the first week in your new house, to help her get adjusted. You will be gone quite a bit with your work, and . . . well . . . she can't see. Shirley will have to learn her way around the house and needs help at first."

"Greg, that's a great idea. Who is she?"

"Her name is Mary Williams. She is a black lady, about 40, has had experience with the blind, is an RN, and an ex-police officer."

"You know how to pick 'em, and are indeed an amazing man! I don't suppose she knows how to shoot, does she?" said Pat with a knowing smile.

"Not only that, but she has a license to carry a concealed weapon."

Pat smiled, yelling goodbye to all of them as he went and wolfed down the sandwich and orange juice. He made the courthouse with ten minutes to spare and picked up another police car along the way. He wanted to drive one of Greg's classic cars today, but was running too late. Capt. Keller said they were going to keep an eye out for his car while he was in court.

He entered the courthouse, checked his gun, and took the stairs two by two to the second floor. The press was arriving, but Herb and several other lawyers were sitting in the front row.

"How goes it, Herb? What are you doing here?"

"Chain Gang is going to take a few uncontested divorces this morning, then start another trial later in the morning. Whenever your jury reaches a verdict, he will stop and bring them to this courtroom."

Pat sat there for about an hour, and then told the bailiff he could be found in the snack bar. No sooner did he get there than he was summoned back to court. About 9:30 the jury was brought back, and the foreman, Ken White, told the judge they were deadlocked. Judge Musselman told them to go back and try again. About 10:30 they came back and once again said they were deadlocked. The judge then gave them what is called the 'Dynamite Charge.'

"Go back in there, take off the gloves, and come to an agreement!"

About 11:30 they were back and the foreman said they still could not reach a verdict.

"If I give you more time, Mr. White, could you reach a verdict?"

"Sir, you could give me a year and I still don't think some of the members of this jury could agree on anything. We are at ten to two for acquittal, but the two members voting for conviction, in my opinion, never will change their minds.

Judge Musselman had a conference with DA Colver, who said ten to two was too strong to warrant a retrial. Ten to two for conviction would be a different story.

Chain Gang really had no choice but to have LaShandra called back and told her she was free to go – after serving 20 days for contempt of court. Tidwell started to say something and the judge shook his finger at her and asked if she wanted to try for 30 days. The Drug Fairy decided to shut up, except for one question.

"Judge, Your Honor, Sir," said Tidwell, laying it on thick. "I don't have no $200.00 to pay. Can't you back up on that?"

"Tell you what I'll do. Since I'm such a generous man, I'll allow you to pay the fine at the rate of $25.00 per day, which is only an extra eight days." Chain Gang smiled. "You were lucky to get a mistrial."

LaShandra started to say something, but when he shook his finger at her again, she wisely shut up. She was finally learning it does not pay to screw with Chain Gang.

As they were taking her away, DA Colver came over to Pat to congratulate him on a fine job trying this case. By this time the judge had left and the courtroom was in an uproar, with the press waiting on him for an interview.

"One question," asked the DA as he shook Pat's hand. "Do you actually believe the B. S. she put out about this Carlos character?"

"Do I believe there was a Carlos? Yes. Do I believe she was an innocent pawn? No, but just because I don't believe her doesn't mean she is guilty. Look, I don't like this woman one bit, and would have bailed out if there were a retrial, but you and I make the system work. We threw the dice and she walked. Tidwell was not acquitted though, so I really don't consider this a win."

"Anytime - - anytime your client doesn't get convicted, it's a win! Believe me, I know!"

"I believe you. And, Dean, you did a great job and acted like a gentleman all through the trial."

"That goes for you, too. Ready to face the lions of the press out there?"

"Let's do it." Pat finished putting his files back in his briefcase. "By the way, have a nice vacation, and don't break a leg."

"Vale, Colorado, here I come."

Pat went through the usual questions, answered them, and then called Zel, Viv, Sandi, and Steve to the side.

"Ladies and you, too, Steve, I have something to tell you, but it has to be off the record for now. Agreed?"

They all agreed his comments from this point on would not be in the news, as he promised them an exclusive.

"I have received a picture of the man we believe to be back of the attempts on the lives of Shirley, Ed, and, of course, yours truly."

"Skinny's brother, Jeffie, I'd bet," interrupted Steve.

"Right, but that's not all. I got together with friends at the Atlanta Police Department and they are having a four-part picture done with Jeffie shown as he looked three years ago, and what he might look like if he had long hair, a mustache and a beard. Their police artist is working on it now. If you will leave your names and phone numbers with Julie, I will instruct her to call you as soon as they come in. You can send over a runner to pick up a copy. This way you can do a story ahead of time and run it the minute you receive the pictures."

"Gosh, Mr. Patton, that sure is nice of you," said Vivienne, "but when do you think they'll be ready?"

"First, it's Pat, remember? Second, I was told I could expect them as early as 2:00 tomorrow afternoon. Please keep in mind, at this time, Jeffie is wanted only for questioning and a warrant for his arrest has not been issued."

The reporters thanked him, and off they went to get their stories of the trial finished and prepare one for the forthcoming pictures of Jeffie. They all assured him they would have a runner at his office by '2:00 tomorrow.'

When Pat walked in the office, Julie looked at him. "Can I help you, sir? Would you like to make an appointment with the mysterious and mostly absent Pat Patton?"

"Okay, Julie, you don't have to rub it in."

"Oh, it's you, Boss! Seriously, what a job you did on the Dope Fairy trial! I got to see about four hours yesterday. It was all over the news. You have these reporters eating out of your hand, but it makes my job so much harder. Now the phone will ring off the hook again. By the way, I got three phone calls from three sexy sounding reporters, and one male, leaving their phone numbers. I understand it's about those pictures Ralph is having made up, and that their calls are on the up and up? But, as the superior secretary that I am, I wanted to check with you first."

"What a speech! And, yes, it was about the pictures. Please call them as soon as the pictures arrive."

"Will do, Boss."

"Please call the Fulton County Jail and see if Louie Lake is still there. I promised I would see him as soon as the trial was over. I could run in this afternoon or tomorrow morning."

"Boss, Capt. Keller is on line two, and while you're talking to him, being I'm the efficient secretary that I am, I'll call Fulton County on line one." Julie tried to conceal her laugh.

"Hi, Capt. What can I do for you?"

"Got some potentially good news for you. I found out the bailiff in Judge Harris Nesbitt's court is still alive."

"I'm glad he's still alive, but who is Judge Harris Nesbitt? I vaguely recall the name."

"He's the judge who presided over Ed's trial back in 1955. Remember, I also read the transcript. Well, I talked to Albert Pickelmire, don't laugh, who was Judge Nesbitt's bailiff for several years, and he told me the Brotherhood had the judge in their pocket. Several Brotherhood members were very wealthy businessmen and contributed heavily to the judge's campaign fund when he ran for reelection, not once, but several times. Mr. Pickelmire said the judge was personal friends of several members and they often had lunch together and belonged to the same clubs. And, get this: Albert said, before the start of Ed's trial, the judge made the remark that no damn coon is going to get away with killing a white man in my court, let alone killing three of them. One of them was the son of Mr. Cain, my best friend. Can you believe that?"

"Wow! Way to go, Capt. Is he willing to help?"

"He sure is, and he said that Cain's son was wild and hung around with trash like Jeb Anderson."

As soon as Pat hung up, Julie buzzed him and said that this would be a good time to see Louie. Tomorrow would be a bad day because some big shots from the State would be visiting the jail. Next, Pat called Shirley and told her about the hung jury. Naturally, she was happy for him, but she had already heard about it on the news.

"Julie, I'm going to grab a legal pad and Louie's file, and head for the Fulton County Jail. It will take me about an hour to get there, and if I don't stay too long, I should be able to miss the five o'clock traffic." When Pat said five o'clock traffic, he had to laugh remembering his Five-O'clock Traffic Bandits case. "Please call Mr. Pickelmire. I'll give you the phone number, and find out when he can see me. If it's tonight or tomorrow night, call Shirley and let her know. Tell her I want her to go with me. She needs to get out of the house. Also, tell my secretary she is getting a raise."

Jeez, Boss, good to have you back," said Julie, laughing at the Pickelmire name. "And I'm sure your secretary will very much appreciate the raise. In fact, I'm sure she will place a giant Hershey Bar in your refrigerator."

"I know, and being the fine secretary that she is, what I asked will be done soon and right. It surely will."

Pat grabbed what he needed and headed out to the parking lot. A police car was driving slowly by his office. Pat waived a thank you to the patrolman, then headed north on I75 to Atlanta in Shirley's Olds. It was a nice car, but how he missed his Mustang.

At the Fulton County Jail, Pat was led into a long narrow room with a row of built-in stools and a counter top that ran the length of the room. The wall, to the right, was a heavy thick-meshed screen, which visitors could talk through when they visited inmates. He was taken by a deputy to one of three closet-sized rooms, at the far end of the visitor's room. It had glass on all sides and a door which could be locked. These rooms also had the meshed screen wall but, in addition, had a two-inch slot above the countertop where attorneys could slide documents to their clients to be read and signed. The glass wall was designed to give attorney/client privacy, but at the same time allowed jailers to keep an eye on them. Louie had a beaming smile when he saw Pat.

"Hi, Louie!"

"Hi, Mr. Patton."

"Do you know the names of the DA and the judge on your case? And were you able to get copies of the charges against you?"

"First, I read all about the Dope Fairy trial. Good job! Especially for a bad client. The verdict came over the radio a little while ago. And, yes, sir, to both of your questions." Louie shoved several pieces of paper out to Pat.

The indictment read pretty much as Louie told him over the phone. The judge was Ryan Bartenslinger and the Assistant DA was Douglas Phillips. Pat agreed there wasn't much to work with. All Louie really wanted was the best plea deal he could get.

"Mr. Patton, there is an envelope, addressed to you, in my property bag at the Jail booking office. In it is a $1,500 money order for your services. Would that be satisfactory?"

"That's more than satisfactory, Louie. I'll get the best deal I can for you."

Louie shoved out a signed release form so Pat could pick up the envelope, which he did on the way out. The next stop was to see Assistant DA Douglas Phillips, who told him that the Telephone Man case was now considered high priority and DA Stanley Hoover had taken it over. Luck was with Pat as the DA was available and agreed to see Pat. He was led into a huge office with awards and commemorative plaques hung all over the walls.

Mr. Hoover warmly greeted Pat, who saw a big cigar-smoking man, well over six feet tall, about fifty years old and distinguished-looking.

"A pleasure to meet you, Mr. Patton. I understand you have been retained on a Fulton County case involving Louie Lake, the Telephone Man. But, of course, in this case he was a very unsuccessful warehouse man." Hoover had a big smile.

"Yes, old Louie's gotten himself into another mess."

"I take it you represented him before?"

"Yes, Sir, that's when he got the name Telephone Man."

"You represented him in the case against the telephone company?"

"Yes, Sir."

"How did it come out?"

"It was dead docketed."

"I see." Mr. Hoover was very impressed with Pat's track record. He had followed both the Five-O'clock Traffic Bandits' case, and the Drug Fairy case in the newspapers, so he was aware of having a high-profile attorney in his office. He also was aware of Pat's love affair with the press.

Better to tread softly, even if he is a novice attorney. I need to run for reelection seven days per week, fifty-two weeks per year. One thing I don't need is unfavorable press.

"Mr. Lake retained me to represent him concerning a jury trial, but as I explained to him, he needs to keep his options open. I also explained I always try to negotiate a plea; in that way, he has a chance to compare the certainty of a plea with the uncertainty of a trial. Today, I'm here to discuss the possibility of a plea, and if the deal is sweet enough, Louie may decide to plea and save us both a lot of work."

If the DA thinks I might actually try this case, and thinks there is even a small possibility of a loss, he might offer a good deal.

"Quite frankly, Mr. Patton, I'm surprised your client would even consider a trial. He was caught red-handed in the warehouse, and even called the press because of the absurd notion the police were out to kill him. He's lucky he's not facing a gun charge, too. We found the guns they tried to hide, but we can't prove possession. Wiped clean of fingerprints, and the serial numbers came up stolen."

"I know, Mr. Hoover, but sometimes things are not what they seem," said Pat with his best mysterious smile.

"Let's see. As you're aware, if he goes to trial and loses, burglary could get him up to 20 years. Also he does have a criminal record," said DA Hoover, trying to look important while thumbing through the file.

"Mr. Hoover, I'll concede he has an arrest record, but if you look closely, he has never been convicted of anything."

That really made the DA sit up and take notice. Apparently this new hot-shot attorney really did do his homework.

"Well, I guess you're right. I was thinking of ten years to serve, which is half of what he could get, but I'll go ten serve eight. Of course you know that's eight years in prison followed by two years' probation. How does that sound?"

"Not good at all, Mr. Hoover. Not good at all." Pat spoke in a somber voice.

"What are you looking at?" asked the surprised DA.

"How about five do two. Look, this man does not have a record; he turned himself in, and think about how much worse it will look on the Police Department if this thing goes to trial. You know the press will be all over it, don't you?"

"First of all, five do two is out of the question - - the judge would never go for it. And second, do you really believe you can get the press to favor a warehouse burglar?"

"As I said before, sometimes things are not what they seem to be, and as far as the press goes, look at the newspaper and listen to radio and TV news tomorrow night. A news story will break about Jeffie Anderson and feature a new and surprising development, including pictures of him."

"What are you talking about? What's that got to do with Louie?"

"That's all I can say for now, but believe me, it will happen."

"Mr. Patton, please have a seat in the waiting room while I talk to Judge Bartenslinger."

Pat followed him out to the waiting room and then Hoover left to find the judge.

Judge Ryan Bartenslinger, also known as Gunslinger, was a man in his 60's, short of six feet tall, and very much overweight. He wore glasses and had white hair. The judge had one more election to go through, and then he would retire. DA Hoover explained what was transpiring.

"Five do two? Preposterous!"

"That's what I told him, but I have a bad feeling about this case right here in my gut. This Patton made a fool out of DA Colver. We both have to think about the next election. This guy has a track record of doing the impossible, and the worst part is he is a favorite of the press. When I asked him about that, he told me to look for a news story about Jeffie Anderson on tomorrow night's news. The way he talked, some surprising new development would be in the newspapers, radio and TV. Judge, I don't like this, but I don't need bad press either."

"You've got a point, Stan. How about this? Tell him I'll accept five do three, but if he goes to trial and loses, I'm going to give him 20 serve 10."

"Thanks, Judge. He would be a fool not to go for that."

DA Hoover rushed back downstairs to see Pat. He went in the back door because he thought of something and needed to check on it. Hoover pulled the files on the two co-defendants, and, sure enough, they had pled to ten serve seven. He immediately called Judge Bartenslinger.

"Judge, Stan, here. Look, we have a problem and are going to have to work together on it. I pulled the files on the two co-defendants on the Lake case, and they both pled guilty and were sentenced to ten serve seven by you. We have to come up with something to justify the difference in sentences, but I think I have that solved. Lake has prior arrests, but no convictions. The other two have criminal convictions, and while neither one have bad records, it would be enough to justify the difference if we ever have to explain it."

"Fine, Stan, as long as our butts are covered."

"Great, Judge! You needed to be aware of it if the subject were ever to come up."

Pat was brought back to DA Hoover's office.

"Mr. Patton, I did what I could on this case, but I could not get the judge to go for five do two. He was very upset that I would even suggest such a thing. Why just last week he yelled, I sentenced the two co-defendants to ten do seven, and I'm not going to treat Lake any differently."

"Then I guess I'll see you in front of a jury," said Pat sadly, and started to get up.

"Wait a minute! I'm not through. Next, I explained to the judge the other two co-defendants had prior criminal convictions. While Lake had some arrests, he had no convictions. Even then, the judge would not go with your suggestion, however, he came close with five do three."

"Thank you, Mr. Hoover. That sounds like a fair compromise to me. I'll advise Louie to seriously consider it, but he will have to make the decision. As soon as I know something, I'll get back to you."

They shook hands and Pat left.

Boy, am I glad that guy is out of here. I sure don't need anything to interfere with my chances for reelection, thought the DA.

I can't believe I pulled off that bluff. There is no way I want to go to trial with this case, thought Pat.

Leaving this late, Pat was sure to catch the five-o'clock traffic. Every time he thought about it, Sammy Joe Washington came into his mind. He hoped Sammy was okay and made a mental note to call Sammy's mother and ask about him. He stopped by a pay phone, called Julie and told her what was going on.

"I got you set up tonight at 7:30 at Jerome and Mickey's with Mr. Pickelmire and your future bride. She was excited about going out again. Capt. Keller called to see how we made out, and when I told him, he insisted on being there, too, but at a separate table with a uniformed police officer. He's looking out after you, Boss.

"That he is, and thanks, Julie. I'll be in bright and early to finish up Ed's Habeas Corpus tomorrow. Hopefully Monday will start a normal week, and I'll be in my new house with the love of my life. Greg hired a lady by the name of Mary Williams to be with her the first week in the new house. Get this, she has experience working with the blind, is an RN, and also an ex-police officer."

"Sounds like Greg is looking out for both of you, too."

"Let me call Shirley and get out of here, because I'm already running late.

"See you in the morning, Boss."

Shirley answered on the 4th ring. "Hi, honey, it's your not-so-secret lover calling."

"Pat, Julie called and told me you're taking me to Jerome & Mickey's tonight. I can't wait to get out again, but Daddy wonders how safe it will be. Where are you?"

"I'm calling from the Fulton County Courthouse and completed a fantastic deal on the Louie Lake case . . . and it may get even better. Dinner is at 7:30. Tell your father Capt. Keller and a uniformed police officer will be there, too. That should make him feel better, but we can't hide the rest of our lives. Maybe the pictures in tomorrow's paper and on TV will break something loose."

"I hope so, Honey. I'll tell Daddy, and hurry on home to me."

"Bye, Hon, and I'll be there as soon as I can, but I know I'll get caught in this traffic."

Pat took off for the jail and luckily was able to see Louie, who was ecstatic over the five serve three. Louie was so happy he almost cried. News had already traveled through the jail that his friends had received ten do seven. Pat had worked a miracle. After Pat told Louie about the story he gave the DA, Louie insisted he was going to send Pat an extra $1000.

Probably in change from telephones.

"Louie, I'm going to wait until after the news story on Jeffie breaks tomorrow to see Hoover again. Maybe he'll go five do two."

CHAPTER 42

The Feeling Returns

Jeffie, Reb, Yanker, and Snake parked their Harleys in front of the Silver Slipper and went inside for a few beers, burgers and fries.

"Ah, ah, Jeffie?"

"What ya want, Reb?"

"Ah, Jeffie, I feel it again. You know, like someone is watching us."

"Look, Dumbass, I don't want to hear it! You understand? I want some time to think, be with friends, have a few beers and some food! Now can that kind of talk."

"Okay, Jeffie, but I, ah, still feel it."

Jeffie shook his head. Some of the girls were already there. He could tell a good time was in store for them. He took out a cigar and ordered a burger, fries, and a beer for both of them. Jeffie had brought $300 with him and stashed the rest - - because he knew once he got to drinking, some broad would try to con him out of the money. They stayed for about three hours and by that time, all four of them had picked up some loose girls, so they all decided to party at Jeffie's house. The girls willingly went with them because they felt like these were real men, especially when on the back of a Harley chopper. Jeffie and his girl went out first, and he told her to put her pocket book in one of his saddlebags. She undid the straps of a saddlebag, and then let out a loud scream! A large rattlesnake had bit her on the hand. It crawled out, fell to the ground, and coiled up for another strike. The snake looked at them, its rattles buzzing away!

"Damn, damn, damn!" yelled Jeffie, as the girl was still screaming hysterically. Snake tried to stomp it with his boot and got bit on the leg for his trouble. Jeffie grabbed a piece of fallen tree limb and killed the snake.

Spike, the bartender, came running out when he heard all the screaming.

"Call the damn ambulance and tell them we need antivenin for two rattlesnake bites," yelled Jeffie.

"Reb, let's get the hell out of here! We don't need to be around when the cops come, and they'll be here in a few minutes."

The boys cranked up their bikes and left, while the other two stayed, Snake because he was bit and Yanker to help him and the hysterical female.

Jeffie led the way to another bar, and then sat next to a window watching their bikes.

"I can't figure it out. Who in hell is after me? And why?"

"I told you, ah, Jeffie, I had that feeling again, but you called me Dumbass."

"Well, you are a dumbass, but maybe you do have something with these feelings. Let me know if you feel that way again, Dumbass," said Jeffie, smiling while softly punching Reb in the arm. Reb smiled back, and knew in his heart he was Jeffie's friend. "Reb, I have an idea of how we can wipe out Piss-Ant, Tight-Ass, and that coon all in one night, and then maybe move to California. Would you like that?"

"Jeffie, you know I'll go anywhere you go."

"How would you like to shoot you a nigger?"

"Yeah, I'd like that!"

"We need to get you a clean gun. Do you know how to shoot a pistol?"

"Yeah. It's, ah, been a few years, but I, ah, shot one a lot on my uncle's farm."

"Okay, we get you, let's say, a 9-mm automatic with a 14-round clip. Shoot the SOB 14 times!"

"Yeah! I'd like that!"

"I'll work on getting a gun tonight, and tomorrow we'll go out in the woods and practice."

They went back to the Silver Slipper and talked to Spike. Snake and the girl got the antivenin and should recover nicely. Spike made some calls for Jeffie, and for $350 he got a deal on a clean 9-mm automatic pistol and 200 rounds of ammo. Then Spike slid an envelope under the table to Jeffie with some of that magic white powder in it, while Jeffie vastly overpaid the bar bill. They picked up two girls. Reb got the same one he had before, while Jeffie got another one, who said, "I'll hang on to my purse, thank you."

* * *

Pat got out of the car, slowly looked around, and thought the O'Kelly's place was really feeling like home to him. How could he have ever found a girl like Shirley, with a family like hers? How blessed he was! He went upstairs and threw his arms around a waiting Shirley. At 6:30, he quickly took a shower and put on more casual clothes for supper with Mr. Pickelmire. Pat hoped he would learn more about the Brotherhood and Jeffie.

When Pat got there, Willie, of all people, was acting as host, and he had a big smile on his face.

"What's going on, Willie? What happened to the waiter's job?" asked Pat.

"First of all, let me tell you how h-a-p-p-y I am to see this l-o-v-e-l-y young lady up and about," said Willie with his usual lisp.

"Thank you, Willie," smiled Shirley. "It's great to hear your voice."

"Now, to answer your question. Oh, I'm s-o-o-o happy!" said Willy in a very excited feminine manner. "I'm working this week as a host. Next week, I'll work cleaning off tables and sweeping floors."

"I don't understand how that could be exciting, Willie." commented Shirley.

"We-l-l-l, wait 'cause I'm not finished. After that, I will have worked and become familiar with all of the main areas in this restaurant. Oh, I'm so excited. Mr. Jerome and Mr. Mickey are going to make me a – a – a manager!" This statement burst out of Willie. He could not hold in the pride of his upcoming promotion. "Oh, I will do them such a good j-o-b!"

Shirley opened her arms to give him a hug, which Willie gladly accepted. Pat shook his hand and told him how happy they were for him, while Willie pointed out Mr. Pickelmire. Pat led Shirley to the table where the ex-bailiff was sitting. Everyone introduced themselves and Willie left after being sure Shirley was comfortable. Shirley always wore dark glasses.

Albert Pickelmire was a small wiry man, about a 5'3", 140 pounds, white hair, about 75, and full of nervous energy. He had a big smile and liked to laugh.

In a flash, Willie had a waiter sent to their table. They ordered and, after some small talk, they got down to business.

"Capt. Keller tells me you were Judge Nesbitt's bailiff back in 1955 when Ed Edwards was being tried for murder."

"Yes, that's right, and I'm willing to tell you what I know, but please don't confuse me with one of those people who loves blacks, because I don't. However, I don't hate anyone either, and I think in a civilized country like ours, we have to be fair to everyone. Justice is supposed to be just, but that wasn't the case in Judge Nesbitt's courtroom. He was very biased against blacks and very lenient with defendants who had money to contribute to his reelection, or influence he could use for personal gain."

"Capt. Keller said something about a very derogatory remark the judge made to you right before the trial."

"Yes, I can remember him saying something like this: 'No coon is going to get away with killing a white man in my court, let alone three of them.' His best friend was Andrew Cain, an undertaker as well as a state senator. One of the white men Edwards killed was Cain's son, Bo."

"Sir, I can't tell you how interesting all of this is to me."

"Cain had money. He's dead now. But, most important to your case is that he was a Brotherhood Board of Directors' member. Of course, nothing was on paper, but over the years, I heard the judge mention it many times."

"I take it you would be willing to make these same statements in court?"

"Yes, sir, I would."

"Shir, please excuse me for a minute as I need to get to a phone to leave a message on Julie's answering machine. She needs to try to get the two eye witnesses, Dickerson and Freeman, back here asap. Judge Musselman gave me the green light by saying he would set up a hearing as soon as I get the information and witnesses I need for it. I'm afraid it might slip my mind. Mr. Pickelmire, you wouldn't mind being left alone for a few minutes with this gorgeous creature, would you?"

"Not at all - - and - - don't hurry back." Mr. Pickelmire made a lecherous grin.

Pat left a blushing Shirley. As he looked back, the two of them were talking away. He was amazed how well Shirley was adjusting to being blind, but she tended to put her hand in front of her face when she was walking to protect it from bumping into some unseen object. She did fairly well eating when Pat told her where different foods were located on her plate by referencing them to a clock's dial. Shirley found that if she kept her left hand on her plate, she could pretty well find what she wanted. She couldn't see Capt. Keller at the next table, but she felt his presence.

When they finished eating, Albert gave Pat a piece of paper with his name, address, and telephone number. Pat gave him a business card, thanked him once again and picked up the tab.

* * *

At the O'Kelly's house, Pat's second home, he called his parents and talked for about 30 minutes, then socialized with Shirley and the O'Kelly's for another 30 minutes before going to bed.

Shirley told her parents how much she enjoyed getting out with people again, and her face was looking so good no one could tell she had been involved in a car bombing. She was looking forward to meeting Mary Williams, who would be with her for the next eight days, Saturday through Friday, at the new house. But Greg had told Mary to come to his house all day Friday so they could get acquainted.

* * *

Lunch for Jeffie and Reb was at the Silver Slipper. Spike had the 9-mm automatic and 200 rounds of ammo, plus a spare clip. They ate, had a few beers and headed for the woods. Jeffie had Reb run about 50 rounds through the gun at distances of between 10 and 50 feet. They had a large cardboard box as a target. Reb surprised him and did well at all distances. If the box were a man, he would be dead many times over. He also had Reb practice loading, unloading, cocking, sliding in a new round from a full clip, and working the safety on and off. When they left, Reb wanted to keep the gun with him.

"Reb, Old Buddy, we don't need you shooting someone before you get Ed the Coon. And always remember, before you shoot him, the gun has to be carefully wiped down while wearing rubber gloves. Then after you kill that black bastard, throw it away!"

"But, I wanna keep it, Jeffie. I never had my own gun before!"

"Listen, Dumbass, and listen good! After you shoot him, bullets can be checked for marks left by the barrel. The cops can link bullets to the gun that fired them. If they find that gun on you, guess what? You fry in the electric chair! But if they later pick you up and don't find a gun, you're in the clear. Understand?"

"Ah, I'm not sure."

"Okay, Dumbass. It's this way. Throw the gun away and go free. Keep it and fry. You understand that? When you fry, you die!"

"Yeah, I understand that."

"Okay, what are you going to do after you shoot him?"

"Ah, throw it away and be free. I don't want to fry and die."

"That's right! You keep it and you fry! You keep it and you die. Again, after you shoot him, what are you gonna do?"

"Ah, Jeffie, I'm gonna throw it away."

"Good! You're either in the clear or in the chair!"

"Ah, Jeffie?"

"What now?"

"Where am I gonna throw it?"

"Who cares? Over a bridge, in a dumpster, or down a sewer drain. If nothing else, pull over beside the road and toss it as far as you can into the woods. But – do not let anyone see you do it! If you do, they might lead the police right to the gun. For now, I keep it, but we're going to practice again right before we do it."

Then Jeffie quickly turned around and put two loads of buckshot from a 12-gauge sawed-off double-barrel shotgun through the box. It looked like a sieve.

"Ah, Jeffie, we got 'em good, didn't we?' said a grinning Reb.

"Yeah, Reb, we got 'em good."

* * *

Pat got up early Friday morning and found Shirley in bed with him. He didn't remember her joining him. She was wrapped around him, sleeping very soundly.

"Shir! Shir! You need to wake up and go to your room before your parents find you here."

"Okay." A groggy Shirley put her arm back around him and promptly went back to sleep.

He had to wake her three times before she got up and went back to her room. Tomorrow night they would be in their own house and in their own bed.

Pat took a three-mile jog, but this time with a .357 Magnum. It was concealed in a wide elastic exercise belt, but it kept trying to slide out. He would have to think of something better for the next time.

When Pat got back he took a quick shower, got dressed, and was eating breakfast when Greg came in.

"Well, I think I had better go to my office today and give my associates a break. They have been covering for me ever since Shirley got hurt."

When the doorbell sounded, Greg said, "It must be Mary Williams, the RN, as the gate guard called to check on her admittance." Mary was black, 41 years old, trim, attractive, intelligent, and had a great smile.

"Mary, I'm Grace, this is my daughter Shirley, and this is Pat, Shirley's fiancé. You met my husband. Today we will work on Shirley's upcoming wedding."

"And mine, too!" piped up Pat with a smile.

"You know what I meant," said Grace while laughing.

"Greg, would it be okay if I borrow the van today so I can pick up Ed at the hospital? He'll be in a wheelchair because of the amputation and really does not have a way to get to his mother's place, where he'll be staying."

"Of course, Pat. You know where the keys are. How's he doing anyway?"

"Just great, considering what he's been through, and thanks for the use of the van."

"This is the 30th, isn't it?" asked Shirley.

"Right, Shir. Why do you ask?"

"Twenty-one more days! Then I get my operation. I'll be able to see you again! New York, here we come!"

"Right you are, Honey," said her father.

Pat and Grace hugged her at the same time.

"I believe God had a reason for this, but he is going to let me see again. I know it in my heart."

They held her tighter, and Greg came over and joined them.

"I can see this is a loving family. I'd like to join in, too, but I'm not sure what kind of a reaction I'd get. A strange black lady hugging her white employers and all."

"Come ahead," welcomed Greg as he reached out to Mary, who threw her arms around them.

Renée came in and heard the tail end of the conversation. "You're not leaving me out of this," she exclaimed. Down went her coat and pocketbook, and she put her arms around everyone.

"This is a good time for a prayer," said Greg. "Father, please bless each and every person in this group, watch over them, guide and direct them through this day and every day. And, Lord, we ask you to guide the fingers of Dr. Orhan when he operates on my beloved daughter. Please, Lord, let her see again, as I have faith You can do it. And, Father please bless the marriage between my daughter and this fine young man she has chosen to be her husband. We ask this in Jesus's name. Amen."

All were moved by Greg's prayer.

* * *

Pat was at the office returning some much-needed phone calls when an Atlanta police officer came in and asked for him. He had 100 printed sheets with Jeffie's picture done in the four ways Pat suggested. What a contrast! It didn't look like the same person when the beard and mustache were added. Ralph and Capt. Tromble one-upped him, however, as he saw on the other side of the sheet were the same four pictures, but with a hat and sunglasses on each of the four poses. They had covered all of the bases. Julie told him the media were sending runners to pick up copies at 2:00.

"Give them each two copies so they won't have to duplicate the pictures on the reverse side."

"Will do, Boss. Just for your information, Chief Keefauver has given the okay for an Atlanta PD car and two uniformed officers to keep an eye on this office and me specifically. They have been cleared by Jonesboro and Clayton County for temporary duty here.

"That's great news! Please make sure you take several copies and pass them out. Chief Keefauver got 100 copies and will take care of the government offices and police department."

* * *

When Pat got to the hospital, Ed was packed up and ready to be released. He really looked good. Except for the loss of the leg, you would never have known he was ending an extended hospital stay. Not being able to get booze didn't hurt either. After Ed signed the release papers, as per hospital policy, a nurse wheeled him out of the hospital and across the parking lot to the van. He noticed Ed looking all around, and Pat was, too.

"Don't worry, I have a .357 Magnum here." He patted his suit coat around the heart area.

"You know, Mr. Patton, I sure enough 'preciates dis, but I has to tell you, I don't think dem mens is done wif me yet."

"You may be right. We all have to be careful."

He thanked the nurse and helped Ed onto the passenger's seat. Pat folded the wheel chair and it was placed in the van and along with Ed's crutches and bag.

* * *

When they got to the area where Ed lived, he asked Pat to pull into the driveway of a friend's house. Pat helped him out and handed him his crutches. They made their way to the door and knocked.

The black man who answered the door was glad to see Ed but was taken back with the sight of Pat. Ed asked his friend if they could come in and he reluctantly agreed. He was a large, older man, wearing glasses.

"Hey, Amos, you still got dat old single-shot 12-gauge dat you was tryin' to sell me a few weeks back?"

Amos nodded toward Pat. "You trust dis white man?"

"Wif my life," answered Ed with a grin. "And I be needin' a couple of dem buckshot shells. It be shootin' okay?"

"I done shot it a few months ago."

311

Amos left them standing and returned with an old beat-up, 12-gauge, single-barrel shotgun, and six shells loaded with buckshot.

"You gots a hacksaw?"

"Yep." He left to retrieve an old hacksaw.

"Mr. Patton, you better go out to the van now, as what I's about to do is illegal and I's don't want you involved."

"Good idea, Ed. What I don't see won't hurt me."

About 20 minutes later Ed came out of the house. Amos was helping Ed with one hand and had a rolled-up blanket in the other. Pat could guess what was in the blanket. They helped Ed into the van, and Amos shook Pat's hand.

"How come the change?" asked Pat after they left."

"I told him you was helpin' me get free and you killed a Brotherhood member, too."

"Is that all?" asked a grinning Pat.

"No. I's also told him dat your great-grandmamma was black."

"You didn't!"

"Sure enough did!"

"I'm not going to ask what is wrapped up in that blanket."

"Best if you don't, but I's not going to let dem bastards kill me without a fight!"

"Don't blame you a bit."

Then Pat briefed him on all he had learned in the past week.

"We have three witnesses - - Freeman, Dickerson, and Pickelmire. There are also court records with gross inconsistencies in them, and a verdict that is inconsistent with the inconsistent evidence! Ed, I have never promised a client anything except that I would work for them, but I really believe you will win this habeas."

"I's can't thank you enough, Mr. Patton, for everything! You knows dat I can't pay you?"

"This one's on the house."

Pat parked the van in front of Ed's mother's place, where he stays, and helped him in the door. The small wooden frame house needed paint, but the yard was well-kept.

When he brought the wheelchair in, Ed gave Pat a big hug and had a tear in his eye. They stood there for a minute, looking at each other, but not saying a word. Then Pat smiled and left.

CHAPTER 43

The Pictures

Snake, still recovering from the snake bite, was laying on a couch at Jeffie's house on Friday afternoon. Getting antivenin in less than 30 minutes after being bitten was the key to a fast recovery. He was drinking beer, smoking cigars, and playing cards with Jeffie, Yanker and Reb. At five o'clock Jeffie turned on Channel 3 News. Zel Murray had a three minute-report, which previewed a 30-minute newscast at six o'clock.

"Jeffie, look at this!" yelled Snake. On the screen were eight pictures of Jeffie, and then the camera gave a close-up view of each one for a few seconds each.

"Damn, damn, damn!" yelled Jeffie in a rage. "Now I won't be able to go nowhere! Yanker, they got all the bases covered!"

"You're going to have to hide out, that's for sure, though they said they only want you for questioning," commented Yanker.

"Yeah, I hear you! Questioning my ass! What I want to know is how they got my name or my picture! How much do they know? And – if they went to the trouble to have all of these pictures made of me, they gotta want me bad! But for what? What do these damn cops have on me?"

"Ah, Jeffie, ah, I don't know," said Reb.

"Of course you don't know, and that's 'cause you're a dumbass!" replied an angry Jeffie.

"Guys, I'm gonna have to accelerate my damn plans. I already got me some ideas on how to get the Coon, Piss-

Ant Patton and old Tight-Ass. Somehow he's back of this and, believe me, he's gonna die, die, die! I'm gonna have to move. I think I'll become a woman, 'cause that would really throw them off. I gotta get what I need for about a week and find a safe place to hide out. Some neighbor is sure to recognize one of these pictures and turn my ass in, and if I allow myself to be taken in for questioning, I may not ever come out. Reb, we gotta find a place to go and I need to think!"

"I'll find you a place," said Yanker and he left.

* * *

When Pat got to the office Friday morning, Julie immediately grabbed him.

"I contacted all of your witnesses, Boss, and Judge Musselman's holding for you."

"Thanks, Julie."

"Hi, Judge, what can I do for you?"

"I just learned I have a one-hour slot open next Wednesday, at 2:00. That's Feb. 4th. Can you have your witnesses and evidence ready by then for the Edward's habeas hearing?"

"Let me check with Julie. Hey, Julie! Are my witnesses going to be back before next Wednesday?"

"Julie's checking on it now, Judge."

A short time later Pat answered, "Yes, we'll have them there. Ed is ready to go, but I haven't filed my motion yet."

"Get it in on Monday and you will be fine."

"Thank you, Judge. We really appreciate your thoughtfulness."

"Bye, Pat. And . . . be careful.

It was Pat now and not Mr. Patton.

"Julie, call Ed. We got us a habeas corpus hearing set up for 2:00 on Wed., Feb. 4th. Sometime today, please stop by the clerk's office and pick up subpoenas for our three witnesses, and tell Ed - - no alcohol."

"Sure, Boss. I know a deputy with the Sheriff's Department who will serve them for me ASAP. Both of the ladies are supposed to be back home by tomorrow afternoon."

"You have a deputy who will do that for you?"

"Sure, Boss, he likes me."

"I wonder why?" Pat smiled, looking over at her pretty face and great body.

"Jeez, Boss, I have no idea."

"Thanks, Julie. Use you're charms and get it done."

Next Friday she would get a $100 bonus, in cash, along with her paycheck.

Pat took care of a few other odds and ends, saw two new clients and, before he knew it, it was time to go.

I hope a normal week is coming up. Everything is coming together. Shirley is out of the hospital, the Tidwell trial is over, and the final move is tomorrow. I'll contact DA Hoover on Monday to see if he will go for the five serve two for Louie. Next week I'll really have to think about Jeffie.

"Hey, Boss, come here quick!" yelled Julie.

Both Pat and Herb ran out of their offices, not knowing what to expect. Julie had the TV turned on and she and Rhonda were watching the preview to the Six-O'clock News. Zel had called and told her to watch for it, because Pat was nice enough to provide the exclusive pictures. Pat and Herb got there in time to see each of the eight individual pictures shown for a few seconds each. Zel also mentioned Pat's name in a favorable way.

"Wow!" exclaimed Herb. "How did you manage to accomplish that? All I know is that Rhonda told me runners were here earlier to pick up some pictures."

Pat explained what was going on and told Julie to give Herb several copies to pass out. Pat also tacked the pictures on their waiting-room bulletin board. It had glass doors that locked, which assured him no one would take down the pictures.

Pat called Shirley to let her know he was on his way home. He was walking out the door when Julie called him back for a phone call from the Fulton County DA.

"Hello, Mr. Hoover. What a pleasant surprise."

"Mr. Patton, you win. I saw the Five-O'clock News preview and the pictures on TV. We will go five serve two on the Lake case. How about a hearing at 9:00 Monday morning?"

"Would right at 9:00 be possible? I'm moving to another house this weekend and need to get back as soon as I can. There will still be lots to do."

"Make it 8:30 and I'll ask the judge to take Lake's plea before he takes the uncontested cases."

"Thank you, Mr. Hoover. I'll be there at 8:30 sharp. It is very kind of you and the judge to work around my schedule. "

"You're welcome and goodbye, Mr. Patton." DA Hoover was glad to get rid of this case. Reelection was all-important.

"Julie, we have the Lake plea at 8:30 Monday morning. Louie will get five do two. I'll go from there back home to help supervise the move."

Pat called Shirley with an update and left. He gassed up the van and ran it through a car wash. When he borrowed something, he liked to return it in better shape than when he borrowed it.

* * *

Shirley was happy he finally got home, and said Mary was very helpful and fit right in. They were working all day on getting things together for the wedding.

Greg came in right after Pat and said, "I talked to Chief Keefauver and he and his wife Patricia are going to meet us at Jerome and Mickey's at 7:30. Lt. Ralph Crawford and his lovely wife Julie will also be there. Willie will have a table for eight reserved for us."

"I wonder if Willie is still messing around with Pick'em-Up-Man? I haven't had time to get on the CB lately. Say, its one minute to Six-O'clock. I'll tune in to Channel 3 News. Y'all need to see this. Did you say Ralph Crawford and his wife, Julie? I owe them a meal."

They watched a more comprehensive story on Jeffie's being wanted for questioning concerning a hit-and-run and a car bombing. The police didn't have enough evidence to convict him of either of those charges, but Jeffie didn't know what they had. Pat, with the Chief's blessing, had talked Zel into running a short story on the beating of two gay men, and the Daytona bombing, right after the story on Jeffie. The thinking was - - if Jeffie had anything to do with any one of them, it might worry him enough to make a mistake. All they had was the similar big man and an even bigger man description, and neighbors describing Johnny 'Reb' Carter as a very big man who was seen leaving his trailer with another man who was big. The Police Department had been watching the burnt-out trailer and the beat-up Camaro, but as far as the police could tell, the men never came back. However, Capt. Keller had a gut feeling the other man might be Jeffie.

* * *

Jeffie was at his house with Reb and Snake when the News at Six with Zel came on. When he saw the stories of the car bombings, Ed's hit-and-run, and the beating of the two gay men, all run together, he was in shock!

"How could they possibly know? How could they?" shouted Jeffie, as he paced back and forth. "Wait a minute! If they had solid evidence linking me to any one of those crimes, there would be an arrest warrant out for me. Right?"

"That's, ah, right, Jeffie."

Jeffie just glared at Reb.

"Then again, they may have a warrant out for me but aren't making it public to catch me off guard."

"Telephone call for you, Jeffie. It's Yanker and he found a place for you to stay."

Jeffie talked to Yanker, gathered up his stuff and, with Reb, went out the back door, yelling, "Snake! If any cops come snooping around, you never heard of no Jeffie. This is Bob Lee's place. Got that?"

"Got it."

Two hours later the police were knocking on the door looking for Jeffie.

"Ain't no one by that name here. I rent from a guy named Bob Lee," said Yanker with a smile showing his missing teeth.

The police left, but they would be back because not one but three neighbors called and said they saw a man there matching Jeffie's description, the one with the long hair, beard and mustache. All of the calls were anonymous because they knew he was trouble.

* * *

Saturday morning Jeffie and Reb got up and went to Geleta's Costume Shop.

"I hope nobody recognizes me from them pictures on TV, even though I shaved, got on this hooded jacket, hat, shades, dark lipstick, and pinned rolled up socks to my shirt to look like I got boobs ."

Jeffie bought everything he needed to fix himself up like a woman, including two wigs of different colors. As they left the shop, Jeffie commented to Reb, "If it worked for brother Skinny, maybe it will work for me, too."

Next they headed for a Goodwill store and bought three nice 'Sunday dresses' that fit Jeffie. Matching pocketbooks were bought, but he found it impossible to find a pair of women's shoes big enough to fit his size 11 ½ feet. A trip to a big woman's store solved that problem, and he also bought a couple pair of extra-large panty hose.

One of the clerks whispered to her male boss, "You can never tell about some people. She sure don't look like no woman. How would you like to pick up something like that in a bar?"

After Goodwill was a trip to K-Mart for a pair of earrings, perfume, a neckless, and a ladies watch. They also found a heavy sweater and a long ladies trench coat.

People stared at this large woman with a definite five-o'clock shadow, but kept their comments to themselves.

* * *

Pat and the O'Kelly's arrived at Jerome and Mickey's before 7:30. Willie was still the host and promptly seated them at their table. A few minutes later the Chief and his wife came in and after ordering drinks, Ralph and Julie arrived.

Small talk went on for a few minutes, and all parties seemed pleased to be together. The Chief's wife Patricia was a very friendly, likeable person, and Ralph was a great guy.

"What's new in Atlanta, Ralph?" asked Pat. "And what's that package you have with you?"

"The package is another hundred pictures of Jeffie," answered Ralph, handing them to Pat. "My dear wife said you were passing them out like M & M candy. As for what's new, Mr. Clean has us wondering. He doesn't fit the profile of the typical serial killer. First he killed up close, which indicated something personal. You know, look 'em in the eye and shoot! Then he stopped the close-range stuff and started using what had to be a rifle, killing at 50 to 100 yards. At no time did he touch a body, or at least we don't think he did, because we found nothing to link anyone to a car, or an apartment except the owners. As the Chief can tell you, close-in crime scenes are much easier to solve because the killer will always bring something into the crime scene and will also take something out. It could be a fingerprint, a hair, or maybe a fiber, like in the Wayne Williams's case, but lots of times there is something there, if only we can find it."

"How do you know it was Mr. Clean using a rifle at long distance?" asked Shirley.

"Germicide General was found in the wounds. Our lab guys suspect he filled hollow-point bullets with it."

"How many victims so far?" asked Greg.

"Eight bodies in less than ten days! At least two of them, the lesbian women, were murdered over two weeks ago, but that is another puzzler. It is very unusual for a serial killer to kill this many in such a short period of time. It's almost put him in the category of a mass murderer. Serial killers normally kill one or two people, then lay off for days, weeks, and even months, until they get stressed out over something and kill again. He's not just a sniper, because he has killed both up close and from a distance. That's assuming it is the same person."

"How many did Wayne Williams kill?" asked Grace.

"Around twenty, but we're still not sure he killed all of the victims he was accused of murdering. He was only convicted of two murders, but we are sure he did several more."

"Mr. Clean will make a mistake and then you'll get him, Honey," commented Julie.

"I sure hope so, but sometimes they never get caught."

"Who hasn't gotten caught?" asked Julie.

"Well, Jack-the-Ripper for one. He killed close to ten women and sent dozens of letters to the press but never was caught. Closer to home we have the Zodiac killer out in San Francisco. He claimed to have killed 30 to 40 people, and also wrote letters to the press, but was never caught."

"I didn't know that," said Shirley.

"And take David Berkowitz, who called himself the Son of Sam. He killed six people in NYC. He got caught, but only because he parked illegally and got a ticket. If it weren't for that and some good police work, he might have killed six more."

"How about the disinfectant?" asked Pat.

"Oh, he's been smart there, too. Germicide General is a brand all the major food stores sell. As you can imagine, that was one of the first things we sent to the lab."

"And no one heard any shots either. I believe he must have some type of silencer," said the Chief.

"You're probably right. Using a .22-caliber firearm does not make as much noise as a larger one, but it can still be heard from quite a distance. Somebody should have heard at least some of the shots," answered Ralph. "And speaking of shots, that was some story in the newspaper, Pat. They printed all eight pictures to boot."

"I haven't seen the paper yet, but we did see the Six-O'clock News."

The Chief continued, "Vivienne ran all of the related stories together as we asked her to do. You know, the Daytona car bombing, Shirley's, ah . . ."

"It's okay, Chief," said Shirley. "You can say Shirley's car bombing."

"Shirley's car bombing," said the Chief, looking a little embarrassed, "the beating of the gay guys, and Ed's hit-and-run. That was really a good story, and maybe it will make life too hot for him to stay in town."

"Any leads yet on Jeffie?' asked Ralph.

"Tips were coming in when I left to come here, or so I was told by our dispatcher. I don't know how many or what they were, but you sure had a good idea, Pat."

"Thanks, Chief."

They enjoyed a good meal and great friendship, but then it was time to go.

"Boss, I almost forgot. A letter came addressed to you today but somehow got mixed up with Herb's mail. It's from Louie Lake."

Pat opened the letter and found a check for $1,000, and a note that read, "I tried, but couldn't get $1,000 worth of coins into this envelope. Louie." That broke Pat up. Friends they were, but Pat did not read the letter out loud because of the blue uniforms.

"Good old Louie came through like he said he would."

"We enjoyed it y'all, but I know Pat for one has to get up early, for the final move into their new house in the morning," commented Greg.

"Jeez, I need to get some rest, too. My boss works me to death," added Julie with a smile. That got them all laughing.

"I take it y'all will be going to church Sunday morning?" asked the Chief.

"Of course," answered Greg, "but why do you ask?"

"Capt. Keller and I, along with our lovely ladies, would like to join you, if that's okay with you."

"Certainly, Chief, we would love to have you," spoke up Grace.

"We plan to have a car follow you to church, park in the lot, and follow you back home. Who knows what these news reports might incite Jeffie or the Confederates to do."

"Thank you, Chief," responded Pat and the O'Kelly's, almost at the same time.

Before we leave, I also need to let you know that Atlanta PD has a man keeping an eye on Ed. We don't want another accident to happen," said Ralph.

With that they all got up and left.

CHAPTER 44

Ed Makes Plans

Jeffie and Reb woke up in an old rental house outside Jonesboro. The property consisted of several acres on a dirt road and was owned by a Brotherhood member. Propane space heaters were used to heat the place, but with no insulation, they had a hard time keeping warm. Frost was on the ground this morning and it was cold. They hadn't thought to bring sheets or blankets, so they had slept in their coats on two old mattresses someone left lying on the floor.

"Jeffie, ah, what are we gonna do today?"

"You're going to go out and buy me several razors, shaving cream, a set of cheap hair clippers, and an old Bible from a used-book store. When you're finished, you can get us something to eat and bring it back here. Then you're going to give me a haircut and I'm going to get a real close shave."

"But, ah, Jeffie, I don't know nothing about cutting no hair."

"Look, Dumbass, all I want you to do is to cut off my hair with the clippers and then I'll shave my face and head. Maybe you had better get a 12- pack of them disposable razors."

"Why are you doin' that?"

"Oh, Reb, sometimes . . .! Man, I got to change my looks.

In that newspaper we picked up, did you see a Jeffie with a shaved head and face? Huh? Did you? And - why do you think I bought those women's clothes?"

"Ah, no, I don't know."

"Here's $40 and a list of what I want. When you get done, stop by the Flying Buzzard and get me two of them buzzard sandwiches, fries, and a large Coke. Get whatever you want for yourself."

Reb read back the list to him with considerable difficultly, even with a lot of help from Jeffie.

"Ah, Jeffie, why do you want me to buy you an old Bible?"

"Now that's the first intelligent question you have asked me in a week or two. The answer is that I'm going to use it when I go to church in the morning."

"You, ah, ah, you in church?" asked Reb, breaking out laughing. "Church? Church?" said Reb laughing all the harder. Finally, it was too much for Jeffie and he had to laugh, too.

"Ah, am I going, too?"

"No, you will wait in the car 'cause this is a job for me alone."

"What church you goin' to?"

"The Solid Rock Christian Church in Jonesboro."

"Say, ah, ain't that where Piss-Ant . . . ? Ah, I get it!"

Jeffie just smiled.

* * *

Ed slept until it warmed up, and then had his mother ask a neighbor to help him get on the sidewalk with his wheelchair. By going out the back door, he didn't have steps to go down, but he couldn't wheel through the grass without help. As soon as he got his strength back and got used to the wheelchair, he felt sure he would be able to do it on his own. Hopefully, in only a few days. He wheeled himself down to the bus stop less than half a block away. He and his friends gathered there every day to drink, look at the women, and tell lies. They noticed he now had a blanket over his legs and figured he was covering his missing leg. They really didn't know Ed.

* * *

Pat was up early on Sat. morning and ate breakfast with the O'Kelly's and Mary. Greg and Grace would stop by the new house later in the morning, then go for a round of golf scheduled for a two o'clock T-Time. The early mornings were cold but sun would warm things up in the afternoon. All in all, it was a great day to play golf and move.

"Shir, I'm going to leave now. I'll be taking the van, so I can pack up some personal things in it. That will leave the Olds for you and Mary. I want to be at my old house before the movers get there. By the way, Eb and Kathy are going to help again.

"Okay, Honey, I'll see you later. I feel quite comfortable with Mary."

"I'll take good care of her, Mr. Patton."

"Please call me Pat."

"Okay, Pat, you got a deal."

Pat got there about the same time as Eb and Kathy. With their help, and the fact that the movers came early, most of the things had been moved by 11:00. Greg and Grace arrived with Shirley and Mary right behind. By noon the last load was ready to be taken to the new house. Greg offered to buy everyone lunch, including the movers, and took orders to call in to the Flying Buzzard. Mary would go along to help with the food, while Shirley road in the van with Pat.

"This is not fun, Honey. I want to roll up my sleeves and help! I'm not used to sitting around and doing nothing."

"A few more weeks, Shir. Only a few more weeks."

Greg, Grace and Mary went inside and got in a special call-in order line.' A very big man was in front of them.

"May I help you, Sir?"

"Yeah, I, ah, called in, ah, an order to be picked up at 12:30."

"Yes, Sir, what's the name?"

"Ah, Carter."

"Coming right up, Sir."

He picked up his order, got into a pickup truck and left.

"Boy, how would you like to face somebody like him in a dark alley?" asked Grace.

"No way," answered Mary. "I'm not sure I would trust my .38 Special to stop someone that big."

They picked up the buzzard sandwiches and went back to the new house. The truck was already unloaded and the movers were putting furniture where Pat wanted it. The things from the basement had previously been unloaded. While there, Greg was beeped by his answering service. He used Pat's phone.

"This is Dr. O'Kelly. You beeped me? Yes? You don't say? That's great news, and thanks for calling!"

"Hey, everybody! Great news. Shirley – your operation has been moved up to Feb. 10th! Dr. Orhan had a cancellation and gave you the slot! He said he was sure a cornea would be available."

Shirley grabbed Pat and they danced around a circle shouting for joy. Then she asked them all to come close and gave them all a big hug.

"The Chief, he really got y'all covered," said Mary, looking out the window. "Two or three times I saw police cars around us, and another one slowly drove by your house."

"Did you notice the one at the Flying Buzzard? He followed us in and then left when we did," asked Grace.

"Sure did," answered Mary. "Just like the old days when I wore a blue uniform."

Greg and Grace finished eating and left for the Lake Spivey Country Club. They all agreed to meet at the Brave Bull at 7:00. Pat, Shirley, Mary, Eb, and Kathy stayed to get the house straight, sheets on the beds, TV hooked up, and a hundred other things. They all loved this house. Pat told Greg he would return the van and pick up the '57 Chevy for a day or two if that was okay with him. Later that afternoon, Pat and Eb got it, and even put the top down for a while, although the weather was really too cool. Things at the new house were going very smoothly and Pat and Eb got some time to arrange things in the shop.

* * *

"Hey, ah, Jeffie, I'm back," yelled Reb. "I, ah, got them buzzard sandwiches you, ah, wanted, and all that other stuff too! All of it."

Jeffie was laying down on a mattress, only it wasn't Jeffie – it was a woman! Reb couldn't see the face, but only the back of the head and dress. Suddenly, she turned around and it was Jeffie!

"Fooled you, didn't I?"

"Ah, yeah, Jeffie. I thought a women was laying there."

"Good. Now let's eat and then I want a haircut and a shave. I'm gonna wear these woman's clothes the rest of the day and tonight to get used to them. Then tomorrow when I see Piss-Ant and the rest of them O'Kelly's, I won't feel so awkward in this outfit."

"Ah, Jeffie, you think of everything," complemented Reb with great admiration.

"Reb, after I get back from church tomorrow, you're gonna get to shoot that gun again."

"Oh, good, good, good." Reb, clapped his hands.

"That ain't all. How would you like to go nigger hunting Monday night?"

"Do I get to shoot 'em?"

"You sure do."

"With my, ah, new gun?"

"Right again."

"I, ah, I can hardly wait! I'm gonna shoot him full of holes, and then I'm gonna throw the gun into a big trash can."

"And you will wear rubber gloves, won't you?"

"Ah, yeah, I'll wear just like you told me."

"We need to steal two cars or trucks early Monday night, as soon as it gets dark."

"Yeah, that will be fun. I like to steal cars and trucks." Reb took a bite out of his buzzard sandwich. "And shoot niggers."

* * *

Shirley started to learn where the furniture was located in each room, and she used her white folding cane to navigate through the house with Mary always near and helping when needed. She told the group to be sure not to move anything from then on, that she and Pat would fine-tune the house after they got back from New York City. Shirley practiced counting steps between objects.

When Shirley and Kathy were outside, a kitten came up to her and started to meow, so they fed it some milk. Shirley asked Mary to go to the neighbors on both sides of the house to see if it belonged to them. They came over and introduced themselves to Shirley and Pat but said they had never seen the cat before. Pat fixed up a cardboard box, about a foot square, as a little house for the cat. Shirley was calling it Whitefoot, because Pat told her the cat was black with one partially white foot. The box had a hole in one side and an old towel in the bottom for a bed. They put the box on the back downstairs porch, which was sheltered by the screened in and roofed deck.

"Aren't I the lucky one," said Pat semi-sarcastically. "We haven't even been here one day and already have a cat!"

Shirley heard him. "Yes, and you're as big a pushover as I am, so why not admit it? Whitefoot, see that big lug over there? He's your daddy. Waive your little paw at him." As Shirley was saying this, she was waving the cat's little paw in the direction of Pat's voice, which made him break out laughing.

* * *

Reb used the electric hair-clippers to cut Jeffie's hair. Jeffie used two of the disposable razors and shaving cream to shave both his face and his head. Reb couldn't help but laugh.

"What are you laughing at, Dumbass?"

"Your head, ah, looks like a cue ball." And Reb laughed again.

Jeffie glared at Reb, who shut up. Then Jeffie put on the wig, earrings, lipstick, and even perfume. He carefully looked at himself in the mirror and decided half of his eyebrows would have to go. He applied a little rouge and eye shadow. Reb was amazed. He really did look like a woman, especially with the stuffed bra. Jeffie practiced a feminine walk and hand movements. He also practiced sitting down in a dress. Like his brother, Skinny, Jeffie was a born actor.

"Okay, Reb, you're taking me out to eat. Here's $20 to pay the bill. I will not talk. I'll fake laryngitis. One more thing before we go."

"Ah, what's that, Jeffie."

"Sit right down here and I'll show you."

"Please, ah, Jeffie, not my hair."

"Not only your hair, Dumbass, your beard, too!"

* * *

Pat and his group arrived at the Brave Bull and were seated. They didn't notice the large bald man with his girlfriend seated at a back table. But – the strangers noticed them!

CHAPTER 45

The Church Service

Sunday morning was a beautiful day that started out at 35° but warmed up to 65° as the day progressed. Pat and Shirley woke up in each other's arms after a night of wild lovemaking.

"It's so good to be in your manly arms again, big boy." Without her dark glasses on, Shirley's eyes had a milkish white color to them.

My poor baby with the beautiful green eyes! Why did this have to happen to you?

"Shirley, I love you so much. I really don't know what I would do without you! Just ten more days and you'll see again! From what your daddy said, it's a slam dunk! Corneal transplants are not that uncommon. Just think, you'll be able to see soon!"

"I so want to see your handsome face again."

"Whatever happens, Honey, I will be here for you."

They cuddled for a little while longer, got their showers and dressed. Mary was up and cooking breakfast, even though she was not paid to be a cook. Mary would go to church with them and was looking forward to it. Finally it was time to leave, and Pat decided to take the 1957 Chevy because it was just plain fun to drive.

* * *

331

Jeffie got up early to make sure he was looking as much like a woman as possible. He had called the church a few days before and found out the service started at 10:45 and let out at 11:45, so worshipers at Solid Rock Jonesboro Christian Church could get a jump on the Baptists in finding an empty table at lunch time. He also found out there were no scheduled church functions or meetings on Monday nights. However, they always had one elder there from 7:00 o'clock to 9:00 PM in case something were to come up, and that was also the time for him, or one of his volunteers, to clean the baptistery. Perfect! He could get in when only one or two people would be there. Now to figure out how to get Piss-Ant and Tight-Ass there.

"Ah, Jeffie, why are you being a woman?"

"'Cause the cops are looking for a man, not a woman, Dumbass."

"Jeffie, ah, what if they figure out who you are?"

"Reb, they're too stupid to figure it out. Besides, I love to get right in their face, daring them to do something about it. After that, I'll kill them. I know you won't understand this, but Indians would be considered brave if they touched their enemies. They called it counting coup. They would strike their enemy but, I'm going to shake hands with mine. Yeah, get right in their face! Then kill them!"

Reb drove him to the local Burger Doodle for breakfast. Jeffie gave him another $20 to pay for it and lunch later. He also had a pad and pencil with him in his pocketbook to write notes. Then he got an idea.

"Hey, Dumbass, how does this whisper sound? Does it sound like I have laryngitis?"

"Ah, Jeffie, I, ah, don't know what this larry-giet-is is, but you sound like, ah, like somebody who has a bad cold and lost his voice!"

"Oh-h-h, Reb, I don't know why I put myself through this, but my whisper sounds real, huh?"

"Yeah, it does."

"Good. Keep the money I gave you for lunch, but I'm going to order and pay, 'cause I want to try out this voice before I use it in church."

"Ah, Jeffie. Why we goin' to church?"

"'Cause I might come back later and need to know the layout of the building, Dumbass. And I told you I like the idea of getting right in their face with them not knowing who I am."

Jeffie ordered and explained he had lost his/her voice. The cashier was very nice and said: "Ma'am, I hope you get it back real soon and thank you for stopping to have breakfast with us."

When they got to their table, Jeffie smiled and whispered that it worked. Even on the way to church, he talked to Reb in a whisper, practicing being a woman with laryngitis. "Reb, you stay in the truck, lay back so no one can see you and take a nap."

Reb pulled his pickup into the church parking lot near the back. They were 15 minutes early for the service but many of the parking spaces were taken up by cars of people attending Sunday School. Jeffie got out, fixed his dress, asked Reb to see if everything was in order, and tried to walk to the entrance with a feminine gate.

"Good morning, Ma'am," said a greeter, who asked Leo to seat Jeffie. He whispered, "I prefer a seat near the rear, what with me being a visitor and all, I don't feel comfortable up front."

The usher said he understood and seated Jeffie in a rear aisle seat, where he had a perfect view of the sanctuary. He started to throw away the introductory package given to prospective new members but decided to hang on to it."

Jeffie could not believe his eyes when the collection plate was handed to him by old man O'Kelly himself. He looked very much like the newspaper pictures.

I didn't really get a good look at him last night at the Brave Bull.

At communion time, Jeffie got another good look at Greg. He was given a plate full of tiny wafers and a container full of grape juice. Jeffie wasn't sure what he was supposed to do with them, but saw people eating a wafer and washing it down with the grape juice, so he did the same.

When the stupid service was over, he saw Pat and the whole O'Kelly clan and burnt their faces into his memory, especially Shirley's.

You and me are going to have us some fun tomorrow night, baby.

Jeffie left the sanctuary and made his way through the crowd to the visitor's desk.

"You have a beautiful building here," whispered Jeffie. "Could someone take me on a short tour?"

Greg, who was an elder in the church, stopped by, shook Jeffie's hand and introduced himself.

This was just too good to be true! I got them all fooled!

The lady at the desk told Greg of Jeffie's request and Greg found Arline Wills, who gave him the grand tour. Jeffie had a good memory and tried to remember everything about the layout of the building.

When he left and got back to the truck, Jeffie grabbed his tablet and pen and started to make notes and draw diagrams of what he saw.

"Ah, Jeffie, I - - -,"

"Not now, Dumbass, can't you see I gotta write some of this info down before I forget it!" said Jeffie in a highly irritated voice.

Several minutes later he put the notes and drawing into his pocketbook.

"Okay, Dumbass, what's your problem?"

"Ah, Jeffie, I did it again."

"You did what again? I swear you're going to drive me nuts!"

"Ah, Jeffie, I had that feeling again."

"Damn, Reb, what feeling?"

"Like, ah, someone was watching us."

"When!"

"Just before you came out and, ah, up to a few minutes ago."

"Damn, damn, damn! Why didn't you tell me when I first came out! Didn't I tell you to let me know just as soon as you had another one of those feelings?" yelled Jeffie as he looked all around.

"I, ah, tried to, but, but you called me a dumbass."

"Ah, hell, do you still have it, the feeling?"

"No."

"Well, be damn sure to tell me next time, for sure."

"I will, Jeffie."

"I found out something interesting from the tour guide. She told me Piss-Ant and Tight-Ass are to be married in the church on March 7th, but have to go through a premarital counseling session with Reverend Hawkins first. That gave me an idea."

* * *

After church the O'Kelly group gathered around for Sunday lunch at the dining room table. Greg got everyone's attention.

"I got a call from Dr. Orhan last night, and I wanted to outline his plan with the two of you," said Greg to Shirley and Pat. "First of all, he is only doing one eye on the 10th and has scheduled the 27th for the other eye."

"Why not both eyes at the same time?" asked Shirley. "If the operation fails, I can't see anyway. It's not like I had at least some vision in my eyes."

"There are two reasons. One is the possibility of rejection. I know, this is 1981, and we have come a long way in medicine, but although it is rare with a cornea transplant these days, it could happen. Your body could decide it doesn't like the new cornea, and Dr. Orhan does not want to fight a possible rejection in both eyes."

"What's the other thing, Greg?" asked Pat.

"Just plain infection. What happens in one eye, many times will affect the other eye. In other words, if one eye were to get infected, there is a good chance the other one could also become infected. Infection is always a possibility, and he would not want to fight an infection in two recently transplanted corneas."

"Right, Daddy. I see, or under my circumstances, should I say I understand." That she could make light of her own plight was a testimony to her character.

335

"The operation, operations will take place in a New York City hospital. You will stay overnight, as a precaution. It is not a serious operation and could actually be done as an outpatient, but not with my daughter. We are taking no chances. I forgot to tell you the procedure should take less than an hour, and your eyes will be patched for about five days. Both eyes will be completed prior to your wedding, Honey."

"Then it looks like we have to make two trips to New York. So what? From the 15th on, when the first patch comes off, I'll at least be able to see with one eye."

When they finished eating, the whole gang went over to Pat and Shirley's new house. When Grace saw how well her daughter was doing, she told Greg they needed to leave, as the kids had many things to do with straightening up. There were still many unopened boxes stacked up in the 3rd bedroom.

After Greg and Grace said their goodbyes, Pat got busy on some of the boxes, but left all of the furniture where it was. They could fine tune it later.

"Pat or Shirley, you have a call from the church office," announced Mary.

"I'll get it," said Pat.

"Yes, this is he. Certainly, I'll tell her. Thank you."

"Who was that?" asked Shirley.

"Reverend Hawkins wants us to come to the church at 7:30 tomorrow night for a counseling session concerning our wedding."

"Right, I've been expecting the call. You did tell her yes, didn't you?"

"I sure did, but it was a he, not a she."

"That's strange. Usually Robin makes those calls. I don't know any men who work in the office." Shirley had an uneasy feeling.

"Most likely a volunteer calling for Reverend Hawkins."

"You're probably right. Honey, I want to practice with my gun again."

Pat unloaded her .38 Special and took out the cylinder as a safety precaution. Shirley practiced pointing and shooting at sounds Pat would make. He would tell her when she was off, but Shirley got to where she was right on target most of the time. However, it would only take once to end up dead. He told her to fire at the sound, and then rapidly fire a little to the right and to the left of it. If the first shot was off the mark, she might get lucky with the 2nd or 3rd shot, and still have three shots left.

Later they turned on some good soft music and Shirley talked to Mary while Pat finished up the Edwards' habeas, which he would have Julie type up and file the next day. She had subpoenaed all of the witnesses to court on Wednesday. Then Ed would be free. The press would be there on this hearing, too, as a man in prison for 26 years for self-defense is big news.

* * *

Jeffie had Reb get a large cardboard box out of a dumpster behind a store, and with a magic marker, drew an outline of a man on it. They set it up in the woods and Jeffie gave Reb the 9mm automatic and 50 rounds of ammo. He had Reb practice firing from the passenger's side window, because that's the side the bus stop is on.

After the first shot, Reb put some Kleenex in his hurting ears. He also practiced pushing the safety on and off, and the same with pushing the slide back and snapping in a fresh round from the clip. When he was finished, Jeffie let loose with a round from the shotgun. The box was quite dead.

When they were done, the boys drove by Ed's bus stop and, sure enough, he was there sitting in his wheelchair drinking liquor with some of his friends.

"There he is, Reb! When you come tomorrow, if he's with any of his black friends, take them out, too! That would be an extra bonus, and that way there are no witnesses. And – don't forget to wear gloves and that stocking over your head."

"I won't, Jeffie, ah, I can hardly wait. Maybe, maybe, ah, them two will be there and I can shoot them, too!"

I'm glad I had Reb practice shooting from the truck. We'll have to steal one with a bench seat like the one he owns, as he can easily slide over, with his left foot on the brake pedal, and cover a good area out of the window. One thing about Reb, he would never rat on me if he got caught. Deliberately, that is, but he isn't too smart. I need to think about that.

"Reb, I read in the paper where Piss-Ant's partner is having his house rebuilt. What say we come back in a few months, when it's finished, and burn it down again?"

"Yeah, ah, Jeffie, that would be fun."

They got something to eat and went home. Jeffie hardly realized he was still in a dress and still whispering. That was the secret of not screwing up - - play the role 24 hours per day. Make it seem natural. He would stay a woman until after he was a long way from here. He had some biker friends in California and would move out there, or possibly Tennessee.

It's a shame I'll have to kill Reb, but the cops will be looking for both of us by tomorrow evening, as Ed will be killed about the same time as I deal with Piss-Ant and Tight-Ass. The big dumbass could never get along by himself, and could be tricked into talking, even though he is loyal as a dog. I'll take him to the old abandoned house down the road and tell him to look down in the well. He'll do anything I tell him. A .38 in the back of the head and then a shove should do it. The well is deep and they may never find his body.

The thought of killing Reb didn't bother Jeffie one bit. It was just a job he had to do.

* * *

Monday morning started out with cold winds and rain. Pat got up, bid Shirley and Mary goodbye and left for his office. He took Shirley's car, as he couldn't bear to get the '57 Chevy out in weather like this. Pat said he would be back by 5:00, because they had the meeting with the preacher.

Julie was at the office when he got there.

"Hey, Boss, it's good to see you back."

"I'm glad to hear that, because I need you to type up this habeas for me. It needs to be filed this afternoon.

"That's what you're paying me those big bucks for. Hint! Hint! Hint!" Julie had a devious smile.

"Look, Julie, you could be a little more subtle than that. By the way, did you hear the weather report for today?"

"Yeah, Boss. This mess is supposed to clear up by noon, the sun will peek out, and then we may have a very nice day. That is if the ground hog doesn't see his shadow."

"What does a groundhog have to do with today?"

"It's Groundhog Day."

"I know that, but he predicts six more weeks of winter, not rain or snow?"

"Well, I thought it sounded good anyway."

"Here, maybe typing this habeas will keep you from driving me completely nuts," said Pat tossing his handwritten habeas on her desk.

"Jeez, Boss, thanks a million." Julie made a fake pout.

As Rhonda was leaving, Pat stopped in to see Herb, who was working on a divorce case.

"Hi, Herb. I've been so busy I've been neglecting you. How's it going?"

"Unlike you with car bombs, arrows, and shootouts following you around, I'm doing good."

"Boy, isn't that the truth. And, it all started with a simple adoption case a few months ago. But at least I didn't get my house burnt down. Say, how is the construction coming?"

"Another two weeks and we should be able to move back. They put a couple of extra men on it, but the interior seems to take as long as the exterior."

"I can understand - - you have sheetrock, wiring, bathrooms, trim, plumbing, heating and air, painting, and several more things."

"Quiet. You're making me tired."

"Julie is typing up Ed's habeas. Would you mind looking it over before it's filed this afternoon?"

"Not at all. I should be here all morning, so bring it by my office. I've been taking in your overflow cases but you are supposed to be taking in mine. I appreciate the business!"

Julie got the habeas done, Herb checked it, and Pat filed it with the clerk's office. He took a copy to the DA's office and gave it to Thelma.

"Pat, you can take it back to Nancy. She has been given the honor of representing the State on this one. DA Colver let her have it, even though you two are good friends. He figures Judge Musselman is going to grant it no matter what we do. Not to mention that he believes Ed was acting in self-defense. From what Shirley told him before she was injured, it was a railroad job and he doesn't want that hanging over an innocent man's head. Let me buzz her. Pat to see you. Okay."

"Hi, Pat. Have a seat. Do any motorcycle riding lately?"

"Truthfully, since Shirley got hurt on the 21st, I haven't had time to hardly go to the bathroom. Here's a copy of the Edwards' Habeas Corpus I just filed."

"Right. It's on for Wednesday. The word came down from the judge that unless we can find a compelling reason for him not to, he is going to grant your petition. Provided you produce the evidence in court you say you have."

"Nancy, I've got it and it will be produced. Two witnesses will testify Ed was attacked in his own home, defended himself, his wife, his home, and shot the man on the ground only when the man raised a rifle to shoot him first. From what I can find out, the trial was a farce! As you can see, we have subpoenaed the bailiff, too, although it is probably overkill."

"No, it's called representing your client. You would be surprised at how many attorneys do as little as possible for their clients."

"No, I wouldn't, but that's sad. If you take the money, you need to work for them, even if it is the county's money for an indigent defendant. Say, it's almost lunch; I'll buy if you have the time."

"I haven't had a better offer. Let's go."

He asked Thelma to let Julie know where he was going. Then they had a good lunch at the Chinese Lullaby. The Atlanta PD car was slowly driving by when he got back to his office.

"Hi, Boss. I have two clients set up from over a week ago, and both are threatening to pay you a retainer."

"I see your Atlanta PD friends are still keeping an eye on you."

"That's because I'm valuable property."

"I'll second that."

"It's a rainy mess outside now, but tonight is supposed to be a mild clear night and a beautiful day tomorrow."

"Good! We have to go to the church tonight to meet with Reverend Hawkins and get our pre-marriage counseling and I didn't want to do it in the rain. Want a Hershey Bar?"

"Thanks, Boss, I love those things, too."

Pat saw his clients, who did pay to retain him, and then he headed for home. Shirley was cooking supper, with a whole lot of help from Mary.

* * *

When Jeffie woke up and looked outside at the rainy mess, he almost called off everything because Ed would not be at the bus stop in the rain and both hits needed to be at the same time. He didn't want the cops following Pat to be on alert, because of word Ed got hit. However, as the morning wore on, things looked much better, and the forecast on TV looked promising for the rest of the day and night.

"Reb, this is it! We do it today. Everything points to a pretty day and night. The Tar Baby has been at the bus stop every day and night since he got out of the hospital last Friday. I never heard of no one hanging out at a bus stop before, but it will make it easier for you to find him. After lunch we ride by to check and if he's there, we steal a pickup for you and a car for me. I'm wanting a plain-Jane type of car nobody will notice."

"Good! Good! Ah, Jeffie, can I have my gun now?"

"Later, Reb, I need to keep it for now. After you kill Ed, drive over to the Jamestown Plaza and park the stolen truck about 10 to 15 spaces away from where we'll park your truck this afternoon. Whoever gets there first will wait on the other one, unless either one of us spots cops. Drive by and look around before you park. You got that?" said Jeffie in his feminine whisper.

"Yeah, I got it. Ah, Jeffie, can I have my gun now?"

"What did I just get done telling you?"

"Ah, later you said, but it is later."

"No, Dumbass! What did I tell you to do after you kill Ed?"

"I don't want to fry, so I gotta throw it away."

"Good, Reb, and after you throw it away?"

"Ah, I go to Jamestown and look for cops, and if I don't see none, then I park a little way from my truck and wait on you."

"Damn! I don't believe it! You're gettin' to be a smart dumbass."

"Aw-w-w, thanks, Jeffie," responded a grateful Reb, like an obedient dog being praised by his master.

"Let's go get lunch. I'll get our tool kit and put it in the truck. You drive, as everyone expects the guy to drive. Let me look in the mirror before we go. I want to be sure this makeup and outfit look okay.

After it's over tonight the cops won't be looking for a female traveling alone.

Jeffie decided to eat lunch at the Silver Slipper to test out the disguise.

"Let me go in first, and you come in a few minutes later. I want to see if any of the regulars recognize me without you. When you come in, sit at my table. I'll do the talking."

Jeffie went in and sat at a table, crossing his legs like he practiced. Spike came over to wait on him.

What will you have, sister?"

"A burger, fries, and a beer," whispered Jeffie.

"Coming right up. You're new here, Honey. What's your name?"

That caught Jeffie by surprise; he had not thought about it.

"My boyfriend will be here in just a minute. Double that order," whispered Jeffie, ignoring his question.

"Look, honey, my name's Spike. Watch these girls in here 'cause they don't like for no strange woman to come in here messin' with their men. Even if you're a big woman."

"Thanks."

"You have a cute voice, Honey. Be back in a minute with your beer."

While he was gone, Reb came in.

"Don't say one word, Dumbass, 'cause they might recognize your voice."

Even Reb looked completely different with a shaved head, no beard, and no Harley hat.

Spike brought the beers and later the food without a word. Everyone was staring at one time or another, but Jeffie and Reb got through lunch without a single person realizing who they were.

"You two ever been in here before?" asked Spike as Jeffie paid the bill. "There is something familiar about you, but I can't put my finger on it."

Jeffie didn't answer, but walked out the door swinging his hips. Reb followed. When they got to the truck, they both broke out laughing. No one recognized either of them.

"Spike even tried to put the make on me!" laughed Jeffie.

"Ah, they didn't know me either. Did they, Jeffie?"

"No, Reb, they didn't know you either. Now, let's go steal us a car and a truck. Charley Mac's Used Car Lot is closed on Monday, so he won't know anything is missing until tomorrow. Let's do it."

"Okay, Jeffie, 'cause, ah, you know I like to steal cars and trucks."

When no cars were coming, Reb used bolt cutters to cut the chain going across the driveway. Quick work was made of the door lock on the Chevy pickup, which Jeffie picked out. Another minute or two and the screwdrivers pried off the plastic cover on the steering column and steering lock-spring. He pushed the starter rod and was off. He told Reb he would stop and fill up the tank. He met Reb at the shopping center, and they went back and got a Chevy V8 four-door sedan. No one paid the slightest bit of attention to them.

"I'll fill this one up, too, and meet you at the house. I'll get us some supper - - a couple of them Flying Buzzard sandwiches, and bring them home. See you there!"

Jeffie was feeling good! He gassed up and picked up the food. Ed lived less than ten mils away, so he decided to check on him. When he went by the bus stop, there sat Ed, drinking with his damn buddies.

Skinny, my brother, it has taken awhile, but we're gonna get them for you tonight! They will die for what they did to you! Die! Die! Die!" hissed Jeffie.

Jeffie gave Reb the 14- shot 9-mm automatic. He also gave him an extra full clip.

If he can't get the job done with 28 shots, he never will.

"Gonna shoot him, ah, 14 times. Ain't I, Jeffie?"

"Yeh, Reb, 14 times."

CHAPTER 46

It's Coming Down!

At 6:45, Ed finished the dinner his mother had fixed for him. He got in his wheelchair and went back to the bus stop. One of his friends was still there. It was cool, and the blanket over his legs felt good. Two other friends had left to get something to eat, and another bottle, but would return because, although chilly, it was a beautiful night. After only a few days, Ed was getting along really well in his wheelchair, without help from anyone.

I wonders how many days before "dey" come again. But come again dey will! I's sure of it, in spite of the regular visits by Atlanta PD patrol cars.

Ed drank very little, but always acted like he was drunk.

* * *

Jeffie wiped the 9-mm clean, and instructed Reb to put on his rubber gloves.

"Reb, it's 6:30 and time to go. I want to be at the church by 7:00 when only one of the elders and possibly a helper will be there." He put on his rubber gloves and wiped the shotgun and shells clean. Then he wiped the .38

Special and ammo clean, along with the switchblade knife he carried. The .38 and knife were put in his purse, while the sawed-off double-barreled shotgun was wrapped in a sweater.

As they went out the door, Jeffie turned and gave Reb a hug. "Good luck, Reb! I'll see you at the parking lot."

"I'll make you, ah, proud of me, Jeffie!"

At 6:45 they were on their way.

* * *

"Mary, it's 6:45. I'll take Shirley to the church now. We're leaving a little early because of a needed gas stop. I also want to run her car through the carwash. That should put us at the church just before the 7:30 meeting. I talked to Shirley and we both agree you deserve a night off."

"Thanks, Pat, but if it's all the same to you, I'll make some popcorn, have a coke, and watch a good movie."

"All alone, huh?"

"Yeah, but Shirley told me she would mention my name to Ed. Maybe you could, too. He sounds like quite a man."

"I'll do it and he is quite a man. See you."

"Have a good time."

* * *

Reb was very excited. He kept the 9-mm automatic on his lap. He even patted and talked to it. As he drove, Reb sang a little song he managed to make up.

"Hi ho, hi ho, it's, ah, off to the bus stop I go,
I'll pull the trigger, and kill me a nigger,
Hi ho, hi ho, hi ho!"

Let's see now. I gotta circle the block and make sure, ah, there ain't no cops. Yeah, ah, shoot 'em at least three times, and then, because, ah, I don't want to fry, I gotta throw my gun away. Jeffie will, ah, get me another one, I jus know it. Maybe I can kill some more with my new gun. Damn, I hope he got his friends with him 'cause

Jeffie said I get to kill them, too! If not, maybe I can shoot him 14 times.

He went past the bus stop and turned right to circle the block like Jeffie told him to do. *He's there! He is there! The Tar Baby is there!* Reb was so excited.

Ed was sitting in his wheelchair at the bus stop talking to his friends. He looked at his watch - - it was 7:15. A pickup truck slowly went by. He could see a big white man behind the steering wheel. The man looked them over good, and then turned right on Ed's street into a neighborhood where no white man ever went.

"Quick, guys! Get away from me!" yelled Ed, clearly and calmly.

"Whatcha mean, man?"

"I said now! I's don't have no time to explain. Go now! At least ten to 15 feet away from me!"

They moved, and Ed waited. Sure enough the pickup was coming again. As the man stopped and rolled down the window on the passenger's side of the truck, Ed cocked the shotgun strapped to his amputated leg.

"Ah, hey, nigger! I got something for you! You're about to die, tar baby!"

"Sorry, redneck, but dis nigger fights back!"

Ed raised the stub of his amputated leg, pointed it at the man in the pickup, and pulled the trigger.

Blam-m-m-m! Reb's gun flew out of his hand as he was blown back into the truck, his face a mass of red! The automatic transmission was in drive and, when Reb was shot, his foot slipped off the brake pedal causing the truck to slowly run off the street and into a parked car.

Seconds later, the Atlanta Police car came by again. It stopped behind the truck with its blue lights flashing as two officers jumped out with guns drawn.

"Hands up where we can see them!" ordered one officer, as he saw the shotgun strapped to Ed's bleeding leg.

Maybe he should tell me to put my leg up, too.

"We don't have to worry about this one!" yelled the 2nd officer, picking up the 9-mm automatic.

"He was tryin' to kill me, officer. Dat redneck was gettin' ready to pull de trigger, but I pulled mine first!"

"It wouldn't have done him one bit of good," said the 2nd officer.

"What do you mean?" asked Ed.

"He didn't have a round in the chamber!"

* * *

Jeffie cut the telephone lines, and then walked into the church. It was 7:05. He saw only one man go through the doorway. *The man is about to find out this isn't going to be his day.* As Jeffie entered the church, a small Honda with dark window tint, parked across the street. He had not noticed it following him. It was about to enter the church parking lot when the driver saw an Oldsmobile Cutlass pull in.

* * *

Mary was sitting on the couch with Whitefoot curled up in her lap. With one hand she petted the cat, which was purring, softly, while she ate popcorn with the other hand. The movie Kramer vs Kramer was on TV, and she was laughing at a scene, when the telephone rang. She looked at the clock; it showed 7:30.

"You reached the Patton residence, Mary speaking."

"This is Reverend Hawkins and I would like to speak to either Pat or Shirley, please."

"Sir, they should have been to your meeting by now because they left about 45 minutes ago."

"What meeting?"

"They told me they were supposed to be at the church for a 7:30 meeting with you. Something to do with counseling before getting married."

"I didn't call a meeting. In fact that's what this call is about, to set one up at a time convenient for both of us."

"Are you calling from the church?"

"No, I'm at home."

"Quickly Reverend, please give me the number at the church!"

She excused herself and dialed the number. A recording said the number was out of order.

I don't like this at all!

Mary dialed Capt. Keller's home number, from a personal phone book laying on the coffee table.

"Keller residence, Dottie speaking."

"This is urgent. I'm Mary Williams and I'm working for Mr. Patton and Shirley O'Kelly. I need to speak to Capt. Keller!"

"I'll get him to the phone right now." An hour seemed to pass until Capt. Keller answered.

"Hi, Mary. What can I do for you?"

"Capt. Keller, I'm so glad I got you. Pat and Shirley were called to their church tonight for a meeting with Reverend Hawkins at 7:30. A few minutes ago, I answered their phone and it was The Reverend saying he never scheduled such a meeting. Then I called the church and got a recording saying the phone is out of order. Capt., I don't like this one bit! My police experience tells me something is very wrong!"

"Thank you, Mary. I'll get a car over there right now!"

"Dottie, stay here! I'll have to run over to Solid Rock Christian Church. Pat and Shirley may be in big trouble," said Capt. Keller as he dialed the dispatcher's number.

"Evette! Get a car over to Solid Rock Christian Church immediately! Tell the officers there could be trouble. On second thought, send two cars, one to the front of the church and another to cover the back. Tell them to go in with guns drawn and also call the EMS. This could very well be Jeffie Anderson going for the kill. Then, please notify the Chief. Bye!"

Capt. Keller grabbed his service revolver and an extra speed-load of six cartridges for his .38 Special and ran out to his car.

On the way to the church, Evette called him on the radio. "I have two cars on the way. I received a call from Atlanta PD. A man tried to kill Ed Edwards less than 30 minutes ago, but Ed killed him instead."

"Damn! It's coming down! Please tell the officers to approach with the utmost caution!"

He raced to the church with blue lights and the siren on.

* * *

Shirley took Pat's arm as he led her across the church parking lot. The lights were on and the door was open.

"I guess we go to Reverend Hawkins' office. You nervous?" asked Pat.

"A little, but I've never been so sure of anything in my whole life."

"I love you, Shir, and know you feel the same way. I will always be there for you. No matter what!"

She reached up and kissed him. "That last comment will get you everything I have to offer, and I will give it willingly."

"A little down-payment after we get home?"

"More than a little, Big Boy, so be prepared!" said Shirley in a sexy caring manner.

They walked arm and arm toward the church office. As they went in, a man was sitting behind a desk.

"He looks like he's asleep. Sir? Sir?"

There was no response from him.

"Shir, stay here." A worried Pat walked around the counter to where the man sat. There was blood on the back of his coat and on his head. Pat felt for a pulse, but found none.

"This man is dead!" Pat drew his .357 Magnum.

"What's happening?" said a worried Shirley as she got her .38 out of her pocketbook.

"Shir, quick, back in the corner," ordered Pat, as he took Shirley by the arm and sat her on a chair in a corner. "No one can get behind you here. Something's wrong! It could be Jeffie or one of the Confederates!"

"Call the police!" yelled Shirley, but Pat had already picked up the phone.

"The line's dead! Stay here! I'm going to go outside to flag down a car. He quickly headed out the doorway with the .357 in his hand. That's when he felt a pain in his head and quickly lost consciousness.

Jeffie was waiting outside the door with the shotgun and hit him in the head with the stock. Jeffie immediately tied Pat's hands as Pat lay on the floor.

"Pat! Pat! Answer me! Please! What's going on?"

"Your dear Piss-Ant can't answer you, my dear, as he . . ."

Bang! Bang! Bang! Shirley shot at the sound and came very close to hitting Jeffie in a vital spot, but she only got some flesh about an inch below his rib cage. She had shot again to the right, and to the left, as Pat had taught her, but missed both times.

"You bitch!" screamed Jeffie who was bleeding but not hurt badly.

Bang! Shirley shot again, but Jeffie was waiting for her this time. He picked Pat up and held him in front of him. Pat was starting to come around, blood running down his neck from a head wound.

"I got your Piss-Ant boyfriend in front of me now! Go ahead and shoot! Fill this dog turd full of lead!" screamed Jeffie.

Jeffie held Pat and the shotgun with his left hand and arm and grabbed a book with his right hand. He didn't want to kill her until after they had their party.

"Pat, Pat! Where are you?"

Jeffie threw the book in the opposite corner of the room. When Shirley shot in the direction of the sound, he dropped Pat and rushed Shirley, grabbing her gun hand and throwing her .38 to the floor.

"I got your fangs now, you little rattlesnake! I didn't kill your Piss-Ant boyfriend because I want him to watch what I'm about to do to you!"

With a sneer on his face, he tied her hands behind her back. Jeffie ripped open her blouse and cut the bra straps, which exposed her breasts.

Then a voice behind him said, "Just like when you raped me, huh, Jeffie?"

He turned around. A small, pretty woman with long dark hair stood with a gun in her hand. Before he could get his shotgun and aim at her, a bullet from a .380 automatic tore into his stomach.

"C-Cindy? You? My Camaro? The s-s-snake?" gasped Jeffie with a look of surprise and disbelief on his face. He was still standing but looked totally confused.

"And this one's for my puppy!" She shot him between the legs. "And these are just for the hell of it!" She shot him in his left arm, the one holding the shotgun, making it fall to the floor. Then another in his right thigh, which made him fall down.

Pat was aware of what was going on but confused. *She's deliberately shooting this woman in non-vital areas, making her die a slow painful death.*

Then he realized. That's not a woman. *It was Jeffie!*

Shirley was trying not to cry. Being tied-up, and unable to see what was going on, almost made her sick. *I've never felt so helpless!*

"Please untie me!" pleaded Pat.

Cindy produced a knife, the rope was cut, and Pat was free. He quickly picked up Shirley's .38 from the floor and went to her.

"What happened?" asked Shirley as Cindy cut her loose.

"Cindy? Jeffie said Cindy? It's you, Cindy, isn't it?" asked Pat. "You saved our lives!"

"I've been following that bastard for weeks trying to get up enough nerve to face him. When I saw Jeffie, dressed as a woman, cutting the telephone lines, I knew he wasn't going to church to pray, and I couldn't wait any longer!" Cindy looked at what she had done and over 25 years of grief poured out at once as she started sobbing almost uncontrollably, dropping her gun.

Pat took both Shirley and Cindy in his arms and held them. Cindy's eyes got big and she pointed to Jeffie. He was raising the shotgun with his good arm and what remaining strength he had! At this range, with a sawed-off shotgun, they would all be hit!

Pat threw the girls aside, and then realized he was still holding Shirley's .38 Special in his hand. Instinct for survival took over as he fired a split-second later, hitting Jeffie in the chest. He pulled the trigger again and again, but got clicks because Shirley's .38 was empty. The chest shot was enough to make Jeffie's shot go wild and tear a hole in the wall. Pat kicked the shotgun away from Jeffie, then took off his coat and used it to cover Shirley's exposed breasts.

Less than a minute later, Capt. Keller arrived with two uniformed police officers on his tail. All had their guns drawn. Two more officers raced to the back of the church.

"Pat, Shirley, are you alright? Who's this other woman?"

"Cindy is the lady who just saved our lives! She's Jeffie's step-daughter and Renee's daughter."

"And the two bodies?"

"The man at the desk is apparently an elder in the church. I've seen him before but don't know his name. The person in the dress is Jeffie, or was Jeffie."

"Pat, are you okay? You have blood running down your forehead," asked the Capt.

"Jeffie hit me in the head with something as I went out to get help. He was about to rape Shirley and then kill both of us, when Cindy came in and wounded him. Although shot five times, he still tried to get us with his shotgun. But . . . I shot first."

"That's funny, because Ed said almost the same thing."

"Ed?"

"Yeah, Jeffie's crime partner, Reb, tried to get Ed while Jeffie was after the two of you, but Ed shot first. He used an illegal weapon and is a convicted felon, but I believe, under the circumstances, Atlanta is going to look the other way."

"I certainly hope so." Pat held Shirley and Cindy, who was getting control of herself. "At any rate, I'll be there to help Ed if needed."

"Hey, Capt.! This guy's still alive!" said an officer, examining the man behind the desk.

"Get the EMS people in here - - here they are now. The man at the desk may still be alive."

Two EMS men immediately started working on the elder.

"A miracle," said Pat. "A few minutes ago there was no pulse!"

"It could have been so faint you couldn't feel it," answered an EMS man.

"Cindy, your mother has wanted to see you for a very long time," said Pat.

"No! No! I'm not good enough! I'm dirty!"

"No, you're not. She wants to see you. Both Shirley and I have talked to her. She has missed you so much."

"Pat, I have another ambulance here to take all three of you to the hospital. You need to be checked out. Please go with these gentlemen. We'll get your statements later."

"This guy, or woman, or whatever, is very dead," said one of the EMS people, looking over Jeffie, whose wig had fallen off.

"Well, Shir, maybe we can go on with our life now." Pat held her while stroking her hair.

After one of the men had bandaged Pat's head, they walked to the ambulance. "Just one second," said Pat as he whispered something to the Capt. And gave him a phone number out of his address book.

"I'll have Evette do it as soon as I can get to my car radio."

"Thanks, Capt."

After they left, as Pat had whispered, the Capt. radioed dispatch and had Evette call Cindy's mother to let her know her daughter was on her way to the hospital.

* * *

When they got there, Ed had finished being checked out. His leg had started bleeding from the recoil of the shotgun strapped to the stub of his leg. He also received a large bruise in his groin and the doctors were concerned the jolt may have broken something loose inside, but Ed was proving to be his usual indestructible self.

Capt. Keller had called the O'Kelly's residence to let them know their daughter and Pat were fine. Greg and

Grace rushed to the hospital along with Mary. All gave Shirley and Pat big hugs, and Shirley made sure Mary met Ed.

When Cindy was finished being checked out, Renée was standing there with tears in her eyes.

"Cindy!" cried a tearful Renée. "Cindy, my baby!"

"Mama!" They both stood looking at each other for a few seconds, and then rushed into each other's arms.

"This nightmare is finally over," said Shirley as she wrapped her arms around Pat. "No more nightmares for us!"

But - she was wrong. So very wrong!

EPILOGUE

On Tue., Feb. 3, 1981, Cindy was back living with Renée. DA Colver decided that even though she violated the law by carrying a pistol without a permit, he would not prosecute. She shot Jeffie to prevent the felony crimes of rape and murder. Greg set her up with a good counselor, and she and Renée are making great progress in getting their lives back together.

On Wed., Feb 4, Pat presented Ed's habeas corpus case in front of Judge Musselman. He had the testimony of Haddie Mae Dickerson and Jenel Freeman, the two eye witnesses to the shooting, Albert Pickelmire, the bailiff in Judge Nesbitt's court who told of bias, and Ed himself. Asst. DA Katman and DA Colver had little to say except they would not oppose the granting of the habeas as there had been a grave miscarriage of justice.

Ed was now completely free, as Fulton County Judge Bartenslinger and DA Hoover would not prosecute the use of an illegal weapon because it was used for self-defense, even if he was a convicted felon. They also wanted no part of bad publicity - -they knew Pat was Ed's attorney and had friends in the press. Mary and Ed make a good team. He enrolled in school to get his GED, and Mary agreed to be his tutor. He was not dumb, just uneducated. His amputated leg did not seem to bother her.

The habeas corpus hearing was heavily attended by the news media. Everyone wanted to know the outcome of a man who spent 26 years in prison for doing nothing more than defending his life and property. A local black organization, Brothers for Brothers, presented Pat with an award for his pro bono, or free, defense of Ed, which also was covered by the media.

With all of the media attention, Pat's business has been better than ever, and he asked Mary if she would be interested in working for him as a paralegal/investigator, as Julie could not keep up with the work. Her experience as a police officer and the fact she was an RN would be of great benefit to his criminal and personal injury practice. In about a year, he planned to expand with a new partner. His firm would then be known as Patton and Patton, and possibly Butterworth, if Herb wanted to come aboard. Mary accepted, and they made room for her in the office.

On Sunday Feb. 8th, the day before Pat's 31st birthday, Greg and Grace had Pat and Shirley over for a birthday party. Pat's parents were also there, coming from Charleston. It was held a day early because Pat would be going to New York with Shirley on his birthday. He was taken blindfolded to Greg's downstairs garage where the blindfold was taken off. There before him sat a completely restored 1969 Shelby Cobra with a 427-cubic inch engine, so beautiful and such a surprise that Pat couldn't talk. He had to take Shirley for a short spin right then and there. What a sweet ride!

The next day they flew to NYC and Shirley was checked into the hospital on the morning of the tenth for her cornea transplant. The right eye was done first and had to be patched for five days. On Mon, Feb. 16th, the bandages were removed by Dr. Pat Kite at Emery Hospital in Atlanta. The first thing Shirley saw was Pat holding a beautiful diamond pendant in front of her. He said he had bought it much earlier, but was keeping it for just this moment. She loved him so.

Eb and Kathy set a date to be married and were to be Pat's best man and Shirley's maid of honor. Eb used every trick he could think of to drive the Cobra, but Pat was very reluctant, as it was not only his baby, but also a partial gift from Greg and Grace, as he contributed only $8,000.

Herb's house was finally finished, and all were invited to a house-warming party. The workmen did a fine job and you could not smell burnt timbers. They made some improvements and now have a two-car garage instead of a carport, and 2 ½ baths instead of 1 ½ baths.

On Feb. 27th, Dr. Orhan performed a successful operation on Shirley's left eye. This time they elected to stay for the weekend and see the city. Shirley loved the word *see*. When the patch was removed, Shirley was ready to go back to work.

On Mon. March 2nd, Willie the Waiter was shot. He was jogging along a deserted road early in the morning before going to work at Jerome and Mickey's, when he was shot in the head with a .22-caliber bullet. The doctors found disinfectant in the wound, so the police attributed this act to the serial killer, Mr. Clean. Willie is in a coma, and according to newspaper reports, is only given a 50/50 chance to live.

The wedding on March the 7th was beautiful, and the reception was a huge success. The couple was scheduled to leave for Hawaii on March 20th. Shirley's eyes looked good, and she was experiencing no problems. Life couldn't be better.

At the end of the reception one of the guests brought Pat and Shirley a wedding present found at the front door of the church. The beautifully wrapped package was addressed to Mr. and Mrs. Patcreep Patton. Apparently it was someone's idea of a joke. Inside was a cat's foot! Black with white on it! Whitefoot!

With boiling rage, Pat opened a typed note, which said, "You stand for everything I despise! You believe you are clever, but ultimately you are helping to destroy the Caucasian race by facilitating blacks escaping punishment for murdering white men. You annihilated two men who were cleansing this country of blacks, homosexuals, and affluent Jews. Now you solemnized a relationship with a rich girl, the daughter of selfish, uncaring individuals. The Anderson brothers failed to eradicate you, but I won't. First though, I'm going to toy with you, like a cat does with a mouse - - before he devours it! Signed – Mr. Clean."

AUTHOR BIOGRAPHY

For 26 years, the author maintained a law practice. He became an attorney, at age 36, the hard way - - by working his way through law school while holding down a full-time job as an avionics technician and working part-time at a motorcycle shop.

Back in 1980's Georgia, most attorneys got their start by signing up to represent individuals on the indigent list. Our Constitution states that no one who is charged with a crime and faces substantial jail time will be denied an attorney. If the accused cannot afford an attorney, the state will provide legal representation. Except for large cities, public defenders were almost unheard of, so legal representation came from members of the Bar. The author represented well over 100 criminal defendants during his career, while also handling adoptions, divorces, bankruptcies, wills, personal injury and various other cases.

Prior to becoming an attorney, he was a farmer, a store clerk, part-owner of an automobile salvage yard, a draftsman, an electronics technician, a motorcycle mechanic, a professional welder, a board operator at a TV station, a customer-relations representative for a photocopy company, and a management trainee for a well-known insurance company. Hobbies have included hunting, boating, flying ultralight airplanes, roller and ice skating, motorcycles, bowling, antique automobiles, scuba diving, weightlifting, jogging, softball, hypnosis, and traveling.

The author has written numerous newspaper articles, been published nationally, and has written several novels. With the exception of a few humorous scenes, the author strived to make prison and the practice of law as realistic as possible. Now retired, he lives on a lake in Georgia.

DON'T MISS BOOK III

OF

THE ADVENTURES OF PAT PATTON SERIES.

<u>Mr. Clean: Serial Killer</u> is the third in <u>The Adventures Of Pat Patton Series</u>. A predator, who loves to play cat and mouse games before the actual kill, has Pat in his sights. Will Pat and his true love survive this latest threat? It was published in May 2018.

www.ingramcontent.com/pod-product-compliance
Lightning Source LLC
Chambersburg PA
CBHW060152260626
47160CB00001B/233